LITTLE FALLS

For Jeanne,
Feel like I've known
you! Best of life.
♡ Joan Di Clemente

Joan Di Clemente

iUniverse, Inc.
New York   Bloomington

LITTLE FALLS

iUniverse books may be ordered through booksellers or by contacting:

iUniverse
1663 Liberty Drive
Bloomington, IN 47403
www.iuniverse.com
1-800-Authors (1-800-288-4677)

Because of the dynamic nature of the Internet, any Web addresses or links contained in this book may have changed since publication and may no longer be valid. The views expressed in this work are solely those of the author and do not necessarily reflect the views of the publisher, and the publisher hereby disclaims any responsibility for them.

ISBN: 978-1-4401-9122-0 (sc)
ISBN: 978-1-4401-9120-6 (dj)
ISBN: 978-1-4401-9121-3 (ebk)

Library of Congress Control Number: 2009912707

Printed in the United States of America

iUniverse rev. date: 4/13/2010

For Emidio and our children

Contents

PROLOGUE

Little Falls is the name of the town in which this fictional story was born. The story grew, along with the six living children of Leo and Margot Lockhart, as their lives imitated the intermittent rapids and calm of Lock 17 on the Erie Canal. From the turn of the century through the early 1930s, this family was a steady spoke in the wheel of daily survival in their town, until the rapids of life thrust them from their tranquility and into the stark reality of relocation for their emotional survival. Five decades of living in the shadow of heartbreaking memories ebbed slowly away with the passing of two generations.

The intent of this story is to present the real life experiences of the family members depicted in *Little Falls*. Using fictional identities, each character melds with the story's moments in time. The choices each one makes along his or her path in life unfolds as part of the whole family scenario. There are the good parts we love to remember and the very human parts we'd like to forget within a family, yet we learn from both.

Researching the history and dynamics of my family members opened up a whole world of awareness, helping to fill in several missing parts left unanswered by the individuals who lived through the history they helped to create. The parts of the whole story were brought about through the help extended by the professional staffs at the Fonda Historical Archives, the Herkimer County Historical Society, and the city clerk of Little Falls city hall.

We were given a tour of the upper chambers in city hall and shown a picture of my godfather in a group photo of town administrators in the 1920s. It didn't matter where our search for information took us—be it Little Falls Library, Holy Family Church and the rectory, or St. Mary's Cemetery on Route 5—every person we interacted with was helpful, interested, and cordial as though we were a family relation!

A Sunday afternoon drive from the motel we stayed at in Little Falls to St. Mary's Hospital in Amsterdam will always remain an unforgettable moment. My mother had received her nursing degree at St. Mary's when it was a Victorian stone building. The new, modern facility was a huge surprise, but the best gift was the delightful sister of St. Joseph who gave of her time to take us on a tour of their alumnae office and chapel. She also insisted on providing us with a delicious lunch. We'll never forget her kindness.

A short distance from Amsterdam is Rotterdam Junction, where my father was born. We had been through the mile-long town back in 1971, so we felt pretty sure of finding my grandmother's home again. It had been next to the firehouse, but there was no firehouse now! Luckily, a family enjoying the summer day in the front yard with their twin sons noticed the blank looks on our faces and filled us in. The firehouse to the left of my father's childhood home burned down. The wind was blowing away from his home, and all that happened was some scorching on the side, which was then covered with vinyl siding by the present occupants. The home on the other side of the firehouse was totally destroyed. My grandmother's home may look a bit different, but the love is still there.

Through the appropriate process, I received a copy of my great-grandfather's military records from the Veterans Administration covering his Civil War term of service in the infantry. Another person's address was listed under "other inquiries." In contacting this lady, I learned she was my maternal grandfather's niece. Our long-distance, east-coast-to-west-coast communications extended over three years, filling in some answers for her as well as for me. My only regret was not to have met her in person; she died in 2006.

It is gratifying to learn that there is a process for protecting information and records of the fragile ones of our society. I learned this when trying to obtain my brother's files from the Commonwealth of Massachusetts. His records were sent to me in 2001 as his next of kin, thirty years after his death.

The following resources, along with the aforementioned military and medical records, help to lend credence to the fictional story of Little Falls: old newspaper clippings, letters saved from my parents' long-distance courtship in 1925, a daily journal in my mother's handwriting for the year 1941, letters written by two of my mother's siblings.

In addition, without the professional support of the iUniverse staff, LITTLE FALLS would never have developed into the quality product you are holding in your hands. Their diligence and guidance made this presentation a rewarding reality.

Little Falls is a view of human nature and the mind when clouded by emotions, insecurity, and self-indulgence, yet counterbalanced by examples of what individuals can endure when life demands it. Some families are a fortress of strength; other families are self-destructive and enjoy tearing each other down.

We each have to strive to preserve the values of the family unit. This is the first view of life a child sees. Which view do you wish your descendents to emulate?

SOMETHING MORE YOU NEED TO DO

You asked me why you've lived so long
Well, I've thought it through and through,
Don't know if this rationale will help
But I'll try to answer you.
You have spoken of days gone by
Of which I have no firsthand knowledge,
You would shake your head and deeply sigh
A sigh, mixed with sorrow and horror.
You would say that I'd never know
Of that which you had been through,
I'd try to lighten it saying, "Such is life!"
But, this angered you.
Your question never left my mind
For when you asked in pain,
I wanted to pound the walls and shout,
"Please don't say it again!"
Instead, I tried to be comforting
Knowing the secrets you let slip out,
Like the confession of an innocent,
You longed for peace without doubt.
The answer came in its purest form
Just before your living was through,
You reached out in a humble gesture of love,
The one thing more you needed to do.

Joan M. Di Clemente

Chapter One

Autumn sunlight gilded the yellow maples as invited guests arrived for the annual Sunday afternoon social at St. Mary's Hospital. The stately Victorian brownstone had been bequeathed to the Sisters of St. Joseph, who then had to find ways to keep it in repair and realize a profit in return. The third floor of the brownstone had been remodeled to serve as housing for student nurses. Being a teaching hospital had definite benefits for patients, given that the majority of the nursing staff were living on site and anxious to fulfill their motto of "Caritas Deus est."

Promptly at two, the chief of surgeons formally began the social by requesting an opening prayer from the chaplain. The introduction of dignitaries and an overview of the hospital's accomplishments were presented by Sister Amadeus, the proctor at St. Mary's. It was an informative twenty minutes and created a feeling of unison between the veteran attendees, visiting parents, and newcomers to Amsterdam's prestigious school of nursing.

The annual social was intended to provide a monitored opportunity for the student nurses to meet the benefactors of the hospital and several physicians practicing beyond the walls of St. Mary's. Sister Amadeus assumed this progressive approach of presenting the upcoming graduates to the right people to assist opportunities for future employment. Humility was difficult for Sister to practice when her pride in the quality of the student nurses and graduates, as the most knowledgeable and proficient in their field, was consistently confirmed wherever they practiced their nursing skills.

Seven student nurses were to graduate in the upcoming spring of 1925. They carried themselves confidently, in their starched white

1

uniforms with unmarked caps perched on their heads, as they circulated among the guests. They conversed cheerfully, never conveying the grueling realities of their profession. Each looked angelic, but the demands of the career they had chosen could be the farthest thing from heaven in the drop of a hat.

Teamwork is stressed in nurses' training, where one does not have to be told what to do but can anticipate what is needed to be done, such as a quick napkin under the gentleman's punch cup on the baby grand piano. No sooner had Sister Amadeus noticed this travesty when a napkin was inconspicuously slipped under the cup by a student nurse, Katherine Lockhart, who began to softly play Chopin's *Moonlight Sonata* on the baby grand piano.

Worried her spontaneous recital might end in humiliation by hitting a series of wrong notes, Katherine swiftly brought the sonata to an appropriate ending as her attention was drawn toward a man brushing road dust off his shoulders in the vestibule. Before a second passed, the supervisor of nurses spotted the late arrival and waved her arms high as she approached the young man.

"Ted! Ted! Over here!" came the excited trill from his Aunt Madie. Her arms were extended toward him as though he was her very own long-lost son. "I'd given up hope and feared some misfortune because you always keep your word! Heaven sakes, Ted, people have come and already left, but thank the Almighty, the most important reason for wanting you here is over there by the piano. No! Not that one. The tall one! Come! Let me properly introduce you. Come on now! You act like you have cement in your shoes."

Aunt Madie had a strong persuasive grip as she steered Ted around and through clusters of people, never giving him a chance to respond or explain his lateness. As they approached the piano, Ted experienced the driest mouth and the emptiest mind he had ever had. He was fairly sure his body was occupying a degree of vertical and horizontal areas because two gray-blue eyes were staring right into his. He knew visibly he was present because under the eyes appeared a nose, and under the nose a mouth spoke to him. Aunt Madie had suddenly disappeared.

"I'm very pleased to meet you, Ted. Your Aunt Madie has been trying to arrange our meeting for a while. Would you like a drink of punch? It's very good."

The young student nurse motioned toward a side table. She proceeded to pour the punch and handed Ted a plate and napkin. His eyes did not leave her as he studied the total picture.

"Thank you. I really needed that drink because the ride from the train station was less than casual. But then, you've never met my cousin, Walter, have you? Incidentally, when Aunt Madie introduced us, she called you, Kate? I thought the invitation she sent me said 'Katherine Lockhart'?"

"My given name is Katherine, but, uh, my baby brother, Sean, calls me Kate. Family and friends call me Kate." She became very self-conscious and looked away from Ted's direct gaze. He struggled for something to say and felt the events that preceded his arrival might be a good topic.

"May I explain my lateness? Friday night I was scheduled to travel to visit my mother in Rotterdam Junction and my cousin, Walter, was planning to drive me on Sunday from there to the social here today. Well, all plans fell through due to the lack of room for a pass holder on the Friday train out of Boston. I had to wait until late Saturday evening, which got me into Schenectady around eight this morning. Then I waited for the connecting train to Amsterdam. Meanwhile, Walter left Rotterdam Junction to meet me in Amsterdam, but he had a flat tire on the way. So I have about half an hour before I leave to catch the train to Boston from here because I need to be back to work at seven tomorrow morning."

By the end of this dialogue, Katherine's eyes were huge, and she was mute. Ted quickly searched for a more meaningful topic and recalled Aunt Madie mentioning that Katherine's mother was born in County Cork. His parents came from Country Kerry, but attempts to stimulate conversation about family didn't go very far except for questions about how many sisters and brothers and the ages of each. Time raced by, and Ted spotted Walter waiting outside to drive him to the station.

"Say, if it would not be too much of an imposition, I'd like to write to you. Would you have the time to answer? With your training and work schedule, I'm sure when you have free time a nap would be your preference. Aunt Madie told me how hard all the student nurses work with studies and duties!"

Ted placed his cup and plate on the sideboard. Katherine asked if he had a pen and withdrew a name card from her pocket. She wrote her posting on the reverse side, and a slow smile crept forth.

"Yes, that would be very pleasant, but only if you put your return address on the envelope," replied Katherine.

Ted realized he hadn't given his address. His attention was diverted to a woman standing nearby who seemed overly interested in their conversation. Katherine also noticed the third party and guided Ted to the center of the floor as she inquired about the length of time it took a letter to travel from Amsterdam to Boston and be delivered to its destination by the postman.

Moving toward the foyer, they joined several other guests bidding their good-byes. Reaching for her hand, Ted stated how pleased he was to have finally met his aunt's favorite student nurse. He spotted Aunt Madie and gave her a wink and wave, mouthing silently that Walter was outside waiting for him. She nodded her understanding.

The air was crisp and fragrant with the smell of the harvested grass piled into high stacks on the open meadows. Driving with his knees and alternating with his hands when shocked by a bump, Walter teased Ted about the flapper he just had high tea with.

"So, Teddy, me boy, was it worth the madness of this weekend's travel regime just to shut up my mother, once and for all?" inquired a smirking cousin Walter.

Ted looked at his cousin, shrugged his shoulders, and lit an overdue cigarette. He felt that to say anything may result in his being misquoted by Walter should he repeat it to his mother, who in turn would repeat it to her sister, Ted's mother. He thought it best to say nothing.

As Katherine watched the roadster vanish down the road until it was obscured by its own cloud of dust, her recollection of Ted was just as cloudy because of the brevity of time spent with him. Was he taller than she? What color were his eyes? Did he have healthy teeth? Now, this is rather silly, she thought. As she recalled their conversation, Ted Bryant's soft-spoken manner seemed a contradiction from Madie's account of his adventurous nature as a self-made man with a promising career with the railroad. Yet he had spent a lot of energy just to be present, having given his word. One can't dismiss determination and perseverance, plus responsibility. A firm hand placed on Katherine's arm jolted her.

"Now what might ya be doin' talking to a perfect stranger?" inquired Margot Lockhart, Katherine's mother. "Who was that young man and why didn't ya introduce him to me?"

Margot's directness always rubbed Katherine the wrong way, yet she owed the woman her very life. This constant mix of feelings fostered both resentment and entrapment for her. Gathering composure, she apologized.

"His name is Ted Bryant and the nephew of Madie Cowan. You met her earlier today. He dropped in to see his aunt on the way to the train station. He had to catch the next train and was in a rush," explained Kate as her face began to burn, giving away her deceit.

Noticing what Margot was doing made Katherine blush all the more. "Ma, what are you doing? You can't just take the linen napkin and those sandwiches and cookies!"

Margot pulled Katherine to the side and glared straight up at her flushed face. "There's plenty here that will go to waste, so I've taken some for the trip home, and a bit to Sean in case ya've forgotten about him."

At this point, Margot placed the linen acquisition on the table and brushed her chestnut wisps upward from her face. She looked overdressed, thought Katherine, for an afternoon tea, with that silly secondhand fox she always wore to special occasions. To continue the conversation would have led to hard feelings.

"Ma, I have to change into my work uniform for duty in twenty minutes," Katherine begged off as she kissed her mother on the cheek.

"Now, ya wait a bit! I came all this way to see ya and ya don't have time for me?"

"Ma, we talked and I told you I can't choose where a nursing position will present itself. Besides, I have to graduate yet, and then obtain my license!" Katherine pleaded.

"Well! It's getting to be a bunch of hooey! Ya just plan on presenting yarself in Little Falls where y'all care for ya father. That's yar duty after all I've done fer ya," Margot directed.

"Listen to yourself," whispered Katherine. "He's still working every day! You talk like he's on his deathbed! Might you be rushing it a bit?"

"Soon enough, Katherine," responded Margot, as she noticed Mr. and Mrs. Dorsey waiting to drive her to the train station. "And don't be getting any ideas about that perfect stranger ya spent more time with than ya mother."

"Good-bye, Mother," sighed Katherine, "and I'm sorry your visit wasn't more pleasant."

Gathering up the linen napkin and its contents, Margot draped her fox wrap over the booty and graciously thanked Sr. Amadeus for the delightful afternoon. Mr. Dorsey was patiently waiting outside and assisted Margot into the Maxwell. The three parents lurched forward, chugged a bit, and then puttered off to the train station, sending the road's autumn mantle into artificial flight.

The Dorseys' daughter, Maureen, had taken to Katherine from the very start of her days at St. Mary's. Being an only child, she loved hearing about Katherine's family which, when told in the right light, provided hours of conversation and laughter. Margot reflected on how she had cautioned Katherine not to confide in Maureen or anyone, no matter how good a friend they seemed to be. Mother and daughter shared a secret which both hid in the depths of their souls, and so it would forever be. Beyond their pledge, Margot harbored an even deeper secret of her own, which she alone would have to answer to God for. As the Maxwell glided to a halt at the depot, Margot retrieved an Irish soda bread from her travel bag in appreciation for the Dorseys' hospitality.

"You're so thoughtful, Mrs. Lockhart! With all you have to do and you think of us! Remember our offer for you and Mr. Lockhart to stay over the night of the girls' graduation. We have plenty of room."

"Ah, yar too kind, Mrs. Dorsey; there's my 'all aboard' and thank ya again for all ya kindness to me, and Katherine. Should Leo and I be able to get away for an overnight, I'll let ya know," answered Margot, knowing already she wouldn't be accepting their invitation.

Chapter Two

Settled into the coach seat for the ride back to Little Falls, Margot reached for her travel bag and took out one tea sandwich and two cookies. The rest would be saved for when she arrived home. She wondered if Sean survived the day with Lenora in charge. That girl is so moody! Why her second daughter was that way puzzled Margot. Those wild movie flicks put ideas in young minds, and with women bobbing their hair, spit curls, legs showing, and the flimsy lace curtain dresses those actresses were wearing, what could you expect, she sighed.

Forming her fox into a pillow, Margot rested her head against the window frame, as her mind drifted along with the passing scenery. Country pastures, farm houses, and cows being herded home at the end of the day transported her back to Millstreet in County Cork. So long ago, yet only yesterday, so it seemed. The realities of life, filled with pain and disillusionment, hadn't beaten her down, it just made her fight all the harder for what she wanted. Fight was one of her innate characteristics along with persistence and an unbelievable dosage of pride. She had more than her share of "looks down the nose" from Yankee aristocrats she had worked for as a domestic during her first seven years in America.

From her earliest recall, she and her older sister, Mary, had been indoctrinated toward one goal by their parents: immigrating to America. The hypnotic rocking of the train held Margot's thoughts on the track of her life's past thirty-one years since leaving Ireland. She found it possible to avoid rehashing all that happened in the past by keeping busy every waking minute of the day, but rare moments of solitude, such as this train ride, resurrected the side she feared God would judge her by.

Prejudice and *contempt* were unknown words in her parents' vocabulary, but the feelings were endured by them all, being children of an emigrant carpenter from England and an Irish mother. This set the Godson family apart from the villagers. Her parents set high standards of behavior so their children were above reproach or criticism. They spoke both Gaelic and the King's language and read and wrote in both.

The six children were sturdy and pleasantly attractive with their fair skin, blue eyes, and range of hair colors from blond, to auburn, to black. They were always adequately clothed due to their mother's skills with homemade muslin and knitted woolens. They learned self-sufficiency from an early age as they assisted their father at his carpentry work and the various chores around their humble one-room dwelling. Margot thought of her own children's lives in contrast. They thought things were tough because there were no frills, just the bare necessities. They had no idea what real poverty was.

The day Mary and Margot departed for America was a day they would never forget. As they hugged their sandy-haired father and raven-haired mother, it felt like what death must evoke when a loved one dies. They had never been separated in all their years from their parents. Now they were leaving the Emerald Isle for a strange country that was not a day's trek away on a donkey, but a whole ocean!

The opportunity for a better life was given to the sisters through the sacrifice of their unselfish parents and the sponsorship of their older brother living in Massachusetts. Each pledged to bring the rest of the family to America, where it didn't matter if you were part this or that. If you were a good worker and lover of freedom and justice, success would be obtainable. The girls had more than their quota of each of these qualifications and never doubted they could meet any challenge.

Employed as live-in maids, Mary and Margot were located near each other in Glens Falls, New York, and would meet on their time off to exchange news and letters from home. Being live-ins, their funds were meager in that meals and lodging were considered part of their earnings. Along with this, they had to manage personal needs and clothing. They were given a uniform to start with and each hoped that an increase in wages or a kindness on their employer's part would make it possible to obtain a second one. It was a trial, Margot recalled, trying to keep the white apron, cuffs, and collar clean, and struggling each night to ready them for the next day. She remembered vividly one day in particular when she and Mary were on Main Street and a ragman plodded along with his cart.

"Excuse me, sir, but might ya happen upon maids' uniforms in your travel?" Margot asked. Mary was horrified that her sister was talking to this tinker of sorts and started pulling Margot away from the cart, exclaiming, "Ya wouldn't be wearing someone else's trash?"

"Well, my heavens, how high horse we've become!" responded Margot.

Meanwhile, the vendor was rummaging through and came up with white collars, cuffs, and a couple of aprons, as well as a navy blue uniform which needed down-sizing.

"See!" squealed Margot, "I'll share with ya, Mary. Ya must be going just as crazy washing yar whites!"

There was an obvious moment of silence before Mary's stuttering response.

"B-by no means; my kind mistress is so ha-happy with my work that sh-she gave me t-two more uniforms."

Margot reached into her secret hiding place for her bosom-warmed purse and paid the vendor. She gathered her parcel, spun around, and glared at Mary. In a rushing gush of Gaelic, she lambasted her older sister for lying and thinking only of her own comfort. Mary burst out in overdue tears from tiredness and the loneliness of being so far from loved ones. She admitted buying two extra uniforms instead of saving the money. The truth hurt but did cleanse the air. The sisters hugged each other, wiped the tears, and reaffirmed their goal.

Finding a place to rent and saving money to free the sisters from the cycle of dependency as live-in maids would require a miracle! The meager money they sent to their parents would not make a reunion possible for perhaps ten years. Mary voiced her fears that their parents would be too old or would die by the time there was enough money to bring them to America.

Margot closed her eyes as she visually recalled what occurred next as she and Mary were sitting on the stone wall outside the Town Hall.

She checked the items purchased from the rag man, and wedged in between was a handmade lace collar. This was the miracle they needed; the special skill of lace making their mother taught them! They could sell handmade lace trim for dresses and make shawls and furniture scarves! Evening hours were generally their own time, as long as they were present in the home if needed. This is what they could do with those evening hours! Mary was willing but wilted when she realized they had no extra money with which to buy thread or needles.

Not to be defeated, Margot came up with the idea of having the customer buy their own thread and color, and she and Mary would set a price for the labor, depending on the size of the item. They borrowed money from their savings to get started with a few samples to entice customers.

A local tailor agreed to display samples of the industrious maids' handiwork after Margot convinced him it would bring women into his shop who wanted to alter an older dress with new lace inserts, cuffs, or collar. Between the tailor's shop and word of mouth, Mary and Margot had more business than they could handle meeting deadlines. They began to regret the finding of their pot of gold, because the lace making took up every available free minute.

"Mary, I don't know ya feelings, but we'll have the money to bring our family to America after this next order is completed, and then I don't ever want to make lace again!" an exhausted, blurry-eyed Margot cried to her older sister as they visited after Sunday Mass in the last pew of St. Michael's Church.

"Now, what might ya be saying? I'm starting to get used to this growth that hangs from my hand day and night," laughed Mary, "but I think yar right and if we never see lace again, it will be too soon!"

They reached their goal and contacted their older brother, Tom, who made the appropriate arrangements for their parents' voyage from Ireland to Glens Falls in the spring of 1898. It was up to Mary and Margot to find housing for their parents and three younger brothers, following a cryptic conversation with Tom who announced he had to manage for himself from here on in and they best learn to do the same. He asked them to extend his welcome to their parents, but at the present time it would not be possible to be in New York when they arrived.

From that time on, Tom saw his parents twice in the intervening years prior to their deaths, as far as Margot could recollect.

Before giving the money to Tom, Margot and Mary made a wise decision and retained some of their savings from the lace making. This was a turning point for the sisters, realizing their needs had changed, and no longer were they those fun-loving youngsters racing through the Millstreet Cemetery scaring their young brothers with the skulls from the overturned graves. It was good that they had used their intuition regarding their money, because Tom didn't keep his monetary promise of contributing toward helping their parents to establish themselves in their new world.

Margot recalled how she and Mary kept an eye on a duplex apartment they could afford on Chestnut Street in Glens Falls, hoping one side or the other would be vacated in time for the arrival of their parents. God was listening, because a month before the planned arrival of their family a vacancy occurred. The sisters moved in and then went on a scavenger hunt for chairs, cots, and a table.

The large, black locomotive that hugged the edge of the duplex's backyard moved slowly along the stockyard's edge, heaped high with coal. The sisters learned to shut out the noise, but the rumbling served as a rather large grandfather clock that shook, rather than chimed its set schedule.

Sharing the same roof for the first time since they left Millstreet seven years ago, the sisters confided in each other about things beyond lace making. One such item centered on male attention, which the sisters discussed at length. Mary's fancy had been captured by a tall, handsome man who visited the oldest son of the family she worked for. He seemed to be coming around more often than necessary, even when the oldest son wasn't at home!

In reply, Margot spoke of the attention given her by the son of the family she was employed by. What she learned was that he had been adopted. It seems his adoptive parents had tried for over five years to have a child, and after adopting him had three children of their own. He was currently working toward his medical degree and would be taking his final training in one of the hospitals in New York City, the name of which she couldn't recall.

He was given the name Joshua by the children's home where he was raised the first two years of his life. His adoptive parents changed his name to Arthur, feeling it would be more acceptable in a Yankee environment combined with their surname of Kirkland. It was assumed his natural mother must have died in childbirth, and his father was so distraught by the loss of her and overwhelmed by the responsibility of caring for the newborn, brought the infant to the local orphanage in the middle of the night, and left him on the steps with a note on which the Star of David was drawn.

Mary was hanging on to every word and begged Margot to continue. Margot added that every time Arthur managed to get her alone, he'd ask her to marry him and then would try to steal a kiss or two. She had been warned by other female domestics of all the games men played with live-in maids, and the poor souls being so far from home and not having any other roof over their heads, became easy prey.

Thinking she best nip this in the bud, Margot told Arthur she was not interested in anyone not of the same faith. She spent a great deal of energy avoiding Arthur within the home, and was relieved when his holiday was over and he went back to the books. In all honesty, she had to admit to Mary that she enjoyed the feeling Arthur gave her just by being near.

Mary thought it all just the most romantic adventure a woman could have had with a future doctor! In her own soul, Margot fought with all her strength to control the urge to give in. Longing to love and be loved at times froze her own moral sense, causing her to feel possessed by a powerful demon who enticed and scoffed at the straight and narrow road she had chosen.

The conductor's call of "Lit-tle Falls" prodded Margot out of her reminiscing as the train's whistle alerted the town to its arrival. She gathered her parcels and made ready to get off. It was quite dark by now, but the lights from the houses lit the way along Albany Street. She spotted Sean looking out the parlor window in anticipation of her arrival.

CHAPTER THREE

Night duty was lonely and quiet. Katherine imagined it was similar to being in purgatory in that you knew others were there, but saw no one. Most of the student nurses took advantage of the quiet to write letters or read their lab notes, but Katherine seldom took the same privilege for fear of being caught with her attention on something other than her duties. She tried to read her daily prayers but couldn't keep her focus, even on the repetition of the familiar words.

The mixed emotions she experienced at the afternoon's social kept creeping to the forefront of her mind. Katherine wished with all her heart that Margot would not talk so much with that Irish brogue! She drew the attention of everyone in the room by wearing that fox on such a warm autumn day, and surely one of the guests must have seen Margot helping herself to a napkin full of sandwiches and cookies! Then, on top of that, since losing her teeth, she was forever adjusting her upper and lower plates! The whole thing was so embarrassing.

Even when Margot wasn't around she caused embarrassment, thought Katherine. Added to her long list was her humiliation when a nurse on laundry duty went throughout the dorm asking if anyone knew who Leslie Levesque was. No one knew the mystery nurse, so the unclaimed uniforms were put back in the laundry room. That night after everyone had gone to bed, Katherine crept down to the laundry room to claim the secondhand uniforms Margot had picked up at a rummage sale for her. Ripping out the former owner's name tags, she sewed in her own by candlelight. Her heart was pounding so loud she feared someone would hear it as she crawled her way up the three flights of stairs in the dark back to her room.

Training for the nursing profession was Katherine's salvation and ticket out of Little Falls. She wanted to be free of all those who made it their business to know everyone's business. Yet some of these same people she loathed were the very ones who supported her and gave her this opportunity. This confused her emotions and usurped her energy each time she entertained leaving them. How could she when her heart was shackled to little Sean?

The ruse devised by Margot to cover Katherine's pregnancy began with the illusion that Margot was gradually growing larger with child, with the help of some batting. Katherine, in turn, stayed close to home toward the end, telling friends she had lots to arrange before leaving for nurse's training in Amsterdam. She let out what clothing she could and wore her mother's large, full-length aprons to conceal her growth when anyone dropped by. The second week in January, Katherine left for St. Mary's School of Nursing, accompanied by her very pregnant-looking mother, who had not planned on feigning the baby's birth in Amsterdam the very next day.

The excitement of packing to leave that eventful day, coupled with the secretive plans of coordinating the availability of a midwife with Dr. Kirkland's help, may have contributed to the slight spotting Katherine noticed on her bloomers. It wasn't time yet; at least not for two or maybe four more weeks. She dismissed it from her mind and told no one.

Margot and Katherine took an early morning train, free of staring female eyes. Twenty minutes out of the range of Little Falls, Katherine felt an intense pain in her back. Then, it stopped as quickly as it started. She assured herself it was due to the excitement, but it happened again!

"Oh! My God!" she whispered huskily, as she grabbed her mother's arm. Panic seized Margot's heart. St. Johnsville was the next stop. They would get off and contact Dr. Kirkland, thought Margot. But, that wouldn't be wise because he may not be available. Dear God in heaven, don't do this to us, she prayed. Think! Think!

Cautiously, Margot whispered words of guidance to calm Katherine's stress. She directed her daughter to inform the conductor that her mother was going into premature labor and to please telegraph ahead to the midwife in Amsterdam their approximate arrival time. Writing the name and address of the midwife, Katherine added a request for transportation, in that by the time they arrived, her mother may not be able to walk very far. The conductor was most expedient, and took it upon himself to arrange transportation, courtesy of the New York Central Railroad.

There was Margot, at the age of forty-six, feigning her daughter's infant son as her own at a time when her husband's health and alcoholism were a town topic. She told everyone that Sean would be a great support to her as she grew older and would help with the care of his ailing father. People seemed to accept it as an act of God, and everyone loves a baby, especially one as adorable as Sean.

Tongues did wag, and Katherine heard plenty in letters from her friends, who wondered just where Margot got the money to send Kate to St. Mary's and adding that now that Margot had this baby and four other children still living at home, her ingenuity would be stretched to the limits. The townspeople knew the lengths Margot went through to make ends meet by renting her carriage house to an itinerant family, doubling and tripling up her own children in bedrooms, and renting two rooms to boarders, along with running a grocery store. The neighbors were exhausted just watching!

This was nothing new to Katherine, but her main focus while reading the letters was to discern any suspicions on the part of the letter writers over some detail she and Margot may have slipped up on. She lived in constant fear of being found out. The sisters at St. Mary's would certainly not want an unwed mother amongst their "pure of heart and soul." Or, if they were to know who the father was, would they be charitable. The nuns lived in a black-and-white world, just like their habits. Katherine was living a lie, and a deliberate lie is a mortal sin.

Her pretense of having pneumonia and needing to postpone her arrival for the start of the January semester for a month was believable. Sister Amadeus was indeed taken with the contrast in Katherine's appearance upon arrival in mid-February, as compared to the early summer interview when she applied for admission. Sr. Amadeus inquired about the attending physician whose care she was under. Katherine was quick to ask if a statement of health from Dr. Kirkland would be acceptable. Being one of Sister Amadeus's favorite doctors, there was no question that this would be more than adequate. She confirmed with Katherine the need to double up on textbook readings to bring her up to par, along with making up all written assignments. The recovering novice assured Sister Superior she had read all the assigned readings during her recovery and was ready to work.

To avoid any slipups, Katherine kept to herself, which was easy to do since she didn't fit in with the other trainees who were out on the husband hunt every free moment. The casual, comfortable friendship of Maureen, a young woman who had befriended her when she first arrived at St. Mary's, was all she needed. Their closeness over the past two years raised some eyebrows. This was part of the reason Katherine sensed Madie kept insisting that she meet her nephew, Ted. Well, she met him and he left her a bit unmoved. Of course, it was not a fair appraisal to make of someone in thirty minutes.

Besides harboring the events which preceded her arrival at St. Mary's, the new knowledge she was acquiring caused more questions. Such was the case during study of Mandel's theory and offspring from incest, which totally caught her off guard one day in class.

"Miss Lockhart! Are you all right?"

"Yes, Sister Regina. I must have a cold coming on," replied Katherine as she held on to the arms of the chair.

"Would you like a glass of water?" offered Sister Regina.

"Thank you. I'm sorry for interrupting your class," apologized Katherine as she attempted to stand.

"Please, just stay and you can copy Maureen's notes for the remaining lecture," offered the kind nun.

Alone with her thoughts, the rushing reality of all that had happened before coming to St. Mary's brought up a whole litany of questions, including her physical difference from her siblings and the fact she bore a healthy son by her father. Of the six children in her family, five had dark brown hair and brown eyes, but Katherine had blue eyes and blonde hair.

To question Margot would be considered disrespectful and would result in a swift slap across the mouth. There were numerous times when Katherine's intelligence presented logical retorts when her mother was in the midst of a rage over one thing or another. But now, as she thought back on the whippings and the time Margot threw her down the cellar stairs, realized she should have been smarter and kept her mouth closed.

Being smart in school helped Katherine to keep her ego intact. Learning came easy to her. She won the spelling bee and math competition in the eighth grade and received two double promotions, allowing her to complete high school at the age of fifteen. She immediately was sent to work at the felt factory making slippers.

In the early spring of her third year of employment, Katherine cut her right hand badly with a leather cutter. Blood wouldn't stop flowing and she fainted. When she awoke, a doctor was bandaging her hand and Margot was by her side. The doctor introduced himself as Dr. Arthur Kirkland, who had recently opened an extension of his Glens Falls practice in Little Falls. Katherine was a bit groggy but remembered feeling comfortable with this stranger, whom her mother seemed to know. The doctor advised Katherine to rest the remainder of the week and visit his office in four days, on the coming Monday.

The floor manager was totally disgusted by the amount of blood covering the ruined stock Katherine had been working on and muttered something about deducting the loss from her pay. The attending doctor thrust some money into the manager's hand and added that Kate would not be able to use her right hand for a long time, so she would have to look for another position. She remembered wanting to stop the doctor's words because she needed the job, but the energy to do so was lacking.

The next few days were painful for Katherine when she accidentally lowered her hand. She deduced that the flow of blood must be exerting pressure on the healing incision.

When Monday came, Katherine recalled how Margot was as nervous as a hen getting her ready for the visit to Dr. Kirkland. The litany of orders ranged from the personal to the absurd.

"Should he be asking why ya work at the factory, ya tell him it is yar choice. And, if he asks anything about yar parents or family, just say, 'I don't know!' Or, if he talks about Glens Falls and yar relatives there, just say, 'Oh, I don't see them except when somebody dies or gets married.'"

"Why would he be asking me anything?" inquired Katherine. "He's only going to see how the cut is healing. I do want to ask him about the lack of feeling in my thumb."

"Just don't be taking up his time. He has more patients than just ya," snapped Margot.

The March winds that Monday morning were true to form, blowing the chill off the canal waters and stinging her nostrils as Katherine scurried to the doctor's office. The nurse directed her to one of the examination rooms which had a distinct antiseptic aroma. Katherine recalled how the tin ceiling curved down about a foot to meet the decorative strip of cherry-colored wood which encircled the walls. The doors and window frames appeared newly refinished, lending a warm glow to the room, as the sunlight reflected off the wooden surfaces.

When Dr. Kirkland entered the room, Katherine jumped, causing him to jump as well. They both laughed. After removing the bandages from her hand, the doctor proceeded to remove the sutures. Katherine was totally absorbed by the gentleness of the doctor's manner. He asked her to move each of her fingers, which gave her the confidence to ask the one question she had about her thumb.

"I was going to ask you why my thumb won't bend or move."

"Been checking things out, have you? It takes time for healing, especially due to the depth of your cut. Had it been just a little nearer your wrist, we would have had a more serious situation. New nerves will have to form, and by the end of next week, I want you to start squeezing this roll of bandages a few times each hour."

"When shall my strength to hold things return?" she asked.

"Each person's healing process is different, but I'd venture three to six months for you," answered the doctor as he rewrapped her hand.

She noticed his little fingers on both hands were crooked, just like hers. He removed his spectacles upon finishing, and his eyes were a gray-blue shade similar to hers. Perhaps this meant she should be a nurse, or even a doctor, but that thought was interrupted by a question from the doctor.

"Now, Miss Lockhart, what are your plans after the incision heals?"

Katherine found this inquiry rather strange in that Dr. Kirkland knew that she had been working at the mill when the accident occurred.

Then she recalled the warnings her mother had made should the doctor be asking questions and carefully phrased her response.

"Once I heal and have back the strength in my hand, I'll see if they'll let me return at the mill. I was making good money doing piecework and was being considered for a supervisor's position. There's not much else around here beyond getting married. We don't have lots of money, so that leaves advanced schooling out. I was a good student and was double promoted, twice!"

Dr. Kirkland assisted Katherine off the examination table and told her to drop by in a couple of months so he could check the healing. She thanked him and offered the money her mother had provided. He said it would cover his fee, including the next checkup.

Katherine's recuperation and relearning to use her hand took time. The timing was perfect in that it allowed Margot the long-awaited opportunity to follow through with a dream. She purchased a local grocery store from its retiring owner, who agreed to stay on for a three-month transition period to help Margot and her sons learn the ins and outs of the business. The home chores were assigned to Katherine to manage with her one good hand and the reluctant help of her younger sisters, Aileen and Lenora.

From day one of this undertaking, Margot didn't feel she needed to pay her sons a wage because she was providing the roof over their heads, along with food and clothing. Bernard and Raymond went along with the arrangement at first because they didn't know if the grocery business would be to their liking.

Katherine recalled hating every moment of being stuck in her parents' home like a servant but enjoyed sleeping later than her brothers, who had to be down at the store stocking the shelves or picking up supplies at 5:30 each morning. Sleeping in until 6:30 AM was her one pleasure until that particular morning when she became aware someone was in the bed with her.

He was drunk and hallucinating, calling Margot's name over and over. She tried to comfort him but the interactions took on a different flavor. Katherine fought as hard as she could, but her strength and injured hand were no match for his sexual determination.

Then, it happened. Katherine pushed her father to the side causing him to fall off the bed. He didn't even know he was on the floor. She left him there and rushed to the wash basin and scrubbed and scrubbed.

She quickly dressed and woke up her younger sisters. They dressed and ate the bread and oatmeal Margot had put out for them. School was not a priority that day. Katherine kept crying and her sisters just looked at her. They sensed it had something to do with their father being on the floor, but then they had seen him on the floor before.

The trio walked to the grocery store. Margot looked at Katherine and flew up the street to her home. The pall engulfed them all. Katherine remembered standing in the back room of the grocery store, frozen to the spot until Margot returned. Surrounded by her brothers and sisters, who tried to comfort her, she stood silently while the little piece of flooring under her feet seemed to slowly melt. Reality dropped her through a nine-month hole where she landed on a fragile limb over a raging waterfall. Now four years later, she finds herself in a situation where she senses the fragile limb is weakening.

The bell for the eleven o'clock rounds abruptly scattered Katherine's reflections, prompting her to prepare the tray of medications. As usual, bedpans were requested by the heaviest patients, and the ones who complained the most if they didn't get their pain medication had to be awoken. The head nurse on duty felt full responsibility was good training for student nurses and tended to disappear rather than help. Thus, Katherine had to manage lifting some patients twice her own weight.

Returning the sterilized hypodermic needles under lock and key, she caught her image in the mirror which lined the rear of the cabinet. Katherine was surprised by how much she resembled the wedding picture of her mother which sat atop of their piano back in Little Falls. Had her mother been as young once? It was difficult to imagine.

All was quiet again and she attempted to write a note of thanks to the Dorseys for their kindness in transporting her mother to and from the train depot. The ink spotted, and she started over on a clean sheet, feeling she was being punished for doing something for herself instead of praying. Once finished, she reached in her pocket and withdrew Ted's Boston address which Madie had given her. Imagine the glamour of living in the city of Boston, and being right near Harvard University!

Katherine had read about the Old North Church and Paul Revere and that the dome of the Massachusetts State House was covered in gold! Now, what was she thinking? No way was she going to waste time on an upstart who may not amount to anything. And from Rotterdam Junction, no less!

She jammed the address back into her pocket. Besides, her mind was set, and once she graduated, there were lots of places she would travel to with all the money made from her nursing career. She wanted a husband with position and money! From what she had seen of Ted and his satchel, it would be some time before both requirements evolved. The cruel honesty of her own thoughts created a feeling of guilt, causing her to open her prayer book and read the Act of Contrition.

CHAPTER FOUR

The connecting train at Schenectady for Boston had mechanical problems, or so the conductor told the passengers as he walked the train punching tickets. Knowing the hours and schedules of the engineers and conductors, Ted Bryant ventured that the real reason was not mechanical, but the result of a few of the crew having a difficult time pulling away from a successful social weekend. He really didn't mind, because it gave him time to think and sort out how and when he could pay back his cousin, Walter, for the loan which helped finance his jaunt to Amsterdam.

Ted's Boston co-workers pointed out that he should buy a new suit if he wished to impress the lovely lady his aunt wanted him to meet. Ted agreed when looking at the frayed cuffs on both the jacket and slacks, yet he had no extra funds set aside for such a luxury. Larry and Sam offered to loan him the funds until the Friday following the trip. With the money borrowed from Walter, Larry and Sam would be repaid. He usually sent his mother two dollars a week, but instead bought a new shirt and tie to go with the suit. He could have used new shoes, but a good polishing took care of that. A sudden jerk of the train alerted the passengers that the crew was on board, and slowly the iron horse steamed out of the depot.

"So, let's see. Where is my record book? Now, if all goes accordingly, seven plus eight, plus three, plus two, aught, carry two..." droned Ted. The sum tallied didn't lessen his debt or assist with repaying it. As for his mother, his sister Ellen would have to reach into her purse a little deeper for a week, being that she still lived at home at the age of thirty. She contributed some weekly, but Ted knew she tended to only exert herself to a point and no more. She had told Ted how some appreciative patrons at a Schenectady hotel, where she worked the switchboard, occasionally tipped her. She was most discreet and could keep her eyes and ears closed to things which could ruin many a reputation.

The train huffed into the Boston terminal at 2:55 AM, and with only four hours before the workday, Ted decided to snooze on the train until the five AM turnabout. The camaraderie he shared with the crew, having worked the line, afforded him this courtesy.

He drifted into a deep sleep and found himself waltzing with a woman in a white marble room with french doors that opened onto a rich, green lawn bordered with elegant ferns and brilliant tropical flowers. Ted looked down into the upturned face of a woman he vaguely recalled. Then, she pushed him away and ripped off her flowing gown, revealing a dazzling white nurse's uniform with a huge red cross on her chest. He awoke from the shakes his conductor friend was giving him.

"Say now, Teddy, my boy! It's me, Charlie. You were really into a deep sleep and mumbling away. You told me to wake you on my last tour of the train."

"Thanks, Charlie. It's been a crazy weekend," Ted mumbled as he checked his watch.

It was 4:30 AM, and he had just enough time to wash up and shave in the water closet and grab some breakfast. He was due to meet with the head manager of the Boston and Maine accounting department at 8 AM. Hopefully, he sighed, this was the day he would be put on full salary and benefits, versus his present status of hourly wage.

The meeting ended with nothing promised but a lot of double talk to keep him hanging on. Ted sensed the head manager had his own problems in that his management skills and charisma were both in storage on some baggage car which hadn't found the right track. But his credentials were from Suffolk University, and that is what dictated administrative choices for management positions. Ted knew the sheepskin was no replacement for know-how, but convincing them he had the know-how was impossible without opportunity.

Some of the interview questions baited Ted into sounding as if he knew more about how to run the department then the present staff.

He offered his observations regarding more efficient ways to record and organize the department's accounts. The head manager, Bob Taggart, seemed quite interested and asked him to work up a chart of responsibilities and work distribution for the entire department as if he were managing it. Ted recognized the trap and downplayed his ideas by categorizing them as purely speculative rather than tested theory. He felt like he had just been played like a ball of yarn being tossed about by the family cat.

With a heavy heart, Ted completed the day and left with the masses that poured out onto Causeway Street. He crossed Causeway to Canal Street on automatic pilot and, lost in his thoughts, found himself on Tremont Street. Backtracking toward Scollay Square, he rounded the corner onto Myrtle Street. Entering the local grocery store, he watched a man about his age lifting his two-year-old up onto his shoulders while an older son was hanging onto the father's left leg. Someday, thought Ted. Suddenly, he was struck with what could be the obstacle which kept Taggart using him for the fill-in jobs and bypassing him for full-time employment.

The majority of the full-timers were long-married, newly married, soon-to-be married, or business school graduates. Well, that's just spiffy! Courting cost money, and the lack of consistent employment was not much to offer a wife. No, thought Ted, there would be no backbreaking work for his wife, or fears about where the next meal would come from or how to keep the roof overhead. Following his father's death, he had seen what his mother endured and had lived with that knowledge since he was six years old. He wanted more out of life and was willing to earn it.

A thought most foreign to Ted's character popped up. What if the prospective wife was not around to go out on dates or be courted in the usual fashion because of her distant residence? She wouldn't see how he lived and the ways he scrimped, because she was in New York preparing for a prestigious profession in nursing.

The truth could be what he chose to tell her. He wouldn't lie, and she would be left to her own imagination to fill in the rest. He paused and shrugged his shoulders. He was assuming a whole lot. What if this new female acquaintance was not interested? Should he pursue this further or wait until he heard from her? Ted decided on the latter and thought back to why he was in the grocery store.

The owner was used to Ted's routine and already had a cut of beef and suet set aside. Ted collected a loaf of bread and two onions and asked the grocer to add it onto his tab. He somberly realized the bread would serve as his suppers until Friday, as he gently cradled it in his arm and headed toward the rooming house.

Entering Beacon Chambers, he draped his suit jacket over the brown bag, nodded to the gents in the sitting room, and climbed the three flights to his room. Breakfast was the only meal offered as part of the boarding fee, and cooking was not allowed in the rooms. The cost of eating out daily was prohibitive for Ted, so he devised a system that had worked, so far.

He used the noise of the radio to camouflage the crackling of the steak in the pan on the hot plate. The aroma of the steak and onions was a real challenge. He placed a large towel along the gapping threshold and opened the window. Sitting on the edge of his bed, Ted consumed the steak and onions, using pieces of bread to clean the pan as best he could. Relighting a half-smoked cigar, he successfully canceled the residual aroma of his supper.

At eight, Ted descended the stairs to the second-floor bathroom and washed off the city's dust as well as the pan. Reflecting on the day's events, he watched the water go down the drain and knew he had to hold on to his hopes and not let them follow the same downward spiral, no matter the aloofness of one such manager, Bob Taggart! Hadn't he proven his dependability and flexibility over the past five years by working all positions in the accounting department? Perhaps he had to be more assertive, but what if it was taken the wrong way? Seniority rules over skill and talent!

Suddenly, a loud banging on the door brought Ted back to the here and now. He had extended his time beyond the allotted ten minutes, as the fellow boarder curtly reminded him through the oak-paneled door. Ted wiped the sink, hid the pan in his towel, and wished the crank a pleasant evening.

Returning to his nine-by-nine abode, Ted thought about joining the male boarders in the sitting room, but he opted to struggle with his battery-powered radio. At night, it was amazing what he could pick up! Maybe Calvin Coolidge's message on the economy was being reviewed, or perhaps he'd pick up some faraway place with a strange-sounding name, as depicted in a popular song of the day.

CHAPTER FIVE

The passing of autumn moved all too swiftly as a few young crimson oaks defied the inevitable outside of Margot's kitchen windows. She turned on the light, stoked the stove, and fetched the dishes for the oatmeal ritual. By 6:00 AM, Aileen and Lenora were scurrying around, quietly completing their assigned before-school chores while attempting not to disturb their sleeping father and baby brother. Bernard and Raymond were already heading down the street to ready the store for the day.

Looking out the window over the soapstone sink, Margot felt a chill as she watched Raymond with his head cast down, dragging way behind the jaunty walk of his older brother. There's something bothering Raymond, she thought, but he wasn't one to let you in on what it might be. His sulking had gone on longer than usual, suggesting it must be something more than he knows how to handle.

In contrast, Bernard's outgoing personality and clever gift of speech and humor appealed to all. He had a good business head and seemed to intuitively know how to handle people. Margot relied heavily on his street smarts but learned not to trust him further than she could throw him! It is a sad moment for a parent when their own flesh and blood steals from them right under their nose.

Perhaps if Raymond was less sullen, people would respond differently toward him, she thought. He had been an excellent math student and did a fine job with her ledgers and journals. He'd have to prove himself a bit more capable of good judgment and common sense before he's able to take on more responsibility. Jealousy is evil, and that is what she surmised was the reason for his contrariness toward his older brother and other siblings.

Drawing herself back to the chores at hand, Margot sent Lenora to ready Sean for breakfast. Then the squeals started along with the thumping of feet through the upstairs hallway. Leo opened his bedroom door as he tucked in his shirt and hushed the children. Their tenants didn't rise until 7:00 AM, which was their time for the bathroom.

Leo scooped up Sean and headed for the kitchen. Aileen and Lenora finished cleaning their dishes and took leave for the walk to St. Mary's School. Margot poured Sean some warm milk and oatmeal and sat next to him, sipping a bit of tea in her saucer. From all outward appearances, it seemed like a well-functioning, harmonious unit, yet each heart harbored its secret of hurt, distrust, and disillusionment.

Margot checked her locket watch and stroked Sean's dark brown hair, softly humming "Oh Danny Boy," his favorite request each time Katherine would play the piano. Leo started to sniffle and blew his nose.

"What? Do ya have a cold?" asked Margot. Leo shrugged, sipped his tea, and broke a piece of bread off the round loaf. "Would ya please use a knife instead of ya hand which just helped blow ya nose! Praise be to Gad! How am I going to live through bringing up yar child properly? I have to leave. I'll see ya around two with Sean; the carriage is in the front hall, and put a hat and coat on him. In case ya didn't notice, it's almost winter."

Putting on her coat, Margot sensed a chill again. As she hastened down Albany Street, taking a right onto Second Street to Main, her thoughts went back to Leo's appearance. She was not prepared for the rapid decline in his behavior since Katherine left for nursing. He seemed to withdraw from longtime friends, preferring to be alone, or with little Sean. His drinking was mostly confined to the weekends since he decided to work the second shift at Gilbert Knitting Mills. He made the decision to care for his young son until he was of age to attend school.

This freedom allowed Margot to operate the store six days a week, using Aileen or Lenora to care for Sean after school in the back room of the store. Leo would bring Sean down after his nap, and then head off to work at the mill with his lunch pail packed with last night's leftovers. It was a comfortable relationship, though a platonic one since Leo had defiled his daughter. Margot would not forgive that, nor could she forgive herself for not foreseeing the danger she put her daughter in. Leo favored Katherine, and Margot had taken advantage of that by sending her in to comfort Leo when he was drunk and loudly begging Margot to come to his bed. She would say to Katherine, "Go and sing a song for yar Pa. He loves yar voice."

Time tends to take care of things, but Margot knew that just when things seemed to reach a degree of normalcy, it was a sign that some ugly monster of life would rear its head. For instance, out of the blue one night, Leo began questioning her about Sean's development and if she thought he was normal. It seemed Leo had overheard a conversation at the mill about a brother who got his sister in the family way, and the child looked like a fish. The family put it in a private sanitarium somewhere, hoping it would die. Another worker told of a father who had raped his daughter and their offspring was retarded. Then Leo really shocked her during another one of his drunken rages by accusing Margot of making up the story about him being Sean's father in order to cover up Katherine's looseness with some young man, adding when he figured out who it was, he'd kill him.

But one Saturday night two years ago was the worst. Leo had been drunk for five days following the celebration of Sean's first birthday. He was singing all the songs he could remember to his beautiful Margot and crying every time he mentioned Katherine. The liquor gained control and a hateful rage took over, with him slamming, kicking, and punching everything within reach. Exhaustion crept in, and the crying and self-deprecation started. Margot tried to calm him down and felt pity watching the quivering shell of the man she once yearned to touch her. He had been such a handsome blade, and quite vain about his curly hair.

It was the umpteenth time she had been through this in varying degrees. She could see the drinking was going to kill him. All he needed was an occasion, a disappointment, a special event, or no better reason than because he wanted a drink and all be damned! Promises made were null and void. That night, she decided to fight fire with fire and give him something besides himself to think about.

"Leo, darlin," she softly spoke. "Come, sit by my side and talk awhile. Ya seem a bit tired."

Such an invitation put in such a gentle manner meant something beyond just sitting, thought Leo, hopefully. Perhaps she has finally missed him and is ready to be reasonable and do wifely things! Stumbling over the parlor rug's fringe, Leo plunked next to Margot.

Holding her breath from the stench of his breath, Margot began by referring back to his concern about whether Sean would grow to be a normal child. This was not what Leo had in mind as he tried to embrace his wife.

"For goodness sake, Leo, I'm trying to put yar mind at peace about something that may be bothering ya," she whispered in his ear, mindful of the tenants upstairs.

"Keep doing that. I like when you whisper in my ear. It makes me feel like going up to the bedroom with you," he slurred.

"Leo, when Bernard was about three months old, a beggar stopped by while I was picking the clothes off the line. He asked me for a handout and I told him we were struggling ourselves. He wanted either money or food but I told him we had neither, and that I was waiting for ya to return shortly. The man had the look of someone with breeding who had fallen on bad times. Bernard was in the laundry basket and the beggar reached down and said he'd take the boy instead. I grabbed at the beggar, pleading that he put Bernard down. He did, but wrapped his arms around my waist and carried me into the stable where he had his way with me. I didn't know whether Katherine was yar baby or his until her coloring was so different from her brothers' and sisters'."

The explanation hung in the air while Leo struggled with his thoughts, processing the full extent of what Margot had said.

"Sean should be just fine! My son! She's not my daughter. Sean won't be like those incest offspring I told you about. We have a healthy boy here! Well, well, well! What do you know! This is something to celebrate."

It sounded as if Leo was congratulating himself for a job well-done through his virility. No mention was made of what Katherine had endured or if she should be told Leo wasn't her father. Margot did not wish to delve into what rights Katherine had. As far as Margot was concerned, Sean was her son and would provide for her and Leo in their old age.

✦ ✦ ✦ ✦ ✦ ✦ ✦

Arriving at the store, Margot found Bernard alone, rushing to and fro servicing early customers. Tying on her apron, Margot pitched right in and refrained from asking about Raymond's whereabouts until nine thirty, when the pace slowed.

"He stopped to talk with a group of kids skipping school with skates slung over their shoulders," responded Bernard.

"But, the lake has not been frozen long enough. I mean, it hasn't been cold enough, long enough," cried Margot, recalling the chilling feelings she had earlier that day. "Dear Gad! Do I have to think for all of ya?"

"Look, Ma. He could use a bit of time with friends, and he promised to be back by ten to give me a break," offered Bernard. "If it will make you feel better, I'll go looking for my nineteen-year-old brother, whose mother found her way from Ireland to America at the age of sixteen! You've got to let him grow!"

"Who might ya think ya are, talking to me like that? Ya shut yar mouth, ya ungrateful pup," snapped Margot. "I'm yar mother and don't ya ever forget it. I gave ya life!"

Their exchange was interrupted by the local sheriff leading a blanket-wrapped Raymond. Margot controlled her first impulse to slap her son for what she considered blatant arrogance and disobedience in deciding to go to the lake instead of the store.

"Well, what do ya have to say fer yarself, Raymond?" she asked loudly as she placed her hands on her hips.

"I'd rather say for him, Mrs. Lockhart, seeing he's been through quite an experience. While on his way to the store with Bernard this morning, he came upon a bunch of wet-behind-the-ears who were determined to skate on an unfrozen lake. Raymond recommended they wait until the middle of December but, seeing they weren't going to listen to him, decided to follow them to the lake in case one fell in. First, he ran to the store to tell Bernard he'd be back by ten.

"Sure enough, just as he arrived at the lake, he heard a frantic yell for help. They told me Raymond took off his jacket and shoes and crawled on his belly on top of the thin ice, reaching the youngster just as he was going under for the second time. Some of the group had run back to town for help, while a couple found long branches to help Raymond pull the victim back to shore. He saved the boy's life! You can be proud of him! Dr. Kirkland asked me to drop by his office with Raymond so he can check him for chills, or frostbite, I guess."

"I'd rather go home and rest awhile," interjected Raymond.

"Son, Dr. Kirkland is checking out the youngster you saved and told me he wanted to make sure you're all right. There's no charge for this, under the circumstances," stated the sheriff, knowing how tight things were for the large family.

Looking back over his shoulder as he guided Raymond out the door, the sheriff added, "Oh, by the way! The newspaper reporter for the Herkimer area plans on putting Raymond's act of bravery in the newspaper. A real celebrity! Come on! Let's go, son."

Margot was speechless as her mindset changed from that of reprimanding Raymond to astonishment over his brave act. Her mouth was still open, as she watched the sheriff help Raymond into the police car. Running to the phone, she rang up Leo and filled him in on their son's heroism. Leo was popping his buttons with "the Lockharts are real men" gushing, when finally she got a word in to ask him to come down as soon as possible to help Bernard with the store. She was going to the doctor's office to make sure Raymond was all right.

Until this moment, she had been trying to find a discreet way to visit Dr. Kirkland to discuss Katherine's employment opportunities upon her graduation and certification as a registered nurse. This would be as good a time as any. She wanted Katherine in Little Falls, just in case Leo slipped faster than expected. His tremors were growing more noticeable.

"Bernard!" she called from the back room. "I'm walking over to the doctor's office and yar Pa will be down with Sean in a short while, to give ya some help."

She went into the water closet to check her appearance in the mirror. She brushed her hair upward and tucked the straggling strands back into the pug at the back of her head. She wore no color on her cheeks or lips, and the days of comparisons to a Gibson Girl seemed so long ago that it was as though it happened to someone else. She attempted a smile, but the pure white pearls which had been an asset to her wholesome face were long gone, having been substituted with an upper and lower set of ill-fitting replacements. She had always been proud of her teeth and cared for them religiously. Their loss was not caused by neglect but by the modern day miracle of toothpaste. The new product was too abrasive and gradually removed the enamel from her teeth. With a sigh, Margot washed her hands, and patted the water on her face.

She called good-bye and went out the rear door of the store. She walked everywhere and had the misshapen feet to prove it, from years of wearing secondhand shoes. The bunions were becoming obvious, where once delicate, slender feet peeked from under the long skirts of her youth.

Margot arrived at Dr. Kirkland's office just before noon and was greeted with a sign on the door that read, "Gone for the day." She turned to leave when a tap on the window called her back. Arthur welcomed Margot in his usual fashion by holding her hands between his. Then he would ask how Ireland's favorite "wild Irish rose" was, and if her daily prayers were being answered.

"Y'all never change, Arthur. I think yar still a bit touched!" They both laughed and Margot asked how Raymond seemed after his cold swim.

"The youngster he saved will have a time of it for a while, but Raymond will be fine after a day of rest. He did not think of himself. It was a very unselfish gesture for such a young man," commented Arthur in a most admirable tone, "and similar to the bravery of a young woman I knew years ago, who always made the best of a bad situation."

"Now, never ya mind the flattery. I have some serious things to share with ya, if ya have the time. If not, I can come back at yar choice of time," she hesitantly said, hoping Arthur could hear her out right then.

"I have about an hour. But then I have a meeting with a young doctor who would be a welcome addition to this office and practice. It would also make my life a bit easier to have coverage for the Little Falls population on the days I am not here due to my affiliation with the New York City hospitals." Arthur pulled up his chair and sat opposite Margot. "Tell me, Margot, what might be troubling you?"

"I haven't wanted to bother ya because it really isn't yar burden, but do ya think I did the right thing? Oh, how would ya know what

I did? Let me go back a bit. Two years ago, when Sean had his first birthday, Leo was drunk for five or six days. He was beside himself, and even accused me of being in cahoots with Katherine to cover up her getting pregnant by some young man, because he still claims to have no memory of forcing himself on her. He feared Sean might be retarded and he just went on and on. It was getting worse as each day passed.

"To stop him from killing himself, I made up a story about a beggar who came by our home for a handout when Bernard was three months old. I told him how the beggar dragged me into the stable and had his way with me and I was afraid to tell Leo at the time. I didn't know if Katherine was Leo's baby or the beggar's until her coloring was so different from her brothers' and sisters'. He believed me, at least for the moment. I am worried about the next time he starts thinking of the money that is being spent on Katherine's education, and starts wondering where it is coming from. Are ya sure, Arthur, that no one knows it is yar generosity and kindness that made this possible for her?"

"Perhaps you should be concerned with Leo turning the situation around and blaming you for the beggar doing what he did. The mind works differently when under the influence of alcohol or drugs. Then, Leo wouldn't feel so guilt-ridden about Katherine, given he might consider it sort of a form of justification for having lived with a tainted wife! Now this is just speculation from his point of view, as you have told me he is searching for some sort of truth which would relieve him from the responsibility of his actions and resolve him from mortal sin. That's what you call it, correct? Don't look at me so strangely, Margot. Other people have the ability to think, just like you.

"Remember the day Kate sliced her hand at the mill, and you were summoned by her supervisor? The expression on your face and the look in your eyes when you found me as the attending doctor betrayed all the denials you could possibly conjure up. Once I saw her, I knew she was our daughter. I will be forever grateful for your gift of Kate. I guess I was that beggar, begging for your love.

"And again, I assure you the funds are in the form of a grant to the hospital from an anonymous donor, with a specific directive to be used for Katherine Lockhart, pending her abilities to maintain honor grades. This removes the suspicion of a 'sugar daddy,' and places the onus on Kate to perform. The money left will be increased to provide for another deserving candidate and so on. The hospital knows there is an end to the money should the donor die. I feel very well with all those prayers from the dear sisters," quipped Arthur.

"Ya can't be angry with me, Arthur, but it is like that saying about a tangled web when you start deceiving. Leo has changed so much since Katherine went to St. Mary's. I'm worried about the tremors. Sometimes he can't hold a cup of tea without slopping it all over. I pretend not to notice. He is such a proud man." She trailed off and cast her eyes down to stop the tears.

Time is a thief stealing away as two friends sat in their older bodies, dealing with the piper's fee. Their conversation moved to the future and Katherine's employment. Arthur had nothing but praise for her nursing capabilities and hoped she might consider continuing toward being a doctor. With that, the other side of Margot peaked.

"Enough is enough. That girl is starting to act like she was born with a silver spoon in her mouth! Between the Dorseys and her high honors grades, we won't be able to talk to her. She's getting all sorts of ideas about moving out of state, and I want her in Little Falls, because she is going to care for Leo when he gets sick," shouted Margot.

"Margot, do you hear what you are saying? You can't control your children's lives as though they are slaves. Your choices do not have to be your children's when they become adults. I read a lovely poem once about how children are not our possessions. They are only loaned to us by God."

Arthur was aware that Margot was worn out from the pretense she was maintaining for all to see. She had so much to lose if the truth be known. Through her efforts, the web was secure, but for how long?

"Why not trust Katherine to do the right thing?" suggested Arthur. "I don't think she will go off to some strange location for her first job. She's tied to her family and her son, but when the time is right, she will leave. You will have to let her. If you interfere too much, Margot, I may have to tell our daughter a story about two people who loved briefly, ever so briefly."

The summation of her visit found Margot a bit agitated. She felt like she had come for absolution and received penance for a lifetime. Bidding Arthur farewell and respectful thanks for listening, she conceded he had given her cause to rethink some things about her attitude. As for Leo, Arthur listed a few doctors who were located in Utica and had success working with all sorts of ailments stemming from alcoholism. He knew the damage was done, and Leo's days were numbered.

Helping Margot on with her coat, Arthur noticed the threadbare collar and multiple strands of silver throughout her chestnut brown hair. Arthur was suddenly taken with Margot's overall physical appearance and inwardly saddened by the demands life had made on her over the years. The contrast between his spouse and her exterior pretense of a devoted wife in the upper echelon of society, and the commoner's appearance borne by Margot, the mother of his only child, caused a sinking feeling in his heart.

Twenty-two years ago, he confided to his adoptive parents his love for a young woman who was in an unhappy marriage. He wanted to take her away with him to a place where her abusive husband wouldn't find her. His parents could not believe what their ears were hearing! Arthur had always done the right thing, never demonstrating an impulsive moment in any of his decisions. Had they known the identity of this abused woman as their former domestic, it would have caused them extensive trauma.

They could not contain their disappointment in their son's shortsightedness by even thinking of becoming involved with a married woman! He would be throwing away his career; tongues would wag, and who'd trust him? Women wouldn't feel safe with him and men wouldn't go to him. There was no place he could go and practice that he would be able to completely avoid his past. They projected over and over the social nuances of the times to the point that Arthur stormed out of their home, angry at himself, at the world, and feeling like a child in the throes of a tantrum. He knew they were right and owed them respect after the years of care and nurturance unselfishly given him. Perhaps Margot would forget their special moment, as though it never happened. He cried softly in the silence of his heart. Rationalizing became easier as time and distance reduced his passion to a one-time memory.

Reflecting back, he realized Margot wouldn't have left Leo but how he wished he had been in Leo's place. Now, all he could do was attempt to give Margot some help for all that she endured alone. He knew what aloneness was.

Life for Dr. Kirkland was rather fragmented and socially depersonalized. The size of his office practice and vanguard specialization in pediatrics placed Herculean demands and constraints on his married life. His socialite wife filled the hours by constantly seeking pleasure in prestigious gatherings and enjoying the monetary benefits of her husband's successful medical status.

Arthur was left with the bills and an empty house most of the time. If he was in Glens Falls, his wife would be at their retreat on Lake George. Should he venture to Lake George, she would leave to visit relatives or friends in Glens Falls or New York City. They never had children, and this drove Arthur further into his career.

Recently, he had reduced his work load and enlisted the services of younger doctors to cover his Glens Falls office and hopefully, the Little Falls area as well. Arthur's dream was to establish connecting medical clinics which serviced all people, not just those who could afford it. This was one reason for setting up practice in Little Falls, with future hopes of extending into Herkimer and Schoharie counties. Not everyone had a means of transportation to the nearest city, but a medical clinic in close proximity which was affordable could reduce epidemics and curb infections from life-threatening injuries.

Arthur's wife had a difficult time with his new role as a crusader when he could have a luxurious suite of offices on Fifth Avenue. To his wife, he was a disappointment; to his Margot, but a friend.

✦ ✦ ✦ ✦ ✦ ✦ ✦ ✦

The sun had moved behind the gray November clouds as Margot briskly walked back to her store. The upper crust of the ground had separated from the lower level, causing a hollow sound under her steps. The leafless trees stood lifeless, leaving only past knowledge as hope that there would be life again, come spring.

The rigors of winter in this section of New York were attested to by the wrapped shrubberies in front of the stately homes. The shutters were closed on the sunless sides, and some hardy souls had already dragged out their horse-drawn sleighs in anticipation of nor'easters which rendered the horseless buggies almost useless.

One can handle the elements, Margot thought, but those hardships imposed by the emotions of human frailties are what reduce the love-filled heart of youth into an atrophied muscle. She learned early in her marriage to Leo what the unhealthy degrees of selfishness and jealousy can do. It was one thing to have the devoted attention of a male suitor, but quite another thing when the license of marriage extended total male dominance over any freedom of choice or preference on the wife's part.

As the spouse of an American-born citizen, she recalled how privileged she felt to be his bride and a member of such a respectable family. Unfortunately, the lineage was taken for granted by Leo. He reveled in being known as a fourth generation American and the son of a Civil War veteran, but exhausted his welcome at the local taverns and most of the clubs by the age of twenty-five. Somehow, he missed the point that honor and respect are earned through personal actions, not through someone else's efforts and sacrifices.

The initial romance of married life and togetherness quickly faded upon the arrival of their son, Bernard. Never during courtship had Leo's alcohol problem surfaced, but in the privacy of their humble dwelling, it consumed the bud of life from Margot's heart. What had she settled for? Why hadn't she seen or been told about this other side of Leo? She felt deceived by his family and friends.

Leo was even envious of the time she spent nursing their son. She reflected on a Saturday afternoon when Bernard was two months old. Leo came home feeling giddy and overly amorous. He wanted to make love right then and there. Margot was not finished nursing, but Leo said she was. He grabbed his son away from her, roughly placing the baby boy in his cradle. Leo proceeded to kiss and suck the milk from her mothering nipples. She pushed him away. He lunged forward pushing her down flat on the bed. She resisted angrily with all her might, smacking Leo in the face and chest. He was not to be deterred, and bit her, leaving a full set of teeth marks on her left breast.

On the Monday following the biting incident, Margot gathered up Bernard and a few belongings and took the train to Glens Falls. She left Leo a note stating she would return in a week and not before, adding he had to stop drinking or it was over as husband and wife. Her family was under the impression that Margot's visit was to show off her handsome son and welcomed her with open arms.

After a couple of days of family hopping, Margot took a stroll over to the neighborhood where she and her sister Mary had worked as domestics. As she neared the home of her former employers, the Kirklands, she spotted a brand new shingle hanging on the porch where old Doc Hawkins had his practice. It read, "Dr. Arthur Kirkland, MD." Margot felt a rush of warmth all over her body. The urge to see Arthur pushed her up the stairs and into the waiting room. Three people were awaiting the good doctor's services as she stood in the doorway. She turned to leave as Dr. Kirkland opened his office door to receive his next patient, but upon spotting Margot, he blurted out, "Dear woman, into my office. I'm so glad you got here this quickly. Please, everyone, come back in two hours, so you won't be exposed. Thank you." Opening a door to the rear room, he spoke to his assistant, "Nurse Atkins, you may leave until 3:30."

Arthur swept Margot into his office. When the coast was clear, they both doubled over with laughter until the tears ran down their cheeks. Gradually, they exchanged news about their lives and families over the span of the past five years. Cautiously, Arthur told Margot how devastated he was by the news of her marriage, but knew her religious preference.

"I'll always have a special place for you in my heart. You were my first love and maybe my last love, Margot. Did I say something wrong? I apologize. Please, don't cry!"

"Oh, Arthur, ya just don't know. It's not what I expected. He drinks so much and it changes him into an ugly person. I had to get away for a while because…he bit me on my breast and I think it is infected."

Protocol went by the wayside, as typically, a nurse would be present for an examination of a female patient. His concern for Margot as a nursing mother superseded good judgment. He directed her to slip off the top of her dress while he assembled swabs, iodine, and gauze. All was going well between doctor and patient until Arthur saw the bite. He was outraged by the extent of the imprint, and found his arms encasing a woman hungry for the gentleness and love he felt for her.

The passion of all the past hopes and dreams welled up in both of them, rendering them helpless souls where nothing mattered except fulfillment. The touch of their lips and the embracing of their bodies had to happen, if only for this one time. It was right…it was right… right?

Arthur kissed and fondled her hair as it cascaded over her shoulders and down her back. Margot loved his touch and never wanted the feeling to stop. She wanted him again and showed him. So long ago, yet it seemed like yesterday.

She knew there would never be another moment such as the moment shared with Arthur. Her choice for better or for worse bound her to Leo, until death.

"Ah, be on with ya," whispered Margot to herself, as she attempted to force her thoughts back to the needs of the present. Reviewing all the facts of the past three years, she prayed nothing had been overlooked that would ruin or crumble all she had worked so hard for in earning a degree of respectability with those high muckety-mucks who looked down their snooty noses and snickered at her brogue. No one must suspect that Sean is not her son.

"Dear God," she sighed, "What is it, a curse? Why do these things continue to happen to us? I no sooner start to go ahead when I find myself further behind! What do you want of me, Gad? How much strength do ya think I have? Now mind ya, I know it could be worse but how much, I don't want to know."

Margot thought about all the spunk she had when she was first married. Nothing could discourage her and persistence would conquer all obstacles, or so she thought. But the curse or whatever it was seemed to have passed on to Katherine right from the day of her birth. On that Christmas Eve of 1902, Leo had promised to be home on time for the special supper Margot had prepared. The blistering wind howled outside the window as Margot kept checking to see if he was coming down the road. By nine, it was apparent Leo had broken his promise and was gathering a bit of his type of holiday spirit at the local tavern.

Bundling up Bernard and wrapping herself in the handmade woolen shawl her mother had sent her as a present, Margot set out for the tavern. It was a moonless night, and the walking was a bit treacherous for one almost ready to give birth any day, plus carrying a robust, sleepy, year-old toddler. She remembered talking to the wind, the moon, and the stars as she stumbled along in an attempt to close out the pain that was mounting.

"Damn ya, Leo Lockhart, and damn myself for having such a temper. Dear Jesus, let me make it to the tavern. Oh, no! I…I'm all wet. Or is it blood? Fast, Margot! Get to the door. I should have waited at home."

She could hear the tenor voice of her husband singing "Sweet Molly Malone," followed by the rambunctious applause of the listening crowd. As Margot pushed open the door, a powerful pain surged from her back around to her full-blown belly. She let out a mournful cry as a rush of people grabbed her son and slowly lowered her to the floor. With one long string of Gaelic, Margot surely damned Leo to his last breath as he fell to his knees by her side. The pain grew intense, and a midwife was summoned as Margot was carried to the back room of the tavern. At approximately 12:09 AM, a healthy baby girl was resting peacefully next to her mother as they both lay atop two tables from the tavern, compliments of the proprietor. It was the first of many times that Leo's friends would be more important to him than the loved ones who were left waiting for his arrival. Then when he did arrive, they were left with cleaning up his vomit and urine from overindulgence.

"Gad is just; Gad is merciful; forgive me," prayed Margot, feeling guilty for the self-pity she found herself indulging in by drudging up past memories.

Rounding the corner on to Main Street, she spotted Bernard talking to a few of his city hall friends outside her store. Bernard surely had the gift of gab and could tell a story like no one else. Bernard had a talent for turning a happening around so people didn't even realize they were seeing a reflection of their own entertaining selves in his humorous stories.

He was a salesman at heart and had a quick, intuitive nature. Quality clothes, impeccable manners, and associates in the right places were most important to Bernard. He had a knack for setting trends, which extended to his toes in the latest dances. Life was sweet in Bernard's eyes, and ready for the plucking. His beaming smile and personality offset the fact that he was bald at an early age due to a childhood bout with smallpox. Most people thought he was much older because of his hair loss and tended to give him more credit than living experience allowed him to have.

Seeing his mother from afar, he bid his friends good-bye, adding for them to keep their lips sealed about his new venture until he had a chance to discuss his political ambitions with his parents. Waiting for his approaching mother, Bernard began to sing "When Irish Eyes Are Smiling," as he waltzed around the sidewalk. Margot could not help but laugh at her full-grown son making a spectacle for her benefit. Bernard grabbed her and swung Margot around a couple of times as she held her balance.

"Get on with ya; yar daft," she laughed, thinking there were so many things about Bernard which were like his father as a young man.

"What might ya be conjuring up? I saw ya talking with those shysters from city hall."

Taxes and the like always irritated Margot, along with the elected officials who were, in her eyes, using her hard-earned money to feather their own nests.

"They're trying to convince me to run for a city hall position in the upcoming election," Bernard casually offered.

"This has been some day! First Raymond becomes a celebrity and now you're going to join the badgers of society! We need to talk over a few things this evening after supper," Margot stated, with more than communication on the agenda.

The supper table that evening was extremely quiet with no one really looking anyone in the eye. It was clear to everyone that things were changing quicker than their family was prepared for.

Change was not limited to their family; it was the tempo of the times since the end of World War I. The world had grown smaller with the use of radio, telephone, airplanes, and movies. All that had been familiar was now becoming old hat. Long skirts were being raised to above the knees. The freedom of the roaring twenties was extremely appealing to young people reared by Victorian parents.

The silence was broken by Sean. "I miss Kate! When will she be home?"

Margot reprimanded the youngster for speaking with food in his mouth and pulled out the day's mail, forgotten in her apron pocket. There was a letter from Katherine with news that topped off the events of the day. Margot read it out loud as the family finished their supper.

It seems Katherine was accepted for an internship at the Brooklyn Hospital on Long Island and would be there over the Christmas holidays. Margot knew this was a wonderful opportunity for her daughter, and only the top student nurses were chosen for training in areas of specialization. As Margot read on, it occurred to her that Arthur may be behind this and felt a bit irritated that he had not even mentioned the possibility during their hour conversation earlier that day! She would be left with explaining Kate's absence to Sean at Christmas. Katherine closed her letter with the hopes of being home in the middle of January for Sean's birthday and before starting her final semester at St. Mary's. Having their attention, Margot took advantage of this rare occasion.

"Raymond, it was a very brave thing ya did saving that drowning youngster, but it could have been yar life that was lost. Ya should have told the sheriff or firemen and let them earn their pay. What would I do if something had happened to ya?"

"You'd still have Bernard and Sean," he responded.

"Why do ya say that? Have ya no feelings for my words? What are ya so angry fer?   Let me help ya, son. I've noticed that someone has been taking money from the store. This someone adds up the parcels bought and charges the customer the correct amount. Then after the customer leaves, writes the sum of the items as one, two, or three dollars less on the receipt, depending on how much the customer spent, so it's not too noticeable.

"We have two things that went wrong here. Raymond, ya weren't adding up the receipts like ya were supposed to be doing to check errors, or ya discovered the difference between supplies and sales and didn't want to snitch. I've already been down this road with Bernard's hand in the till, so it's something I watch for, and I know who the little devil is! Lenora, what have ya got to say fer yarself?"

"I'll tell you why I took the money! I should be paid for working after school each day. I need clothes in the styles other girls are wearing, not hand-me-downs from a sister who's eight years older. You take all sorts of care of Katherine. Katherine this! Katherine that! People ought to know what Katherine really is!"

"Shut yar mouth. We have little ears listening, to say nothing about the MacArthurs upstairs! What has gotten into each of ya? Can't ya see how hard I'm working?" pleaded Margot in a loud whisper. "We can't count on yar pa. His health is bad,"

Lenora just about jumped out of her skin and screamed with every vein in her slender neck sticking out.

"Pa is a drunk! He makes himself ill and I'm sick of him and you pretending!"

Margot lost control and slammed Lenora so hard with her hand that she knocked her off the chair and into the side of the black-bellied stove. Bernard and Raymond rushed to help her up as Sean screamed at the top of his lungs. Aileen wet her pants and was busy wiping the floor. The upstairs tenant, Mr. MacArthur, came rushing into the kitchen.

"May I be of help?" he inquired, wild-eyed.

Margot was scarlet with anger but gathered a clear state of mind.

"Thank ya, Mr. MacArthur. We were afraid Lenora had burned herself when she tipped her chair too far back and fell toward the stove. Is she hurt, Bernard? Let me see. I'll get some shaved ice from the ice box. Thank ya, Mr. MacArthur. We can take care of her."

As Mr. MacArthur closed his upstairs door, Margot grabbed Lenora's arm. "Ya go geet whatever ya bought with the money. Yar a little sneak. Yar not to be trusted and never will be again. Y'all get a job somewhere else and pay rent to live here."

No one argued or took up Lenora's cause. Yet each felt the same resentment toward Margot's idea that she could use them to work for nothing. There was no future for them, just bondage. Each had their own plan for getting out from under.

Being on a roll, Margot made a clean sweep as she continued.

"Bernard, so ya will be takin' my money another way, as a city hall official, if elected. Well, learn from this, and don't put yar hands into the city's till."

With this, Bernard rose to leave. He was tired of walking on eggshells.

"Ya come back here, this minute," Margot demanded. "We don't need any more disgrace. Yar father takes care of that for all of us. If yar elected, ya will be working for all the people of Little Falls and must not do anything to cause criticism of yarself or yar family."

She made the sign of the cross and wished him success, adding that she hoped his father's alcoholism would not be the reason should he lose the election.

"May I leave, now?" Bernard requested.

She waved her hand in dismissal.

Rushing out the front door, Bernard hoped he wasn't too late to catch his father on break between shifts at the mill. Leo was playing cards with a couple of co-workers by the small kerosene heater just inside the huge sliding factory doors. Catching sight of Bernard racing up the path, Leo closed his hand and placed some money on the barrel. His first thought was that something bad had happened to Raymond following his icy dip in the lake, but Bernard put his father's fears to rest when he told about the support and encouragement he received from his friends to run in the upcoming election. The newspapers might get hold of the rumor and he wanted his parents to know beforehand. Leo was elated and shook his son's hand as though he had already been elected.

"Son, do you know what this means to me? We'll show those highbrows what the Lockhart men are made of. You're a leader, just like your grandfather was during the Civil War. Who knows where this could lead! Congress, the Senate, even president!"

At this point, Bernard brought up the possibility of losing the election, in an attempt to bring his father back to reality. Leo stepped back a pace and looked at his firstborn.

"You're starting to sound like your mother! Lockharts are winners!"

The next few days, Bernard covered every public gathering of people that numbered more than two, encouraging the voters to write in his name on their ballots. It was a close race, but he won and was the youngest elected candidate the town had ever had. There was so much to learn and no room for error, yet he wanted it so much he could taste it!

Margot was astounded by Bernard's victory and cut out the newspaper clippings on the election, as well as Raymond's heroic rescue of the youngster from Mirror Lake. She knew how surprised Katherine would be to hear of all that had transpired and included the clippings in her letter. She told Katherine that a special gift would be arriving before she left for Long Island. It was a combination Christmas and birthday gift, and they hoped she'd like it. Lenora had picked it out.

✦ ✦ ✦ ✦ ✦ ✦ ✦ ✦

The day at the hospital had been exhausting, and Katherine felt as though she was coming down with a cold. She had cut her finger on a pin while changing a patient's bandages the day before and the scratch seemed infected. Epsom salts might help, she thought. Mail had been left on her bureau, and she wanted to read it but was too tired.

"No, it wouldn't be right if something was wrong with Sean and I waited until tomorrow. What kind of a mother am I? But I don't feel like a mother. I don't know what I am. Let's see what's in Ma's letter."

She read the clippings and was left breathless. What is going on back home? There was never any talk about Bernard going into government! Whatever possessed Raymond to go after the youngster in that icy lake? And what is Lenora doing picking out a gift for her? Things are different somehow, and changing so much; she really didn't know the people in this letter. Instead of happiness for Bernard and relief that Raymond was safe or gratitude for Lenora's maturity, Katherine felt empty due to not being part of their daily world. She felt as if she didn't belong where she was; didn't feel as if she belonged anywhere.

Searching for a handkerchief to wipe her tears, she opened the dresser drawer and spotted a folded piece of paper with Ted's Boston address on it in Madie's handwriting. Impulsively, she gathered paper and pen and wrote to this nephew of her supervisor, who perhaps might not even recall meeting her. At least the news from home could give her something to write about, along with her upcoming internship.

Katherine realized guiltily that a note of congratulations was appropriate to send to Bernard. So, upon completing Ted's note, she briefly penned her wishes for Bernard's success, omitting her own interpretation of why he was so motivated to be a public figure. She knew how hard he tried to impress and win the affections of a certain austere young daughter of one of the wealthiest families in town. The young woman was willing to cooperate, but her parents had better plans for their delicate, well-bred daughter than just a flamboyant, "good time Charlie" store clerk. Bernard's election would certainly get their attention.

Katherine fell asleep, fully dressed, on top of her bed. Two days later she awoke to find herself in quarantine, having picked up a potent staph infection from her patient. Her finger was bandaged with a splint to allow the incision to heal. The attending physician had lanced it hoping to bring her fever under control. Maureen was standing next to her bed. "What happened?" Katherine asked groggily.

"I found you on your bed in a deep sleep. You wouldn't wake up and were as hot as a firecracker! I was so scared, I sent for Sister Amadeus. She noticed your finger and knew what had happened."

"Did you call my parents?"

"We were going to if your fever didn't break, but you responded to the alcohol rubs and the medication. You'll be weak for a couple of days, then good as new and a bit more careful," chided Maureen.

"Who gave me the alcohol rubs?" inquired Katherine.

"I did. When I saw the stretch marks, I knew how you got them. No one else need know."

Katherine turned toward the wall and cried.

"Oh, by the way, I mailed the two letters you had written. You were holding them in your hand, addressed, stamped, sealed, and ready to go. Hope that's what you wanted."

CHAPTER SIX

The fall winds of Boston whipped around the swift-moving form of a man hurrying so as not to be late for the punch-in at the Boston and Maine. Ted had taken time to check his mail cubicle as he left Beacon Chambers and was surprised to find a letter with the posting of Little Falls. To read it immediately would make him later than he already was, thus he tucked it inside his suit jacket, next to his heart.

Just in the nick of time, he punched in on the number of the man he was filling in for. Standing in front of the large oak wheel with its brass punch arm, Ted saw it differently today than every other day. It seemed to represent the earth upon which was listed a number for all of its occupants. When one's time was up, the number was assigned to the next person, who then resumed the related tasks of life. It didn't matter who you were but rather that the work be completed. There was no escape because the tie that binds is money, for survival.

The rush was on in the freight and accounting departments due to the increased shipping and travel anticipated for the upcoming Christmas season. Along with this confusion was the preparation for the end of the year profit and loss statements. Ted was part of the team assigned to collecting and organizing the information for the head accountant. He perceived this as an opportunity to make a favorable impression through precise categorizing, accurate computations, and thoroughness.

As was his practice, Ted removed his jacket and placed it on the back of his chair. The letter from the inner pocket fell to the floor and throughout the morning his chair rolled over it. Larry, Ted's co-worker, spotted the powder-blue envelope and, upon picking it up noted the

Little Falls return address, the fluid female writing, and the faint aroma of perfume. Could it be that shy, dependable Ted is corresponding with a woman? Larry told Sam about his find, and together they plotted how to give the letter back to Ted.

The day ended and Ted chatted lightly with Sam and Larry as they punched out. They kidded Ted about having the bed all to himself and not waking up in the morning with a mouthful of a wife's flowing hair. One good thing about the hair, Ted chided, was they both could save their wife's trimmings for their fast-approaching need for toupees, as he mockingly smoothed his generous dose of dark brown hair.

Beacon Chambers was a welcome sight after the race of the day. Ted nodded to the gents by the fireplace in the sitting room and ascended the three flights, two steps at a time. He removed his topcoat and reached into the inner pocket of his suit jacket. The letter wasn't there! He donned his topcoat and retraced his steps back to the B & M but knew it was pointless because of the frigid winds that were scattering anything and everything in their path.

Honesty would be best. He should just write Katherine that he lost her letter even before opening it. What would she think of a man who can't even hold on to an envelope that made a three-hundred mile journey via a public mailbox, to the hands of a postal worker in Schenectady, who stuffed it into the U.S. mail pouch bound for Boston, which was then hand-sorted and passed on to the mail carrier for delivery to Myrtle Street? Better to wait and think of a way to write her without giving away the fact he never read the letter. That was one of the conversations they had the day they met, regarding how long it took for a letter to reach its destination!

Ted climbed the three flights with a heavy heart and an empty stomach. He didn't feel like eating but needed something to warm him. He heated water and made some tea. He decided to turn in early, and checked his collar and cuffs for the next day.

The heat had dropped earlier than usual, and Ted quieted the relentless wind that buffeted the loose-fitting window sash with stuffed paper. He closed his eyes and imagined a cozy cottage for two near a rippling stream, which was backed by a range of green-covered mountains in the distance. The living room would have a large hearth with comfortable fireside chairs. The windows would be tight and draft-free. The list of specifics rambled for a couple of minutes more, but sleep canceled the continuation.

Upon awakening at dawn, Ted observed a blanket of white on the window ledge. The first snowfall of the season and Thanksgiving is next week! He dressed under the covers and slipped on his socks and shoes. Using a piece of cardboard, he shoveled the fluffy snow into his cooking pot, added some water, boiled two eggs, and used the remainder of the hot water to shave. The stale bread tasted great after soaking it in the soft-boiled eggs. Now he was ready for flapjacks and some brewed coffee. One good thing about the boarding house was the courtesy breakfast each morning.

The walk to work was fun for Ted, reminding him of the trudges to school in the snow when he was a youngster in Rotterdam Junction. The one-room schoolhouse smelled like baked potatoes in the winter, because many students carried a hot spud in each hand to ward off freezing fingers on the way. The potatoes were placed on top of the potbellied stove in a cast-iron skillet. Then they served as lunch for the students. Potatoes seemed to taste better back then, thought Ted.

Having punched in, he spotted a large envelope resting atop his desk. It had the logo of the president of the Boston and Maine Railroad on the upper left corner. Ted felt faint. He looked at the envelope as though it was a python ready to launch at his throat. Larry and Sam were quietly observing from a distance and began to feel a bit rotten.

"Morning, Ted. What's that you've got there?" asked Larry.

"I was just about to open this envelope. It seems to be from the president's office."

"Here, let me do it for you. You seem a bit shaky," winked Sam, retrieving a light blue envelope from the parcel.

Ted noticed it was still sealed. Evidently the finder was just returning it to him. He sensed more was going on here by the way his co-workers were hovering over his shoulders.

At this point, both Sam and Larry were splitting at the seams with glee and curiosity. They had pulled a good one on him, but he dared not let them know how he had searched in the dark and bitter cold the night before for the lost letter. Surely, it would be fodder for his friends for at least another six months, or perhaps forever should it never amount to anything with Katherine.

He chose to laugh also, and warned them to be on their guard. Putting the letter in his pants pocket, he was about to pick up the president's envelope when Bob Taggart spotted the familiar logo as he passed Ted's desk. He inquired as to what association Ted had with the president that warranted such a large envelope.

"A letter addressed to me was found by someone who put it in this envelope to return it to me, I assume," Ted answered meekly.

"I feel it is important for me to know what is going on in my department, especially when any contact occurs between my staff and the president's office," sputtered Taggart.

Larry, feeling a bit uncomfortable, thought they'd better get Ted off the fire.

"Ted sure is relieved to have that letter back because his fiancée was forwarding details about his upcoming trip to Little Falls to meet her parents."

Ted was speechless having not read the letter, and having only met Katherine once. Taggart offered his hand in congratulations, which clued Ted in to continuing the charade. Switching back to his usual demeanor, Taggart urged them to burn the night oils if necessary to stay on schedule for the end-of-the-year deadline.

The trio returned to their desks and focused on their assignments without a sound for the remaining hours prior to lunch. They met outside and walked to their favorite lunch stand bursting with laughter and imitating Taggart's bulging eyes when he learned of Ted's betrothal. Though Sam and Larry coaxed him, Ted refrained from opening the letter for them to view, telling them he would fill them in, in good time.

The afternoon crawled by until finally everyone had punched out except Ted. He wanted to read Katherine's letter in private, and didn't want to take a chance on losing it again. He was surprised to learn of Bernard's election, and recalled a Schenectady broadcast on his wireless several evenings ago announcing a sweeping win in Little Falls by a write-in candidate. That could have been about Katherine's brother! She had told him a little about her brothers and sisters that day in September. He couldn't imagine what it must be like to have three times as many people in a family as there were in his. He recalled how one of Katherine's sisters had died at eleven months old, just like his older sister, Monica. They had that in common, and now he could tell her how he heard parts of Bernard's good news on the wireless before the static attack. As for Raymond's heroics, it brought back sad memories for Ted of a childhood friend's death. He died alone, when attempting a winter shortcut over the local swimming hole on the way to Ted's home.

He felt proud of his association with such a capable woman chosen for an internship at Brooklyn Hospital. A pang of sadness pushed at his heart when reading she would be away from home at Christmastime on her twenty-third birthday. He knew from their first meeting how close she was to her family and especially her younger brother, Sean.

All the way to Beacon Chambers, Ted thought of how to start the letter and what to say. He gathered the stationery, pen, ink, and blotter, as his thoughts raced through possible ways to meet Katherine again. Waiting until his next scheduled time off could take months based on all the different jobs he had been given recently, covering for deaths, sicknesses, and unforeseen circumstances. Nothing ventured thus nothing gained was a philosophy Ted believed. He propped his pillow against the iron bed frame and prepared to write a lengthy letter when a knock at the door interrupted. It was an old friend from his hometown who was staying overnight in one of the transient rooms. He had a letter from Ted's mother. They talked for over half an hour when they decided to go to the Bell in Hand for a brew. Ted knew he could get some stew while at the tavern, in that he wasn't a drinker.

Upon returning to his room, Ted reassessed what he should write in the letter. He did not want to divulge information on Katherine's background Aunt Madie had given him. He decided to focus on the goals he had set for himself in order to acquaint this intelligent woman with his character and qualifications, should she consider him a worthy suitor. He began to write with his usual precise Palmer Method motion of rhythmic circles at the start of each sentence and each multisyllable word. The content of the letter was congratulatory for the three oldest Lockhart's accomplishments.

Ted briefly described his current position and added he hoped it would become permanent, thus affording him dependable and consistent wages which would allow him to live in a larger dwelling than his present nine-by-nine-foot room at Beacon Chambers. He was confident that what he left unsaid could be interpreted. Katherine would deduce he was not in a position of being able to commit to anything except survival at the present time.

Courting was a luxury, and Ted's luxury would only extend as deep as the cost of stationery, ink, and stamps. His trips to New York would be governed by the whims of his employer, who might need him to cover for someone in Concord, New Hampshire, or Portland, Maine. Occasionally, he was able to wangle a pass on the New York Central. All these restricting specifics would emerge throughout future correspondence, should Katherine still wish to exchange letters after this first presentation of honest reality, in the life and times of Ted Bryant. Past experience had proven Murphy's Law time and again for Ted, and so he learned not to speculate or anticipate out loud. He was very closed-mouthed and seldom verbalized just for the sake of talking. When he spoke, it was with purpose and meaning.

The nonsense hour of midnight arrived, and Ted ended on a hopeful note that perhaps one of his jobs would take him to Union Station in New York City during Katherine's internship. Should it materialize, he would wire her pending receipt of the Long Island address, in her next letter. He hesitated at the presumption being drawn here on his part and closed with:

"If you care to answer this letter I should be more than pleased to hear from you. Please tell me something about your work as I know it must be interesting, and I know that you are working hard to obtain your RN title. Meanwhile, I shall take your advice and not work too hard, and beg to remain, Your friend, Ted F. Bryant."

He mailed the letter on his way to work the following morning feeling as though his very soul dropped into the mail slot.

Thanksgiving Day, Ted traveled by train to Salem, arriving at his cousin Bill's home just an hour before the ceremonial carving of the golden roasted turkey. Bill's wife Emma was a fantastic cook, and Ted always looked forward to their invitation to visit. In appreciation for their kindness, Ted was prepared with a link of Italian salami from the North End, and chocolates for the rest of the family and their invited guests.

It was so homey and pleasant sharing the holiday with good folks, even though he knew eventually Emma would get around to asking him about his social activities. She was always trying to match him up with someone from her church. Ted usually dreaded this invasion but startled them this time with casual conversation about the lovely young nurse he met at the September social at St. Mary's.

He watched as all eyebrows moved up in surprised arches. He mentioned how thoughtful his mother had been in helping to arrange a ride for him to Amsterdam with his cousin Walter, as well as Aunt Madie's part in arranging the meeting with Katherine. Then, for good measure, he added the part about Bernard being elected to city hall on a write-in vote!

While they were still trying to find their voices, Ted thanked them again for their hospitality and apologized for talking for a straight thirty minutes. He dismissed himself from the table, stating he would be taking the five fifteen, which left him a scant forty minutes to help with the dishes before rushing to the depot. Between cleaning off the table, the washing and rinsing in the kitchen, and quick hugs and kisses, Ted avoided Emma's questions about the future.

On the return trip to Boston, Ted found himself laughing as he recalled the looks on Bill's and Emma's faces as he talked about Katherine and her family. He took out her latest letter and reread the dates she would be in New York City. Yes, it could be worked out. They could meet at Grand Central Station and spend the afternoon together. Then Ted would catch the connecting train to Schenectady and spend the Christmas holidays with his mother and sister in Rotterdam Junction. That will mean gifts for Christmas, a restaurant for lunch with Katherine, and paid fare on the New York Central.

He would need to be extra frugal the next three weeks, working every possible hour he could arrange. Family men usually soaked up all the extra work at this time of year. Well, he couldn't blame them for being industrious for their families.

Each day dragged by, seeming to be forty-eight hours in length. Would December 23 ever come? The nights of sleep seemed only four hours long, the first of which was always tortured by unknown fears and self-doubts. Indecision about what to give as a Christmas gift was compounded by the fact it was also Katherine's birthday. A woman's guidance was needed at a time like this, but his sister or mother might read more into it than it meant, at least at this juncture of a new relationship.

Fourteen days into December, Ted tried to recall what pleased the dearest woman in his life. He remembered giving his mother a locket when he was eighteen. From that day on, she always wore it when dressing in her best. That was it! Plus, she has a sweet tooth. Everyone likes chocolates! Yes! It's settled. Locket! Chocolate!

✦ ✦ ✦ ✦ ✦ ✦ ✦ ✦

The train pulled in exactly on time at eleven forty-five as Ted checked his pocket watch. He wished the conductor and porter a Merry Christmas and proceeded to the round information counter, in the main hall of Grand Central Station. Katherine was due to arrive at twelve noon.

He had rehearsed his words, but should he hug or kiss her or shake hands? If he was holding something in both hands, this would take care of the decision to shake or hug. As he was deep in thought, Ted didn't see the young woman and man approaching from the left. The man interrupted Ted's preoccupation by asking for a light. This required Ted to put both handheld items on the ground next to his satchel. As he lit the cigarette for this stranger, Ted spotted Katherine standing there smiling. She moved to his side, linking her arm in his, and introduced the smoking stranger as her brother, Bernard.

Ted wasn't the only one feeling a bit restless that Katherine was going to be away from home for Christmas and her birthday. The Lockhart family had sent their Christmas wishes by way of Bernard, and provided a chaperone for her when learning of Ted's Grand Central rendezvous.

"You're not put out about this?" asked Bernard.

"It's perfectly fine by me, and I should have given more thought to Katherine's safety, in that New York City is definitely not Little Falls," responded Ted.

Bernard was so congenial that Ted's disappointment of not having Katherine all to himself was short-lived. It actually made the whole encounter more relaxed and enjoyable. Lunch was Bernard's treat, and he wouldn't hear otherwise from Ted. During lunch, Bernard offered to see Kate back to her nursing quarters after Ted caught his connecting train for Schenectady. This would allow them all more time to enjoy the city together.

The weather was fairly mild, except for some windy corners. The threesome strolled along Fifth Avenue, admiring the holiday decorations and latest trends in the store windows. They stopped for coffee and dessert, aware time was running short.

Ted presented Katherine with her birthday and Christmas gifts. The expression on her face as she opened each was similar to the wonderment of a child. Katherine fingered the gold-filled locket with the rhinestone floral inlay.

"Here, would you like me to help you put on the locket?" offered Ted.

"No thank you. I'm going to put it under the tree at my parents' home just like I was there for Christmas. Would you do that for me Bernard?" she begged. "This way I know it will be safe and won't get lost while I'm here in New York City."

As she opened the second package, it was obvious this one was staying with her.

"Oh, I can share these with the girls at the hospital. They love chocolates; and I have plans for the container they came in." With a slight hint of coquettishness, Katherine spoke for only Ted to hear, "I plan to keep your letters in it."

Ted checked his watch and was shocked at the time. He quickly paid the waiter despite Bernard's objections. They raced each other to Grand Central Station, arriving not a minute too soon.

"Aren't you going to kiss my sister good-bye?" laughed Bernard.

Ted swiftly embraced Katherine, kissed her on the cheek, hopped on the train and drifted off in the direction of Schenectady. He watched until the brother and sister looked like two little people in a toy train station display at Macy's.

After all the days of waiting, it was over so quickly! Ted enjoyed Katherine's and Bernard's company, and the family had certainly put him in his place. How could he have been so short-sighted regarding her safety by asking her to meet a once-met-man in Grand Central Station? If it had been his sister or daughter, would he want her meeting a man in New York City? What a cluck he was!

He was used to looking out for number one since being on his own at fourteen years of age. Reproaching himself, he vowed to take off the blinders and observe the periphery because half a view was like having half a mind. Yet, he thought, Katherine did appear pleased with his intentions and gifts.

CHAPTER SEVEN

The holidays passed swiftly, for which Ted was most grateful. Being alone exaggerated the number of couples he observed and the shared affection which glowed around them. Ted longed for this feeling of belonging to someone. For him, the start of 1926 presented the return of the worker he was filling in for, which bumped Ted back to his former position. A chronic period of depression ensued, coupled with the germ of loneliness. It almost did Ted in; his saving grace was his need to appear confident in Katherine's eyes.

In answering her letters, he was not afraid to venture into the discussion and long-range prospects of their relationship. He had to find a way to convey how important she was becoming to him, yet feared he could be misinterpreting Katherine's view of his financial limitations. The ploy of only telling her what she needed to know had turned on him. The three hundred miles separating them had to be bridged through sincerity. Yet he had to buy time until his ideas of permanent employment, a substantial salary, and suitable living quarters became a reality.

The first week of February, Ted wrote Katherine about the emptiness of his bachelor life. He told how he wished for a magic carpet they could use at their disposal, to shuttle at whim between Little Falls and Boston. They toyed with each other by putting secret codes in their letters, hoping the other would figure it out. Ted teasingly threatened her by suggesting, "Your letters might be used as evidence against you some day."

He wasn't prepared for Katherine's reaction. Her salutation was back to being formal, and the stiffness of the content was similar to what one would write to a new acquaintance or twice-removed cousin. What could he do to erase his written words? He had no idea she was so sensitive a person. Perhaps, being away from home in a demanding environment like Brooklyn Hospital was starting to take its toll on her. Katherine would have to take the state test for licensing as a registered nurse following graduation from nursing school in four months. That's why she reacted like she did to the teasing. She's got a lot on her mind, too, he concluded.

Weather is always a good topic to open a conversation with, so why not a letter? With two feet of snow in Boston, Ted filled six pages with hopes and dreams, admitting he would lose his "vocal acquaintance" trying to say these same words face-to-face. To lighten it up a bit, he submitted a ditty for a serious nurse's critique:

Doctor Smith fell in a well,

And sank without a moan

He should have tended to the sick

And let the well alone.

Fearful the total content of his letter may not be as clear as he hoped, and dreading he might offend Katherine again, he closed with, "Afraid some of the Boston mist from outdoors is creeping into the space where my brain should be, so please make allowances."

The mail cubicle at Beacon Chambers was empty for eight consecutive days. Ted submerged himself in work and accepted all the overtime he could accrue. He walked to and from work despite the near-zero temperatures. The pounds had crept on the past five years since trading the yard for the desk; a predisposition he attempted to curb by smoking.

The first week of March came in like a lion, and brought with it the long-awaited letter from Little Falls. Katherine was home in Little Falls. She had completed the internship, and spent the past weekend with Maureen Dorsey in Amsterdam. They went to the movies Saturday night and saw *A Thief in Paradise,* and on Sunday afternoon had tea with the sisters at St. Mary's Hospital. She apologized for breaking the promise to write twice a week but needed time to sort out all that was occurring in her life.

The pen couldn't write fast enough for Ted's response that night. He knew the words had to convey his understanding of what they both were struggling with.

"You say, 'so many things are bound to happen in a lifetime to make one's opinions change'—true! I think your friend that told you it was necessary to live under the same roof, might have spoken from experience. Yet there is a world of truth in it. I can agree with you, completely, that should one find themselves married to someone, with opposite ideals or tastes, along with having nothing in common, that would be a tragedy in itself! About my ideas, would you care to have me change them, regarding you? Answering your question of when I started wishing about spending our lives together, it was December 23, in Grand Central Station when you slipped your arm in mine."

The response from Katherine reflected the woman he thought he had known before the unfortunate teasing. Her unrelenting side was also back as she urged Ted to give up smoking during Lent. He held off until the last week of the forty days, and proudly reported in his March 26 letter that he wasn't smoking. Adding a postscript, he said he was going to Rotterdam Junction for Easter.

Unknowingly, he upset Katherine by conveying in his April 7 letter how he spoke about her and their friendship to his mother and sister during his Easter visit. Katherine's response, dated April 13, lambasted Ted for his insensitivity by mentioning her not only to his mother and sister, but his Aunt Madie, who then repeated it all to Katherine at St. Mary's! Then the real reason she was upset presented itself in her closing statement.

"If you could travel to Rotterdam Junction and extend your weekend to Tuesday, why couldn't you find time to visit Little Falls?" she wrote. "With all the time spent talking about me, you could have been here, had lunch, and been back in Rotterdam Junction for supper!"

Ted had hoped to journey over to Little Falls, but the digging of the outhouse at his mother's took longer than anticipated. Instead, his money went to buy replacement boards, new hinges for the outhouse door, and glass for a couple of broken windowpanes in his mother's living room.

The only thing to do was to face the music, surmised Ted. He wrote Katherine he was arriving in Little Falls on Saturday, April 17, and would be staying at the Reiman Hotel through the nineteenth. He felt pretty sure he could find Albany Street and looked forward to meeting her parents. So much for the overtime money he had just earned. He shrugged his shoulders and thought, easy come, easy go!

The letter arrived April 16, and shocked Katherine. "Who does he think he is, telling me rather than asking? And what makes him think I'm sitting on my hands waiting for him with nothing to do?" screeched Katherine as she rumpled the letter. Even her parents were taken aback by his presumptuous attitude. But that's how he was, she would soon learn, when bent on setting the record straight. His laid-back demeanor belied his stubborn nature.

The accommodations at the Reiman were basic, matching Ted's conservative nature. A wake-up knock at seven found Ted already up, clean-shirted, and shaved. He slipped on his suit jacket and looked out the window wondering which direction Albany Street was. Following a light breakfast of coffee and toast, Ted conversed with some locals who obligingly gave him directions.

Walking up Albany Street, Ted was surprised at the sizes of the Victorian homes with their peaked roofs, chimneys, and large porches, in contrast to his mother's home with its lean-to and outhouse. He imagined these folks had water closets and running water, wishing his mother had the same conveniences. Halfway up the street it was easy to pick out his destination, as he noticed two youngsters shouting toward a home as he passed every tree or hitch. As he reached the front steps of his destination, the home appeared deserted. He twisted the doorbell and heard a bunch of giggles and a hushing sound.

The door opened, and Katherine greeted him with reserve, introducing Ted to her parents and siblings. Breakfast was deliciously prepared and served on three huge platters. Ted loved the browned potato slices and pork. He couldn't stop raving and eating the homemade breads.

Everyone satisfied, the younger siblings started cleaning the flatware from the table while the older ones carried the dishware. Leo engaged Ted in shoptalk and guided him to the parlor, taking the opportunity to bend fresh ears about his father's Civil War bravery. Ted was astonished to learn that Nathan was still active and marched in the local parades in his Civil War uniform. A call from the kitchen requested Leo's help with something or other. Katherine entered with her coat and gloves.

"Ted, would you like to tour the grand metropolis of downtown Little Falls? My mother has to be at her store by ten to relieve the clerks who covered for her this morning. We could accompany her to the store and then explore the rest on our own."

"Fine with me," Ted responded. "Great day to be out with the sun, and I'd enjoy seeing your hometown with a native guide."

Margot assembled her treasures into the hallmark satchel she carried everywhere recently. Ted kept offering to carry it for her, but Margot would not hear of it. All she treasured, along with the store's books and petty cash, were contained within. Realizing she couldn't trust even her own flesh and blood ate at her subconscious, causing her to become a bit eccentric and secretive beyond what was necessary.

Upon entering Margot's store, the aroma of fresh ground coffee along with the wedges of cheese and links of salami tickled Ted's hunger, even though breakfast was only one hour behind him. He enjoyed touring the premises including the walk-in icebox and storage room. Ted continued his tour with the able guide steering him in and out of all the stores while she introduced him to the people she felt mattered.

After two hours, they exhausted every nook and cranny as well as their feet. The couple stood by the side of the canal as they enjoyed the clear sky and warmth of the sun, attempting to have a private conversation. It proved impossible as the locals were out in full force after such a hard winter. Each stopped to inquire about Katherine's well-being and her upcoming graduation, along with questions about Ted's job and their recommendations about how the railroad should be run.

The longer they stood there, the more people would talk. They decided to beg off by stating they were expected back home and made the gesture to depart several times. This did not discourage some; they just kept walking right along with them, clear up to the Lockhart's home. Ted was used to this type of friendliness, being from such a small town himself where everyone knew everyone's business whether you wanted them to or not.

Safely inside, the couple sat on the window seat, holding hands as they watched Sean and his playmates in a game of kick ball. Ted was comfortable in the Lockhart's home. It was appointed in fashionable taste but with an inclination of being a bit oversized in decorative lamps and picture frames. The colors didn't blend, but each in its own fashion was made of quality materials. Ted thought it could be the way the sunlight reflected in the room, or it could be his slight color-blindness. Yet as he looked at Katherine, the sunlight looked great on her hair and skin.

"Katherine, you would like my mother. She has had a hard life without my father, but you'd never guess it. She smiles and sings, and still enjoys a good Irish jig. What a cook! Apple pies like no one else's. If I lived at home, I'd be fifty to eighty pounds heavier, and when I visit, five to eight pounds plague me for a month until I starve them off." Ted paused and looked out the window, and then continued. "She has a special gift. She tells people things by reading their tea leaves and cards but warns them not to believe anything she says."

"I don't believe in fortune-telling. It really is frowned upon by the church, you know," said Katherine.

"True, but the people always return to tell her how accurate she was. Things she couldn't know about, she tells them." Ted paused, observing Katherine's expression as she watched Sean tumbling on the lawn. She seemed so far away and he doubted she was listening. He continued. "I'm aware of the doctrine, but not everything can be satisfied by human interpretation of what Jesus intended for each of us by the examples he used to try and show us. We also acknowledge he intended us to use free will. For instance, why am I sitting here with you? Why did we grow to this point with three hundred miles between us? What is it that draws us together? There are certainly several other willing male suitors for you to consider. I noticed quite a few eyeing you today!"

"I don't believe anyone notices me. It was being with a stranger to these parts that drew attention to me," retorted Katherine.

"You're switching tracks constantly on me," responded Ted. "There are many parts to each of us, and I'm attempting to condense twenty-eight years of living and my tiny family's importance to me in a rare uninterrupted piece of quiet, which hasn't occurred but this once, since arriving here!"

"Don't raise your voice to me. You're in my parents' home and will not upset them with our relationship, such as it is."

Sean raced into the parlor. Katherine stretched out her arms to embrace him, but the youngster headed for Ted. "Please pitch me a ball like the Boston Braves, Ted." Perfect timing not denied, Ted excused himself, stating he would like the pleasure of continuing their conversation later.

Katherine whipped around the dining room table setting it for dinner and thinking Ted's words over and over; I'm pleased to meet you, Lenora. Katherine has mentioned you often in her letters, that's how I feel I know you. You're quite a dancer, I hear! Won the Charleston contest with your brother, Bernard, right?

"So pleasant and gentlemanly!" commented Katherine to herself sarcastically.

I'm so pleased to meet you, Mrs. Lockhart. Haven't we met before? I remember! I saw you at the social in September at St. Mary's Hospital. Sorry, I didn't know you were Katherine's mother, but I was in a rush to make the train. Hope my being here now is not too much trouble?

"Sugar wouldn't melt in your mouth," grumbled Katherine.

Margot had prepared a delicious roast beef, leaving explicit orders as to when it was to be put in the oven, along with the times for each of the accompanying vegetables and potatoes. Roast beef was a rare treat and generally reserved for holidays and wakes. The total experience with the family around the table kept Ted laughing through dessert. Following the ritual cleaning up, Bernard and Ted went outside for a smoke while Lenora and Aileen spied on them from the stoop, hoping to catch Raymond asking for a cigarette.

It was obvious to Margot that Katherine was unusually sullen and not that enthralled with Ted's visit.

"Why don't you suggest a movie so the two of ya can have some time alone," offered Margot. "I think *The Snob* is at the Rialto, and starts at six thirty."

"Ma, please! He isn't interested in me. The only reason he's here is because I wrote an angry letter when I found out from Madie that he extended his Easter visit to Rotterdam Junction through Tuesday, and couldn't find time to visit Little Falls!"

"Ya hush up and listen. He owes ya no explanation. Yar acting high and mighty, after his coming all the way to offer an apology he doesn't have to give. Yar just another of many young women he probably is familiar with. Did ya ever hear that ya catch more with honey than vinegar? Ya've been showing yar jealousy on yar face every time he pays attention to yar sisters or Sean. It isn't very pretty when yar face looks like the wrong end of Patty's pig!"

"And when did you suddenly change your tune about my seeing 'that perfect stranger'!" asked Katherine, quoting Margot's words from the first time she had seen Ted at the St. Mary's social.

"He's good-looking and very polite. Ya could do worse!"

"And the fact both his parents came from Ireland doesn't matter." Katherine sarcastically implied.

With that, Katherine left the kitchen, pushing the swinging door so forcefully that it slammed against the edge of the china closet in the dining room. A couple of large chargers Margot had leaning against the cabinet's rear wall came crashing forward onto the tea cups and saucers. An obvious quiet preceded rushing feet as Lenora and Aileen scurried to clean up the broken china.

Upon hearing the crashing of broken dishes, the smokers entered to see if they could assist. Leo distracted Ted with a political discussion regarding unions. With her coat over her shoulders, Katherine reappeared and loudly asked, "Who's interested in a movie? It starts at six thirty, so we'll have to rush. It's my treat."

The family members knew not to answer in the affirmative, leaving Ted isolated in his response.

"You hit upon my weakness, Katherine. I'd enjoy accompanying you, but it's my treat!"

"Dutch," offered Katherine.

"Deal," responded Ted.

He had learned that to disagree or question a Lockhart was a waste of valuable time, and though he hadn't observed anger between any of them, the need to win appeared malevolent in nature. They didn't like being questioned about why they decided this or that. Instead, they would look at you with a straight, flat stare which tended to make the receiver feel like an idiot.

This was observed close-up following the tour of Bernard's office at city hall earlier that day. Ted learned how Bernard procured the position and was flying by the seat of his pants to learn the ropes. Ted asked Bernard some questions about process and cross-referencing each department's accounts for public disclosure, only to be cut off with a fast comment about people cottoned to city hall, accompanied by that straight, flat stare.

Here we have a public servant, thought Ted when he and Katherine left Bernard's office, who doesn't know what he's doing, yet is pretending to know it all. This was a reckless attitude for an adult in a public position. There was no doubt in Ted's mind that Bernard would have it all mastered in no time provided his cockiness didn't turn people off.

This need to be the best was evident as Ted observed the children and parents around the supper table. He enjoyed their spontaneous spirits and jovial nature, but one was left with a feeling that, if rubbed the wrong way, the converse would surface. A couple of times Ted observed the sharpness of Margot's looks at Leo, especially when he suggested something to ward off the night's chill.

As Ted helped Katherine on with her coat, Bernard came bounding down the hall stairs. "I'll give you both a ride," he offered.

"That's not necessary," replied Ted. "It's a nice, calm night, if Katherine doesn't mind walking?"

"Never mind Katherine's walking," laughed Bernard. "It's you who will be worn out after three trips. And besides, it feels like rain. Say, take my car!"

"Sorry, but I don't drive. I always take a train like a loyal employee."

As this exchange transpired, the members of the family resembled an audience at a tennis match looking back and forth as each speaker spoke.

"Before the movie is over, please decide," begged Katherine.

"It's settled. I'll drop you both off and pick you up after the flick. I'll drive you back to the Reiman after we bring Kate home, Ted."

The theater was quite full, placing the couple on a side aisle at the rear. A local resident was sleeping off his liquid supper, and at the most important moments in the dialog would let out a loud snore. Ted and Katherine were laughing so hard the tears rolled down their cheeks. It was a great relief mechanism for them both. Halfway through the flick, Ted suggested they go to the Reiman for a cup of coffee. Katherine agreed, having already seen the movie twice in Amsterdam.

The coffee urn was still plugged in and the last of the hotel's supper patrons were sparsely scattered at far corners of the dining room. The waiter motioned for the couple to enter and seated them next to the fireplace where the remaining embers emitted some warmth. Ted ordered for them, asking for a couple of the special desserts. Rice pudding was all that was left. "Rice is nice," responded Ted.

The coffees and puddings were served to the very quiet couple gazing into the dying fire. The waiter returned with a lighted candle for the table and complimentary chocolates. Jarred out of their melancholy by the waiter's kindness, both thanked him at the same time.

"I think my jaw is worn out from talking to your family all day. Thankfully, rice pudding won't require too much action. Just think, if the dessert was butter crunch toffee marble cake, I'd start choking to death and you'd have to try and save me."

Ted noticed tears in Katherine's eyes and reached across the table to hold her hand.

"Have I offended you, Katherine?"

"No, no! It's not you. It's me. I'm just a bit tired. You've been most thoughtful, and it wasn't easy being descended upon by my family. One of them at a time is bad enough!"

"Oh, it was a lot of fun. They certainly have a great amount of energy and confidence, so it seems. They are very proud of your and Bernard's accomplishments. You both are great examples of what hard work can bring."

"You've done well, yourself," exclaimed Katherine.

"At a much slower pace, though. I'm twenty-eight years old and have to double step all the time to stay ahead of the twenty-two-year-olds fresh out of business school. I'd rather talk about our future plans and our friendship."

"Some future in Little Falls!" whispered Katherine. "There is sporadic money in home care. I'm glad this is the last semester of training. You take what comes along and wait for the next case. It can be rather depressing caring for people who you know will die no matter how much care you give them. I pretend each of them is Jesus and imagine how I'd care for him in his human form."

"Perhaps when you obtain your license, more opportunities will present themselves. You could work at a hospital or a doctor's office."

"I should have such luck! The doctors have had their nurses forever, and only if one of them dies is there an opening! The nearest hospitals in Herkimer or Albany would require my living nearby, and the salary is so sparse, I'd have to steal to eat."

"What about St. Mary's Hospital?"

"The sisters would be relentless in trying to convince me to join the Order of St. Joseph," Katherine said casually. "I've thought about it, but my brothers always tease me by saying, 'Nun whatsoever!'"

"That definitely is not an option. It is contrary to my plans, as I started to explain before you again switched tracks. Let's be honest now that we are face-to-face. Katherine, look at me, please! Is there a future for us together?"

"My parents want me to stay in Little Falls. Mostly it's my mother's insistence because of my father's health," responded Katherine.

"All aboard for another switch," sighed Ted.

"Please refrain from making little of what I'm saying," glared Katherine as she pulled on her coat and reached for her purse and gloves. "You have but yourself to be concerned about. I have a family who, to use your term, is always switching tracks. They go from one shenanigan to the other, and I never know where the next embarrassment will come from."

"They seem capable of managing for themselves quite well," offered Ted. "Should they get into Dutch, they will learn how to handle it. Surely you've made mistakes, yourself?"

"What do you mean by that?"

"Haven't you gone to confession with something on your conscience that only you and God knew about and asked for forgiveness? Did you ever say as a kid, 'Bless me Father, for I have sinned. I stole a banana and ate the skin'?"

Katherine's eyes were downcast and she was shaking her head.

"Katherine, listen to me. Focus on us as husband and wife because this is my purpose here. The woman I marry will not work but care for her children and husband. We won't be wealthy or own an estate, but our children won't go hungry. One more thing, I'd like to ask for your hand in marriage, and if all goes according to plan, I will bring your engagement ring this coming Christmas. We will wed the following April, if all this meets with your approval and acceptance."

Stunned by Ted's normally no-action persona suddenly taking total action with a planned agenda, she had dismissed his intentions as simply entertainment until some other woman came along.

"This has been some visit, Ted," Katherine cautiously responded. "May I tell my parents your plans, or is this just between you and me?"

"I'm not looking for an answer from your parents! What is your answer? Then together we will decide when and who should know our plans," stated Ted.

Taken aback a bit as though chastised, Katherine answered, "Yes, I believe we could be happy as husband and wife, but we need to know each other better. I'd like to meet your family, too. What if your mother doesn't approve of me?"

"My mother is happy if I'm happy, and if you are my wife, she will love you. Besides, I'm sure my Aunt Madie has laid the foundation regarding your qualifications as a suitable partner!"

"You make it sound so simple, Ted. Experience has caused me to expect the worst and..."

"Stop where you are before your track-switching causes a collision. The only obstacle I can imagine that would derail my proposal to you would be your decision to discontinue our journey toward sharing the remainder of our life together."

Reaching for her gloved hand, Ted continued, "Katherine, look at me. You're the most beautiful woman I have ever known. I mean that from the depths of my heart and soul. In addition, you're intelligent and industrious. My only concern is measuring up to your expectations. See! You're not alone in the confidence struggle."

Having observed a subtle change in Katherine's expression, suggesting she was gathering a defense against his seeing clear through to the core of her insecurities, Ted suggested they both make a novena to help them through the coming months of decision.

"You surprise me, Ted, suggesting that there is another power which can intervene or assist you. You seem so in control of what you want to happen and when it will happen."

"God helps those who help themselves, and he is much too busy with the rest of the world to be concerned with one man and woman. That's why he gave us free will. He wants us to use our intelligence and not wait for someone else to decide for us." Ted could feel color rising in his cheeks and longed for a cigarette.

"My heavens," exclaimed Katherine. "Bernard is expecting us to be outside the theater around nine, and that gives us five minutes to walk back there."

Ted motioned to the waiter and paid the receipt. The couple hurried along in silence. Suddenly, Ted pulled Katherine into a dark storefront and kissed her long and strongly. There was no objection from Katherine.

"Words can certainly complicate things," Ted softly whispered as he caressed her. Time stood still. She wished Bernard was not waiting.

As they approached the theater's entrance, Bernard was nowhere in sight. Ted fumbled the package of cigarettes in his pocket and asked permission to smoke. Katherine realized her words of disdain toward smoking would be poor timing at this moment.

"After feeling how slender you are when I embraced you, I can sneak you into my room at the Reiman in my suitcase. What do you say? Good idea? Not so good. Then will you have breakfast with me following the eight o'clock Mass at St. Mary's Church tomorrow morning? My train leaves at one." Before Katherine responded, a car pulled up to the curb.

"Hey! You two! Am I supposed to keep this cab waiting or could you say your good-byes in the backseat?" called a grinning Bernard.

"Oh my God, Bernard, are you the town crier?" Katherine said, wrapping her coat around her as she entered the car. Ted sat in the front with Bernard.

The lights were all on at the Lockhart home making it stand out like a beacon in the otherwise darkened neighborhood. Katherine alighted from the car and extended her hand to Ted. Shaking it, she wished him a pleasant trip back to Boston. Bernard remained in the car.

Not to be put off, Ted loudly asked, "Aren't you going to Mass tomorrow? And what about my invitation to breakfast? My train leaves at one, so you'll still have the rest of Sunday to yourself."

By now, lights were coming on in the nearby homes with forms in the windows looking for the origin of the voices and the running motor.

"Really, Ted! I don't want you to get tired of me in just one weekend!"

"Perhaps you are the one who is tired," answered Ted. "I'm going to stay here until you answer."

"Good Lord, yes!"

Katherine firmly closed the front door as silence resumed and the neighbors returned to their beds. Bernard drove Ted to the Reiman Hotel.

Sunday was the perfect spring day, teasing with promise of the warm summer sun. St. Mary's eight o'clock Mass was almost filled, with the older generation in the majority. Ted and Katherine sat halfway back on the bride's side.

Ted leaned over and whispered, "You'll look like an angel in white at the altar this time next year."

Katherine could feel the flush of her cheeks, and the embarrassment that someone might notice her blushing made the rush even worse. Some angel, she thought. If you had any idea what the real situation is, and if you did find out how would you feel toward me? Dear Lord, what am I to do? Will my whole life be a lie?

The remaining four hours raced by. There was the occasional quiet that Katherine dreaded when her inner thoughts screamed, and she feared Ted might hear them. Walking toward the depot, he told Katherine of his loneliness when he first left home, and how his pride wouldn't let him go back no matter how hard it got. There was a definite hint of warning in this telling that Katherine didn't catch, being entrenched in her own mission to escape.

The smoking locomotive slowly powered forward as waving arms tried to slow down its velocity. Ted finally got the window to open and leaned out shouting over the engine, "Katherine, please thank your parents again for me, and my future brother-in-law, for transporting me to and fro."

Appearing not to hear, Katherine just kept waving, fearing that one of her neighbors may have heard Ted and would repeat it to her mother.

CHAPTER EIGHT

The newness of spring made everything bearable. Optimism saturated Ted's thoughts and behavior during the busy hours of work, causing his co-workers to slyly smile while envisioning Cupid's arrow aimed at its new victim.

In the quiet of the night, Ted would panic and argue in his subconscious about the ridiculousness of the situation he had created. He had allowed himself to be bullied and shoved into the pretense of a romantic relationship, just to divert the wrath of his boss. With deep doubts and memories of his own father's shortcomings as a husband and a parent, Ted would break out in a sweat. Whenever his thoughts went to that level of recall, Ted would jump out of bed, smoke a cigarette, and read a book until his thoughts were drowned by the author's words. Any idle moment had to be immediately occupied with structure or exhaustion, for fear he would weaken, and forego any further involvement with Katherine.

The Boston Braves were playing on April 24, and Ted joined the exuberant crowd at Braves Field as they cheered and yelled at everything, making sure they got their money's worth. Ted especially enjoyed the food served by the vendors which completed the ambiance of the outing. Following the game, his married buddies played a few hands of poker with mad-money they concealed from their wives. Ted's limit was one hand, and he exited before anyone noticed he was gone.

Walking through Boston Common, Ted had never seen a more beautiful array of colors, and it wasn't May yet! The greens were greener and the blossoming trees and bulbs were as though some artist had touched them up with enriched hues. He was compelled to capture the gracefulness, if only in a black-and-white photo. He took a loan from his savings for a box camera and a roll of film, writing a promissory note of repayment.

From a novice's point of view, the photos captured the moment but could only hint at how the real thing grabbed at all the senses. Times like this caused Ted to humbly reflect on how limited we are in respect to the grandeur of the One who created all that we take for granted.

While sharing his first photo venture with his buddies at lunch in the North Station Cafeteria, he sensed someone looking over his shoulder.

"Pictures of trees, shrubs, and buildings, eh Ted!" droned Taggart. "What about your sweetheart in Little Falls?"

"Well, you see, Mr. Taggart, I just purchased the camera a couple of weeks ago and will be taking it to Little Falls in June," quietly explained Ted.

"Drop by my office after lunch," directed Taggart.

Ted slumped down as Taggart huffed on his way. They all were quiet for a moment and then started conversations about random happenings at home with children, spouses, or in-laws.

Ted's mind bordered between numbness and runaway possibilities of what his meeting with Taggart would yield. Arriving at the door of Taggart's office felt like a walk down death row.

"Mr. Taggart," Ted called as he poked his upper body through the jarred door.

"Come in and shut the door," responded Taggart. "Don't bother sitting. This won't take but a second. I want you to know you weren't my first choice, but the capable young man I wanted has accepted a position with the New York Central. You'll be starting next Monday as a salaried employee. Don't disappoint me; any questions?"

"Two," Ted managed to mouth. "What is the position and salary?"

"On your lunchtime tomorrow, go down to the business office and find out. Now, if there are no further questions, I have a department to run," he mumbled as he shuffled about and thumbed through the disorganized piles of reports on his desktop.

Ted mumbled something about doing his best for the department as he backed out the door. His comment received a grunt from Taggart.

Ted sent a note to a woman from the business office he had once dated, asking if she knew what his new position and salary were. Her response arrived in the four o'clock mail basket. Hourly wages at eighty-eight cents was three cents more than he estimated, and the position of third assistant to the head accountant had not been anticipated, given Taggart's demeanor. He felt it best to check it out the next day and not say anything in his planned letter to Katherine that evening. It was a very long night of restless sleep, resulting in baggy eyes come sunrise.

The morning dragged with lunch break delayed by the unexpected visit of the Boston Fire Department. Someone had discovered a burning trash bucket in one of the bathrooms, resulting in a rush to file important papers. Finally, the routine was resumed, and Ted quickly ate his lunch of bread and fruit at his desk and rushed to the business office to verify his position and benefits. The one week paid vacation would work out just perfectly for a honeymoon the end of next April; he learned later that it was only after one full year of employment.

As Ted read the completed authorization of his full-time employment and signed the acceptance form, an idea crossed his mind. No need to live at Beacon Chambers anymore! He could move to a flat. His sister Ellen had recently procured a job in Lawrence at a telegraph office and hated living in a rooming house. They could live together, share expenses, and save money!

That thought had to hold until he saw Ellen this coming weekend. Tonight, he would write Katherine about the good news regarding his job and salary increase. He knew he would have to extend beyond being just a purveyor of good news and designed an application for her to complete for the lifelong occupation as his wife. If she replied in a serious manner, Ted's confidence would be renewed. If she responded in a frivolous vein, that would be most disappointing. Nevertheless, this was how he chose to chance what he desired. As he wrote the conclusion of his letter, he tried to clarify by explaining:

"Am afraid I'm a poor talker, especially when I have something I want to say and sometimes can't find words to express my thoughts."

No sooner had Ted mailed his letter to Katherine and returned to Beacon Chambers, than he was called to the phone.

"Ned? It's Ellen," she answered using his nickname. "I spotted a flat for rent on South Broadway in Lawrence this morning. It's on the way to where I work and a short distance from the train station. I was wondering if you are interested in sharing it with me."

"Sis, I don't believe it! This morning I was given a full-time position, which commences this coming Monday, and I thought about asking you if you'd like to share a flat together!"

Ellen was relieved having put a deposit on the flat to secure her intent for fear someone might snatch it. Thursday night Ted and Ellen sealed the deal with their new landlord and moved in the following Saturday. It didn't take long with the sparse belongings the sister and brother possessed. They slept on the floor the following two weeks until they were able to purchase mattresses.

The multitude of items required in getting the flat up and running astounded Ellen and Ted. The stove and icebox were provided by the landlord, but the cooking utensils, flatware, and dishes were their responsibility. Friends offered odd pieces of furniture and incomplete sets of dishes and faded towels. Neither Ted nor Ellen was too proud to accept.

On the second Saturday in Lawrence, just before dropping off to sleep, a wave of guilt descended over Ted when he realized a week and a half had passed since his last letter to Katherine. He hadn't picked up his mail at Beacon Chambers since checking out! No problem. The six o'clock train to North Station would allow him time to walk to Myrtle Street and make it back to work by seven forty-five. That's what he'd do on Monday. Then, with a start, he sat straight up! He hadn't sent Katherine his new address! He grabbed a pen and went hunting for stationery to no avail. A brown paper bag was the only paper he saw, and he was no Abe Lincoln.

Sunday raced by amid attending church and working out a financial agreement with Ellen. Between rent, food, and utilities, and the ratio of Ted's salary to Ellen's, a compromise was reached. Ellen assumed the majority of house-cleaning and cooking to offset her reduced share of the rent.

On Monday, Ted picked up the mail at Beacon Chambers with time to grab some breakfast with friends still boarding there. His mail contained three letters from Katherine, including one wondering if her application had been rejected as a future wife. Stopping at the telegraph counter in North Station, Ted wired her the minimum words:

DON'T WORRY DEAR GOOD NEWS LETTER TO FOLLOW.
LOVE TED

That evening, Ted found the stationery and wrote a lengthy letter, describing the flat and what had transpired over the past two weeks.

"Your feelings and approval of what has occurred are very important to me. Do you feel I did the right thing renting a flat? It is good preparation for a man anticipating sharing a dwelling with a wife. Ellen and I have a good system worked out, at least on paper. The proof will be in the trial run."

The contents of Ted's upbeat letter did not have the positive effect he had hoped. Katherine's mind began to race wildly over thoughts about what would happen after they married next April. Would his sister, Ellen, remain in the second bedroom? Would Katherine then be assigned the home chores while Ellen and Ted went off each day to work? Would she be required to cook each night? Ted did say his wife would not work! If Ted thought he was going to have a live-in maid with other fringe benefits, he had another thought coming! She was a professionally trained woman who deserved more respect than being closed up in a flat in some godforsaken mill town in Lawrence, Massachusetts. She could stay in Little Falls and have the same misery! Why didn't he take a flat in Boston? It sounds so much better than Lawrence!

There was a lot at risk, for if Katherine disapproved of Ted's living arrangement, it would certainly change their timeline of a December engagement and April wedding. It could cancel the possibility of it ever happening! People were already asking about her beau from Boston, and even her mother was making extra sacrifices in anticipation of her first daughter's marriage. A few cents here and a dollar there would help out with the expense of a wedding when the time came.

Feeling she really didn't need this irritation at a time in her life when the future should appear as a golden door gradually opening to a multitude of radiant rays of hope and possibilities, Katherine put Ted's letter in the June page of her calendar. She'd see him in June and set him straight to his face. He had kept her waiting two weeks, and surely he knew she had been frantic with finishing up at nursing school and preparing for her license examination.

The evening went swiftly for Katherine, having to iron her uniforms for the next three days. She was scheduled to assist in surgery at eight in the morning and then attend to the patient as his private nurse until his scheduled release on Friday.

The appendectomy was uncomplicated and was completed just as the textbooks recounted. Following surgery, Katherine proceeded to pull down her mask. The operating surgeon looked at her and offered a suggestion.

"You know, Miss Lockhart, you are a fairly attractive woman and would be even more so if you got rid of all that hair on your face. Drop by my office after you scrub up, and I'll be glad to show you what can be achieved."

The room seemed to become as large as an amphitheater with thousands of people shouting, pointing, and laughing at the hairy-faced nurse in the center. The glaring of the overhead surgery lights felt like it was searing Katherine's skin and roasting the outer layer until it crumbled like burned bacon. She felt her legs start to give and steadied herself against the gurney. Her embarrassment was evidenced by the inflamed blushing. She looked straight at the insensitive surgeon and spoke.

"Thank you for your concern, Dr. Young. I've seen your wife. When you've had success with her face, I might consider enlisting your professional services."

The surgeon left in a rather abrupt fashion, signaling the attending St. Joseph nun to follow him. He wrote a request that Miss Lockhart not be assigned to assist him ever again in the operating room, or be assigned to any of his patients. Sister Noreen was shocked but wiser than the surgeon expected and agreed to his request. She knew his reputation regarding young nurses and felt Miss Lockhart was one of the luckier ones in being removed from his sight.

The remaining days through June graduation were tense whenever Katherine was in near proximity to Dr. Young. He would mention to anyone near enough to hear him that recent studies continue to support the theory that Homo sapiens are thought to be descendants of the ape family. This, he contended, seemed to be based on some people being more hairy than others. Occasionally, a banana would be left for Katherine to happen upon during her shift.

Not only was it upsetting to Katherine, but to the sisters, who espouse all are created in the image and likeness of God. God is perfect, thus are we not nearer to that image? But Dr. Young was clever enough only to quote the journals, not to support the theories.

The deviousness of Dr. Young reached the ears of Dr. Kirkland, having overheard some of the nurses chatting during his daily rounds. Meeting with Sister Amadeus, he inquired about the gossip and dropped a hint that Dr. Young had been one of the doctors he was intending to recommend as a consulting specialist for Brooklyn Hospital. Hearing this type of pettiness put questions in Arthur's mind regarding the professionalism of Dr. Young.

Sister Amadeus thought Katherine Lockhart's approach was just as petty, given the wife was the innocent victim. She noted that Katherine had changed since this encounter, keeping to herself more than usual.

"You know, Dr. Kirkland, Katherine has an unknown benefactor who has provided for her nursing education. St. Mary's is most indebted to this unknown Samaritan because the scholarship will benefit other deserving individuals as long as the benefactor lives. Katherine is the first to receive this scholarship but not the most deserving. My observations leave me with the impression that Miss Lockhart thinks she is above the cut of the cloth from which others are made. Instead of humility and compassion for all God's creatures, I sense her sorting those that are worth her efforts and those who are not. She may have the intelligence to learn all the scientific and medical processes and terminology, but a kind heart is lacking. She is not, innately, a nurse."

"Perhaps it is due to her inexperience or youthful age," suggested Dr. Kirkland.

"Offer whatever you think, but I've seen a lot of young women since being head of this training program, and someone put a tourniquet on her heart a long time ago. She seems to care, but only because she knows it is part of the nursing picture. Though Dr. Young was inappropriate in his embarrassing Miss Lockhart in front of other people, she didn't hesitate in her reaction or stop to consider anything but getting even."

"I understand she is the valedictorian for her graduating class. Do you know what her topic will be?" inquired Dr. Kirkland.

"We request a copy one week prior to her presentation. The *Amsterdam Recorder* always prints the speeches. We like to prevent problems before they happen."

"Yes, I can appreciate wanting to monitor the bud of youthful enthusiasm," chuckled the doctor.

A student nurse knocked and entered with afternoon tea and biscuits for Sr. Amadeus and guest. Dr. Kirkland was always treated with respect, even though his wife never included St. Mary's in any of her fundraising ventures.

"If I may suggest something, Sister, has anyone discussed this incident with Miss Lockhart, or suggested that she apologize to Dr. Young?"

"She is not easy to talk with," responded Sr. Amadeus. "She'll listen and she appears to accept what you are saying, but you cannot be sure. In classes, she responds perfectly in both oral and written work. Her independent, expressive writing is intricate but tends toward being overly euphoric. She does have the highest grades in her graduating class."

"Do you sense she is destined for the sisterhood?" he hesitantly asked.

"Not from what I can gather from the mail she receives from a suitor in Boston. He is the nephew of Madie Cowan, one of our supervisors. I'm sure he will be more aggressive following her graduation," Sister smugly stated.

"Well, Sister, I'd suggest that Kate Lockhart should meet with Dr. Young in your presence and apologize."

"If you don't mind, Doctor, I'd rather let it rest. I've already suggested that Katherine speak with her confessor regarding forgiveness for not turning the other cheek."

"I understand your premise, but there is a worldlier one, of my concern. Next time I see Miss Lockhart, be aware I will convey it to her. You never know when your path will cross with someone from your past. I've learned this from personal experience," he responded. "I must be on my way, and I appreciate the time you are always willing to extend me, Sister."

"Well, Dr. Kirkland, you may not be a Catholic but you are a Christian man," commented an admiring nun.

As Dr. Kirkland gathered up his medical bag and coat at the front desk, he noticed Katherine coming on duty. He watched as she signed in at the nurses' desk and gathered the keys from the retiring nurse. He opened the conversation with congratulations on her fast-approaching graduation.

"Do you mind if I ask what your plans are?" inquired the doctor.

Katherine replied she hoped to work on home cases that Dr. Stanley had already been directing her way during holidays and vacations.

"Would you be interested in a position in New York City?" offered Dr. Kirkland.

"Not really. Especially if, well, I've heard Dr. Young is interested in going to New York City. It would be just my luck…No, New York City is not for me," stammered Katherine.

"You don't particularly want to be anywhere Dr. Young might be?"

"Why are you asking me these questions, Dr. Kirkland?" she inquired, rather uneasily.

"I overheard something about an encounter you had with Dr. Young. It seems you said something about his wife. It really is not my place to say anything, yet my experience has taught me that you never know when you may cross paths with Dr. Young again in your future. My suggestion would be to apologize, even if you are right."

Katherine started to cry and turned away from Dr. Kirkland. He wanted to reach out and touch her quivering shoulders but kept his place.

"I'm sorry, Kate, that I upset you so much. I was only trying to help you realize the world is a small place. It is hard enough being in nursing, caring for people who are too sick or unconscious and unaware of the vigil you keep over them." Dr. Kirkland attempted to slow her tears.

"No, no! Dr. Kirkland, that's not why I'm crying," sobbed Katherine. "It's just that in the past month a lot of things have piled up in my personal life, along with the responsibilities of finishing my training. I don't want to disappoint my family. Yet I question my capabilities of caring for the lives of the ill when I can be upset by such an insignificant thing as an attack on my vanity."

"That's a forward step, Kate. To thyself be true," offered Dr. Kirkland.

Katherine suddenly felt vulnerable and quickly regained a controlling stance.

"Yes, you are right. Be true to self…well…I won't apologize because Dr. Young has to be true to himself, also. He is a pompous ass! Excuse me, but my patients are waiting."

"She is her mother's daughter," sighed Dr. Kirkland to himself.

During the quiet of that evening, Katherine read four letters Ted had written since he moved to Lawrence. He made no mention of her failure to write back other than writing that he hoped she wasn't working too hard. He hoped that following her graduation, they could spend two or three days together to discuss their future plans.

The feeling of suffocation was too overpowering. Katherine had to slow it all down. She did not have the strength to handle the realities surfacing in her adult life. For too long she had pretended nothing had happened and it all would work out. She found herself blaming her mother. Surely Margot had known. Hadn't she relied on her to soothe Leo when he had been drinking? It made everything calm again. Sean belonged to her parents, not her. She had only helped out. Margot said Sean would help care for Leo as he grew old. It was all going to be fine. It had to be. Besides, Sean was perfect.

Katherine's mind surged with anxiety thinking of how she could conceal the stretch marks from Ted, once she became his wife. She would feign shyness. Making love in the dark is a bit Victorian but not unusual for a good Catholic girl. Hopefully she would become pregnant fairly soon after they married. Oh, why was she kidding herself? Truth is the only redeemer; but how much human truth would be needed to change that which only God could forgive?

Following rounds, Katherine completed the patients' charts and wrote a brief letter to Ted, confirming her availability to spend time together the weekend following graduation. She suggested that he not buy a lot of furniture for the apartment but rather to concentrate on a few quality pieces, such as a double bed, a dresser, and a kitchen table with two chairs. Then, she added, the remainder of furniture could be purchased with money from wedding gifts and funds she hoped to earn during the coming ten months.

Katherine chose not to refer to or include Ellen in her letters. She was hoping it would evolve into Ted's own idea to inform his sister that she needed to be in her own apartment by the time they got back from their honeymoon in Europe. But what if Ellen insists on staying or Ted hasn't the backbone to ask his sister to move out?

The more Katherine thought about what could happen, her heart began to pound faster and faster. Her temples pulsed as she clasped the sides of her jaw trying to hold back the pounding in her neck. She suddenly slammed her fists repeatedly into a pile of clean towels resting in a laundry basket next to the nurses' desk in an attempt to release her fury.

Why, she thought, did she always have to be the one to adjust, please or endure when others seemed to be doing just as they wanted when they wanted! Well, one day God would make them all pay for their sins. Taking out her prayer book, Katherine prayed for the remainder of her shift.

Chapter Nine

The train was twenty minutes ahead of schedule. Katherine raced into the Little Falls depot, scanning the arrivals for Ted. Bernard was two steps behind her and spotted the unsuspecting bachelor using the phone. They approached him from behind, plotting the abduction of his valise, as he leaned forward on the counter talking with someone who appeared hard-of-hearing.

"Listen please, Mrs. O'Toole! No, I'm not at the pool! Tell my mother, my mother! No, I don't have a brother! Just tell my mother… Hello! Mrs. O'Toole?"

It would've been a successful capture, but Ted's connection was cut off. Spinning around, he surmised what was going on.

"Well, what do you know? Thought Boston was a place to be on your guard, but Little Falls? Officer! Officer! Over here, please. Citizen's arrest," called Ted. By now several eyes were turning toward the three, who were acting like a group of Keystone Cops.

"Cut it out, Ted," begged Katherine. "It wouldn't do for the Professional Examination Bureau to hear I was arrested for bag-snatching! Then I'd never get my nursing license!"

Bernard kept repeating, "Yeh!" over and over with a big cigar bouncing up and down out of the corner of his mouth. Safely out of the depot and into Bernard's car, Ted hugged Katherine and kissed her.

Supper at the Lockhart's was light and quick, because Bernard had arranged for Ted and Katherine to spend the evening with him and his heartthrob, Lily. Rushing them out and into the car, Bernard sped toward Herkimer as Katherine brought Ted up to the present, describing the flowers and decorations used at Institute Hall on the night of her graduation from St. Mary's School of Nursing.

"Would you believe the florist suspended our class motto from the ceiling right above the seven of us? 'Deus Caritas Est' was formed out of rosebuds with blue ribbons here and there. The whole hall was decorated in old rose and old blue just like the invitation I sent you. It was elegant and in such good taste!" Katherine dreamily recounted.

"Wish I could have been there for you. How did your farewell address go? Were you nervous?" inquired Ted.

"The last month and a half was very busy. Then there was a humiliating incident with one of the surgeons at St. Mary's. I'd rather not go into details about it because we have more important things to discuss," Katherine quickly added. "My farewell address will be in the *Amsterdam Reporter* in a couple of weeks."

"That's great! But what did the doctor do to cause you humiliation?"

"This particular doctor, who will remain nameless, cheats on his wife. He thinks he is the cat's pajamas with all the student nurses. I could eat peanuts off his balding head, he's so short!"

"So this doctor is not one of your favorite people. What did he do?"

"A very respectable doctor gave me some valuable advice. He said, 'To thy self be true', and in my speech, the focus on personal honor, self-respect, and integrity was just what I needed to teach that uncouth doctor a lesson. I summed up the qualities a person must possess to administer to all God's children. I used the direct quote as written: 'This above all: to thine own self be true, And it must follow as the night the day, Thou canst not then be false to any man.' This certainly identified the shallowness of this supposed doctor and emphasized the need for each nurse to embody the summary of all perfection."

"Do you suppose you got through to this doctor, or might you have made a few people uncomfortable, especially those who are not perfect?" inquired Ted.

"Our motto 'Deus Caritas Est' is for the times when we stumble and fall out of the grace of God. He will forgive us because he is the divine physician who went about doing well to all. We must constantly strive to live in God's image with goodness embodied in our every deed," concluded Katherine.

"You are still angry with this doctor. Perhaps, if you told me what upset you, we could sort it out," suggested Ted.

"It's no longer important. Lots of people were there when he made the comment and they know what he's like."

"What comment?" Ted asked. That Lockhart 'are you an idiot' look came across Katherine's face as she turned and looked directly in his eyes.

"If I felt it was important enough to repeat, I would. It is not. Let's end this discussion unless you, like most men, need to have your way. Thus, if you choose to pursue this ridiculous topic of conversation, you will find yourself talking to yourself, because I won't answer. Are the next two days going to be devoted to our future, or some idiot's ignorance?"

"Wow! Listen! I don't mean to interrupt, but Lily is going to meet you both for the first time. How about relaxing and thinking happy thoughts," suggested Bernard, as he pulled into a side yard on the outskirts of Herkimer.

"Thought you were picking up Lily?" Katherine exclaimed. "Doesn't she live in that lovely Georgian House?"

"Lily's here at her friend's home. Her parents still won't accept our dating. It's easier for her if we do it this way."

"Bernard! How can you stoop to this? Who do her parents think they are? This is 1925, not 1825! She should put her foot down. After all, she's not eighteen!" replied his shocked sister.

"This is not your business, Kate. Please make her feel comfortable, because if all goes well with my political career, she will be your sister-in-law," Bernard firmly stated.

Two beeps on his horn and the front porch light came on. The door opened and a slender form appeared on the stoop. Bernard bounded up the steps and wrapped his arms around Lily. He guided her to the car like a fragile piece of china.

Katherine and Ted were distanced from each other in the backseat so as not to make the timid creature uncomfortable. Upon entering the car, Lily sat facing straight forward. Bernard entered and began the introductions.

"Lily, I'd like you to meet my sister, Kate," The front seat passenger made a nod of her head.

"This is her beau, Ted Bryant, from Boston." Another nod of the head followed.

The vehicle proceeded toward its destination. Bernard planned on going to Wright's where they could enjoy some good dance music. A soft voice broke the silence.

"Bernard, I must be back at Trudy's home no later than ten. Her parents are at a wedding with my parents, and they are picking me up to go home with them. My father prefers that I not sleep over at Trudy's due to her having three grown brothers still living at home."

"For heavens sake, Lily, that only gives us an hour and forty minutes. We can't go anywhere and be back in that time! You told me you'd figure a way to stay overnight."

"Bernard Lockhart! I won't have you talking to me that way after all I've gone through trying to please you."

"Please me! All we do is please your parents because I'm not good enough. Well, I'm tired of it," grouched Bernard.

"Where are you going, Bernard?" asked a sobbing Lily as the car made a U-turn and retraced the route it had just traveled.

"We're going back to Trudy's. Thought this would be more pleasant," Bernard said as he lit a cigarette and handed it to Lily.

"Say! We passed what looked like a Ma and Pa diner in that last block. Bet we could get some coffee and dessert and use the time to get acquainted with Lily," suggested Ted.

The diner was still open and the foursome settled on a booth. The decor was well worn, so the male escorts used their handkerchiefs to brush off the booth seats before their ladies sat down. The owner took their order and stated that the diner closed in thirty minutes.

In the brighter light, Katherine surveyed in detail the object of Bernard's infatuation. On the surface, Lily oozed refinement, from her light brown hair down to her T-strap pumps. Her enormous violet-blue eyes and long lashes dominated her face, drawing attention away from the rather long, pointed nose and thin lips. She was extremely slender, evidenced by her collarbone poking through her lavender sheath. A silver beaded purse with deep purple pansies dangled from a wrist that suggested nothing heavier than a teacup had ever been lifted. Lily's hands and manicured fingernails caused Katherine to keep her hands beneath the table.

"Lily, it is a pleasure to meet you and I hope we can get you back on time before your parents return from the wedding," attempted Ted in opening some sort of conversation.

"It wasn't very polite to leave Trudy alone while I went out. I told Bernard ahead of time that she should come along, but his car won't hold five or six people like Daddy's."

Ted felt like a third wheel and waited for someone else to say something.

"Bernard wanted us to meet you because, from what he has indicated, you could be our sister-in-law someday soon, provided we get married also," Katherine offered awkwardly.

"Bernard! Whatever are you saying to people? You know we are just friends, and it will never amount to more than that. Daddy is too powerful," Lily exclaimed with eyes that grew even larger than normal.

"Guess I got carried away, Lily, thinking my younger sister might get married before me. Hope you don't mind my assumption, Ted?" Bernard said apologetically.

"It generally is the course of events when a man displays consistent interest in a special young woman," Ted offered whimsically with a circular motion of his hands. This caused even Lily to giggle.

Their refreshments arrived and they were quiet for a period, but the invisible waves of feelings were hanging like the steam on the diner's windows. Lily played with her pie and ice cream as her companions dutifully wasted naught. She appeared to smell a foul odor by the wrinkles which bridged her nose. Bernard paid the tab, and Lily was out the door before any of them.

The drive back to Trudy's was painfully quiet with each in separate chambers of thoughts. As they arrived at Trudy's, two cars were in front of the house. Cutting the motor, Bernard glided to a silent stop.

"Daddy and Mommy have returned already!" Lily gasped.

At the same time, they all noticed Trudy, motioning from her bedroom window, to go around to the back of the house. Following the directive, Bernard and Lily bent down low and crept around to the back door. They learned Trudy had concocted a story that Lily was resting following a migraine attack. Trudy bought time by pretending she was having a conversation with Lily, while the parents visited and occasionally called up the stairs asking when Lily was coming down so they could be on their way. That was the longest twenty minutes Trudy said she had ever lived through. Lily kissed Bernard and snuck up the backstairs to the bedroom.

On the way back to Little Falls, Bernard explained that reelection would cement his chances of marrying Lily. By then, she would be twenty-five, an age when people start considering a woman destined for spinsterhood. Her parents would be more accepting then. Katherine cringed at Bernard's honesty yet knew it was so, with her twenty-fourth birthday not that far off.

Ted dozed off with the rocking and bobbing of the car. He had been up since four in the morning. Arriving at the Reiman, Bernard shook Ted, who awoke and mumbled he would appreciate it if Katherine would join him for breakfast at 8:30 in the main dining room. Katherine accepted.

Driving up Albany Street, Katherine observed her brother's profile and felt sadness in her heart for him. He appeared a bit haggard after his evening, which undoubtedly disappointed him on all counts.

"Lily is rather delicate, Bernard," Katherine offered cautiously.

"What do you mean by that?"

"I can't imagine her hand-washing bedsheets and clothes with those lovely hands or beating a rug over the clothesline."

"I wouldn't want her to. We'll send out the laundry and have a cleaning lady." Bernard gallantly predicted.

"What about cooking and buying groceries?" inquired a prodding sister?

"I like cooking. Besides, Lily becomes nauseous around raw meat. That would be my responsibility," dismissed an ardent Bernard.

"And childbirth? Do you think she wants children and could have children?"

"Now, just a minute; have you and Ted had these discussions? Would you like me asking him these questions?" responded Bernard.

"I wouldn't mind, because I'd know you were just concerned about my happiness and whether I am realistic about what's involved in being married," stammered Katherine.

"Then your conclusions will probably be the same as mine. How does anyone know how it will all work out? It's a chance you take, just like gambling. It's the roll of the dice or the draw of the cards, my dear," offered Bernard. "Better call it a night and get your beauty sleep. Oh, by the way, does Ted know about Sean? They seem to have taken to one another."

"Do you intend to have a loose tongue?"

"No, Katherine, but a plan of some sort may be a good idea, if Ted is becoming important to you," warned Bernard.

Peeking in to check on Sean, Katherine was taken aback by how grown up he looked in his bed. He was no longer a baby and next year would go to school. Maybe Margot would let her take Sean to the first day of school.

"No! I can't do that," Katherine cautioned herself. "I'd better let things stay as they are. But helping out with outfits would be acceptable, like a gift." Sleep was elusive, causing her to toss and turn, as Bernard's words kept repeating. She had to protect whatever dignity was left, but how?

Ted met Katherine halfway up Albany Street and they began to discuss the events of the previous evening on their way to breakfast at the Reiman. The dining room was rather full, canceling any privacy the couple may have hoped for.

Katherine guided Ted's conversation away from anything of a personal nature by suggesting that busy ears of the waiters or patrons might hear and repeat whatever was overheard just for the excitement of it. Ted became a bit paranoid by the time breakfast was finished, and worried he might have talked in his sleep, loud enough for someone to have heard. He had visions of the patrons on either side of his rented room, standing on their beds with their ear pressed to the bottom of their water glass as it rested against their adjoining walls. Small towns can sometimes be a bit trying.

"I was hoping to take you on a train ride to Schenectady this weekend, where we'd hitch a ride to Rotterdam Junction with my cousin, Walter, so you could meet Maggie Bryant. But, when I called Mrs. O'Toole, my mother's neighbor who has one of the three phones in Rotterdam Junction, she told me my mother was assisting a midwife with the birth of her own baby. That's a switch! Maybe next time," offered Ted.

"That would have been a pleasant thing to do. I'd love to meet your mother and find out the truth about you," teased Katherine.

"How about a picnic lunch instead?" suggested Ted. "I've brought my new camera, and they make picnic lunches at this hotel. Do you know of a spot where there are no ears around?"

"We could go over to the high school grounds. There are some beautiful, old trees there," suggested Katherine.

"We need to make our first purchase together," Ted decided.

"What might that be?" asked Katherine.

"A picnic cloth, and preferably a washable one because I can be rather clumsy."

"We can go to Colewards, down the street in the next block. Their prices are fair. Or I could go home and get a cloth," offered Katherine.

Ted guided Katherine toward Colewards. It was the most attractive of all the cloths, they decided. Both were doubly pleased when they learned its cost was only forty-five cents. Ted was prepared to pay at least ten cents more.

Picking up the picnic lunch, the couple made their way to the largest tree on the school grounds while keeping a wary eye on those huge clouds that had moved in over the past hour. After a few snapshots and conversation, hoping to beat the rain, they stubbornly laid out their picnic cloth. They hurriedly consumed the lunch as drops of summer rain soaked their last mouthfuls. Running to the front of the school building, they huddled under the sparse overhang.

"There is something to be said for this location," offered Ted. "No ears. And necessity deems we stand close to each other. A rather nice arrangement and couldn't have planned it better myself. Thank you, St. Catherine!"

"Sometimes I think you're dippy, Ted," sighed Katherine. "You know, after meeting Lily last night and wondering about her future with Bernard, it made me think of some things we should discuss."

"For instance?" prompted Ted.

"For instance, I want to work until I become pregnant. And what if certain chores, like laundry, are too much for me to do the last few weeks before I have the baby? And after I have the baby, what will we do?"

"How did our mothers manage?" asked Ted.

"My mother had her sisters to help her, but if we move to Boston or Lawrence, I'll be on my own."

"My sister, Ellen, will be there, at least at night and weekends," offered Ted.

"Excuse me, but why should your sister be required to cook our meals or do our laundry after a hard day's work? You can't ask her or expect her to do that! Why should she leave her apartment each night or weekend to come to our home when she has her own life and needs? Really, Ted!"

"Ellen will be living with us, Katherine," replied a solemn Ted. "She will be with us until she marries or chooses another arrangement."

"I would be most uncomfortable sharing your bed each night knowing your sister was in the next room, if you understand what I'm saying," Katherine said with crossed fingers and toes.

"I thought I did, but sharing the rent affords me the opportunity to save toward our engagement and wedding. After we're married you will not and should not have to work. That I'm firm about!" Ted answered resolutely.

"But your sister can't be expected to do our laundry and cooking, plus be kept awake by a crying baby during the night," Katherine expounded.

"Right now, I wish I didn't have ears!" Ted exclaimed. "We're not even engaged and already we have a crying baby!"

"Please do not make little of what I'm saying," chided Katherine.

"Let's slow down. We don't even know if Ellen will want to stay when we get married. I never discussed it with her but would never make her feel she wasn't welcomed. She's put a lot of effort into making the flat livable," stated Ted.

"But, it's hers and yours. Where will I fit in? I've had to share my whole life with nothing to call my own, not even a bed," cried Katherine.

"Your parents have a lovely home with impressive furniture, which is a lot nicer than what I had growing up!"

"God, Ted! Are you blind? All that furniture is secondhand stuff my mother picks up at house sales. It's so embarrassing to see her trudging up the street with some piece of furniture, or a picture frame, or a lamp! We don't have but the money to cover our needs from week to week, and sometimes not even that. Grief! My nurse's uniforms are secondhand!"

"How did your parents manage the money for your training at St. Mary's?"

"It was a scholarship. I couldn't believe it. I felt like it was a miracle after all that happened."

"After all what happened?" asked Ted.

"I had an accident at the slipper factory and cut my hand badly. Maybe someone at the slipper factory felt sorry for me," Katherine offered offhandedly, showing the scar.

"You worked in a slipper factory? How long? Why did you decide to go into nursing?" inquired Ted. "There are so many things I don't know about you."

"Which question do I answer first?" asked Katherine. Perhaps it is better this way, she thought. I'll tell Ted about Sean and it will be a purification of my inner soul.

Her story came pouring out, but the participants and circumstances were changed to protect the guilty. How could Ted ever look at her father without disgust if he knew the truth? Thus, she fabricated a small-town romance with a baseline of social discrimination. Lily's reaction to Bernard's wishes to marry her despite her parents' reservations gave Katherine a theme. She adapted it to create her own story, mixing incidents and half-truths.

"I had always had a crush on Larry, a longtime chum of my brother's. Larry's family owned the slipper factory. All the girls in town were aware of this Romeo's flings and considered him a good catch, due to his family's wealth. Larry and I used to talk a lot but just as friends.

"While I was recovering from cutting my hand, he stopped by to see how I was. No one else was at home, and there he stood with flowers and candy at the front door. I was just about to wash my hair and apologized for how awful I must have looked.

"Larry said, 'Dear girl! How do you propose to wash all that hair with one hand and get the soap out? Let me do the honors.'

"He was insistent. We were so giddy. All I could think of was this millionaire's son washing my hair in the kitchen sink. I'm ashamed to say, but a lot more occurred than washing hair. Before I knew it, we were into the forbidden parts that were a sin to even think about. I was so taken with the attention and excitement, nothing of consequence crossed my mind.

"Larry suggested we keep our love quiet until he graduated the following June. Then he would tell his parents of his plans to marry me. I recall he switched the conversation and asked me to the Saturday night dance at the Knights of Columbus Hall.

"I remember him saying, 'You'll be my girl from now on. Everyone will know we're a couple.' Then he grew sullen and added, 'Perhaps we should start off slowly. Could Bernard drive you to the K of C dance Saturday night?' I was so enthralled that he wanted me to be his girl and his future wife, I agreed to the arrangement, asking how I would get home after the dance.

"Larry's response was, 'Everyone knows that a good girl always goes home with the man she came to the social with.' Then he added, 'I'll have my car so we can have some privacy together during the evening. Remember to be sure Bernard knows he is to drive you home.'

"It wasn't easy finding something to wear that fit over the large bandage on my hand. My sister, Lenora, fixed my hair and helped me dress. Larry sent a corsage, which was beautiful! My parents did not like the idea of him sending me flowers and warned about his reputation. I really didn't want to hear anything that would spoil the joy I was experiencing.

"When we got to the K of C, Larry's car was already parked in front, so Bernard pulled right up behind him. I expected the person in the driver's seat to be Larry and glided up to the door, chanting his college song. A distraught face, streaked with tears of grief, blankly looked back at me. It was Larry's father, Mr. Upton! He looked at me without any expression in his eyes.

"'They say Larry is dead. I thought he might show up here knowing the way he loves music and dancing. Then, I could tell them they all were wrong about him being dead!'

94

"I remember shouting, 'Oh, dear God!' A horrible, sharp pain went thorough my chest, near my heart. Bernard stood behind me and held me up, unable to believe what he just heard about his friend.

"The Upton Family held a closed wake at their home, followed by internment in the family mosque. The local paper reported the circumstances of the horse-riding accident, and listed the cause of death as being the result of a broken neck. Larry died instantly.

"Three weeks after Larry's death, I suspected I might be pregnant. My mother was shocked beyond words. It took a bit of time before she calmed down, but when she did, there was never any doubt that the baby would be welcomed and loved. She said it was a gift from God; our own flesh and blood.

"I didn't want the Uptons involved, but my mother felt it might bring comfort to know their son was still alive in the coming birth of my baby. We asked to visit, and received a prompt invitation.

"We presented our calling card and the butler led us into the parlor where Mrs. Upton was seated by the window overlooking the garden. My mother offered condolences and the understanding of losing a child, having lost baby Colleen. Mrs. Upton remained rigid and erect, almost like a statue. She inquired if there was another reason why we wanted to extend our sympathies in person.

"Her directness took us back a bit. You wouldn't believe my mother. She is not intimidated by anyone, and told Mrs. Upton that Larry was very fond of me and we had planned to marry after his graduation in June.

"Mrs. Upton answered my mother in a rather snotty fashion, saying, 'My dear woman, I can assure you Lawrence had plans but marriage was not one of them. He was scheduled to tour Europe this summer, prior to continuing his studies in the fall at Oxford.'

"I felt my mother shouldn't be bearing the whole burden and told Mrs. Upton, again, about Larry's plan to tell his parents of our desire to be together, when he graduated in June. Then I added that by then, I would have had to tell him I was carrying his child. It was almost like she couldn't hear what we were trying to tell her.

"Mrs. Upton was silent for a period of time which felt like an hour. She got up out of her chair and walked toward the marble fireplace. When she turned to speak to us, her face was stern and her eyelids were flaming red from suppressed tears. In a rather threatening tone of voice, she told us to heed carefully what she was about to say.

"'My son has many friends who would testify to your daughter's loose morals and if asked, would swear that any one of them could be the baby's father. Or if that approach is too distasteful for you, a rumor could be circulated that Leo Lockhart impregnated his own daughter. A lot of people know about his philandering and drinking and would believe it! Perhaps a rumor that one of Katherine's brothers fathered the child would be less devastating, or was it one of those transient boarders from Ireland you take in for money, Mrs. Lockhart?'

"My mother jumped to her feet and I feared she might strike Mrs. Upton! But, Mrs. Upton wasn't finished with us. She glared at us and continued by saying neither she nor her husband would have ever accepted a mix of their blood with our type. Lawrence needed an equal mate of similar breeding and social background, adding she hoped we were quite clear on how things stood.

"I'll never forget the strength my mother had for the both of us. Looking out the window toward the stables where the Uptons housed their prize-winning stallions, she said to Mrs. Upton, 'Ya've been around horses too long and yar a gaddamn jackass! I feel sorry for ya because y'all never have any rights to the baby even if ya take a fancy down the road. No one will believe ya. Ya not only lost a son, ya've lost a grandchild.' We then let ourselves out the door and never looked back."

"Did you go away to have the baby?" asked a rather numb Ted.

"That took a whole lot of advance planning. Someone advised my mother to arrange an interview for me with St. Mary's School of Nursing in July. It seemed crazy because we had no money! My mother went with me for the interview and pretended she was pregnant. As she was well practiced with being pregnant, no one suspected differently. I didn't look like I was in the family way until about the seventh month. I stayed close to home planning for the baby but told my friends I was getting prepared to leave for nurse's training.

"When the scholarship was offered through an unknown philanthropist, I thought it was from the Uptons and suggested this to my mother. She spit on the floor and said if it were, we would not accept it. Then, a day or two later she told me she knew it wasn't from

96

them because it was given to a Catholic hospital and the Uptons were Presbyterians. The rest is not easy to talk about at this time, but I used a bout with pneumonia as a pretense for delaying my start in January at St. Mary's. The recovery from Sean's birth took longer than we expected, so I stayed with my aunt in Glens Falls until the middle of February."

A stunned Ted hung his head and rubbed his forehead. Slowly he placed his arms around Katherine and hugged her for a long time. When he was composed enough, he looked at her. To Katherine's astonishment, he had been crying.

"This changes nothing, Katherine. I fell in love with you. With your public acceptance of my proposal in December, we'll marry the end of April. Our honeymoon will be on the conservative side, because I'll suggest that Ellen keep the present apartment and I'll look for a new one for us. This will require all the trappings, from furniture to dishes."

"You don't have to do that, Ted," said a sheepish Katherine.

"Yes, I do! I want you to pick out things you like and send me the description or manufacturer's name and I'll find the same or near same in Boston. Let's list by importance the items you feel we will need. It stopped raining! Let me walk you home. And I don't think you need to let anyone know you told me about what happened; not even your parents. Let the present status quo remain."

The feeling of peace Ted had given Katherine by his understanding and support established a genuine respect for the man she had once considered a real bozo. She saw him in a different light and listened to what he had to say with a newfound respect.

Locating a few sheets of paper and pencil was not an easy task in the Lockhart home, but once in hand, the couple began to draft a plan. Ted was meticulous and organized, which are definite assets for an accountant. Together they planned precisely what was necessary to set up a livable flat based on Ted's recent experience and Katherine's domestic knowledge. They calculated the cost, and formed a grid of expenses covering the next ten months.

A budget per month was planned for each of them. Katherine's was based on the hopes of at least two weeks of work per month. Ted's was definite given his new position and known salary.

The next day, following eight o'clock Mass at St. Mary's Church, the couple reviewed their plan and put on the finishing touches over breakfast at the Reiman. The budget meant sacrifice in all aspects. Spontaneous trips to Little Falls would be history. They would have to cut back on personal indulgences including movies, eating out, and cigarettes. Ted knew by rolling his own he'd save quite a bit.

The issue of an engagement ring was discussed, with Katherine stating it was not necessary. Ted wouldn't hear of that and insisted she let him know her preferences. He couldn't promise a large gem but would do the best he could.

"I almost forgot to give you your graduation present, Katherine! Wait right here while I go upstairs for my belongings to check out."

"I'll wait for you in the lobby," Katherine offered.

Rushing to his room, Ted placed the blue velvet ring box containing Katherine's birthstone in his pants pocket. Gathering his valise and suit jacket, he descended the stairs. His legs seemed unsteady, causing him to pause and lean against the wall. A need for air forced him to breathe deeply, resulting in a few moments of light headedness. He pretended to be searching his pockets for something as another hotel patron passed him on the stairs. Finally, the incident subsided and he continued downward. He thought perhaps the three cups of coffee caused the rush.

As he approached Katherine, she looked at him, strangely. "Do you feel all right, Ted? You're very pale and you have perspiration on your brow!"

"Just in a rush, dear. Let's start walking. I have something besides a good-bye kiss to give you at the depot."

CHAPTER TEN

Independence Day was lacking in celebration for Katherine, who was attending to a young man dying of a kidney disorder. The patient's family knew his days were numbered, and having him at home was the best known medicine of the day.

"Too bad you have to be stuck here with me, Miss Lockhart," spoke the shivering form in the bed.

"You're awake!" responded Katherine. "Let me rearrange your pillow so you can sit up a bit, if you'd like to."

"Thanks, but what would you be doing today, if you weren't here?" asked the patient.

"I'd be beside someone else's bed, plumping their pillow," smiled the nurse. "Would you like something to drink or eat?"

She went down to the kitchen to prepare a tray for her patient. Returning to the bedroom, the wasted form of the twenty-three-year-old was in a deep sleep. Placing the tray at the side of the bed, she checked his pulse and temperature. They were stable. Just that brief conversation had exhausted him.

Looking at the sleeping young man who was almost the same age as she, Katherine grieved when thinking about his life being almost over. She fingered a small red, white, and blue ribbon topped with a brass eagle which was pinned to her waistband. Her grandfather had given it to her on July 4, when she was twelve and he seventy-two. Some live so long, and others don't have the privilege.

Taking out Ted's latest letter, she reread every word for the eighth time. Correspondence between the melancholy lovers had grown intimate and a bit sensual, replacing the physical interactions the miles denied. Katherine had to hide all the letters for chance the invasive searching of younger sisters or a curious mother would have it all over the house that Ted took her letters to bed with him and would smell her perfume as though she were there, next to him, kissing and caressing until the wee hours of the morning!

A few days later, her patient suffered a convulsion and died. This tainted the remaining summer for Katherine. The weather didn't make it any easier. Mother Nature covered the sun with threatening clouds topped with heavy downpours each weekend. Many social or travel plans were canceled or rained out.

Things seemed to grow out of proportion from Katherine's point of view. A letter from Ted added to her feeling of incompetence, by mentioning that his mother was apprehensive about their relationship after foreseeing a lot of suffering close to Ted when reading the cards. Just why he chose to tell her this bothered her. Was he having second thoughts about what she told him in confidence, or was his mother that gifted that she knew Katherine had contrived the story about the fictitious Larry?

The fondness and respect Ted evidenced toward his mother was a threat to Katherine. She was tired of having to share, or be the recipient of secondhand this or that, or leftovers no one else wanted. This time it was going to be different. Katherine vowed her needs were to come first.

A carefully worded response informed Ted that the suffering his mother may have seen could be related to her caring for so many ill people as a nurse and not associated with their relationship. Then, she suggested it was about time Ted arranged for her to meet his mother.

She added toward the end of her letter, "Usually, gifted people such as your mother obtain clearer impressions when their subject for the reading of the cards is present, not unknown or miles away. Of course, I don't believe in any of this and consider it a sin, as a true Roman Catholic, but with respect for the age of your mother and the possibility she is very lonely, we should humor her and make her feel important."

Labor Day seemed the apropos time to arrange an introduction. Ted solicited Cousin Walter for a ride from Schenectady to Rotterdam Junction. A connecting train out of Little Falls deposited Katherine in

Schenectady where an unshaven and disheveled Ted greeted her. His train ride from Boston had been hectic with holiday travelers partying the whole time.

Walter was reliably on time and loaded their parcels in the backseat. Katherine quickly learned why Ted had no voice the first time she met him. She was positive the right side of the car was going to meet every tree trunk, bush, and boulder between Schenectady and Rotterdam Junction. Between looking at his passengers when he talked instead of out the windshield, and closing his eyes when he laughed, Katherine thought for sure this is what being close to death must feel like.

Arriving at Maggie's home, a jovial white-haired woman in a beige dress and a full-length white apron came running up the incline shouting, "My son! My son! Ted! Ted!" Her arms were extended upward reaching for the sky. Her face was flushed, and by the time she was halfway up the road, she was out of breath and panting inaudible words.

Ted looked at Katherine with a crooked smile and a shrug of his shoulders. He walked forward and embraced his mother, who kissed his cheek and laughed right from her toes.

Despite the jealousy Katherine harbored for this woman she had never met, she caught herself laughing and enjoying Maggie's genuine excitement and greeting. They all crowded into the tiny kitchen and persuaded Walter to stay for lunch. The sweet biscuits Katherine had made were placed on the same plate with Maggie's apple tarts. Egg salad sandwiches with homemade mayonnaise were already prepared and waiting in the icebox.

A small, round table was set in the front parlor with a lovely handmade tablecloth and matching napkins. Katherine examined the delicate embroidery depicting a weeping willow on the edge of a pond with two swans. There were four or five vases with fresh-cut flowers throughout the room, and a love seat between the two front windows.

Ted and Walter gathered four chairs around the table as Maggie brought in the lunch plates. Katherine followed with the teacups and saucers. With all assembled within arms reach, the young adults did well by Maggie's efforts, emptying the plate of sandwiches. A second pot of tea was prepared to accompany the dessert.

"Aunt Maggie, please read my tea leaves and only tell me the good things. When will my ship come in? And will I marry a woman with money?" Walter taunted. "I'm only fooling, Auntie. Would you like me to do anything or get anything for you, while I'm here?" he asked.

"Great idea!" interrupted Ted. "We'll be back in a little while."

Katherine didn't want to be left alone with Maggie, but it all happened so quickly. Ted and Walter both were gone before she could ask to go with them. She started to pick up their used plates, but Maggie insisted she sit and talk for a while.

"Ted has never brought a young woman to meet me until now. You must mean a lot to him, Katherine, but then you know this."

"Thank you. I'm fond of Ted, also," Katherine answered, feeling color glowing on her cheeks.

"Let me have your teacup after you have turned it upside down and rotated it one full turn," Maggie directed.

"If you don't mind, Mrs. Bryant, I'd rather not participate in this activity," Katherine hesitantly said.

"Fine, dear. Do me a favor then, and fetch the kettle so I may warm up my tea."

As Katherine left the room, she carried out the dirty dishes to place them in the sink but found no faucets. Befuddled, she put the dishes on the kitchen table and picked up the kettle. As she returned to the parlor, Maggie was looking at the inside of Katherine's teacup.

"With all these leaves in your cup, you may want to rinse it out before you have more tea," Maggie quickly commented, covering her real purpose for looking.

"What do you do about washing dishes? I couldn't find any faucets," asked Katherine.

Maggie laughed cheerfully and explained there was no plumbing, only a pump. The pump in the kitchen no longer worked, so they get water from the outside well.

"If there is no plumbing, where is your toilet and bathtub?"

"Oh, how thoughtless of me; you've been here over two hours and I never told you, in case you needed to use it! Follow me," Maggie motioned as she went through the kitchen, then the summer kitchen, and opened the back door. About forty feet away from the house stood the outhouse. She handed Katherine some paper.

Back in the house, Katherine asked to wash her hands. Maggie gave her a small porcelain bowl filled with sudsy water. When Katherine finished, Maggie threw it outside behind the house. Meanwhile, more water was warming on the stove to wash and rinse the lunch dishes.

Placing two large porcelain basins on the kitchen table, Maggie washed the dishes in one then rinsed them in the other. While drying each dish, Katherine realized the daily struggles this woman must have with laundry and bathing, to say nothing about pumping and carrying all the water into the house. It must be hell in winter using that outhouse!

As the women worked together, each cautiously spoke about the past and present. The younger with purpose and reason, the older with knowledge and fear of what she read in Katherine's tea leaves.

Ted returned with arms laden with groceries for his mother. Walter carried chopped wood for the stove and a new water pail.

"Ted! You didn't have to do that," sighed a grateful Maggie. "How did you do that? The general store is closed today!"

"Mr. Gordon opened the store for us," Ted said as he hugged his mother.

Checking his pocket watch, Ted mentioned to Walter that it would be best to leave for the train no later than three thirty, so the drive back for Walter would still be during daylight. When Maggie heard this, she insisted on whipping up some of her fried potatoes for them to take on the train.

While Maggie sang and banged the pots in the kitchen, Ted pumped the player piano as Walter searched for Aunt Maggie's favorite songs. Watching all of this occur was an eye-opener for Katherine. There was an invisible form of communication between them all. She compared it to her family, where no one did anything for another unless screamed at, pushed, or embarrassed into it.

The moment for departure came as Walter checked the radiator's water and kicked the car tires. Katherine saw Ted slip his cousin some money and wondered how the funds for the groceries and gas affected their agreed-to budget. Ted must have worked a lot of overtime to afford the trip for her to meet his mother. Katherine couldn't help but wonder why everything was such a struggle and why some people have so much, and others so little.

The farewells were brief with Ted reminding his mother that Ellen would be home for Thanksgiving and he, Christmas afternoon. Maggie thanked Katherine for coming and said she hoped to see her again. Then, handing the tin filled with the potato supper to Katherine, she warned her to guard it with her life from the monger she was with, because he was just like his father, "God rest his soul!"

With an hour to wait before the train, Ted excused himself, taking his suitcase with him. Katherine was anxious for him to return, because the aroma from the tin was tempting her. He appeared after ten minutes, having shaved and changed his shirt. Sitting outside the station, they enjoyed the last rays of daylight. They opened the tin, and found two forks and cloth napkins on a wooden plate with the potatoes below.

"What do you think of my mother?" asked Ted.

"She is dedicated to you and your sister. Having two children is a lot different than having six. But, Ted, can't you arrange to put plumbing in her home? She must have a hard time, especially in the winter!"

"It would be very expensive to have someone dig a waste basin, let alone purchase the pipes, faucets, and toilet with its flush tank. Of course, if you want to postpone our plans for another year, I could use the money for the improvements. We had the roof done last year and that set me back a bit."

"How about moving to another house?" suggested Katherine.

"I asked my mother to consider moving years ago, but she said she came to the home as a young bride and will leave only when she dies. She really wants it to stay the way my father left it. I think she believes his spirit lives there still, along with baby Monica," Ted softly explained, as if praying.

"Really, Ted! You're not serious? You are! Incidentally, your mother tried to read my tea leaves and I refused. Do you think I upset her?"

"It would take more than that to upset her," Ted answered. "We best head for our trains." The train to Boston was already loading passengers and the train to Little Falls was just pulling in.

"Ted, when did you decide not to visit over Thanksgiving?" Katherine asked.

Looking down at his suitcase, Ted shook his head.

"Why do I have to say the same thing over and over? The world I live in is the same one you live in, I think! You work and get paid so you have money to pay your expenses. You pay your expenses; the money is gone. You start over and repeat the process. If you have fewer expenses one week, you save the money. The next week your expenses may be higher, thus draining the savings. If I'm going to save for all the things we want in order to marry, one of us has to sacrifice!"

"Don't talk down to me, Ted. Naturally I understand, but I would think you'd consult with me instead of deciding these things with your sister," Katherine answered, fighting the urge to tear up. "How do you plan to be with both your mother and me on Christmas?"

"I need to make decisions, Katherine, without wondering if you'll approve. You must trust in my abilities to know what the best choice is. The choice of Christmas over Thanksgiving is obvious, don't you agree? Christmas Eve will be with you and Christmas afternoon, God allowing, I'll be with my mother."

Both sat on their separate trains reflecting on the road ahead of them, wondering if walking it together would be better than alone.

Alone with her thoughts following Ted's visit, Katherine came to her own conclusion regarding the role of being a wife. The strong, spirited ones, like her mother, wind up doing it all and wearing themselves out before their time. But, a shrinking violet with a delicate disposition, like her brother's Lily, gets all sorts of attention and dedication from their male suitor or husband.

When she told Ted that story about Sean being Larry Upton's son, his reaction was just as she would have wanted it to be. Yet, Katherine was left with the realization that the consideration Ted displayed was elicited through her lying. She would never know how he truly would have reacted with the truth. Katherine's purpose was to cover all possible demons whose ugly heads might surface regarding Sean's father, either in the form of a malicious gossiper or a slip of the tongue by her own family.

If only Maureen were nearby. Katherine missed her companionship and relied heavily on her good sense. She decided to invite her to Little Falls the weekend following Thanksgiving. Maureen wrote back suggesting Katherine visit Amsterdam, because her father had been under the weather recently and she wanted to keep an eye on him. He tended to do too much, especially where his prized trotters were concerned.

The reunion was a welcome reprieve for both young women. The pace at St. Mary's Hospital was unrelenting, pushing Maureen to her limits. Katherine was thinner by ten pounds with the round-the-clock cases. All the two friends wanted to do was sit, eat, and talk.

Mr. and Mrs. Dorsey were pleased that Katherine came to visit. They managed to grab a few moments of opportunity to tell her how reclusive their daughter had become since Katherine's graduation. Except for work, Maureen seemed not to have any other interest, or any suitors.

Katherine tried to explain the physical strain and responsibility factors which drain a nurse. The life of each patient rests with the nurse's ability to recognize any change that threatens recovery. Mrs. Dorsey appeared to understand but wanted grandchildren, not an exhausted nurse. The conversation came to an abrupt halt as Maureen entered with cider and pumpkin pie. Katherine picked up the slack with talk of Ted.

"Therefore, Maureen, should Ted ask me to marry, would you consent to being my maid of honor?"

"Oh, it would be wonderful for you when he does ask, and he will. I just know he will! What about your sisters? Would their feelings be hurt if I was your choice?"

"If I had an older sister, she would be my choice, but you are my choice. I need your knowledge to help me with choices like a wedding dress and honeymoon clothes!"

"This will be so much fun! Let's go down to Bergman's and see the latest styles. They have samples as well as catalogs," suggested Maureen. Her parents were elated to see the spark back in their daughter's eyes.

Following the exploratory trip and the review of several catalogs, Maureen and Katherine had made up their minds. White was definitely the future bride's choice of color, and dusty rose suited her maid of honor. Wanting to be a bit daring, they chose matching black malines picture hats and flapper-length skirts. That would be top draw and definitely Fifth Avenue. Elegance was the order of the day. The collection of notes Maureen made while they fantasized over choices took about an hour to sort and tally, leaving the two of them adrift on the ocean of doom when the estimated cost was reached.

"How will I ever be able to order those things? The store wants a deposit, and even that would be too much!" cried Katherine. "Then, on top of that, I need clothes for the honeymoon!"

"Let's think about it. We're the same size, and I already have a gorgeous dress that was only worn once. Remember the formal dinner the night before graduation? My parents surprised me with the latest style—a beaded dress with a drop waist in dusty rose, remember? So, who needs two dusty rose-colored dresses? No one in your family has seen it, so I can wear that as your maid of honor. The picture hat will look super with it."

"That solves your problem, but I'm still in the same dilemma," sighed Katherine.

"I want to buy your wedding dress for you, as my wedding present to you. I love you, Katherine, and want you to be happy. Then, we'll swap. I'll take the white dress and give you the beaded dusty rose dress to wear on your honeymoon and other social parties in Boston. I'll tell my folks we traded because the rose dress looked better on you, and the white dress looked better with my dark hair. You'll have to buy your own underwear, though!"

Katherine threw a pillow at Maureen, who blocked it with a kick of her legs. What a ruckus, as the Dorseys sat in their living room enjoying the sounds of life, despite the jarring of the crystal chandelier in the dining room. Out of respect for the parents and the hour, the friends quieted down. The conversation finally centered on Sean and Ted. Katherine conveyed the story she had told Ted about Sean being her son. Maureen's mouth dropped open.

"Oh, Katherine, what if he learns the truth some day? What if somehow someone slips up," whispered Maureen.

"If it happens, and I don't think it shall, having covered every possible rumor a person might concoct, then I'll face the truth. Hopefully by then, Ted will love me enough to trust I thought it was the most respectful thing to do regarding my family," offered Katherine. "I also have my mother to think of and all the sacrifices she made for me. I owe her so much, and will never be able to repay her. This way, we can still be a respectable family unit."

"I understand why you did it. You're really torn between love and hate for your mother, Katherine. I can sense that. Have you ever asked her why she went to such lengths to conceal what he did to you, when she could have just made your father leave?"

"What are you saying, Maureen?" asked Katherine, feeling exposed. "Don't you believe that's what happened?"

"I don't doubt that's what happened, but your mother is a strong person with plenty of helpers between your brothers and sisters. Why would she continue to live with a man who raped his own daughter?"

Not being able to answer that part herself, Katherine speculated by continuing, "Maureen, think! We're Catholics in a largely Protestant town and members of a well-known family. Could we continue to live in Little Falls if everyone knew why my mother kicked my father out? She believes in her marriage vows, for better or for worse, for richer or poorer, in sickness and health, till death do we part."

"Guess that's where we differ. I will bow to no man and never will," Maureen emphasized with a pointing finger.

"Will you still be in my wedding?"

"Give me a hug and I'll think about it, silly," demanded Maureen.

Returning home, Katherine was refreshed and in control. The clouds over her eyes had lifted with the help of her dear friend. As could be expected, the guilt of wanting worldly goods, and spending the money rather than giving the money to the poor, crept into Katherine's subconscious and she feared what the retribution might be for being so vain.

Christmas Eve finally arrived and was storybook perfect. A soft, fluffy snow drifted past the window as Katherine searched for Bernard's car. He had gone to pick Ted up at the Reiman Hotel.

The candles in the neighbors' windows seemed to be lighting the way for Jesus. Carolers were singing in front of the Lockhart's home with noticeable frost escaping on their breath. Katherine and Lenora offered them some hot tea and cookies, which they gladly accepted.

Bernard came in stomping his feet and grabbed a cup of tea. He handed Katherine a parcel and an envelope.

"Where is Ted?" asked Katherine.

"No Ted!" answered Bernard. "The letter is supposed to explain it."

Katherine was shaking and had a difficult time opening a simple envelope, ripping part of the letter in the process.

"Dearest Katherine,

> Just as I was about to leave for the train, a messenger delivered a telegram from Father Shea, my mother's pastor. Mother had a mild stroke and lost her speech, but all else seems fine.

> You can't feel anger toward me, dearest, though I know you are disappointed. I'm sure you would have made the same choice, had it been one of your parents.

> I've sent your Christmas present in care of an old chum who is a conductor on the New York Central and lives in Albany. He promised to see that it would be at the Reiman for Bernard to pick up, in place of me.

> Wish I were inside the box but instead my heart is. Please don't open the smallest blue box. I want to be present to share the moment with you, and will be, as soon as humanly possible.

Happy Birthday and Merry Christmas!

Love,

Ted

P.S. Please thank Bernard for me, and say hello to Sean."

A deep, sinking disappointment bottomed out in the pit of Katherine's stomach. She thanked Bernard and put the brown paper-wrapped box under the tree, and went up to the room she shared with Lenora and Aileen.

Alone in the dark, Katherine prayed the rosary in hopes of shutting out the overwhelming emptiness. All her preparations for this special Christmas were dashed. There always seemed to be something or someone to pull her up short when her focus became too self-centered.

This pattern shocked Katherine every time it occurred. She felt selfish and not very pleasing in the eyes of God, who knew what she was thinking as she read Ted's letter, in that it might make her life a lot smoother if his mother died. Then, Ted's head would have his own thoughts, not what his mother saw in the cards.

"What does that say about me?" Katherine said to herself. She didn't like what she felt, knowing that the jealousy part of her personality could often consume her rational thinking.

Wiping her eyes, she prayed for God's forgiveness on the eve of this most blessed holy day, and rejoined her family as they finished trimming the tree.

Chapter Eleven

The snow continued to fall throughout the night, clearing at sunrise on Christmas morning. The sound of sleigh bells could be heard, as neighbors hitched up their teams and offered sleigh rides to walking church-goers. It put everyone in the true Christmas spirit by slowing them down long enough to wish each other holiday cheer and a prosperous New Year.

The lazy hour following Christmas dinner was interrupted by the phone. Dr. Kirkland was at the Leroys' home due to old Edwin Leroy overdoing the snow shoveling. Katherine's services were requested by the doctor because the Leroys' daughter was out of town until the following day.

Mrs. Leroy, being a semi-invalid, required certain services that Mr. Leroy presently was unable to assist her with. Dr. Kirkland prescribed total rest in order to allow time to assess any damage Mr. Leroy may have suffered from what appeared to be a mild stroke.

Bundling up, Katherine trudged over to the Leroys' home on John Street. Passing the Quirks' home, she recalled how the widow was found frozen to death in her favorite chair about four winters ago. Ever since that tragedy, neighbors were more watchful of the older residents living alone. They took turns dropping by to check that the stove had the necessary fuel it needed and that there was food in the house.

Having lived on John Street during her preteen years, Katherine knew the Leroys. She told herself working on Christmas Day didn't bother her. She felt like that was the true spirit of what Christmas should be.

Mrs. Leroy was waiting for Katherine by the front porch window in her wheelchair and opened the door, handing her the written orders left by Dr. Kirkland. The wheelchair did not prevent Mrs. Leroy from maintaining an orderly home. Her hands were never idle, and it was evidenced by the needlework throughout the home. Even under the stress of concern about her husband, she had managed to make a soup for his supper.

Sitting with the elderly neighbors, Katherine engaged Mr. Leroy in conversation to assess if he had experienced additional side effects since Dr. Kirkland had left. He sat rather rigid with no facial expression, though he seemed aware of what was going on.

Offering to keep an eye on the soup while it finished cooking, Katherine prepared a pot of tea and set a tray for the Leroys. Tears welled up in Katherine's eyes as she thought of how this Christmas was supposed to be. It was her twenty-fourth birthday and here she was, just like any other day. The soup started to boil over, and she quickly moved the pot off the burner.

They were all startled by the sound of the door knocker. Katherine raced to the door and opened it to find Ted down on one knee with an opened ring box in his right hand.

"Katherine, will you marry me?" asked her breathless suitor.

"What? But how did y ...? Yes!" cried Katherine.

"Is everything all right, Katherine?" called Mrs. Leroy, as she rolled her wheelchair to the front door.

"Mrs. Leroy, this is Ted Bryant, and he just asked me to be his wife!"

"Come in! Come in, young man. You can't marry her tonight. She's caring for us until tomorrow. After four in the afternoon, you can get married. Would you like some soup and tea with us?"

Ted got up off his knee and entered. "It's a pleasure to meet you, Mrs. Leroy, and is that Mr. Leroy?"

"Edwin! This is Katherine's young man," said Mrs. Leroy in a very loud voice. He nodded and extended a shaky hand to Ted.

"Now, how about that soup and tea," Mrs. Leroy said in Katherine's direction.

"But first, would you and Mr. Leroy be witness to Katherine's acceptance of this ring?" Ted requested, as he placed it on Katherine's finger and kissed her gently.

"Edwin, it's like that special Christmas you asked me to be your wife," Mrs. Leroy loudly said to her husband.

"I'll never forget that you said, yes," Mr. Leroy softly answered.

Mr. Leroy was going to be all right, thought Katherine as she prepared the kitchen table, placing a lighted candle in the center. She overheard Ted telling the Leroys about his mother's stroke, and how a neighbor was staying with her so he could travel from Rotterdam Junction to Little Falls in order to give Katherine the diamond on her birthday. Feeling rather thoughtless, Katherine entered the parlor and inquired about his mother's condition.

"Like I was just telling these nice folks, there comes a time when you have to slow down, do less, or let others do for you. Mom is doing a lot better, thanks to the kindness of God. Mrs. O'Keefe is staying with her tonight and I'll be staying with a friend of mine who is the engineer on the train that brought me here. His mother's place is on the other side of the tracks. Then, we head back at four thirty in the morning."

"Supper is ready. Ted, would you please assist Mrs. Leroy to the kitchen table. I'll help Mr. Leroy with his soup."

The foursome sat in the kitchen eating by candlelight. A gentle hand with a sparkling star dabbed the dribbling away between Mr. Leroy's mouthfuls. Perhaps a good night's rest would reduce the telltale signs of stroke, hoped Katherine.

Ted later assisted Mr. Leroy in his preparations for bed. Katherine helped Mrs. Leroy with her hair, which she religiously brushed and braided each night.

"Katherine, I almost forgot to tell you that Dr. Kirkland left a present for you on the table near the front door. He felt so bad having to bother you, not only being Christmas but your birthday! A real Christmas angel," sighed Mrs. Leroy.

When all was quiet and the dishes cleaned up, Ted and Katherine sat looking at each other in the light of the candle.

"Is this what you generally do on these home cases?"

"This is easy. They're lovely people and not at all demanding," answered Katherine.

"How serious was Mr. Leroy's stroke? Did he have a stroke or heart problem prior to this incident?" asked Ted, inquiring more for his own information regarding his mother's stroke.

"Dr. Kirkland asked me to watch for any additional signs or marked changes. Mr. Leroy seemed to be a bit more in control of his left hand and his speech after he had some supper," Katherine replied.

"Your folks were hesitant to tell me where you were until I showed them the ring box. Sorry I had to unwrap it, but I guess you have been pretty close-mouthed about our plans," Ted concluded.

"I have my reasons. Will you be able to visit for a day before returning to Boston?" Katherine asked hopefully.

"I have to discuss this with you, because the way I see it, these extra days I'm taking due to my mother's stroke really cut into our honeymoon plans. I'll only have accrued four days by April for our wedding. Had we decided on September or later, I'd have seven days by then. So, one day for the wedding and three days that meet the weekend would allow us to go to Atlantic City and return to Lawrence by Sunday, giving me time to ready myself for the Monday workday. Of course, you would be on your own on until I arrive home after work Monday evening."

"I thought Paris in the spring would be an unforgettable honeymoon!" The words rushed out before Katherine could control her disappointment.

"I'm afraid the only way you'll see Paris is if it is extremely clear as you look across the Atlantic Ocean from the Atlantic City Boardwalk. You haven't said anything about your engagement ring. Do you like it?" Ted asked.

"It's lovely and in very good taste; very delicate with the open work on either side of the diamond," Katherine responded, as she turned her hand from side to side.

"The jeweler at W. B. Horn said that quality is what counts in a diamond. A larger one, say one carat, could cost half the price of your diamond in a lesser quality. I trusted his judgment in relation to my wallet," related a beaming Ted.

"Speaking of judgment, how did you get here with all that snow?" asked Katherine.

"Hopped the mail train which plows through just about anything. The engineer saw my lantern when he slowed down at the mail pouch pickup point and recognized me. Tomorrow, as I said, we head back. He'll let me off about a mile from home, near the schoolhouse I attended centuries ago. You didn't say anything about your Christmas present! I saw it opened under your parents' tree."

"Honestly, I don't know where my mind is. Of course, it was more than you should have done. The watch is very smart and will go with my street clothes. I use this pocket watch with the second hand when on duty."

"I didn't even think about the need for a second hand. See, you need to help me with a lot of things I don't know. I'm just a country boy trying to make a living."

"Stop it, Ted. Don't belittle yourself. You've done quite well given the fact you've been on your own since just a kid. I need to check on Mr. Leroy, so perhaps we should say good night."

"Do I deserve a good-bye kiss before I go out into the cold, stormy, wind-chilling blizzard?"

"For goodness sakes, the stars are out!" whispered Katherine, as she joined in an embrace and kiss that promised a lot more than the surroundings would allow. Helping Ted with his coat and scarf, Katherine felt less than deserving thinking about all he went through to fulfill his promise to give her the engagement ring on her birthday.

"Ted, please don't be concerned about arranging to come back to see me before returning to Boston. Your safety is more important to me. No more of these boyhood shenanigans of hopping trains. I can learn to be more understanding when things don't always work out as we want them. I'm so very proud of you. No wonder your mother thinks the world of you. Please thank her for sharing you this Christmas, and I hope she is better real soon."

Ted had been patient for a long time waiting for the shell that Katherine had tucked herself into would crack a little to let her express sincere emotions. This was a start, and it was the best Christmas present Katherine could have given him.

"Whatever you wish, Katherine. Things always work out. It may not be exactly the way we want it to be, but down the line we learn it wasn't all that important as we made it out to be."

"What is important is that I check on Mr. Leroy and give him his medicine. Now, good night, and thank you again, Ted, for making this the best Christmas and birthday of my life."

The air was crisp and clear with the stars sparkling like the diamond on her hand. Katherine wanted to cry, but controlled the urge as Ted cautiously descended the icy stairs waving back every few feet until out of view. Leaning her forehead against the cold doorjamb, Katherine prayed, "Dear Jesus, I don't deserve this kind of goodness. Ted thinks I'm so special, but I'm nothing but a selfish, self-centered bitch! Please help me to be a better person, and protect Ted from harm." Katherine blessed herself and softly closed the heavy oak door.

Mr. Leroy was resting peacefully, as was Mrs. Leroy. Dr. Kirkland told Katherine, in the orders he left, not to awaken Mr. Leroy for the medication for fear awakening him from a deep sleep could do more harm than good.

Making a comfortable bed on the sofa, Katherine donned her coat and covered her legs with the hand-crocheted throw Mrs. Leroy had placed there for her use. Try as she may, her mind wouldn't rest. It flashed vivid cameos of times she had only been interested in what she wanted and wouldn't relent until whatever that was, was obtained. If she didn't get what she wanted, then everyone in close proximity suffered her anger for days.

One time in particular was when students in grades six through eight competed in the areas of math and spelling. Katherine, as a sixth grader, outdid every sixth, seventh, and eighth grade student in both spelling and math. She begged her parents for a new pair of shoes to wear the day of the award ceremony, but funds were not available for such. Katherine refused to go, and screamed and cried the whole day prior until her eyes were puffed like protruding Ping-Pong balls.

Margot washed, starched, and ironed Katherine's best outfit, applying black boot polish on the shoes to cover the worn-out toes and heels. Next, she washed Katherine's hair and had her sit near the stove while supper was prepared, to assist the drying of her waist-length hair.

Katherine's complaining didn't lessen, and after listening to the wailing for some time, Margot sent Katherine to bed without supper.

She showed them all when the school principal gave her a double promotion to grade eight! Yet, there she was, still pouting in the picture taken that day, which her mother continued to display on the wall. She had tried crossing her ankles to hide the worst shoe, but they came out as clear and ugly in the photograph as they truly were. The shoes were not the focus of the picture, for anyone would be more taken with "Katherine's face looking like the wrong end of Patty's pig," as offered by Margot.

Pulling the throw around her shoulders, Katherine thought, there I go again! Why do I think I'm smarter and can do everything more perfect then everyone else? I don't feel that sure of myself, because my insides jump and my heart pounds in my throat and temples when I'm in the limelight or when I have to support my opinions. Guess I'm fearful of meeting someone smarter and better than me. They're out there, waiting…to challenge…question…laugh at me…betray…

The rising sun flashed on her closed lids. With a start, Katherine sat up, reorienting herself with the surroundings, and not believing it was after six. Quietly, she cracked open the bedroom door and was surprised to see Mrs. Leroy already in her wheelchair. Whispering a morning greeting, Mrs. Leroy motioned toward the water closet. Katherine obliged, and then helped her settle back into bed to rest until seven. Katherine went down to the cellar to stoke the embers and add a few shovels of coal to the furnace. Opening the damper, the draft picked up the fire, then she closed it a bit to create a steady flow of heat.

Back upstairs, Katherine checked the radiators to see if they were warming up. She spotted the gift on the hall table that Dr. Kirkland had left for her. Removing the wrapping, she opened a slim box which held a black leather kit. Inside the envelope-style kit were the instruments a nurse would use for removing surgical bandages and stitches. She now had her very own set! Tucked behind the scissors and tweezers was a note: "Thank you for being so kind and compassionate. Happy Birthday, Dr. Kirkland." She wondered how he knew it was her birthday. Maybe he saw it on her records, or someone told him.

Katherine thought about her four years of training at St. Mary's and how she pushed to be the best. In her soul-searching quest, she found herself in the middle of an inner one-way conversation: "My speech at graduation must have made everyone think that I'm out of touch with reality and adrift in the clouds. How lofty and idealistic I must have seemed, and no one stopped me! If they had tried to offer advice, I honestly would have considered them jealous of my intelligence, or envious that they were not given the honor to deliver the farewell address for our class. Sweet Jesus, forgive my arrogance!

"I've got to stop blaming all my slipups, mistakes, or bad times on my family, or Ted's mother, or anyone else whom I perceive as getting in my way. I've got to accept my own mistakes and learn from them. People make mistakes all the time; my family will continue to make their mistakes, and when I live in Massachusetts, I won't know about it unless they tell me. And they won't know about my mistakes unless I tell them. They won't know about our ups and downs as newlyweds, and why should they?

"From the size of my diamond, Ted is operating on a rigid budget. He must be telling the truth about what it costs to live in the Boston area. Money is tight, but the benefits of steady employment with the railroad are the trade-off, so he says. I'll have to adjust my highfalutin ideas, as my mother calls them, to a lower level. Visions of a maid and groundskeeper to help me maintain our future residence are now laughable. I'm ridiculous. Who do I think I am? No more upper crust pretenses when my friends ask me where Ted and I will be living. I'll respond that we'll be taking up residence in Lawrence until I familiarize myself with the Boston area."

Chapter Twelve

The postman was kept busy delivering envelopes and small packages to the Albany Street residence. Each parcel was carefully examined and recorded by Katherine in her gift registry. She noted specifics and initial impressions for future reference when writing each thank you note. She displayed silver and glass stemware on a sideboard in the parlor. Personal items, such as lace lingerie, were quickly packed away.

The replies acknowledging attendance at the wedding were sparse. Because the wedding was on a Tuesday, only the members of the wedding party were able to get the time off from their employment. The majority of the invited guests either had no means of transportation on a weekday, or would not attend without a spouse.

The wedding brunch was to be held at the Hotel Utica following a nuptial Mass. The hotel was over twenty miles from Little Falls, further reducing the number of local neighbors who could attend. This worked out favorably for Katherine's parents, who could just about manage to finance a wedding breakfast for a sparse few guests. Doing it small but with style would play well in the local newspaper, concluded Katherine and Margot, following hours of anxiety over the impending costs.

The other fly in the ointment was the disappointment that neither Ted's mother, Maggie, nor his sister, Ellen, could afford to attend the wedding. Funds were not available for Maggie to buy appropriate clothing, let alone stay a day or two at a hotel! Ellen was saving for her own wedding and knew Ted couldn't finance anyone else's needs, given his own set of circumstances.

Pandemonium soaked every fiber of their brains the day before the wedding. As in any event which focuses attention on all members of a family, people were overreacting and half-hearing what was being said. In between the verbal exchanges, well-intentioned neighbors dropped off homemade jams and pies, or just came by to gawk at the gifts. Courtesy was hard to extend when time was needed to accomplish so many last-minute details.

Keeping an eye on Leo, who offered a bit of the spirits to whoever walked through the front door, was wearing Margot down. Her temples were pounding as she checked the clock. It was time for supper, and she turned off the porch light, the hall light, and the parlor's torch light.

"Why'd ya do that for, Ma?" whined a slightly flushed Lenora.

"Geet into the kitchen with the lot of ya! Geet! Geet! Now, I've been observing a bit of nipping going on by the older members, and I'll have none of it! I expect each of ya to get washed up and to bed by nine. Supper's in the pot and damn any one of ya that brings me shame on my daughter's wedding day!" Margot stood firmly by the kitchen table with one hand on her hip and the curse of hell's fire shooting from her eyes.

A few self-conscious coughs followed by the quick shuffling of dishes and chairs preceded a very quiet meal. The ritual following supper, of the washing, drying, and sweeping was speedily completed.

"Kate! You won't be home for supper when you get married!" Sean exclaimed.

"Does that mean I can never come back for a visit and eat here again?" inquired Katherine.

"You know what I mean, don't you?" the embarrassed six-year-old whispered.

"I know all too well, and I love you so much for saying what you said," replied Katherine.

The morning of the wedding day was cool and crisp after a night of heavy spring rain. The air was clean and pure, and nature's colors appeared surrealistically mounted on a background of reality, as the rising sun pushed the clouds away.

Looking out the bedroom window, Katherine imagined she could see Ted standing by his window at the Reiman, experiencing the same feelings and excitement. It was going to be a perfect wedding. A soft tap on the bedroom door interrupted Katherine's thoughts.

"Come in," called Katherine.

"Kate, I'll miss you not living here anymore," sniffed Sean.

"I'll not be that far away. And besides, you can come and visit Ted and me on all your school vacations," promised Katherine.

"Ma said you and Ted may have your own children to worry about, and for me not to bother you," repeated the innocent child.

"You will never bother me, Sean. I love you with all my heart. Now, remember to obey Ma and Pa. They need you to help them around the house and store. I want you to learn all you can in school so you can take care of yourself, like Bernard, Raymond, and Ted."

Another knock found Aileen and Lenora pushing each other aside as they entered.

"Ma said you only have forty minutes until we all leave for St. Mary's. May we help?" asked Lenora.

"Tell me if I got all the hairs tucked in neatly," directed Katherine.

"Everything is fine. No, wait! One is hanging," reported Lenora as she completed the tuck. She gave Katherine a big hug; then ran from the room.

"She's been weepy all morning," said Aileen.

"I want to give you each something; here is one for Lenora, too. They're hand-carved rosary beads from Ireland. Please remember me when you pray the rosary. I'm going to need those prayers!" Katherine sighed.

"If you feel that worried, don't get married!" whined Aileen.

Another knock on the door, and Maureen arrived to claim all responsibilities as maid of honor. Approaching Katherine, she placed her hands on the future bride's shoulders, and looked intently into her eyes.

"I'm here to tell you I've got a car outside with the motor running. We can get away from all of this and drive to some foreign country," gestured a dramatic Maureen.

"Are you here to help or hinder?" asked Katherine, motioning to Aileen and Sean to leave the room, as she readied to put on her wedding dress.

"By the way, I brought a change of clothes so you can take this dress I'm wearing on your honeymoon, as we planned."

"Are you sure that's what you want to do?" asked Katherine.

"I told you, I'll never wear it again," replied a somber Maureen, "and your white dress will remain with me forever as a token of our friendship. I'll always be there when you need me, Katherine."

"Let's hope I never have to impose on your friendship," Katherine replied with an uneasy feeling about the way Maureen was staring at her. "Besides, it's for you to be married in, also!"

Pretending not to be uncomfortable, Katherine donned her dress and the black malines picture hat and scarf, and swung around with arms posed in a mannequin's stance.

"What do you think?" Katherine asked Maureen.

"I think it looks like Fifth Avenue. Let's go!" shrieked Maureen.

Everyone was ready and waiting as the young women descended the steps. Several neighbors, who had watched Katherine grow up, seemed to consider themselves as having had a hand in the success of the moment, as they stood smiling and waving at each other outside the Lockharts' house.

Bernard stood waiting at attention like the doorman at the Ritz, and flamboyantly opened the car door for Katherine. Maureen opened her own door and jumped in the front passenger seat. A strange aura encased Katherine's senses. People spoke, but their speech was garbled. All her doubts were now playing in the front of her head like a newsreel at the movies. Perhaps she and Ted should have waited longer than four months. What if he was the total opposite of what she thought he was? The car came to a halt in front of St. Mary's Church.

"Cold feet?" asked Bernard, "Should I have Father Kielty come out here to the car?"

Finally, with the shaking controlled, Katherine stood next to Ted as Father Kielty's voice echoed in the spacious chamber. A feeling of being disconnected and cut off from all that was familiar seemed to sweep down and suck the breath out of Katherine's lungs. Seeming to sense this panic, Father took both Katherine's and Ted's hands in his.

"Just as God extends his hand toward man, as depicted in Michelangelo's painting in the Sistine Chapel, you have but to reach out in prayer and he is there for you, always," prayed Father, as he made the sign of the cross on both of their foreheads.

At the conclusion of the service, Katherine placed a small bouquet of irises, and white baby's breath on the Blessed Virgin's altar. Outside the church, the newly married couple greeted well-wishers as Bernard attempted to guide the bride and groom toward his car. A storm of rice rained on them all. Looking over at Sean, Katherine noticed he was throwing from a box of barley, and began laughing so hard the tears rained as she ran to hug him.

The gaiety came to a deafening quiet as the couple sat in the backseat holding hands and feeling like strangers who had just met. In the front seats, Bernard and Maureen were enjoying the levity of their independence, which would still be intact after this day was over, as they beeped the horn and sang in harmony, "Those wedding bells are breaking up that old gang of mine."

✦ ✦ ✦ ✦ ✦ ✦

The Hotel Utica presented a lovely wedding brunch that any bride and groom would be pleased with. Margot and Leo were impressed and felt they indeed had gotten their money's worth. Unfortunately, the hotel had allowed only two hours before another engagement occupied the room, adjoining the Crystal Ballroom. A courtesy suite was provided for the bridal couple to change into their travel attire for their honeymoon.

Margot had purposely tried to avoid inviting anyone back to their home for fear Leo would start toasting everyone. But, here they all stood in the main lobby of the hotel at two in the afternoon.

"Folks, if ya'd like a spot of tea and some Irish bread or apple pie, stop by our home on Albany Street between four and six," offered Margot.

Bernard drove Katherine and Ted to the train station and the total entourage from the wedding followed. The train was leaving at 3:45 for connecting points to Atlantic City. Ted opened the coach windows for last-minute exchanges as he and Katherine looked out upon all the merriment and antics of their well-wishers. Leo boarded the train and motioned for Katherine so he could speak with her in private.

'Pa, you better leave before the train starts moving!" cautioned Katherine, fearful her father might try jumping off, since he still didn't accept his limitations.

"Katherine, please listen. I'm sorry for all the pain I've caused you. You don't have to forgive me now, but maybe one day you will. Perhaps, if you knew I wasn't your father, it would lessen the stigma. This is my wedding gift to you."

"You're not…my…father? Pa, what are you saying?" as she reached for Leo's arm to steady herself.

"Don't let your mother know I told you, but after I die, find out the truth; promise you won't say anything until then," a gaunt and solemn Leo begged, as he pulled away from Katherine.

"I promise!" whispered Katherine, keeping her shock under control.

The train's locomotive was fired and ready to leave. With the assistance of the conductor, Leo alighted intact.

Returning to Ted's side, Katherine joined in the waving as the train moved slowly in the direction of the couple's future. She watched until the countryside's brush blocked any familiar view of Little Falls. Ted held her firmly with one arm around her waist, realizing she was struggling to hold back the tears.

"Ted, our wedding was lovely, wasn't it?" she finally managed to say.

"The best wedding I've ever had!" answered Ted.

"Ted! What are you, a bluebeard?" exclaimed Katherine.

"You'll find out soon enough," he teased, "and be the envy of all your women friends. Incidentally, we'll be getting off in Albany to stay overnight at my friend's home. He's out of town for the remainder of the week and offered his place. I thought you'd be more comfortable in a private home rather than a hotel for our first night together."

"But what if someone tries to reach us in an emergency?" Katherine asked.

"Bernard knows, and I gave him the address should he need to get in touch for some reason." Ted refrained from adding that his mother also knew.

They arrived at the bungalow at dusk. Ted located the hidden key and turned on the entrance light. He showed Katherine all around the bachelor's home, and placed their suitcases and overnight bags in the guest room.

The home was charming and lacked the clutter and oversized furniture of her parents' home. The rattan sofa and chairs had colorful blue and white striped cushions that gave one the feeling of being in a seaside cottage, minus the sand or the view.

"Fred is a real character," Ted chuckled, breaking the silence which was obvious now that they were alone for the first time as husband and wife. "He collects odds and ends from sidewalk sales and refinishes the pieces. When he tires of something, he sets it out on Saturday, puts a 'for sale' sign up, and then uses the money when he sells it to look for his next treasure."

"He is talented; very good at upholstering and painting, plus his choice of colors..." a distant-minded bride replied.

Ted suddenly embraced and kissed his new bride. Katherine felt the need to push him away for fear someone may be watching, but Ted sensed the push and shut off the light. It was a long and pleasurable night with no thought of oversleeping, missing a train, forgetting to give a patient the medicine, or who they would have to answer to. It was their own world now, and the embracing couple was going to make the most of these precious days before life called its trump.

Awakening before Ted, Katherine attempted to prepare breakfast in a stranger's kitchen only to find the icebox disconnected and empty. The gas was turned off and there was no hot water, only cold, with no way to warm it. She knew this would be no problem for Ted, after his years of roughing it at his home in Rotterdam Junction. But how was she going to launder the bed sheets?

"Will he ever wake up?" Katherine whispered to herself. "Perhaps by banging a few cupboard doors he may wake up." It didn't work. Returning to the bathroom, Katherine sponged and dressed for their afternoon travel plans.

Around ten, Ted appeared in pajama bottoms with his shaving gear in hand. "Sorry I slept so long! Why didn't you wake me?"

"I was planning to when breakfast was ready, but the cupboards are bare!"

"I forgot to mention that Fred has the first penny he ever made. He did leave on the cold water, didn't he?" Ted asked.

"Thank God! That he did," answered Katherine.

"Let's soak the sheets in the wash tub while I shave. Then, we'll hang them on the porch. Its still enclosed from the winter, so no one will steal them," Ted glibly added.

"Were you reading my mind? I had planned to pack them and mail them back to your friend. I've been worried about what to do with the bed sheets since last night!" responded a blushing Katherine.

"You're not serious? You were worried about the sheets?" an amused Ted responded.

"Don't make fun of me. Those sheets are very personal and a private matter. Nobody's business but ours," Katherine answered in a hoity-toity fashion.

"I'll make note of how sensitive you are about bed sheets. Does that also include coverlets and blankets?"

"Ted Bryant, I expect a degree of courtesy and respect in matters of a private nature. I've heard some doctors discussing very personal issues with each other concerning their home life and wives. I will not be a topic of discussion with the men and women at Fred's place of employment."

"Are you hungry?" Ted inquired.

"I haven't eaten since the night before we got married, except for the small piece of chicken at our reception," Katherine responded, almost crying.

"First, I'll dump the sheets in the tub. Next, I'll shave. Then, we'll pop down the street one block to a nifty diner. Give me fifteen minutes," a rushing figure was shouting as he moved swiftly from bedroom, to tub, to bathroom.

Twelve minutes later, the hungry couple walked quickly to partake of the breakfast menu at the diner before the noon crowd descended from the capitol building nearby. Returning to the bungalow, Ted wrung out the sheets and Katherine hung them.

"Did you know that cold water creates fewer wrinkles in cotton? And when they hang to dry, sometimes they don't even need to be ironed."

"You're spoofing with me," responded Katherine. "Who do you think washes my uniforms, the maid?"

"Are we having our first discourse over the mere subject of cotton? Or is it the labor of cleanliness?" inquired Ted.

"Look! If you lived with other people who were absolute pigs the way they kept their clothes and personal selves, you'd understand," Katherine answered.

"Now, you shouldn't talk about the good nuns that way," Ted interjected, in an attempt to lighten up an exchange he could not understand from where it came or was going.

"It's not the nuns I'm talking about! It's that group of people I lived with," screamed Katherine.'

"Could we not yell? We don't have a lot of time. We need to finish packing and leave within the next half hour," requested Ted softly, hoping to lower the decibels.

"Well! Isn't your life simple! You just breeze in and out of friends' homes for an overnight. Before me, who did you breeze in and out with?" Katherine inquired, wide-eyed.

"I won't dignify that question with a response. Get ready, please, and we'll not continue this train of pointless conversation."

"So, what I say or ask is pointless?" shrieked Katherine.

"Stop; I'm leaving in ten minutes. Be ready," replied Ted.

Katherine couldn't stop the tears, and finally applied cold compresses to counteract the red eyelids. She had already packed while Ted was shaving and washing the sheets. Picking up her bags in the hallway, she waited on the front porch.

Ted exited, placing the key back in its hiding place. He looked at Katherine and started walking toward the corner taxi stand. She grabbed her bags and followed. On the remainder of the trip to Atlantic City, neither spoke to the other. Each was left to sort the words exchanged and contemplate why anger was the choice of expression.

Reflecting on the times the words in his letters were often misinterpreted by Katherine, Ted had dismissed it by rationalizing that face-to-face conversation would remove the language glitches. He noticed a pattern emerging around perceptions made by Katherine at times when she might be feeling insecure or insulted.

If she wasn't being complimented or the center of attention, then her guard was up for the first hint of what she perceived as being criticism, reacting similar to an insulted Frenchman who challenges a duel. In Katherine's case, the choice of weapon was her mouth. Ted felt rather chauvinistic coming to this conclusion.

He reviewed his words again and again, and they were not insulting but chit-chat shallow, to be honest. Perhaps it is a matter of establishing trust. Where does this distrust come from, Ted wondered?

The reticent female form next to him stared out the train window, occasionally sniffing and wiping her nose. She seemed like a total stranger, not the lovely woman he stood at the altar with twenty-eight hours ago, and held passionately in his arms all night!

He had never seen this coldness before in Katherine, but then, she had never witnessed him really angry. If today was upsetting for her, he had better clue her in to his temper's potential. She's not the only creature fighting the devil within, he thought. He excused himself and went out on the platform to smoke a cigarette.

"And that's another thing. If I want a cigarette, I'm going to have it, damn it!" Ted said out loud to himself.

CHAPTER THIRTEEN

Ted was out of town on the date of their first anniversary, dampening the romance of the milestone. On his return trip, a mechanical problem with the train's brake system occurred just as it pulled into Little Falls. It was estimated that the repairs would take approximately two to three hours due to the need to fetch a part from up the line. The passengers were free to get off, and would be summoned by four whistles a half hour before departure.

Ted knew exactly what he wanted to do with the time, and for starters recalled the department store Katherine had taken him to on the main street. He found a silk crepe blouse in a soft rose that looked just like what Katherine would choose and had it gift wrapped. Next, he called Margot's store pretending he was calling from Boston, and livened up the day when he walked in thirty minutes later. Sean ran home to retrieve a couple of tardy letters to Katherine and a small box of things Margot felt her daughter may want, along with a box containing homemade preserves and a link of hard sausage for Ted to bring back to Lawrence.

"Who would have imagined! Of all places for the brakes to break! How did everyone look?" inquired Katherine as she and Ted sat by candlelight enjoying the delayed celebration.

"If you mean Sean, he is taller and slimmer. Everybody else seems the same. I told your mother we would try to visit this coming Christmas for your twenty-seventh birthday."

"Oh, could we, Ted, really? Perhaps I'll be working by then, but I'll worry about that when it happens," Katherine added.

She had interviewed for every possible nursing position within Lawrence that she could reach by walking or by trolley or train. Language tended to be a barrier when cases involved the immigrant population. Ted didn't want her working nights or in a public hospital. His restrictions, combined with hers, eliminated several opportunities.

At last, on December second, a Doctor Porter called and requested that Katherine drop by to discuss starting on the first of February as his office nurse. The present nurse was leaving at the end of January, as she was in a family way.

Nurse Watkins was thirty-two years old, and so delighted with finally being pregnant, she didn't seem to mind that it was Dr. Porter who suggested she leave before she began to show. He felt it would make his male patients uncomfortable.

Katherine and Ted were hoping for a child but were in no hurry. They wanted a better flat, but with one income up to now, had not even entertained looking at other rentals. This position with Dr. Porter would enable them to consider a residential area of single and two-family homes in place of the tenement area they presently lived in.

Unable to control themselves, they searched casually the second and third weeks of December, and to their surprise located the ideal flat in a two-family home, within walking distance to both Dr. Porter's office and the train station. They postponed their holiday trip to New York and moved in the weekend following Christmas.

The second week of January, Katherine found certain food odors repulsive. Butter tasted rotten and meats smelled rotten! She blamed it on the icebox and drove the ice man crazy in demanding an explanation on where he procured his ice.

"I smell rotten fish, Mr. Mossier!" claimed Katherine, with hands on her hips.

"Excuse me, lady. You seem like a nice lady, but I don't bring you used ice! I've been doing this many years now, and I think you should see a doctor," exclaimed the ice man.

"You think I'm crazy?" shrieked Katherine, "Well, I never in my life…"

"Lady, you're going to have a baby!" answered the man.

"I'm what? A baby! Oh, you think so? I'm so sorry, Mr. Mossier, for bothering you so. It never occurred to me that it was me!" Katherine answered.

"And, if you're not having a baby, I'll eat the next block of ice I bring you. We have five children of our own and my wife acted strange each time!"

When Ted arrived home that evening, Katherine conveyed the ice man's diagnosis. He couldn't stop laughing. Katherine didn't find it as amusing; given the fact Dr. Porter would not be open to having a nurse in the family way just a month behind his nurse of eight years. If the ice man's diagnosis was correct, she'd have to decline the job and enlist the doctor's services instead.

"You'll have the baby at a hospital and receive the best care possible," promised Ted.

"It will be so expensive," Katherine said.

"We have eight months or so to plan. No problem. If Joe Blow can do it, so can I," Ted said with a shrug of his shoulders.

"Who's Joe Blow?"

"Just your everyday blot, trying to make a living," responded Ted as he lit his pipe.

They hadn't planned on their landlord raising their rent in anticipation of additional water usage for laundry with a new baby around. Four months after the birth of their daughter, Teresa, Katherine learned she was pregnant with their second child.

The bills from Teresa's hospital birth were not yet fully paid, and the rent increase narrowed their funds. Katherine decided to have a home birth with Dr. Porter's assistance. The birth was complicated due to the size of the ten pound, three ounces baby boy. After seeing what Katherine went through to give him a daughter and son, Ted vowed to himself there would be no more children. Katherine was too fragile to endure such suffering. The children needed a mother, not a corpse.

He concealed the financial strain the untimely pregnancies caused. With the October crash following Teresa Ann's birth in August of 1929, businesses were suffering from the lack of a cash flow, wages were frozen, and no one made waves for fear of being laid off, if they were fortunate enough to have a job! The domino effect was rapid.

Margot wrote from Little Falls that she feared for her business, as customers were unable to pay their running tabs. She wasn't able to stock the store with a variety of goods because vendors wanted cash upon delivery. Credit was no longer an acceptable commodity.

Ted occasionally missed sending his mother money to help with the tax payments on her home, but would make up the shortage by doubling the amount until he caught up. It was a constant game of borrowing from one pocket to fill another.

Times were hard all over but people made due, and the goodness they sowed when affluent with a couple of dollars loaned to a friend would filter back from the least expected sources. Ted discovered this when a letter arrived at work from a young man he had befriended when living at Beacon Chambers.

The young man heard through the grapevine that Ted was now the father of two children and knew the money he owed Ted would come in handy. Ted felt like he had just struck it rich in a gold mine when he received the envelope! Cautiously, Ted figured the most expeditious way to use the money without raising Katherine's imagination beyond the seventy dollars. He paid back the eighteen dollars owed his friends, and on the way home stopped by the furniture store to buy his daughter a stroller. Next, he would be passing by Dr. Porter's office, and if he was still open, it would be the sign to give the good doctor the remainder of the money. Just as Ted was playing this fate game, Dr. Porter walked out his door.

"Good evening, Ted. What's that–an empty stroller? Are you looking for another baby? Two in thirteen months would be enough for some!" the doctor joked as he shook Ted's hand.

"Dr. Porter, I have some money toward our bill. I could come back tomorrow if this isn't a good time."

"No, no! Come in!" Doctor Porter replied, surprised. "Did you rob a bank?"

Ted told the doctor about his friend's kindness, which allowed him to pay back his co-workers and buy the stroller.

"And so you're putting it to good use, I see! Well, let's see. Yes, I believe twenty-five should settle our account," concluded the doctor.

It was more than twice that as Ted recalled, but the old saying that a bird in the hand is worth two in a bush must have governed the doctor's decision. Arriving home, Ted felt relieved having the bills off his back.

"Katherine, come look outside!" called Ted.

With a baby in her arms and a toddler hugging her leg, Katherine looked out the parlor window at the stroller, nodding her approval. This would allow the whole family to go out together for walks on the weekend. By the time Sonny grew out of the baby carriage, Teresa Ann would be too big for the stroller.

"Where did you get the money?" she inquired.

"It's a story I'll tell you after supper. But first I want you to use the remainder of the money for whatever you wish."

Not since her working days did Katherine have her own money. She was so delighted she couldn't decide where to hide it. Ted suggested one of her medical books and she agreed.

"Should the landlord ask where the stroller came from, tell her someone I work with lost her baby to smallpox and gave us the stroller," instructed Ted.

The repetition of the phrase, "easy come, easy go" kept running in his head throughout the evening. Just before Ted dozed off to sleep, Katherine said she would use her money to buy Sean a complete Boy Scout uniform and mail it to him for his first troop meeting in September.

Ted woke up in the middle of the night from a nightmare in which a seedy individual had stolen the brown paper package containing Sean's new uniform. It was snowing and Sean was running around in his underwear shoveling through snow banks looking for his uniform. Ted decided he would have a friend drop off the package in Little Falls rather than use the mail.

A few days later, Ted received a letter from his mother telling about thefts from mailboxes and churches' poor boxes in several surrounding towns. Wooden fences were being stolen at night to be used for fuel. She suggested that he not send her cash in the mail and to hold on to it until she visited at Christmas. This was the first he knew of his mother's intention to visit for the holidays. How could he break the news to Katherine when she was planning for them to go to Little Falls for Christmas?

Arriving home from work one evening a few days after receiving his mother's letter, Katherine's greeting seemed a bit frosty.

"Did the children give you a hard time today, dear?" cautiously inquired Ted.

"Your supper is ready, as usual." Katherine responded.

"I'm missing some part of this conversation," Ted said more or less to himself.

"My, aren't we coy!" Katherine replied.

"That's me! I'm even coy when I'm not trying to be! Now, will you please tell me what you're upset about?" he asked.

"This is what is upsetting," Katherine said as she tossed the letter on the table.

"You promised we'd go to Little Falls for the holidays. It's been almost four years since I've spent time with my family, and you promised we'd go back this year. It doesn't even cost you money for train tickets! You're just lazy. I'm fed up with your tiredness. For a thirty-four-year-old you act like you're sixty! Another thing, we're scraping by and sacrificing, but what is your sister Ellen doing to help her mother out? She's a stay-at-home wife with no children. She could get a job and send money to her mother. Or better still, why couldn't your mother live with Ellen and her husband?"

"Katherine, sit down, please," implored Ted. "I'm tired from looking at numbers all day, along with the other responsibilities of my job. Next, you and the children may still go to Little Falls for the holidays and stay as long as you're comfortable with being there. Lastly, my mother won't leave her home to live with anyone. When she comes at Christmas, my sister can help out with entertaining our mother while I'm at work."

"Why didn't you tell me about your plans before?" inquired Katherine.

"I'm waiting to find out if there will be room for you and the children on the train, along with which days passes are allowed during the holidays, and if there would be cargo space for the carriages. An answer still hasn't come back, because paying customers are more desirable due to the tight money situation of the times. Unfortunately, no friend has recently given me any money."

"If they owe it to you, ask for it!" she demanded. "Our pockets could use some change, and we'd have enough if you didn't send money to Rotterdam Junction!"

"I knew you'd get to that sooner or later," sighed Ted. "I've never let my mother know how tight things were for me when living on my own. Now you know because you are living it with me, but she is still unaware, and it isn't her burden to ever know. She thinks that working in an office versus a blue-collar job automatically means success. She brags to everyone about my position with the B & M. Thank heavens she is close to the vest about her money matters, because if these same people knew the small amount I send her, they'd peg me as a cheap so-and-so or a big joke putting on airs."

"How much are you sending each week, Ted?" asked Katherine.

"It's just enough to pay the taxes on the house, which comes to forty-two dollars a year."

"That's less than a dollar a week!" a dumbfounded wife deduced upon a quick estimation thus negating what she thought was about five times the amount Ted was sending each week! This left her wondering just what he was doing with the rest of the money.

"I make and handle the money; you spend it. Seems like a kindly arrangement."

"I don't waste any of it. I am very frugal. How much have we saved so far?" asked Katherine?

"You're joking," exclaimed Ted. "I just explained there is no money beyond that which our daily needs demand. Each time you dip into the teapot to buy Teresa Ann a frilly this or that or Sonny a blue this or that to match his eyes, it's gone. Something else is left wanting."

"Don't you want us to look nice? People form opinions about what kind of man you are as a provider," stammered Katherine. "This is a professional neighborhood, and I won't be looked down upon."

"Then, we'll move to a location where no one has seen our old clothes and everything will be new again," shouted Ted. "Isn't that what you're really upset about, Katherine? That you didn't marry a 'ball of fire' is starting to dawn on you. As a matter of fact, I didn't even have a dime to give a poor fellow today who was begging outside North Station. When he approached me, I told him I was working that side of the street myself!"

135

"You didn't! You wouldn't! Why I never..!" Katherine muttered.

"By the way, the landlord stopped me on my way in tonight to inform me that the rent will increase another two dollars, starting in March. I'm serious about looking for a more reasonable flat after New Year's. And now, I'm tired and am going to bed."

"You didn't eat your supper, after I spent two hours preparing it," Katherine sniffed.

The distance between the couple in bed was growing wider with each passing week. His reserve was prompted by the fear of another child, and hers was from the feelings of entrapment and disappointment.

✦ ✦ ✦ ✦ ✦ ✦

The holiday trip to Little Falls opened Katherine's eyes. The spirit of Christmas was present only because of her children and Sean. She had taken that away from Ted by insisting on being with her family.

There were definite changes in Lenora's and Bernard's attitudes and behaviors. They seemed self-centered, and enjoyed being inebriated to the point of no intelligence, and scoffed at Katherine's prudishness. The group they chummed around with smoked and drank, plus seemed to be morally loose. One young man in particular couldn't keep away from Lenora, and appeared to enjoy when she was drunk because it was the only time she'd let him come near her. The one night Katherine went out with her siblings was the last time for the remainder of her stay. This was not how she envisioned her Christmas holiday with her family. How she wished Ted was with her.

Margot had changed, as well. There were no spontaneous Irish folk songs, though she'd hum when holding the grandchildren. While readying the children for bed the fourth night of Katherine's stay, daughter and mother attempted to catch up on the times distance had robbed them of.

"Where have the years gone, Katherine? I thought there were so many more years of energy left, but doing it on my own is wearing me down," admitted Margot.

"Lenora and Aileen help around the house, don't they? I do hope you are giving Aileen something for working at the store," inquired Katherine.

"Yes, yes, yes! I know she won't work for nothing, and Lenora is not worth the room she takes up around here with all her late nights. Since she lost her job at the Mill Store, she's in bed until noon and then is out of the house until two or three in the morning! Dear Lord, why do ya curse me with the worst possible family? Will my debt ever be paid?"

"What debt, Ma?" quickly asked Katherine.

"Aw, never ya mind. I'm just tired and worried about having the money to pay the delivery man. The one blessing is that everyone is practically in the same boat, so we're grateful for whatever little we can give or get."

"Ma, what do you think of Lenora's boyfriend, Hank?"

"He's a gaddamn German and a Protestant! I told him not to show his face around here. I won't have the likes of his kind thinking he can even touch one of my daughters. And I don't want to hear anymore about him."

"What if he was a Catholic German?" teased Katherine.

"That would be the day Jesus comes down from the cross! Are you daft? His kind is bent on taking over the world by getting into every young woman's underdrawers!"

"I wish you wouldn't talk so crudely. The children have ears, and besides all a lady has to say is no!" Katherine replied, surprised at her own response.

"I'm afraid it's not that simple for some who are hungry for love and tenderness," Margot softly responded.

"Is Bernard any nearer to asking Lily the big question?" asked Katherine.

"Lily this and Lily that! Now there's a real dilly. I don't know where my children find these people. From what I hear, her father lost a million when the stock market collapsed, but he has enough rental real estate to keep him from being wiped out. He let several of the staff go from their department store, and it's now opened only three days a week," replied Margot, sounding more like her old self. "What about you, Katherine?" Margot asked.

"What about me? You see for yourself! I'm busy with the children and feeling stronger. Sonny's birth took a lot out of me, and I think Ted is finished with babies." Katherine added.

"A marriage needs shared affection. When it's not there, part of ya shrivels up and dies; I know," an insightful Margot stated.

"It was all going so well between us before the expense of the children, but money is a constant issue, and Ted doesn't want me to work."

"There'll be plenty of time for that when yar children are in school and older. Believe me, once ya start working, men get used to not having to worry about handing over their total paycheck and start fretting it away on self-indulgences," her mother offered.

"Ted's not like that. He handles all the money and does a fine job of it even though it's tight from week to week. The flat we're in is too expensive since the landlord raised our rent twice already, and plans to up it again in March. So, we'll probably have a new address shortly," Katherine discretely added, yet conveyed a lot more than she realized.

In an attempt to take the focus off herself, Katherine asked, "Have you heard from Raymond, recently?"

"We received season's greetings and scant notes about a nurse he is serious about. I expect they'll marry in Herkimer somewhere. He's a loner if there ever was one; Bernard drives up every couple of months and spends the weekend with him. Seems Raymond wants to go to college and is taking courses to advance him. Well, he's smart enough to be good at whatever he chooses, but I don't understand why he doesn't come around to visit," Margot shared.

Katherine was looking at her mother for what seemed like the first time. She was aging and seemed a lot grayer than Katherine felt she should be in just a short four years since she last saw her.

"Katherine, I have something for ya," Margot said as she left the room. She returned with a framed picture of Sean in his Boy Scout uniform, sitting on the window seat.

"It's just lovely, Ma! Thank you so much. How did you ever get him to sit still long enough?" laughed Katherine.

"The man who comes through with the pony agreed to take the indoor picture for the same price, if I purchased two, which is just what I needed. And I had to pay an extra twenty-five cents for Sean to sit on the pony. Everyone has a gimmick!"

"May I pay you for the picture?" offered Katherine.

"Let's say its yar birthday present for the past couple of years," said Margot.

"Thank you. I hope our visit hasn't been too much of a burden. I plan to leave the day after New Year's, if that is all right with you. If I can do anything to help out at the store, or do any mending for you, please let me earn my stay," offered Katherine.

"What I'd appreciate is if ya would talk with Bernard about a town rumor that his hands are not clean like they used to be, and that he plays favorites. I don't want any shame brought on this family beyond what we already have had. Your father's family avoids us like the plague since his drinking became a public embarrassment," Margot humbly added.

"Pa doesn't look well, and he's lost a lot of weight. Could he be drinking again on the sly?" Katherine asked.

"He's not drinking and he's not eating. Sean does a good job of getting him to take some supper after everyone is out of the kitchen. Sometimes his hands shake so, he can't keep the food on the fork or spoon, and Sean will feed him. Other times he is fine," explained Margot.

"I thought they were playing cards or something, and that's why they wanted the kitchen to themselves. Getting back to Bernard, what makes you think he would discuss anything about his life with me?" asked Katherine.

"He respects both you and Ted, and always asks to read yar letters."

"Should he confide in me, I won't tell you anything," Katherine stated.

"And why should ya. Perhaps by telling ya, it may make him stop to think about what he is doing and prevent trouble, if it's not too late. The other night when Bernard came home he was drunk, though he claimed he wasn't, and rambled on that he could fool some of the people most of the time and the rest of the people all of the time, but he couldn't fool the fool he is. I thought it was the drink talking, but the rumor makes me think there's more to it," Margot sadly answered.

"Just starting a conversation will be difficult after the words I had with both Lenora and Bernard about their drinking Saturday night. Aren't they afraid of getting caught?" Katherine asked somberly

"Every one of them lies for the other. But blood is thicker than water, and in their hearts they know yar right. I need yar help," Margot begged.

"Ma, I'm just about able to take care of myself and Ted. I doubt myself all the time, and at the low times I just can't stop crying. There's no one to help me with the children, and Ted is always exhausted; he works long hours and is all used up by the time he gets home," Katherine confided.

"What if Lenora were to visit with you for a few months to help with the children and housework?" asked Margot.

"You need her here. And besides, we can't afford another mouth to feed. Lenora may be skinny, but she can eat, to say nothing about her other habits! If Aileen or Sean would like to visit for a couple of weeks during the summer, that would be fine," offered Katherine knowing her mother was trying to put distance between Lenora and Hank.

Margot depended on Aileen for helping her at the store and at home, plus Sean basically took care of Leo, so she quickly changed the subject.

"Did you go through the things Ted took home to you from your old bedroom dresser? I was so surprised when he dropped by. He stayed only about a half hour. I had packed the box to ship to you, but he offered to hand deliver it."

"I put it in my closet after removing your note and the perishables. Thank you for saving my things. I'll look through them when I get back home," Katherine replied.

"Then you didn't see the newspaper clipping of your nuptials. Let's go into my bedroom so we won't awaken the children. I didn't want to send it when ya were newly married because, well, I'll get my copy for ya," said Margot as she rummaged through a special box of mementos.

"I meant to ask you to save me a copy and then I forgot about it. What's this? 'Monkey skin' georgette!' Why would anyone describe my wedding dress in those terms? You're so right, Ma! I would have died of embarrassment."

"The day the article appeared in the *Tribune,* a few know-it-alls dropped in the store with left-handed congratulations. They also commented on yar dress being white. They said they didn't realize you were born in Ireland and an immigrant! I said you were born here. They said, 'Didn't you know that only immigrants get married in white?' So I said, 'Ya wore white, too?' They seemed insulted and turned to leave when I thanked them for their goodwill wishes and gave them each a sample box of a new laxative a salesman had left at the store that very morning."

"You didn't!" Katherine laughed, imagining the whole scene.

"And that, I did!" a cocky Margot responded with her hands on her hips. The next day, Katherine talked Aileen into keeping an eye on Teresa Ann while Sonny was napping so she could visit the library to check the past issues of the *Little Falls Tribune*. She located the date of the publication following her wedding and leafed through the four-and-a-half-year-old edition, recognizing familiar names of people and places. Then, the social section and a name jumped off the page.

> "Dr. Keith Young, resident Surgeon at St. Mary's Hospital in Amsterdam, spent the last week in April at the home of his twin brother, Albert Young, senior reporter for the *Little Falls Tribune*."

Katherine read the article again and again. It was so innocent in appearance, yet she knew better. Dr. Young must have heard she was getting married in Little Falls the end of April. The odds are he coerced his twin brother into doctoring the announcement by putting that 'monkey skin' addition into her wedding dress description.

"Dr. Kirkland was right!" she fumed. "One never knows when paths may again cross. Well, Dr. Young, it ends here. No one will ever see my wedding pictures or this newspaper clipping. This is the end, you scheming, despicable, sleazy bastard! You've just had your last pound of flesh." Carefully, she folded the extracted page upon which her wedding announcement and photo appeared, slid it up the sleeve of her coat, and slammed the newspaper archive journal closed.

"HUSH!" a voice responded from the opposite side of the room. Katherine placed the adjusted journal into its appropriate space and quietly exited by the side door.

✦ ✦ ✦ ✦ ✦ ✦ ✦ ✦

Katherine packed her children's tiny clothes, as she readied herself to say good-bye and travel back to her own life. The evening prior, Bernard and Katherine had walked the carriage and stroller to the depot for loading into the baggage car, in advance of her morning departure. Being alone with her brother afforded the opportunity to check out Margot's concerns. Bernard was excellent at blocking any openings in their casual conversation which would allow Katherine entrance to prod his conscience. According to Bernard, Little Falls was managing to care for its residents, and at least eighty percent of the properties should remain with their present owners, despite the Depression.

He speculated about the future of Little Falls and its industry, and was confident he would be part of its progress. He knew several high-level business people and was learning a lot from them regarding trends in the economy and the risks they took in the past to build their fortunes. If Bernard was concerned about anything, or uneasy regarding his position at city hall, there was not a hint of any problem. He still thought all was right with the world, and the love of his life, Lily, was worth a million.

As for their brother, Raymond, his goal seemed to be to get as far away from Little Falls as possible. The room Raymond is renting in Herkimer, as described by Bernard, is neat and orderly with everything in its assigned spot. Raymond even posts his daily routine on the closet door. No drinking; no smoking, and he goes to Mass daily.

"What about this Carol he's smitten with?" Katherine asked Bernard with a hint of jealousy.

"She's a real intelligent lady. Carol's petite with dark brown hair and beautiful brown eyes. Her parents have Irish roots, and her three brothers all went to college. She is in her last year of nurse's training. I told Raymond to hold on to that one. She'd bring some quality to this family, if she were a member!" concluded Bernard.

Katherine found no clues of panic or impending doom when reviewing her previous evening's conversation with Bernard. His troubles, if he had any, seemed to be as water off a duck's back. The packing completed, she made one final check in the mirror.

"So, she'd bring some quality to this family, if Raymond married his Carol! What am I?" a threatened sister asked, "Yesterday's chopped liver?"

The excitement of being back with Ted lasted a brief two weeks. While she was in Little Falls, Ted had scouted around the various train routes from Boston, and located a six-family home with a third floor flat for half the rent they were presently paying.

The second floor jaunt up the stairs with two children was challenging, argued Katherine, but Ted showed her the numbers and what it could save them. He explained that shoes, clothes, and food costs would increase as the children grew. They needed to think ahead and have some savings for unforeseen needs.

"Don't you think in the future you'll make more than you're making now?" asked Katherine.

"You can't second-guess something like that. The reality is what is in the pay envelope now."

"Change your job! Look around for a better-paying position. For God's sake, Ted! Take a chance and don't be such a stick in the mud!" Katherine shouted, wide-eyed.

"I should be more like Bernard and Raymond?" asked Ted. "If I didn't have the responsibility of other lives depending on me, I could."

"So, now it's the children and I who are holding you back! Is that what you are saying?" Katherine asked in an elevated tone.

"No, that's not what I'm saying! It's just that this is the only way to have security in these unsure times. This job with the Boston and Maine provides opportunity based on seniority and ability to do the work. It also is heading toward offering pensions and helping with work-related injuries. Rails are the future, and won't go away within my lifetime. They're a down-to-earth service for the everyday person's needs."

"I'll have to start all over again in a new location. How near are the stores and church?" asked Katherine.

"Pardon the point, but you're not in this alone," Ted interjected.

Katherine turned on her heels and locked herself in the bathroom. For over an hour, Ted played with the children and prepared them for bed. Teresa Ann used her potty and Sonny got a clean diaper. Teresa Ann said her prayers as Sonny played with his stuffed bear in his crib. Ted covered them with their favorite blankets, kissed them both, and turned out the light.

Sitting in the dark parlor with just the glow from the radio dial and his pipe, Ted wondered what Katherine's next move might be, but at the moment the energy to counter-challenge wasn't there. He turned the radio up just loud enough to barely hear and fought the temptation to drift off while watching the smoke from his pipe dance and tumble in the light of the crescent dial.

Peeking out of the bathroom door, Katherine could hear the radio and knew Ted would be preoccupied for another thirty minutes. She began wringing her hands and then rubbed her face with cleansing cream. She wanted to strike out at something. The feeling of entrapment had returned. She had to do something to show she was not totally controlled.

Being the dependable, dutiful wife who did only what her husband wanted was beginning to repulse her. What good was compliance when her needs were always postponed because of the children, or lack of money or Ted's rationalizing! She looked dowdy, like someone's old-maid aunt, next to Lenora and her friends when she visited Little Falls over the Christmas holidays. She had given up her career and dreams for what; for this? It wasn't getting better; only worse! Well, she thought, things are going to change.

Turning up the volume ever so slightly, Ted listened as the national news droned on. The newsman commented on the possibility of the governor of New York receiving the Democratic nomination as their candidate in the upcoming November presidential election. Roosevelt's political performance since 1928 suggested he was in tune with the everyday struggle Americans were experiencing. Europe was a different situation with all countries keeping a close eye on Germany's Nazi party and its aggressive leader. There was a bit of news regarding Amelia Earhart's solo flight in the spring. Ted had mixed feelings about a woman in a man's role, and felt it wasn't a natural thing for a lady to be doing. This gender interruption brought him back to the present situation of Katherine in the bathroom. Plus, nature was calling.

"Katherine, will you be coming out soon? I'd prefer not to have to use the potty chair. Katherine, do you hear me?"

"Yes, I hear you," Katherine responded, as she languished over her reflection and all its imperfections in the bathroom mirror.

The door opened allowing about four inches for Ted to fathom Katherine's latest tantrum. She had cut off her waist-length hair to just below her earlobes. Stifling his shock and disappointment, he opened the door all the way.

"Do me a favor, Ted, and please trim the back evenly. I can't manage to see it with this hand mirror."

"Do you want the sides to be longer than the back? The girls at work have bobs like Lenora's, and that's how it's cut," Ted offered as he accepted the scissors.

"I'm not interested in having what Lenora has. I suppose she's impressed you with her exotic charm. Why is it men are fascinated with women who behave like whores?"

"What I'll do is trim the straggling strands, but you'll need a hairdresser to shape and thin it," suggested Ted.

"When did you become so observant about women's hairstyles? My, we do have hidden talents!" Katherine responded.

"I need to use the bathroom," replied Ted, as he removed two dollars from his wallet and laid it on the sink's rim.

"Keep your money. I'm selling my hair in exchange for a styling at Mildred's Salon.

"I'll have none of that poor talk. We can manage a haircut," Ted calmly stated.

"You certainly had me fooled. And now it's too late. The deed is done," Katherine responded smugly, pushing past Ted.

CHAPTER FOURTEEN

As sparse as the Bryant's belongings were, it was no easy task for the movers Ted hired to trek three flights of stairs carrying the double dresser and the chifforobe. Not having an automobile, Ted enlisted the help of a couple of bachelor co-workers who were willing to use their cars to transport wooden boxes and small items in exchange for a home-cooked meal.

The new landlord allowed space in the cellar for the carriages and boxes of items there was no room for in the small closets. Once settled in, Katherine found a few benefits to the third-floor flat. The laundry dried quicker, but she had to use twice the number of clothespins due to the unobstructed wind. The wind also cooled the rooms. This would be a blessing during the warm summer, but presently, in February, it was like being in a walk-in icebox. They quickly learned the heat from the furnace couldn't reach the top floor, thus life was confined to the surrounding area of the kitchen stove.

Knitting sweaters, kneesocks, and mittens helped Katherine to reduce the boredom and confinement of winter. Frequently, her depression welled up, causing her mind's eye to see the rooms as filled with filthy junk furniture, and the air to constantly stink of dirty diapers. These feelings paralyzed all physical energy, reducing Katherine's brain to confused mush. She would keep the children in bed with her until ten or eleven in the morning, dozing off in between their playing and squabbles.

In a panic, she would rush to fix the children's lunch and wash Ted's shirts. The diapers would be boiled with soap chips in one pot, and Ted's nicotine-stained handkerchiefs in another. Working in her nightclothes until around four in the afternoon, Katherine would dress only to avoid criticism from Ted when he arrived home from work. This habit of not dressing prevented her from going out for groceries or taking a walk with the children. For a while, Ted bought her excuses that Teresa needed to potty train, Sonny was teething or Katherine had menstrual pains, until he realized the consistency of the routine.

The winter weekends found Ted and Katherine confined to the four walls of the kitchen. Church was out of the question for Katherine, because she felt she didn't have anything to wear. Ted wasn't that strict about all the rules of the Catholic Church, except for Easter and Christmas, thus didn't care if they took turns going or not, seeing they couldn't go together with the children. They would all go together when the children were bigger, he rationalized.

On a Sunday near the end of March, around two in the afternoon, a knock came at their door. Katherine scooted toward her bedroom, checking the napping children in their room as she went by. She was still in her bathrobe, feigning a migraine to ward off any sexual ideas Ted might be entertaining. Listening by the bedroom door, Katherine could hear a jovial exchange between Ted and an unfamiliar voice.

"You finally got here, you old son of a gun," a rejuvenated Ted exclaimed in a loud voice.

This was intended to be a warning to Katherine that the person was not a stranger who would go away, but a visitor, who would be staying awhile. Quietly, she closed the children's bedroom door.

Scurrying around the room, Katherine made the double bed and searched for a presentable outfit. Ted knocked at the bedroom door and entered, employing a changed personality.

"Do you feel better, Katherine, and well enough to meet my cousin Charlie?" he half-pleaded.

"I'd love to meet your cousin Charlie! I've heard so many wonderful things about this brilliant relative!" answered Katherine in a theatrical voice.

"Just get dressed and put on a pot of coffee," seethed Ted. "Charlie brought an apple pie his mother made for us."

Quickly, Katherine dressed and arranged her hair.

"I'll be right there," she called toward the living room, as she piled the dirty dishes into a basin and concealed them behind a large pastry board under the sink.

Checking the pot roast in the oven, Katherine noticed that Ted had put more than the usual amount of potatoes and carrots in with the meat. Entering the parlor, Katherine was pleasantly taken by the handsome man waiting to meet her.

"This is a definite pleasure to finally meet you, Katherine," Charlie said as he gently kissed her cheek.

"Why, thank you, Charles. Ted is very fond of you and is as proud of your accomplishments as if they were his own," Katherine said.

"Now, what are you telling this unsuspecting creature about me, Ted?" Charlie asked with a wink of his right eye toward Katherine.

"Only that you graduated with honors from Harvard and Suffolk Law, and share a very successful legal practice with the son of the Mayor of Boston. You know all the right people and the sky's the limit!" responded Katherine as she winked her left eye at Charlie. "Now, if you'll excuse me, I'll prepare the cups for coffee and check on the children. I believe they're awake from their nap. Oh, and do plan on staying for supper. We won't take no for an answer."

Katherine couldn't help but chuckle at the contrast in Ted compared to what was transpiring before Charlie's arrival. She was also surprised at the change in herself. The doom of the day was gone, and thoughts about leaving Ted seemed stupid. She readied the children and introduced them to Cousin Charlie.

During the course of dinner and catching up on relatives and various issues of the day, Charlie spoke of a great source of inner peace he had recently discovered as a member of the Third Order of St. Francis. He described his loneliness and fears which could render him almost dysfunctional when faced with a legal case he doubted the ability to handle. Yet, once he put his trust in the Lord and learned how to pray, the inner peace and strength he experienced were astounding!

"But is this Order recognized by the Pope?" inquired Katherine.

"Just ask your pastor, and if they don't already have members, you can contact my parish in Salem. They will instruct your pastor on how to organize a new branch of the society and provide the robes, for a small fee. I remember paying two dollars," Charlie explained.

"What robes?" asked Ted.

"It's similar to a monk's robe. It's dark brown with a hood and rope belt, just like the pictures you see of St. Francis. You wear it at the meetings, along with a scapular you're given as a member. When we die, we are supposed to be buried in the robe with the scapular."

The approach of evening had darkened the windows and the winter cold was noticeable. Katherine brought Charlie's cashmere jacket from the closet.

"Here's your coat! What's your hurry," laughed Katherine.

"The heat is used up by the time it arrives up here on the third floor, so we just layer the clothes," explained Ted.

"Have you considered moving?" Charlie inquired.

"That's a moot topic," quickly responded Ted. "Until a higher-paying position is available at the Boston and Maine, this is where we stay!" He tried to conceal the worn edges of his slacks under the table while Charlie smoked Ted's last cigarette.

Katherine pushed the two men out of the kitchen, insisting that they use the remainder of their visit to catch up on relatives and the good old days. She put Sonny to bed, tidied up the kitchen, and helped Teresa into her pajamas, sending her in to say good night to her daddy and Uncle Charlie.

Ted retrieved Charlie's topcoat from the closet for him, and then carried Teresa to her bedroom.

"Katherine, I promise to call you directly the next time before visiting," Charlie said as he put on his topcoat.

"You're welcome anytime, Charles, and thank your mother for the pie. A call would be appreciated next time, and could save you a long trip, just in case we aren't home," suggested Katherine, hoping he didn't notice they didn't have a phone at present.

"Ted said he knew you both would be home today when I saw him last Friday. Got to go and catch the last train to Salem."

Katherine was speechless. Ted had deliberately not told her Charlie was coming for a visit. He wanted to embarrass her! That's why he came home with the meat and vegetables from the North End last Friday night. He was prepared to present himself as the perfect host. What had he told Charlie about her? What was all that talk about loneliness and fear?

"That goddamn son of a bitch! Making me out to be sick in the head when I slave to make this a home when it's a goddamn sty! Oh, sweet Jesus! Well, I'm not taking this sitting down," she ranted out loud, while slamming and banging every possible cupboard. The children began to cry.

"Stop it, Katherine," yelled Ted, as he returned from seeing Charlie out.

A cup went sailing across the kitchen toward Ted, striking the exhaust pipe over the stove. Next, a plate followed. He reached her side and wrapped his arms around her as she fainted and slumped to the floor.

The second-floor tenants were banging at the back door, asking if everything was all right. Ted lowered Katherine flat on the floor and opened the door. The Italian-speaking neighbor rushed to the form on the floor, as her husband sized up Ted. She listened for Katherine's heart and felt her neck for a pulse, motioning with gestures for Ted to get a glass of water and a wet face cloth.

Slowly, Katherine gained consciousness as the neighbors blessed themselves. Ted thanked them for their help and kindness as he ushered them out the door. They both glanced back over their shoulders at the reclining Katherine. The husband pushed his face near to Ted's and shook his index finger while mumbling, "no noisa!"

The following Tuesday, around eight thirty in the morning, a note from the landlord was slipped under the Bryant's front door, stating their frequent arguments were upsetting the tenants and their children. Ted and Katherine were given until April to vacate the third-floor apartment.

Returning from work that evening, Ted found the flat in darkness and no one at home. As he entered the bedroom, he found all Katherine's bureau drawers open and mostly empty. Rushing to the children's room, Ted found their closet empty and Teresa Ann's stuffed bear gone. Tears began to drip out of his tired lids as he walked to the kitchen. On the table were two notes. The first was from the landlord, and the second from Katherine.

Dear Ted,

It pains me deeply to make a decision such as the one I made today. Please understand why I had to leave.

It is clear to me that what you are content with is not even near what my expectations are. Your complacency brings nothing to look forward to. Perhaps the children and I are too much responsibility for you.

You and I no longer seem able to talk or understand each other. When we do talk, we get caught up in the words. Perhaps we were just meant to write letters to each other, rather than be married.

Please find a first-floor flat; the stairs are really a strain on my heart, according to what I surmised from the doctor's suggestions a couple of months ago. I wanted to tell you but didn't want to add to your problems.

Inviting Charles on Sunday and not telling me made it clear that you only see what you want to see. I used some of the rent money to buy my train ticket.

Still waiting,

Katherine

The following day, Ted sent a telegram to his in-laws' residence in Little Falls, along with a money order to alleviate the burden Katherine was putting on them. He borrowed the money from his cousin Charlie, who willingly gave it, accompanied by a sigh of relief that it wasn't his life in such an upheaval.

Over the next three weeks, Ted scoured the papers, contacting every possible rental. They were all either worse than what they had, or more expensive than Ted could afford.

Finally, there was a new listing in the Porter Square area of Cambridge. Ted recalled Stanley O'Neil's conversation about his cousin Skip's political campaigning up and down Massachusetts Avenue, and asked if he knew where Cambridge Terrace was located.

"Sure I know where it is. I pass it every day as I walk to the Porter Square train station! I have my car today because of a few errands that need to be done on the way home. If you can view the flat tonight, I'll drive you right to the front door. How's that for service?" chuckled Stanley.

Even the owner said it was the only night available that week for a viewing. Ted took both happenings as a positive omen but didn't want to get his hopes up.

On the way to view the rental, Stanley had to stop at St. Peter's Rectory on Concord Avenue to pick up the soiled altar cloths and other whites his wife laundered for the rectory. Ted took the opportunity while waiting for Stanley, to light a candle in the church. As he knelt to pray, the soft glow of the candles brought back memories of his years spent as an altar boy at St. Mary's Church in Rotterdam Junction. He recalled how earnestly his mother prayed that he would become a priest.

"Ted! I'm ready," whispered Stanley from the side door exit. "Let's take a fast drive down to the local grocery. I have to pick up the wife some special cheese, and you can get an idea of how far the train station is from Cambridge Terrace."

It was less than half the distance Ted was used to walking from his Lawrence flat. He thanked his friend and slipped a dollar into Stanley's coat pocket, despite the objections. As he mounted the front steps to the Cambridge Terrace rental, the door opened and a man in a policeman's uniform greeted him.

"You must be Ted Bryant," greeted the officer as he extended his hand. "This is my parents', well, now it's my mother's home, and I'm showing the flat for her. She has not been too well since my father's death. It was a shock to all of us."

The policeman unlocked the second floor door and Ted was delighted with the size of the two bedrooms, the large dining room, plus the sun porch. He tried hard to conceal his immediate liking and asked about the rent.

"First, I'd like to explain that this may not be for a long period of time. It all depends on how my mother recovers from her present health problems. So, you're sure of a few months to a year, because it is tough to sell a home with so many people out of work. The rent is bi-weekly, for that reason," the officer said as he wrote a sum on a sheet of paper and signed his name under it.

"I'll take it! Do you want a deposit?" asked Ted, anxiously.

"Ten dollars would be a good retainer, which will then be applied toward your first month's rent. You said on the phone that you worked for the Boston and Maine Railroad and you folks have two toddlers. I recall you saying your wife was a nurse. Does she work?"

"She would like to work, but I feel she needs to be home with the children, at least until they attend school. At the moment, Katherine is in New York with the children visiting her family. When would it be possible to move in?"

"I need to fix the kitchen faucet and a couple of windows on my next day off. How about in two weeks? Give me a call at my home," the officer said, jotting his number down. "'I'll introduce you to my mother, but then I have to leave for work."

Ted knew that working at night was not his bag of wax and praised the public servant for his dedication.

"I have no choice in the matter. We take turns and rotate beats. Make sure you call, and in fact, call me next Wednesday. I might get it done this weekend."

Walking back to the Porter Square train station, Ted was impressed with the neighborhood and knew Katherine would like it, even though she stressed the need to be on the first floor, per her doctor's suggestion. Like other issues in Katherine's life, Ted made it a practice to follow up on the original source to glean the truth, due to her tendency to embellish.

It was true that the physician advised Katherine not to run up and down the three flights more than necessary, because she was so slender and did have a tendency toward palpitation when upset or stressed. It wasn't due to a weak heart, but rather her disposition as a result of working herself into a snit. The physician had explained it to Ted as Katherine's reaction to stress. There must have been an occasion of deep disappointment or betrayal somewhere in her past, the doctor speculated, or she could be the type of person who tends to create her own stress.

Ted didn't have all the pieces to Katherine's puzzle, so was not about to share what he did know with the doctor. What Ted was most concerned about was her strength to care for and love their children. The physician assured him that Katherine seemed to be a good mother, and the only concern would be her insecurities rubbing off on the children, by setting unrealistic behavior demands on them, or punishing them undeservedly.

Thanking the doctor for his insights, Ted pondered his own confusion over the cock-and-bull story Katherine told him about Larry Upton being Sean's father. When Ted had to wait for the train to be fixed a few years back in Little Falls, it afforded him the opportunity to visit the local library to research the newspaper accounts of Larry's demise. The archives held a wealth of information on the Upton family and their son's unfortunate death. The story told of a bunch of kids enjoying a toboggan run following a snowstorm. Lawrence Upton lost control of his stirring and hit a huge boulder hidden under a drift, breaking his neck and fracturing his skull. He died instantly at the tender age of ten, in 1912.

The absence of Katherine and the children allowed Ted to regroup his emotions. He made a promise to himself that Katherine would not destroy him or his children, if he could help it. She was by nature, self-centered, yet he couldn't help loving her when she allowed him into her heart. Unfortunately, those times were generally after he did something she had been nagging him to do, or when he gave her a gift, or received a pay raise. These occasions were rare, thus the sexual rewards were sparse. Guess you could say, he pondered, it was partly his fault by not being a ball of fire and a giant financial success.

Maybe his cousin Charlie was on to something with the Third Order of St. Francis. It was worth a try. A person could do many worse things with one night a week, than spending it in church. He'd have to discuss this with Katherine when she returned. Perhaps it would bring them back together and help to break down the barriers which were growing between them.

✦ ✦ ✦ ✦ ✦ ✦ ✦ ✦

"Hello! Mother Lockhart! This is Ted. How is everyone?"

"Just fine, Ted. Wait while I tell Katherine yar on the phone. She's putting the children to bed." A pause ensued, followed by quick steps approaching the phone.

"Hello! Ted? Is everything all right?" asked Katherine.

"I'm just fine! I found a flat in Cambridge in a two-family. It's not far from stores, the trolley, the depot, or church."

"First floor?" asked Katherine.

"No, second," Ted hesitantly answered.

"If you feel it is right for us, please go ahead and put a deposit on it."

"Do you want to know what it has for rooms?" Ted asked, excitedly.

"When I return, we can talk," answered Katherine. "I have so much to tell you, but right now is not the time. We can go back tomorrow. We've been here long enough. Incidentally, is the rent more?"

"I have to arrange the closure of our present living quarters and secure the agreement of occupancy with the new landlord. As for the rent, it is a bit more but workable given the hopeful development of an opening in my department," Ted said, refraining from telling her about the suicide of a close co-worker.

"Did you hear about the Lindbergh's baby son?" asked Katherine. "You can't trust anyone these days. Don't worry, I'm very protective of our children and will be extra cautious on the return trip."

"I was planning to come up for you and the children the weekend after next, and we can come back to the new flat together. I'll be able to help with the children," Ted offered.

"That's so long from now! Things are in a bit of a mess here. Take my word for it." sighed Katherine.

"Would you like to go to Rotterdam Junction with the children for a few days? I know my mother would welcome the company," Ted suggested. The silence on Katherine's end of the phone was answer enough.

"Guess not!" said Ted, responding to his own suggestion. "Thought you might be uncomfortable returning to Lawrence under the circumstances, and just caring for the children is enough work. I don't mind the packing and moving. Besides, I'm thinking of getting rid of a lot of the odd pieces and just taking the bedroom furniture and the kitchen set."

"What will we do for sitting in the parlor?" Katherine gingerly asked.

"I was thinking this new place is large enough for a couch, a couple of comfortable chairs, and a floor lamp," Ted offhandedly answered.

"Sure! We can wait until you come, but please bring some money to replace what I've had to borrow, which will be about thirty dollars."

Ted hadn't planned on selling his wireless radio, but that would bring at least ten dollars. Now he'd have to figure where to get twenty more and…

"Ted! Ted! Are you there?" Katherine's voice squeaked over the line.

"Sorry. I guess we lost the connection for a few seconds. I'll drop you a letter and a diagram of the flat so you can tell me where you want the beds and dressers," Ted concluded.

"Good night, Ted. I love you, and the children miss you dearly," she said, quickly hanging up the receiver.

Settling in didn't take but a few days. Prior to moving, Ted had asked Mr. Miller, owner of the secondhand store, to give him a price on the love seat, the Morris chair, an oak desk, and various other small pieces of furniture. Mr. Miller spotted Ted's wireless and a foot stove he knew was quite old and offered a fair price for the whole lot. Ted was pleased with the offer and relieved he had less to move.

Following Katherine's markings on the diagram, Ted had the movers place the bedroom furniture as desired. As he prepared to set up the pantry, he suddenly realized an icebox was needed. Luckily, there were a couple of furniture and appliance stores nearby with lots of reclaimed items from Harvard University students who rented flats, got caught up in socializing, and flunked out.

Ted found a two-year-old Kelvinator which bragged it would keep ice cream and ice cubes in their preferred frozen state. It could be delivered for an additional dollar tacked on to the price, which he took advantage of. As he was about to leave the store, a handsome dining room table with six chairs and a plush maroon velvet couch caught his attention.

"You're a man with an eye for real quality; and the price is right!" said the persuasive store owner.

"Perhaps, but will my wife think so?" pondered Ted. "I wasn't prepared to buy anything but the refrigerator."

"No problem! You can pay me so much each week, and when I deliver the couch and the dining room set with your paid-for refrigerator this coming Friday, I'll know where to pick them up if you falter on the payments. But I know you won't, because I'm a judge of character. So, what's to hurt? I won't charge for the delivery!" the store owner offered, while rubbing his hands together.

Walking back up Walnut Street to Cambridge Terrace, all sorts of doubts about his quick decisions on the Kelvinator and furniture raced around his brain, plus questions about the thirty dollars he had to come up with for Little Falls next Saturday. Two days until payday and twelve dollars right off the top goes to pay back Charlie and Fred, both of whom had been more than patient. Then, the following week the rent will be due and Katherine will be back with the children and their needs.

There was only one resource left, and he had promised not to touch it. The next day at lunchtime, he stopped by the cashier on the seventh floor with his savings book and drew out thirty dollars, leaving twenty-two in reserve. Returning to the accounting department on the eighth floor, a note from his boss was on top of a pile of work Ted had yet to address. Opening it, he saw the familiar sprawl in headline letters: SEE ME.

Taggart was his usual self, and circumvented the real reason for his note by starting with mention of some sort of police investigation that was underway regarding Stollard's suicide. Taggart was agitated because of the time it was taking away from the concentration of his staff on their assigned tasks.

"And before we know it, people will be taking off on spring vacations or to get married and are not the least bit concerned about completing their jobs before they go!" griped Taggart.

And your point is…? Ted found himself wanting to say but refrained from escalating Taggart's blood pressure to new heights.

"Now, I know you have a tendency to travel to New York to see your relatives over weekends, but with this new position, I'll need your presence on Saturdays and Sundays when deadlines need to be met. Is that clear?" sputtered Taggart, as he suddenly stood up.

"You must be offering me Rich Stollard's position. Did the reason for his suicide have any connection to his job?" asked Ted.

"Now what do you mean by making a remark like that?" Taggart asked.

"There should be no reason for weekend work schedules unless the staff is not applying themselves when on the job, which I perceive not to be the case. I'd like your permission to rearrange the recording process and responsibilities," stated Ted.

"I don't want anything changed. I set this method up, and it's proven to be the most efficient way for getting the job done," directed Taggart.

"I'll check with the business office during my lunchtime regarding my salary rate. Is there anything else, Mr. Taggart?"

"You're a strange one, Bryant. You've just repeated part of my conversation to you when I first hired you. Please don't get too cocky!"

"Yes, I recall you told me I wasn't your first choice. This time, I know I am," Ted retorted, surprised by his own courage.

"Well, yes! Perhaps it was callous of me to say that then, and you have surprised me with your capabilities. Uh, uh, keep up the good work," grumbled Taggart as he extended his hand.

Ted shook Taggart's hand firmly, hoping to convey they were now gentlemen, as opposed to the subservient position he felt prior to this meeting. Ted was well aware of the huge number of people out of work and barely surviving, yet here he was, protected by his union. A prayer formed on his lips as he walked back to his desk, thanking God for the positive turn of events,

Arriving on time, Ted found Bernard in casual clothes waiting for him at the Little Falls depot. Usually his fashionable brother-in-law was decked to the nines, complete with cufflinks and tiepin.

"Hey, Ted! Good to see you," greeted Bernard. "I've got my father's jalopy. I sold mine."

Ted began to sense what Katherine must have meant when she said things were really a mess at her parents' home.

"I've got to tell you something, Ted," started Bernard as they drove toward Albany Street. "I've had to resign my position at City Hall due to an unfortunate combination of circumstances. I chose to help out someone who was in debt and was close to losing everything. This person is very important politically, and made it seem like the right thing to do. Never in my wildest dreams did I expect an audit! They found a shortage of cash, and someone from across the street in another office building even claims to have seen me taking money out of the office vault late one night. Seems this person saw my office lights come on and described the person who opened the vault as bald like me."

"Wait, wait a minute," interrupted Ted. "What money? How much? There are lots of bald men! God, Bernard! Who could convince you to do something like that?"

"I couldn't tell the police, and I certainly won't involve you by telling you. So, I'm going to accept my punishment and move on," responded Bernard.

"Hold it! Did you take the money?" asked Ted.

"No! I thought about what this prominent person requested and tried to figure a way to protect myself, it being such a large amount. Finally, I decided to borrow from Peter to pay Paul through the use of an in-house transfer between accounts, because it was to be paid back in three days. I put the transfer paper under my desk blotter, feeling I needed the night to sleep on it before taking any action. I left my office around seven that evening.

"Someone entered my office later that evening, knew the combination to the vault, and removed the exact amount of money as I had written on the transfer sheet. When I arrived for work the next morning, there was an auditor going through my books, and his assistant found my handwritten transfer under the desk blotter. The rest is clear; the transfer amount matched the shortage in the vault.

"Presently, I'm waiting for my hearing. My lawyer advises me to plead guilty or I'll have to name names, which would ruin lots of lives, and realistically, whoever masterminded this could see fit to have me silenced forever," concluded Bernard.

"But, what about your political future, if you're saddled with a jail record?" asked Ted?

"Getting through today and tomorrow is as far as I can think for the present, Ted," answered a very humbled Bernard.

Arriving at their destination, the Lockhart home looked tattered, and needed to be painted badly. Upon entering, Ted was surprised to find just the bare minimum in furniture and the absence of carpets.

Katherine flew down the stairs into Ted's arms. She was as near to tears as her next breath. Close behind came Teresa Ann, one step at a time, followed by Sonny, sliding down the stairs on his tummy and knees. Ted couldn't hug them enough.

"Ted!" Katherine began.

"Yes, he told me," responded Ted.

The whole house was hushed and somber. Margot's appearance shocked Ted the most. Her total stature had changed from being full of spunk to one of dragging her form, foot by foot. She had been injured deeply, and this wound could not be dressed. It was injured pride with no cure available.

After the children went to sleep and suitcases were packed for the trip back to Massachusetts, Katherine filled Ted in on the shame her parents were experiencing. People were not patronizing their store. Sean's schoolmates avoided him and wouldn't let him join in their softball games.

"Ted, my family has to move or they'll die from loneliness," sobbed Katherine. "Their own relatives avoid them!"

"Where will they move to?" asked Ted.

"Perhaps they'll go to Glens Falls for the time being. Ma's sisters live there still. Times are so bad!"

"Let's get some rest. Tomorrow will be a long day for us. Here's the money you asked for," Ted nonchalantly added.

"This will help so much. I had no idea all this was happening here. My mother didn't want to bother us," Katherine whispered as she kissed her husband.

The new flat on Cambridge Terrace thrilled Katherine, and the children didn't seem to notice any difference since their bedroom contained the same familiar furniture and toys. Ted's spontaneous choice of the dining room table and chairs, along with the maroon couch, pleased Katherine. The greatest treasure of all was the Kelvinator! Katherine felt liberated from the block of ice and seemed at peace with the world.

Ted spared her the knowledge of having bought the furniture and couch on time. He had decided to give her two dollars every two weeks for her own needs, knowing she would remind him, which in turn would remind him to pay the rent and the furniture bill.

Exploring her new environment, Katherine quickly learned the names of the owners of the multiple stores that graced the Massachusetts Avenue area around her neighborhood, as well as which ones to avoid. Having children made it easier to meet people, and for Katherine it was the crutch she needed to help her be more sociable.

While walking the children along an unexplored section of Massachusetts Avenue, Katherine noticed a grocery store for sale. She learned the original owner was deceased a mere three months and his family decided to sell the store. Within the next block, she noticed an apartment for rent. Would her parents consider moving to Cambridge? She could hardly wait for Ted to come home to share her plan with him.

Reflecting on the total situation, Ted felt it was overall a good solution, provided Katherine could remain neutral around her family. He had certain reservations as to whether they were helpful or destructive to one another based on what Katherine had unknowingly shared when recounting past history, and what he observed himself when the whole family gathered together.

They phoned Margot and discussed the relocation idea. If she wanted to visit for the purpose of seeing the store firsthand, they had room for her. Within the hour, Margot phoned back and asked if she could come Thursday, requesting that Katherine inform the present owners of the Lockharts' interest in their store. Margot arrived prepared to act, with cash in hand. By Friday's end, she was to be the new owner of the grocery store and renter of the vacant apartment in the next block.

Unbeknownst to Katherine and Ted, Margot had already considered moving nearby. She knew Leo's health was deteriorating and, as a nurse, Katherine could help with his care. In addition, making Aileen and Sean toe the mark was increasingly difficult for Leo and Margot. Their early years were catching up with them from both the pleasures and weaknesses of the flesh as well as from enduring the demands of the flesh through childbirth and hard physical work. Margot's vision of her status in life when she reached her late fifties was to be one of a lady of leisure, doted on by her children and grandchildren. Instead, she was struggling to survive with an almost-invalid husband and an eleven-year-old son.

Arriving back in Little Falls, Margot compiled her assets. She had the remainder of the month to tie all the loose ends together. The need to leave with her head held high was paramount. No one would say the Lockhart family left because of the shame their son brought them, she told herself, and sought a way to set the record straight. Her take-charge method frightened Leo, yet his broken spirit could not protest. Both Aileen and Sean were relieved by the thought of escaping the humiliation, and welcomed the adventure, never having been beyond Little Falls. Lenora's attitude, being twenty-three years old, was another story.

Margot engaged the services of a reputable lawyer and longtime family friend to draw up a cover letter to accompany her bank check, made payable to the City of Little Falls for the amount that Bernard had been charged with taking. The letter clearly stated the check was not an admission of guilt but rather a gesture of respect for the people of Little Falls, and that the Lockhart family was confident that one day the truth would be known. This gesture emptied Margot's life savings, along with the amount she had withdrawn to purchase the store in Massachusetts.

She gave the lawyer power of attorney to sell the contents of her store and business and the Albany Street home. The lawyer's fee was to be an agreed-to percentage of the total realized, thus being in his best interest to coordinate a profitable sale. The remaining funds, after the fee, were to be wired to Margot's new account at the North Cambridge Savings and Loan Bank in Porter Square.

In the window of the Little Falls grocery store, a discreet for sale sign was posted with the name of the lawyer as the contact. As usual, the local busybodies drifted in and out, salivating with gossip fever.

"You're not leaving after all these years of establishing such a fine reputation!" crooned Mrs. Fardy.

"Yes, 'tis a necessary decision I've made. Leo is not well, and my daughter, Katherine, being a nurse, wants to care for her father," Margot responded in the most sophisticated voice she could conjure up.

"But, isn't she living in Boston somewhere? That means you'll be moving, and at such a time!" replied the prying customer.

"God doesn't let us pick our times. We just have to follow and abide by his will," responded Margot.

"I was referring to Bernard's upcoming hearing. He will fight the charges, won't he?" Mrs. Fardy prodded.

"Even if he is accused and sentenced, he is innocent, and so was Jesus, if you happen to recall!" snapped Margot in return.

"Dear, dear Mrs. Lockhart, Bernard is a man; Jesus is God's son! You're not putting your son on the same footing as Christ?" sneered Mrs. Fardy.

"By no means, mind ya; I'm jest saying that the bastards who lied about Jesus are alive and live right here in Little Falls. If yar here to purchase something please do, because I could use the money. If not, thank ya for dropping by," concluded Margot, as she opened a fly strip and hung it next to the intrusive gossiper.

Margo's departure plan was simple. No need to drag it out for months and try to sell the home on her own, when she could be in a new location where the economy was not as stressed. Her only fear was that no one would buy the store's contents or the Albany Street home. Then she would be faced with the expense of storing everything, plus having an unoccupied home, which is easy prey for vandals. She had to stop herself from thinking negatively and said a few prayers. It was hard to have faith that things would turn out well, when at present it was difficult to distinguish if this was life or hell.

The final Saturday before sunrise, five members of the Lockhart family left their Albany Street home, never to return. Bernard and Raymond waved until the car was out of their vision, and then readied the crates and pieces of furniture to be transported to Massachusetts. They worked side by side, not saying a word, until Bernard banged his fist into the wall.

"What's up with you? Swatting bugs?" asked Raymond.

"Goddamn! I'm a fool, Raymond, and an embarrassment to our parents. We might not have had the greatest life, with Pa and all, but it was the best Ma could do! Damn! Do you know what Ma did? She paid back the missing money out of her life's savings!" cried Bernard with his arms hanging limply by his sides like bread dough.

"Let's not discuss this, Bernard, because I have my own opinion about why you did what you did. I'm sorry to admit a sort of satisfaction that you were taken down a peg," ventured Raymond, with his feet firmly placed and ready for a physical reaction.

"Thanks a lot, brother!" Bernard angrily responded. "The fact I'll be going to jail doesn't upset you but rather gives you satisfaction. That's all I need to hear!"

"You can hold your own, Bernard. I've seen how you operate when bent on having your way. You'll manage, and hopefully be the wiser for brownnosing," affirmed the younger brother.

"Brownnosing; if some jerk hadn't robbed the vault, you'd be standing in line to shake my hand in less than two years from now, at the White House!" yelled Bernard.

"So for now, Bernard, I'll stand in line each Sunday to shake your hand through prison bars. Wake up, Bernard! This is no one's fault but yours. You overplayed your hand. Lie to yourself, if you must, but do me a favor and take off the rose-colored glasses. This whole event was staged to get rid of you by discrediting your reputation," Raymond said, attempting to convey how clearly others saw what was behind the whole fiasco.

"But why put all that effort into deceiving me for so long?" Bernard mumbled.

"Despite yourself, Bernard, people really like you, and your personality is perfect for a politician. But you have one flaw. You're basically honest, yet an opportunist. Whoever masterminded this topple knew you'd never just take the money without thinking of a strategy for covering it until it was paid back. They also knew how hungry you were for success and power, thus you'd take the bait to have one of the high rollers in your debt. You convicted yourself in your own handwriting when you wrote that transfer. If you now try to draw them in by naming names, which they knew you would never do, they have but to deny or counter with slander."

"When did my kid brother become so smart?" asked Bernard.

"I just hope Lily is worth it all, Bernard. I'll be at the hearing and will keep my mouth shut. I used to be jealous of how much attention Ma gave you when we were kids, but at this moment, I'm one lucky son of a gun, and wouldn't trade places with you," Raymond concluded.

"You're so serious, Raymond! It will all work out, you'll see. Right now, let's get this stuff into the vestibule. My friend should be here any minute with the truck. I'm supposed to phone Katherine at her Cambridge home after we finish packing to let her know how much of this stuff you and I got into the truck. I think she's afraid the truck driver will sell some of the furniture between here and Massachusetts. Raymond! Smile! Life's too short; loosen up!" laughed Bernard, as he put Raymond in a headlock.

CHAPTER FIFTEEN

The sunrise brightened the horizon as the travelers motored through the neighborhood they no longer would call their home. Methodically, Leo guided the steering wheel, banking a left onto John Street.

"Are ya daft, Leo? You want to go right!" Margot motioned with her hand.

"Bear with me, Margot. Let's take a few last minutes to say good-bye to the memory of our first home together," responded Leo.

"Don't break down on me, Leo! Ya hold yar head high and proud. If ya want to cry, wait until after the town's limits, when Lenora will drive for ya," Margot ordered.

"Margot, darling, have you no heart? I was born here, and always thought I'd be buried here," Leo pleaded.

"Well ya certainly tried to rush the buried part, but for now it seems God wants us somewhere else. It's sad for all of us. Now, turn this damn contraption around and get through Main Street before some nosy so-and-so sees us," she directed.

Margot wanted to make the most of the daylight and clear sky, given the Mohawk Trail's reputation for icy conditions. Margot was never comfortable with the transition from horse and buggy and trains to the motor car; she detested the way they took over the roads. When she wanted to cross the street, it didn't matter what the traffic dictated. Margot would put up her hand as she stepped into the road, while onlookers held their breath. Several drivers undoubtedly aged prematurely from the experience.

Despite the sadness of their journey, the countryside forced its beauty through the car's inner gloom. Lenora pulled off the road at a vista point overlooking an apple orchard.

"My eyes are going buggy and need a rest," explained Lenora.

"Wish I had a camera. This is unbelievable!" Aileen exclaimed.

"Seeing we've stopped, let's have an early lunch," suggested Margot.

Leo and Sean took the usual male walk off to the heavy brush, while the females readied the food. Together, the five broke off pieces of the homemade bread, and salted their hard-boiled eggs.

"Pa, you'll have to drive after lunch because we need gas in the next town," Leonora offered between chews, in that she didn't have a license and had difficulty parking a car in tight spots.

"Ma, what's Uncle Thomas like?" Sean asked.

"I know what he was like as my big brother but haven't seen him for over thirty-five years," replied Margot.

"It was kind of him to let us stop at his home on our way to Cambridge," added Leo.

"And sure, it took a bit of convincing! I promised to cook some of our mother's old favorite recipes. As a bachelor, I can just imagine how he lives and eats!" Margot concluded.

Back on the road with a full tank, Leo pulled over to let Lenora drive the remainder of the way to Fitchburg, Massachusetts. Margot filled the time telling her family about their uncle's broken heart and reclusive lifestyle. Thomas was the first of their family to leave Ireland, bent on making his fortune in America. He sent money home regularly, and helped sponsor part of Mary's and Margot's trip to Glens Falls. When his sisters brought news of his sweetheart's marriage to a rival friend, Thomas stopped sending money to his parents and never responded to their letters.

Thomas made no exceptions, and when notified about the deaths of his parents, he begged off attending the funerals. He said he wanted to keep the last memory of them as it was when he looked on their hopeful faces when he left for America.

"His presence and comfort would have been appreciated during those difficult years, as well as some money during our parents' long illnesses. Some cronies that visited Thomas told us that he was a wealthy farmer. Then he seemed to disappear, and my letters and Christmas cards came back. My sisters and I didn't know if he died or moved back to Ireland.

"Then, this past Christmas, Thomas sent me a card! I said to myself, that old goat is still kicking! Mind ya, he mentions not a word about the past thirty-five years, but writes like he saw me yesterday! To top it all off, the writing in the card looked like a woman's handwriting!"

"So, what did he say?" coached Aileen.

"Seems one of his horses kicked him in the head, and when his helper took him to the doctor, they asked who his next of kin was and he gave my name. Well, he mended, but it got him thinking about death, so he says, and asked me to visit in the near future because he wanted to talk with me about something. I wrote back saying ya father wasn't well and it would be easier if he visited us. Never heard a thing back! Then, when all this hell rolled over us, I remembered hearing that Fitchburg was on the way to Cambridge and so, ya have it."

Following the detailed road map Thomas's neighbor sent them, they arrived at their destination. Knocking at the door, Margot tried to get a peek at the interior. To her surprise, the rooms looked empty.

"Faith and begora, is it you, Margot?" came a voice from the side porch. A bent form arose from a rocking chair and, swinging a cane in a sweeping motion, walked toward her.

"Thomas! Thomas!" cried Margot. The brother and sister embraced as tears streamed down their weathered cheeks.

"Come inside, all of you. My friend, Molly, has made a pot of chicken and dumplings. You must be worn to a tether from that long drive," said Thomas, as he motioned toward the kitchen.

There were two chairs at the table with several soup bowls, spoons, and cloth napkins on the sideboard. A pot of water simmered alongside the stew, ready for tea when needed. Fresh baked rolls were covered by a gingham cloth, with fresh butter in a bowl, ready for the spreading.

"This is so kind of you, Thomas," Leo said as he reached for Thomas's hand. There was no reaction to Leo's gesture as Thomas attempted to locate one of the chairs.

"How long have you been without your vision, Uncle Thomas?" asked Lenora.

"Hush, girl!" Margot gestured with both hands raised to the ceiling.

"For about four summers, but I'm learning to live with it. Seems there is some pressure on my eyes from the blow to my head. It didn't happen at the time the horse kicked me, so the doctor wants to wait to see if it is just a temporary condition, as he calls it. My neighbors have been so helpful, and I never did anything for a one of them, ever!" Thomas concluded, tearfully.

Leo and his children took their soup bowls and sat on the hall stairs, leaving Margot and Thomas to enjoy the only two seats in the whole house. Upstairs, they found five cots set up in one bedroom, each prepared with sheets, pillow, and blanket. In the bathroom, five cloths and towels were waiting for use with Uncle Thomas's own towel on a separate wall rack. His hairbrush was tied with a string for easy retrieval should he drop it. A tin cup on another string hung from a hook next to the sink.

The weary retired, as Margot and Thomas reminisced about Ireland and their relatives. Margot refrained from sharing anything about their own present hardship, and talked only about the good things and her grandchildren.

"What if yar sight never returns?" asked Margot.

"Molly has been like the wife I never had, and she wants to care for me. She lives in the farmhouse up the road. Her husband died three years ago. I don't love her like my Kathleen, but at my age, to even have someone is a blessing. What she sees in me I'll never know. I plan to leave this house and land to her. I want to be buried with our parents in Glens Falls. Promise me this will be so when the time comes. Molly is at me to marry, fearful folks might get the wrong idea about us. But, my heart was pledged to one woman whom I'll marry in the next life."

"And what if Kathleen won't have ya, even then?" Margot said, playing the devil's advocate. "What if her husband has some objections?"

"So be it!" Thomas responded with a bang of his cane on the floor.

The next morning, everything was straightened up as though they hadn't been there. Farewells were brief and the promise confirmed again. Margot remembered her parents' cemetery lot number, which gave Thomas great comfort.

As the Lockhart family drove away, the bent form waved from the front porch, as a female figure was crossing the field in the direction of Thomas's home. Margot chuckled and felt Molly just might win this battle.

"So, Margot darling, what was Thomas's question?" inquired Leo.

"That I would make sure he is buried with our parents in Glens Falls, when he dies. The poor soul spent most of his life on a dream that never happened, and apart from the only people who cared about him. Now he wants to spend eternity buried with them!" sighed Margot, shaking her head.

✦ ✦ ✦ ✦ ✦ ✦ ✦ ✦

The apartment's convenient location on the Mass Avenue trolley line, and Margot's present financial limitations, are what justified her quick decision to subject the five of them to endure the closeness of the one-bedroom apartment. The apartment was a block from her store, and within walking distance to the church, the school, and her daughter, Katherine. Also, the city hospital was nearby, should Leo take a sudden turn for the worst.

Arranging the furniture took but a few hours. Three cots, a couch, a side chair, a round oak table with six chairs and matching buffet, the master bedroom furniture, a console radio, an RCA record player with its records, and a coat rack. The remainder, which consisted of wooden crates filled with clothes, linens, dishes, pots and pans, and cherished family pictures in Victorian frames, took almost a week due to several arguments over turf.

Margot was unrelenting, insisting the living room remain the formal room it was intended for. Lenora and Aileen tried to convince their parents to use the living room as the master bedroom, and the intended bedroom could be shared by them with a freestanding screen to section off Sean's cot. That would leave the large entrance foyer for the record player, the buffet, and extra chairs. They pleaded that the intended dining room could hold the couch, side chair, and radio in a cozy fashion.

Margot was set in her mind and would hear none of it. Lenora and Aileen were to sleep in the foyer area, using the buffet and coat rack for their clothes. Sean would sleep in the intended dining room, using the lower drawers of the in-wall china closet for his clothes. The master bedroom choked with the oversized Victorian bed, dresser, and vanity, making it necessary to sit on the bed when extending the dresser drawers. The vanity argued with an ill-placed radiator, reducing the space needed to walk past the foot of the bed. The couch, with its matching side chair, and the record player, sat breathing comfortably in the generous living room, as the treasured family pictures looked down from the walls.

Several unpacked wooden crates were relegated to the bathroom directly across the public hallway from the Lockhart's apartment. It was a generous-sized bathroom with a white marble sink, a medicine cabinet, and the proverbial claw-footed tub. A rectangular linen closet was located to the left of the entrance door, and was used to store tools and odd things, like rat poison. The walls and ceiling were covered in tin with an embossed design of alternate clam shells and a flower medallion, all painted in faded beige. A light hung from the center of the room from which a pull chain ended with a large glass ball, tending to elude the hand in favor of the forehead or eyeball of night visitors. Though across the hall, at least this bathroom was not shared with other tenants, which the Lockhart family had done for years with their extra-income borders in Little Falls.

The first week raced by, between the store and settling into the apartment and before Margot realized it, she had to locate the school records for Sean's and Aileen's registration at St. John's Parochial School on Rindge Avenue. Margot called from the drugstore's pay phone and arranged a meeting for the coming Monday with Sr. Mary John. During the registration meeting, Sister Superior warned that the transition for Sean and Aileen could result in some educational differences, which might present the need to retain the children.

"Might it be better to see first what they can do before ya pass judgment or suppose?" suggested Margot.

"Why, yes! And we shall! I was only forewarning you because we are in a highly motivated environment, with Harvard and the Massachusetts Institute of Technology almost in our neighborhood," replied Sister

Mary John, with her hands concealed within the oversized sleeves of her Dominican habit.

"My daughter, Katherine, is a registered nurse. My oldest son served twelve years in political office, and I own my own business. My son, Sean, and my daughter, Aileen, work in the store, waiting on customers, making change, stocking the shelves, and checking the inventory. All of that takes a good brain. Ya won't be keeping them back. All ya have to worry about is keeping up with them! Thank ya. They'll be in school, tomorrow," responded Margot in a highbrow fashion.

That evening, Margot lay the law down for both Sean and Aileen regarding what her expectations were regarding daily attendance and homework.

"And I won't be humiliated by either of ya failing. We've all had enough humiliation for a lifetime. Now, eat up and get washed and in bed by nine."

Lenora listened quietly, feeling so trapped between working at the store and now having to help her siblings with their nightly homework. She felt like her life was over as her stomach turned sour. Why hadn't she stayed in New York? Why didn't she think about going to live with Aunt Mary and Uncle Jim in Glens Falls? That's what she decided to propose.

While washing the supper dishes, Lenora started to muster up the strength to tell Margot her plan, but was interrupted by a loud knock at the door. There stood Hank, looking as if he had walked across Europe in a dust storm.

"I thought I'd lost you forever!" spouted a dust-covered and exhausted Hank.

"What's the meaning of this?" Margot snapped.

"Ma, this is Hank Snyder, a friend from Long Island. I met him while he was visiting his cousin, Andrew Schramm. You know his aunt, who makes that lovely lace," replied Lenora.

"Stop right there! How did ya find us?" asked Margot. "And, if ya don't mind my saying, ya look like ya died and forgot to lie down!"

"Bernard told me where you went. I planned to stay at my cousin's for a week in Little Falls and stopped by your Albany Street home. It was empty! What happened? Lenora, I came to ask you to marry me but had to hitchhike here for over fourteen hours. I must look a mess!" Hank rambled.

"You, geet out of here, now. No Protestant is marrying my daughter. Geet!" Margot shouted, attempting to slam the door.

"You're not getting rid of me, Mrs. Lockhart! I love Lenora and I believe she loves me, and if it's a Catholic you'll allow to marry her, then that's what I'll become. I'll be back as a Catholic!" responded the determined suitor.

"They won't have the likes of you!" shouted Margot.

Lenora was hysterical as Margot kept pushing her away from the door. Running to the parlor, Lenora attempted to open the window, but it wouldn't budge. She banged on the window and Hank looked up. He threw her a kiss and made the sign of the Christian cross and smiled.

"Is there such a thing as a guardian angel?" Lenora wondered out loud.

Spotting a telephone sign outside the corner drugstore, Hank used the phone number Bernard had given him for the Bryant household. Ted answered and listened to Hank's recount of the past fourteen hours, and his encounter with Margot, until he ran out of nickels for the phone.

"Why don't you stay the night with us and look for a place tomorrow," offered Ted.

Katherine was appalled to think Ted would offer to have a perfect stranger stay in their home! What do they know about him? And from what she had observed of him the night she went out with Bernard and Lenora, Hank was a major groper, the way he was all over her sister!

"You won't be alone with him. I'm here tonight, and tomorrow's Saturday. We can afford to help out a suffering soul who happens to be in love with another Lockhart woman. I understand his pain," Ted said with a grin. "I'm going to meet him halfway along Mass Avenue."

"I'll get a sheet and blanket. He'll need a pillow. I don't believe we're doing this; My God!" Katherine exclaimed.

"Thanks, Katherine. I'll be back in about twenty minutes with Lenora's Hank."

✦ ✦ ✦ ✦ ✦ ✦ ✦ ✦

Over the next few weeks, short notes from Bernard, and shorter notes from Raymond, kept Margot abreast of the progress being made by the lawyer in organizing a plea for leniency. She was heartbroken that Bernard would not fight the whole damn lot of them. She couldn't stop the nagging thoughts that perhaps there was more to Bernard's situation than met the eye, yet knew she would never be privy to it.

There was that Thanksgiving when Ted and Katherine visited for the holiday weekend, and Margot overheard a private conversation that was not meant for everyone's ears. Katherine had questioned Bernard about his activities on a particular date in October. Bernard was abrupt with Katherine, and retorted by asking her what she was doing on that same day. Then he laughed, and told Katherine he knew exactly where he was; at the Capitol Theatre in Ilion, New York, enjoying a very good concert. Could that have been the start of Bernard's downfall? What difference would it make now? What's done is done!

Sorting through the mail, Margot noticed a familiar script peeking out of the pile. With a shaking hand, she removed the letter and carefully read and reread it.

Dear Mrs. Lockhart,

It has come to my attention that you and your family have vacated the residence on Albany Street and have placed your home for sale in the capable hands of Albert Gifford, Esquire.

This letter is intended to be my official offer for your viewing and acceptance or refusal. A copy of this letter is being shared with Mr. Gifford.

My offer for the dwelling on Albany Street is in keeping with the present selling prices of surrounding homes in the same neighborhood. For the land upon which stands a seven-room home with a free-standing carriage barn: $3,342.

The residence will be used by my apprentice, Dr. Hanrahan, to provide a dwelling for his family and his new practice in the town of Little Falls. I'll be retiring from active practice to pursue my research in a leisurely fashion and will provide Dr. Hanrahan support, as needed.

Please advise Mr. Gifford as to your acceptance or refusal of the above offer, as I am negotiating the purchase for Dr. Hanrahan. He is still managing my Glens Falls practice until the new physician takes over in January of 1934.

Respectfully yours,

Arthur Kirkland, M.D.

Tears welled up and ran down Margot's cheek. Gathering paper, pen, and ink, Margot wrote Mr. Gifford of her acceptance, stating she and Leo were in agreement on the offer and looked forward to receiving the necessary papers for signing in order to transfer ownership to Dr. Hanrahan and his family.

Margot wanted to ask about the progress being made on the sale of her former store's contents but kept the letter pure to the topic. Paying store rent was opted for in place of storage, because Margot felt seeing the counters and cases would help sell them. Unfortunately, she was beginning to doubt her theory. Yet, until the landlord either raised the rent or forced her to empty the store, she would postpone the moment of decision until Bernard's hearing. Let those Little Falls busybodies wonder.

Her present venture was slowly building a positive reputation in the Cambridge neighborhood, having to overcome hearsay of the former owner's tendency of playing favorites and leaning on the scales. True or not, Margot placed the scales so customers could see her hands. Then, addressing sly remarks regarding favoritism, she placed posters in the window advertising the quantity received of specific hard-to-obtain items, with an end-of-day tally as to how many were left.

"Now," thought Margot, "if someone who has nothing else to do wants to sit across the street and count the number of people who come out with a specific item, let them. Next thing they'll want to know is how often I change my bloomers!"

Each day brought some person or diversion to help Margot briefly to keep her mind off the changes in Leo. His grimaces tended to frighten young children at the store, who would hide behind their mother's skirt or coat. A crushed Leo would slowly shuffle out of the store, balancing himself with his cane in one hand, and the other against the storefront.

Father Smith, from St. John's Rectory, happened to be buying apples as Leo shuffled past the store.

"Say, Mrs. Lockhart, do you know anything about that poor soul?"

"Yes, I know quite a lot about that poor soul, Father. He's my husband, and God decided Leo should pay for his sins now, instead of in death!"

"Put my foot in my mouth that time!" the young priest stammered.

"Ah, Father! Don't be so humble when yar being honest. Leo is the father of our six living children. He hasn't had a drink in fourteen years. Do you know Aileen or Sean Lockhart at St. John's Elementary School?" Margot asked.

"Sean Lockhart is his son?" responded Father Smith.

"Yes, he is. Ya seem surprised!" Margot responded, taken aback.

"Sean is an excellent student and should go to college once he completes high school. Why, he is an all-around kind of young man, a great athlete and well-liked by his classmates. You folks have done a fine job with the lad!" the priest added.

"I depend on Sean to help with his father. Ya know he feeds his father each morning and night because the 'poor soul' can't steady a spoon or fork to get the food into his mouth. He also shaves his father and dresses him before leaving for school. I don't know how I'd manage if he wasn't here," Margot stated, hoping to convince the priest that charity begins at home.

"Aren't there other male family members who can help? That's a lot to expect of a boy his age!" said Father Smith.

"My son-in-law, Ted, helps me out with the evening hours at the store. On the weekends, he also visits Leo, but Ted has to help my daughter, Katherine, who is not that strong since the birth of her two children. All my daughters help with the laundry, because Leo has a lot of nighttime accidents, if you know what I mean, Father."

"Indeed, you don't have to say any more. Would it be all right with you and your husband if I brought him Communion?" asked the priest.

"Thank ya, Father. I'll ask Leo and let you know. Please don't be saying things to Sean about college. That's a ways off, and I need him to help me in my old age," Margot said.

"He may do it now, but may want something for himself as he gets older," suggested the priest.

"He owes it to me for taking care of him from the time he was born!" snapped Margot.

"But, don't parents do that?" the priest asked.

"That's all I have to say about this and I thank you for your concern. Now, I need to be attending to the store's needs. Drop in again, Father, when you need apples," Margot stated.

Margot did not plan on such a brain-picking encounter, and found herself in a rather foul mood. The newspaper truck dropped off the daily papers with a loud plunk, bringing her back to the endless tasks at hand.

The headlines shouted success regarding Roosevelt's master plan for putting the unemployed back to work, with national pride the emphasis more than ever before. The Depression and the droughts hit the overall economy in a domino manner. Even the experts who saw it coming hadn't fully anticipated the present outcome.

The common man knew what it was, though. It wasn't just the lack of employment and money; it was the intense changes forced upon the generation of the times. The world was moving fast with continual inventions and hyped competition from international advances. It was a matter of personal pride, the foundation upon which the United States was nurtured. The country needed a strong leader, and each Democrat prayed Roosevelt was the one. The atrocities of the First World War changed the game plan for all future conflicts, and the United States was determined to stay on top.

As Margot scanned the newspaper, she noticed an editorial about the progress being made to appeal prohibition with the Twenty-First

Amendment. Congress was hoping for a decision before the year's end. This was not good news for Margot. She had seen the worst side of alcohol firsthand, and understood all too well the negative effect it had on certain members of her family, Leo notwithstanding.

Her routine was constant and didn't allow for any such weaknesses or self-indulgence as alcohol. Margot had no patience or time for those who wasted their lives. Yet, charity begins at home, and having not kicked Leo out a long time ago, she felt that one compromise was enough compassion for a lifetime. She didn't need anyone telling her what God considered acceptable compassion, because she'd meet him eye-to-eye one day and find that out herself. But for now she had things to do and chores for Sean and Aileen.

"Hey Ma, I've got to write a report and need to go to Larry's house," shouted Sean, arriving on the scene from school. "Pa is resting and I emptied the trash. I'll be back by four to help you clean up and close."

"Wait! Ya were supposed to stack the shelves and break down the empty cans and cartons!" called Margot after the fleeting Sean.

"I will! I will! Oh, Al Capp wants a couple of Cokes. I'll deliver them to his studio on my way. Here's his money."

"I don't like you hanging around that artist, and I don't care if he thinks you look like Lil' Abner! Where's Aileen?" Margot asked.

"She's talking with some friends at the end of the block and will help you. I asked her to help extra in my place until I get back, okay?" begged Sean.

"Sean, is Lenora at the apartment?" asked Margot.

"Ma, I've got to run. No, she isn't." shouted Sean in forward motion.

Since Hank had made his appearance, Lenora would disappear on her day off from the store. She never said where she went or with whom. A few times she had feigned visiting Katherine and the children but got caught in her deception when Katherine dropped by the store with the children. Margot wondered if it was deliberate on Katherine's part, but refrained from feeding into the jealousy her oldest daughter had for the younger sisters.

The energy needed to complete all the related tasks associated with a business were more demanding under Massachusetts standards.

Margot had no time for idle chatter or jealous siblings, because her energies were used for survival. There were new licensing rules and regulations for refrigeration of perishables, as well as the vendors' handling of same. Margot tended to become a bit feisty with having to comply, knowing that over the past years she had never contaminated or poisoned anyone, at least to her knowledge.

"Hello, Mama! Great day! What is my assignment, today? You look very neat in your crisp, new store dress!" an exhilarated Aileen offered, dancing her way between the bins of potatoes and vegetables.

"And, when did ya kiss the Blarney Stone? Is it a new dress for a school social, y'all be wanting?" asked Margot.

"I'm just in a good mood. Got the highest grade in the history test! Have you heard about Lenora and Hank?" sang Aileen.

"My ears are closed, and I don't want ya talking about yar sister. She'll be the death of me, with her goings-on. Just like her father! Ya don't have to tell me anything. I either already know it, or can just use my imagination with that one! Now, don't be wasting my time and yars. Keep yarself in line, Aileen! That's what we each have to answer to Gad for!" warned Margot.

Margot wondered if this news about Lenora and Hank would mean they would have to move again. Maybe it's just that someone has a wicked tongue and is mean-spirited. Margot couldn't focus and had difficulty adding up a customer's purchases. Finally, there was a lull.

"Aileen, may I speak with ya in the back room," called Margot.

"Sure!" chirped Aileen, tossing her head, and swinging her pageboy from side to side.

"What did ya hear about Lenora and Hank?"

"I thought you wanted me to MYOB!" Aileen teased.

"Never mind the pig Latin!" replied Margot, attempting to convey some knowledge of her daughter's world.

"It's not pig Latin. It's an abbreviation for…"

"Answer what I asked ya," an impatient mother demanded.

"Well, my friend Cindy's mother works at St. John's Rectory as a cook, and recently, each Thursday from four to five, Lenora and Hank meet with a priest. Hank is preparing to receive the sacraments to become a Catholic! And this is the best part! They're going to be married as soon as Hank completes whatever it is he has to know," Aileen conveyed feeling ever so grownup being in the know.

"He better have a job, because they're not living with us!" Margot responded.

"Ma, you know how you always refer to Hank as that goddamn German? He was born in New York—in the Bronx! Both Lenora and Hank are Americans."

"Ya don't need to be telling me what I know! He's not Irish!" Margot answered with disgust.

"But, Sean's friend, Norah, is Irish and you don't like her family because they're from Sligo!" Aileen said, exercising her observed flaw in Margot's reasoning.

"I'll thank ya to shut yar mouth and get on with yar chores or… no allowance! What are they teaching at that school? Have they changed the commandment from 'Honor they father and mother' to 'decide when ya wish to honor yar parents'?" shouted Margot.

"No, Ma. What they are telling us is that we're all equal because we are made in the image of God and we are all his children," answered Aileen.

"I won't be needing ya to teach me my catechism! I knew it before ya was even spit!" snapped Margot.

"Oh, Ma, no one can talk with you because your ears are closed," said Aileen, pushing her luck beyond Margot's patience.

With that comment, a bag of potatoes went flying directly at Aileen, who agilely sidestepped from years of practice.

"Wow!" exclaimed the postman as the sack landed at his feet. "Here's your mail. How much do you want for the mashed potatoes?"

Margot just glared at the postman and shifted alternately to Aileen. The store was so quiet one could hear the stacked onions as they started to loosen their positions in the bin.

"Aileen, catch those onions," shouted Margot as she accepted the mail from the carrier. Watching as the postman continued on his way, Margot turned and grabbed her daughter's arm.

"Aileen! Don't ya ever embarrass me again in front of a perfect stranger," seethed Margot.

"But, Ma, you threw the potatoes," claimed Aileen.

"It was yar fault. Ya drove me to it! And shut yar gaddamn mouth or I'll shut it for ya. Ya learn a little respect or I'll yank all that hair right out of yar head," rumbled Margot in her Irish whisper. She looked in disgust as Aileen bawled her eyes out.

"Get in the back room and clean up yar face. Who wants to look at a face that looks like the wrong end of a pig? Yar the most ungrateful daughter a mother ever had, and don't think I haven't noticed the money you've been skimming from the cash register!" warned Margot.

Focusing on the mail in her hand, Margot opened the lawyer's letter first.

"Well here's another kettle of fish! Dear Gad, I've got to get the last of the furniture out of our Albany Street home. And not only that, but the cases and counters. The gaddamn building was sold where we had our store. It needs to be emptied by the end of next month, it says!"

Sean returned from his friend's house and received the tail end of Margot's frustrations.

"So nice of ya to finally arrive!" greeted Margot, sarcastically.

"I'm only three minutes late!" Sean replied.

"Ya best learn now, that life doesn't wait!"

"Yes Ma. I'll stack the shelves and crush the cartons." Sean answered.

"Aileen! We have customers that need help."

"Yes, Ma," Aileen called, entering with arms filled with oatmeal boxes.

Continuing to sort through the mail, Margot began to second-guess leaving Little Falls. Perhaps she should have waited until after the hearing. No news from either of her sons made her wonder if Bernard were contriving some stupid plan of leaving the country, instead of facing the inevitable.

It is true that the Good Shepherd left his flock to locate one lost sheep, but sacrificing the whole family for one son's shortsightedness now seemed pointless. Margot was experiencing a feeling that, up to now, was foreign to her nature. Doubt was rattling her brain, in that, could it be stubborn pride guided her decision versus wisdom? Her decision to uproot and relocate at such a tumultuous time was starting to take a toll on all of them, like fish out of water.

Chapter Sixteen

Day by day, each member of the family maneuvered their way through the economic turmoil and international unrest of 1934 thrust upon them through radio waves, movie newsreels, or the corner newsstand's headlines. They endured this reality given they still had their freedom of choice and independence, in contrast to Bernard's current status. He had a new address for the next two years, compliments of the State of New York's penal system.

They wrote to Bernard, attempting to keep him connected to what was once a family, despite the fragility of its members. They wrote to Raymond but he seldom wrote back, leaving the letter-writing to his wife, Carol. The occasional letters from Carol sounded mostly obligatory and filled with how well Raymond was doing in his studies and employment. She never mentioned any concerns about the health of their first son until the most recent letter included a newspaper clipping of his death and her brief account of what happened.

The family was shocked, and grieved for the loss Raymond and Carol were enduring. Then, the family's shock turned to puzzlement as to why Raymond had not contacted them so they could have arranged to attend the infant's funeral. After the puzzlement, anger took over in the form of unreasonable speculations.

The phone calls between Margot, Lenora, and Katherine, since the arrival of Carol's letter, were driving Ted crazy. He could only imagine what half of the conversation was, but what he heard Katherine saying in response made him boil!

"Katherine, hang up the phone! Tell your mother I have to use the phone, and other people waiting for the phone deserve a turn."

"This is really not your concern, Ted!"

"Hang up the phone now!"

"Ma, Ted needs to use the phone. Call me tomorrow."

Walking out to the kitchen, Katherine began to wash the supper dishes nosily and muttered to herself.

"Katherine, just sit with me awhile at the table. I want you to recall a conversation we had when I returned from Raymond's wedding, two years ago."

"Oh, I recall how elegant you said it was," Katherine sarcastically replied.

"And, do you remember all the excuses each member of your family came up with for not attending?" prodded Ted.

"We didn't make up excuses. They were real reasons!" Katherine retorted.

"They were excuses, because Raymond had planned it so none of us would have had any expenses beyond getting ourselves there," Ted offered.

"I said it then, and I'll say it now; we did Raymond and Carol a favor by not showing up. We used the transportation money in addition to whatever other expenses the traveling might have incurred, and purchased real nice wedding gifts for their home," Katherine haughtily answered.

"He didn't want presents; he wanted his family to meet his bride and her family. Their wedding invitation was sent two months ahead of time, and you each spent those two months acting like you could read Raymond's mind. You convinced yourselves he would be relieved if he didn't have to concern himself with any of you! Personally, I believe you and Lenora couldn't stand the competition of being in the same room with a beautiful woman, and Carol is beautiful!" said Ted.

"Ted Bryant! You take that back!" shouted Katherine.

"Sorry if the truth hurts! You, Lenora, and Aileen are even jealous of each other! It is obvious to me and probably others. I can understand why your mother didn't want to go without your father. Yet, I don't recall either you or Lenora offering to stay with your father so your mother could attend Raymond's wedding," Ted said, adding fuel to Katherine's anger.

"What has come over you?" Katherine cried. "If you had such strong feelings about all this, why didn't you speak up and say you and I would attend and represent the family?" Katherine said, expressing her first thoughts and wishes to be present at her brother's wedding.

"It wasn't my son or brother. And if I had, you would have insisted on leaving the children with your parents unless you could buy all new clothes and shoes for them!" her husband offered.

"And that is precisely another reason why I chose not to go! We'd look like the poor relations of the family!" Katherine banged the tabletop and stood up.

At this eventual point of all their confrontations which evolved around money, Ted put his hands in his pockets, pulled out the lining, and shrugged his shoulders.

"You're welcome to whatever I have. At the moment, it's just lint!"

"That's the story of our life," Katherine snapped.

"You know, Katherine, honesty would have been a better way to have approached your brother's wedding. I just told Raymond I was representing the family because of my railroad pass, and that money was extremely tight for your parents. Plus, all of them were living in an apartment intended for two. He cried, Katherine, and that is not what a person who doesn't care one way or the other about family would do. He knows that your mother sacrificed everything to pay Bernard's debt.

"So, I'd speculate that Raymond and Carol chose not to stress all of you by calling about their grief when they knew we would not be able to go to New York at the drop of a hat. There is nothing to stop you from writing them, or better still, calling them," suggested Ted.

"What will I say to Carol if she answers the phone? I haven't even met her!" Katherine pondered.

"Call on your training as a nurse. How would you comfort a mother who's lost her baby?" Ted asked.

"There are no words…" Katherine whispered.

"Just give them a call. The words will come," encouraged Ted. "Remember how we felt when you suffered a miscarriage four months ago? Raymond and Carol knew and loved their child, and watched the infant die! You and I lost a being that might have been, not a child that lived and was loved," Ted interjected.

Searching through the desk drawers, Katherine located the address. "Operator, I'd like to place a person-to-person call to Mohawk, New York. Yes, Raymond Lockhart. Yes, I'll wait. Operator! Operator! That's all right. I'll speak to his wife. Hello! Hello! Carol? Hello, Carol. This is Katherine Bryant, Raymond's sister. We received your letter. Carol! Carol! Oh! Please don't cry. I didn't want to make you cry. Carol, I'm so very sorry. I know you both loved your son, and he is now an angel in heaven. You and Raymond have your own personal angel to put in a good word for you both to God. Yes, I'll say hello to Ted for you. Yes, I'll write. Good night.

"Oh, Ted! If only they were nearer so I could have been of some help," Katherine cried as she hung up the receiver.

"It was not as you, Lenora, and your mother were imagining. Raymond and Carol were not spiteful because you didn't attend their wedding. People filled with grief don't always think clearly, or have the presence of mind while in their pain to realize the need to explain themselves to others. They can just about manage to get through the day," explained Ted.

"Raymond wasn't the same after our baby sister, Colleen died," Katherine recalled. "When she first died, he would go to the cemetery every free moment so she wouldn't be alone. I don't want to talk about this anymore."

"I hope you will write soon so they know others understand what it is to lose a child," suggested Ted.

"I said let's not talk about this anymore. And I'm not going to write about losing a child. I know what you're up to, Ted Bryant! You think I never got over having to give my baby to my mother!" Katherine replied.

"Well, there are different types of losses which can affect us our whole lives," offered Ted, wishing he hadn't started down this path.

"Listen, if you're looking for something to make me feel guiltier than I already feel you've succeeded. Jesus Christ, Ted! Just when I think we're getting along, you pull some stunt like this. Do you realize the state we'd be in with a couple of more children to care for? We're just about hanging on now, and I want our children to be able to have things, like piano and dancing lessons. With the mischief Sonny gets into, we've got a long road! The medical bill from his stitches after he jumped the ice truck cost more than a week of groceries! Lucky for us, my mother owns the grocery store!" Katherine retorted, ready for whatever was to come next.

"This was your third miscarriage, and I'm wondering if you've caused them by taking harsh laxatives I found in the trash," Ted challenged.

"Now you wait just a minute. I'm starting to get the picture. The death of Raymond's son is just an excuse to vent your suspicions. For your information, Leonora asked me to put them in our trash so Hank wouldn't see what she was doing. Some trusting soul you are!"

"What's she doing?" asked Ted.

"You know, some people have trouble with constipation. It is personal and private," responded Katherine attempting to wipe the table clean.

"Why don't I believe you, Katherine?"

"I don't really care if you do or don't. If you need to know more, ask Lenora about her piles and constipation. Right now, I have to concentrate on what to write in the letter to Carol and Raymond, after I wash the supper dishes," Katherine answered.

✦ ✦ ✦ ✦ ✦ ✦ ✦

Someone who has had their independence taken away by an illness, physical injury, or a temporary confinement, tends to gain a deep respect for things they previously took for granted. Bernard's daily routine under the guidance of the prison guards intensified his appreciation of all he could remember. The gradual toughening of his skin over the years in political office assisted Bernard's endurance. What worried him most was his fear of losing all decency due to the crudeness of some of the inmates he rubbed elbows with in the close confines of prison.

Mail communication with his family, along with Raymond's loyalty on visitor's day, helped Bernard to hold on. Lily tried to visit him, but he refused to see her and returned her letters unopened. He instructed Raymond to explain to Lily how it would pain him deeply for her to see him under such circumstances, and to read her letters would cause him to weaken and become unable to endure.

Carol and Raymond invited Lily to their home, in order to explain the intent of Bernard's request. She surprised them by quickly accepting, and asked if the coming Sunday would be convenient. Raymond arranged to pick Lily up at the Mohawk depot at noon.

"Hi, Lily, remember me, Bernard's brother?"

"Silly! Who would forget such a handsome man," teased Lily. "This is so kind of you and your wife. I have so many questions to ask you about Bernard, and something to tell you, but I'll wait until Carol is present."

"We'll be at my home in about ten minutes. It's not much, but it's ours, and Carol is expecting again. We lost our first son last fall."

"Oh, I'm so sorry. I didn't know."

"I didn't tell my parents how sick Richard was, and then he went to heaven. It all happened so quickly! My sister, Katherine, claims our son is an angel watching over us. We sure could use some divine intervention."

"You, me, and Bernard," interjected Lily.

Raymond glanced toward Lily, who seemed to be miles away in thought. He changed the subject by pointing out local points of interest and quoting the historic significance of each.

"Here we are. Let me take that package for you. Watch your step, Lily, and don't use the banister. I've got to fix it. Hello, Carol!"

"I'm in the kitchen," called the budding mother.

"Hello, Carol," called Lily as she walked toward the kitchen, "we've never met, but Bernard told me what a wonderful woman Raymond married. Thank you for inviting me to your home."

Carol was totally taken by the poised creature with her elegant clothing and cameo complexion. In contrast, Carol found herself straightening her hair and removing her apron, while trying to hide a glob of mashed potatoes on the toe of her left shoe.

"Please take a seat in the parlor and I'll bring you a cup of tea while the food finishes cooking," Carol offered, as she put on the tea kettle.

"Please let me help," offered Lily. "I'd prefer to drink the tea in the kitchen so I may keep you company. Don't fuss on my account."

"Well, why not. Come on into my messy kitchen. I'm like a mad scientist when preparing food. Raymond cleans up after me. Do you want a cup of tea, Raymond?" asked Carol.

"No, I'll check the roast and potatoes, and it is my expert opinion as I gaze upon the golden browned spuds, that we should put the tea on the dining room table, because the food is ready," Raymond said, lifting the roasting pan from the oven.

Conversation flowed in between the enjoyment of the roast and vegetables. Lily finally directed the conversation onto a new path. She spoke of having learned about a side of her father that shook her very constitution.

"You can't mean, you don't mean…Lily, are you saying it was your father who set Bernard up?" gasped Raymond.

"Yes! I'm saying just that because of a conversation I overheard. If I were to ask my father, he would deny it," Lily answered, misty-eyed.

"When did you hear this conversation?" asked Carol.

"About three months ago. Some man I've never seen before visited my father at our home. My father was most upset that this man was so brazen to come to our home, and tried to get him to leave, stating he would see him at the office. I stayed close by the phone in the study just in case the police needed to be summoned. The man was relentless and insisted that he be paid immediately for something my father had him do several months ago. My father told him to get out. That's when some of the things the man said in anger made me realize Bernard was victimized."

"Why would he do that to Bernard?" asked Raymond.

"Bernard is very much like my father. As a self-made man from humble roots, Daddy didn't want me to slip back into what he called 'gutter life,' from whence he came. May God forgive me but I let him influence me. I really do love your brother, but the stories Daddy told me about being poor just made me a coward, especially after living in luxury all my life. I owe Bernard so much for being patient with me for the past ten years. I never wanted any other man, but Daddy made it clear he'd cut me off from the family if I defied him by marrying Bernard.

"Now I don't have any respect for my father, and I hope Bernard will still want me. Please, Raymond, tell him I found out part of the truth and hope it's not too late for us," begged Lily.

+ + + + + + +

Raymond could hardly wait for the next visiting day to come. Carol packed him a nice lunch and kissed him long and hard, as she felt the veil of sadness being lifted off of his soul.

"This is just the news Bernard needs to give him the strength to endure the remaining nine months. It's about time some good is happening," Raymond attempted to say between Carol's kisses.

Bernard greeted Raymond as if he had already heard about Lily's discovery. Instead, he had good news of his own. His exemplary behavior and cooperation earned him an earlier release date, narrowing the remaining nine months down to ninety days.

The brothers talked of the future for the first time in the positive. Raymond repeated Lily's story, and Bernard hung his head.

"She knows most of it. Her father begged me for the money stating all would be ruined if people found out he had used their investments in his company to play the stock market and lost. I believed him, and filled out the transfer for a temporary loan from my department, which would be paid back when he sold some real estate holdings within the next three days. He baited me with his promise to approve of my marriage to Lily, and support for my candidacy for state senator. I left the transfer under my desk blotter overnight in order to sort it all through in my mind. It felt similar to selling my soul to the devil. I left the office around 7:00 PM. The person who entered my office pretending to be me knew the safe's combination and that the transfer was under my blotter. He took the exact same amount from the safe, and left my handwritten transfer on top of my desk to burn me. Having an auditor waiting as I walked into my office the following morning was a setup if ever there was one.

"The person in the building across from the town hall, who was the main witness, claimed he saw me in my office around nine at night taking money out of the safe. But my office window is higher than the windows in the building across the way, unless it was someone who was on the roof looking downward.

"That's it, Raymond! The person who claims he saw me take the money out of the safe must be the same person who stole the money. He may have been using binoculars, and saw me put the ledgers in the safe and saw the turns I made to open the safe! No one would have seen this person on the roof because it was dark and overcast that night at 7:00 PM, and he had a clear view with all the lights on in my section of the town hall. He saw everything I did!

"Hiring a lawyer with my meager savings against a millionaire's endless resources seemed senseless to me. I opted to hold on to whatever Lily might still feel toward me rather than try to discredit her father, whom no one in her eyes could hold a candle to. Now, as things have turned out, I think it was a wise decision, hey brother?"

"When you are released, where will you live, and how will you get a job?" Raymond asked.

"One day at a time, and one thing at a time. First, please tell Lily nothing between us has changed. Second, tell her to get ready for a honeymoon. Third, will you and Carol witness our marriage?"

"We'd be honored! This is great! Do you want me to tell Ma and Pa?" asked Raymond.

"No, I would like to just show up and surprise them all in Cambridge. Maybe that's where Lily and I will live to get a new start. Perhaps Ma could use me at the store while I'm looking for a permanent job," Bernard speculated.

The matter-of-fact manner that Bernard adopted early in life used to grate on Raymond's sensitive nature, but now he saw it as the strength which assisted his brother through his incarceration. This temporary setback had only strengthened Bernard.

"Ma wrote me a long letter and brought me up to date on all that's going on. Can't believe Hank convinced Lenora to marry him, but it's been almost two years, and both are still alive. He is so jealous of anyone who even looks at Lenora. I've had to step in several times to keep Hank from getting his head bashed by some fullback. What do you think he weighs soaking wet? One forty?" offered Bernard.

"I can't say. But he's strong and mean when angry enough!" acknowledged Raymond.

"Ma and Pa took the loss of your son real hard, from what they said in my letter. I wrote them there is nothing that will stop a Lockhart from trying again. When is Carol expecting the baby?" inquired Bernard.

"She thinks it will be in four months or so. God, Bernard! That still hurts so bad, watching the last breath leave his body. It was Colleen all over again." Raymond said, trying to hold back the tears.

"Hey, Raymond, it's all right to cry. I've cried many a night in this hellhole. Promise you won't tell anyone, though."

"Guess we're all spinning since leaving Little Falls," Raymond replied.

"Let me say it for you, Raymond. I made a mess of things for the whole family, but never did I ask Ma to bail me out. It was her own stubborn decision, and I hope to make it up to her. I'll make her proud of me one day," Bernard stated.

"Bernard, how about me driving you to Cambridge, when you leave this place? We can visit the family and you can look for an apartment to live in with Lily after you two are married. I can manage a long weekend before Carol's last month before the baby. Will you need some money to hold you over?" offered Raymond.

"I have some money. Lily opened an account in her name with my meager nine hundred in savings. She has her own money through an inheritance and an allowance her father gives her. When she marries, the monthly allowance goes into a fund which is to be used toward a college education for the children of her marriage. Should there be no children, the money reverts back to her father's estate and is given to whatever charity he designates in his will," explained Bernard.

"What a sleuth! He has figured all the angles!" laughed Raymond

"Yeah, and I made a big mistake by thinking I was smarter. He hit my weakest point, and I betrayed myself by not sticking with my instincts. He would have been jealous of any male who took his daughter from him," surmised Bernard.

"You may be my older, smarter brother, but let me clue you in on another possibility. While you were enjoying your vacation behind locked doors, your archenemy sponsored a young political upstart from Utica with a Yale diploma, whom, by all newspaper accounts is bound for the Senate. You were in the way, Bernard, and not a cooperative player. With a criminal record, you're out of the game for life. That's my opinion.

"What I still don't understand though, is why didn't you fight the charges and go to trial? You could have stood on your overall record and won, instead of pleading guilty!" pondered Raymond.

"Let it rest, Raymond. A lot of people were grateful I didn't drag them through the mud with me. There was a lot going on, and Lily's father was only a fraction of it. I had bailed several locals out of tight situations using the treasury's money, and they always paid me back, and no one was the wiser. Damn! Ted warned me years ago and I laughed at him," responded Bernard.

Chapter Seventeen

There was an air of reticent anticipation throughout the country in the midthirties, which seeped slowly through the upper stratosphere of unpredictability down onto the staunch individuals bent on surviving but another day. Radios hummed with progressive news from the Vatican. Corner newsstands chronicled the event with large, black-print headlines. The Holy Father sanctioned the rhythm system for practicing married Catholics. The age of female liberation took off with full abandonment, armed with calendars, crossed fingers, and trust in the long-awaited edict.

For some, it worked. For others, the theory proved to have side effects which resulted in a baby nine months down the line. Such was the situation in countless homes, and the Bryant household was no exception. Just as expected, when it rains, it pours. Their landlord decided to sell the two-family dwelling on Cambridge Terrace. Ted and Katherine made an offer to buy, but their hopes were quickly dashed when they learned what the owner's asking price was.

Another search; another move; another mouth to feed, and another reason for discord grew, due to Katherine's insistence that they find a first-floor rental. Her heart was palpitating often, accompanied by fainting spells which required aromatic spirits to revive her. Complete exhaustion from such an attack found her in bed for the next few days. Ted felt extremely guilty for putting her through the ordeal of bearing another child, yet Katherine seemed to be looking forward to having the baby as evidenced by the knitting of booties and carriage shawls each evening.

With time quickly running out, Ted spotted a first-floor flat advertised in the *Boston Sunday Globe* and was on the doorstep at nine that morning. The rent was five dollars more a month, but only two blocks away from St. John's School. He put down a deposit, knowing he would have to curb Katherine's inclination of spending money, especially now with the third child on the way.

Having St. John's Church a short distance away pleased Katherine. She would spend an hour or more each day reading her special prayers in the lower church. Kneeling most of the hour, she would offer up the pain she felt from the enlarged varicose veins in her legs to the suffering form of Jesus as he hung nailed to his cross. She believed God was just, and prayed she would be exonerated on the Day of Judgment, when each soul would be called upon to account for their sins.

"Thy will be done; into thy hands I commend my spirit," prayed Katherine, as she concluded her daily litany.

✦ ✦ ✦ ✦ ✦ ✦ ✦ ✦

The birth of a baby girl was a partial relief for Katherine and Ted. If Teresa Ann was any measure, another daughter would be a pleasure, in contrast to Sonny's perpetual motion and tantrums. The two o'clock feeding had always been Ted's way of alleviating the drain on Katherine with their first two children, but that was when he was thirty-three—now he was forty. After dozing off one night and almost letting baby Rosalie slide out of his arms, Ted offered to do it all, from bottles to bath, on Saturdays and Sundays. This seemed a fair exchange to Katherine, given she could sneak some shut-eye during the baby's naps while the older children were at school.

For the first time in a long time, the Bryant family was working together and enjoying the innocence of their baby. Everything seemed new again with each growth milestone, from the first tooth, to the first word and step. It was a first-time experience for Teresa Ann and Sonny, who spoiled their baby sister with love and attention, until it became a task and interrupted their playtime with friends.

Over the next three years, the Haskell Street dwelling was becoming cramped with three growing children in one bedroom. Teresa's and Sonny's schedule was different, being several years older than Rosalie.

Katherine began to overreact to Sonny's presence in the bedroom when the budding eleven-year-old Teresa Ann was dressing. It was all too reminiscent of Katherine's early years, and she vowed her daughter was not going to be offended by any male, at any age! Sonny, being a male, was guilty in her mind, even if he hadn't thought or done anything.

Margot had been present a couple of times when Katherine lost control over Sonny's forgetting to close the bathroom door while relieving himself. Sonny responded that the urinals at school are not private, thus he didn't see what the big deal was all about. This earned him a swift hand across his mouth.

Margot thought Katherine's family needed a larger place to live, but who could afford it in this economy? She pondered this one day, walking her routine path along Beech Street, onto Elm Street heading toward Davis Square. Rounding the corner onto Elm Street, she spotted a FOR SALE sign on a single-family home, wedged between two triple-decker homes. Her legs couldn't carry her fast enough to Haskell Street.

"Katherine! Katherine!" shouted Margot as she knocked on their front door.

"What's wrong? Is it Pa?" a panicked Katherine yelled as she ran to let her mother in, while Ted stood at the stove making up a batch of fried eggs and onions for their ritual Saturday lunch.

"Katherine! Ya've got to get there right away before someone else buys it! I'll loan ya and Ted the down payment. It has four bedrooms and an apartment on the top floor with its own bedroom!" Margot added this point, hopeful it would be where she would live when Leo died.

"Ma, Ma! Calm down! You're all flushed. Here, have some lunch and a cup of tea. Tell us more about your find," offered Katherine.

Margot could hardly contain herself. In between bites of her lunch, she coached Ted on what he should ask the realtor, and what to look for in the structure of the home, the roof, and cellar. Gathering Rosalie up for a carriage ride, the trio retraced the path back to Elm Street.

The realtor was still there overseeing the replacement of three single windows in the front living room, where originally a large, leaded stained glass window had weakened over the years. Recognizing Margot, he approached the breathless walkers and exchanged information about the home being sold as part of an estate. He knew with the present economy, the home could sit for a long time. The price was negotiated and repairs agreed upon. The Bryants were now the owners of their first home.

✦ ✦ ✦ ✦ ✦ ✦ ✦ ✦

In October of 1940, Margot decided to sell her business in order to care for Leo. There were more and more days when he could not put one foot in front of the other. Leo spent most of his day sitting, with Margot creating a schedule in order to attend to his daily needs. This worked well until he became deadweight and Margot could not lift him.

Sean graduated from St. John's and went to work for the First National grocery store, with hopes of progressing to store manager in a few years. During his lunch break, he would run the mile from Davis Square to help Margot with Leo. The routine allowed for no postponement of his responsibility, and Sean never seemed to mind the restrictions. Neither of his sisters' husbands was available to help during the day.

One morning, Leo didn't get up and just stared into space, frantically yelling Sean's name. This continued sporadically over time, until Sean arrived and held his father's hand. Leo would then fall into a deep sleep, but when he would awaken, he would resume the routine.

Their family physician advised hospitalization; because it was evident Leo was starving to death. All his faculties were stating to fail.

"What can they do for him that we can't do?" Margot asked the doctor. "He's not going to get any better!"

"No, he won't get better, but he could be made a bit more comfortable. We would give him medicine to lessen his pain," suggested the doctor.

"My daughter is a nurse. Would she be able to provide the right care her father needs?" inquired Margot.

"It is a lot to expect of one person. At the hospital they work in teams to lift the patient and…" responded the doctor as Margot interrupted.

"I asked if my daughter could care for him." Margot blankly asked.

"Yes, she could administer the medicine and care for him as a registered nurse," the physician replied.

"Then, that would be what my husband would want. He made me promise to let him die in his own bed. So be it," affirmed Margot.

"I'll write a prescription. Should your daughter have any questions, here are my phone numbers for my office and the hospital," offered the doctor.

It was three days before Margot called Katherine in a panic. Upon arriving at her parents' apartment with three-year-old Rosalie, Katherine was appalled by the stench of impending death. Her father's bedsores were gangrenous, and the skin was falling off his back when she attempted to turn him on his side. Katherine jumped back in shock.

"Oh, sweet Jesus, remove this suffering soul from his agony," cried Katherine. Her father's eyes focused on her.

"Don't cry, Katherine. Don't cry."

"Pa!"

He fell into a deep sleep. Katherine watched his emaciated chest rise and sink. Her tears wouldn't stop.

"Katherine, come. Have a cup of tea," Sean offered.

"I don't want tea! Why didn't you call me when things got so bad? His skin is rotting off his back! Didn't you clean him like I showed you?" Katherine asked.

"I tried, Katherine, but I had to go to work. Ma has no strength left to lift him. We did our best," Sean explained.

"Do you realize I could lose my nurse's license if Pa's doctor finds out I'm a nurse?" Katherine cried.

"He knows ya're a nurse. I told him ya would take care of yar father and give him this medicine," Margot quietly offered.

"What medicine? When did you decide this?" Katherine gasped.

"Three days ago. Dr. Charles wanted to put Leo in the hospital, but yar Pa's last wish is to die in his own bed," Margot calmly answered.

"If you told him I'd take care of Pa, that means nursing care! Now, I'll surely lose my license for not reporting his deteriorating condition!

What is wrong with you?" Katherine sobbed in between blowing her nose.

Rosalie started to cry when she heard her mother's voice raised in anger. A scream came from the front bedroom.

"Sean! Sean!"

Rushing to his father's bedside, Sean returned with an expressionless face.

"Ma, go down to the drugstore and phone the doctor. Pa is going fast. Katherine, this will be no place for Rosalie in a few moments. Why don't you go home, and I'll explain it all to the doctor," Sean offered.

That evening, supper was simple, quick, and very quiet at the Bryant home. After the children were in bed, Katherine went to her bedroom and knelt to say her daily prayers. A knock came on the bedroom door and Katherine turned to look, expecting to see one of the children. To her shocked eyes it was her father, who raised his hand in a slow wave.

"Pa! What are you doing here?" Katherine cried.

He was gone just as quickly as he came. Katherine collapsed on the floor with such deep sobbing that Ted heard her above his ritual evening radio program.

"Katherine, what's wrong?" Ted asked, rushing into their bedroom.

"Ted, my father…He was standing right there and waving good-bye to me!"

"I'll go over to see how he is," offered Ted.

"If he dies, they are going to blame me. I'll lose my license. Why did my mother do this to me?" cried Katherine.

"I hear the telephone ringing. Look, just sit here and rest a bit and I'll see who is calling."

Ted rushed down the stairs to answer the phone. The message was as he expected. He fixed Katherine a cup of coffee.

"Drink this, and then I'll tell you what the call was about," he said, handing Katherine the cup.

Katherine sipped the coffee, rubbing the rim of the cup with her fingertips. Shivers shook her body.

"Katherine, your father died about ten minutes ago. The doctor was with him and wrote out the death certificate, listing the causes as heart failure and complications from liver disease," Ted related as he held Katherine.

✦ ✦ ✦ ✦ ✦ ✦ ✦

The wake was held in Lenora's flat, because Katherine couldn't deal with the mixed emotions of hate, love, and the sorrow of not having told Sean the truth. There were so many unresolved issues that had been avoided or denied, and now none of it made any sense or seemed to matter.

Nothing mattered to Katherine for several months. She drifted from day to day, sleeping when Rosalie napped, and staying up well past midnight to catch up on chores not done during the day. Every time she closed her eyes, she'd see her father's face.

Margot decided Katherine had to stop wading in her own self-pity and confronted her daughter.

"Katherine, when you see your father's face, is it of a young or old Leo?"

"Don't torture me. I want to block it out!" Katherine curtly answered.

"Yar right when ya say I let him die, but it was his request to let it go the way God intended it for him. When I'd watch him as he slept, I'd see the slow decaying of a man whose handsome face and strong body once sent shivers through me. He'd never be whole again. I made the decision to just let him sleep, rather than force him awake to take water or broth. Surely, I need to think it was God and not the devil that heard his screams and took pity on him," responded Margot.

"It's not funny, Ma! Well, now you're finally rid of him, and you almost finished my reputation with your selfishness," chided Katherine.

"Why are ya always so righteous? That part of ya is very much like yar father. He made decisions with his own interest first," Margot stated.

"I'm nothing like my father. No alcohol passes my lips after watching what it does in this family!" snapped Katherine.

"Get off yar high horse. Your father is still living, and ya even know him. I'm tired of yar 'better than thou' behavior. Ya could have come each day to help with Leo, but yar too busy, or under the weather with your heart. There is not a damn thing wrong with ya except a rotten disposition!" replied Margot.

"I don't have to listen to this. You'll eat your words when I keel over," replied Katherine in an attempt to gain just a wee bit of pity from her mother.

"I'll be long gone, Katherine, when that happens. Y'all outlive us all. Let's hope ya won't outlive all who might care about ya," warned Margot.

"Don't be putting your curse on me. If you think you've told me something to shock me, Pa already told me he wasn't my father the day Ted and I married."

"Did he tell you who it was?" asked Katherine.

"No, he told me to ask you, but not until after he died," answered Katherine.

"That was kind of him. It's Dr. Kirkland, Katherine," Margot confessed.

Ted tried to alleviate the emotional burden, but the doctor's advice to hire a domestic to help Katherine with the chores and children was beyond his wallet. Instead, he arranged to send the whitewash and shirts to the laundry, and for the weekly groceries to be delivered by S. S. Pierce. This helped Katherine's depression in a way Ted never could have imagined.

The delivery man found a sympathetic ear in Katherine, and the weekly deliveries turned into a romantic rendezvous. Neither Katherine nor the delivery man appeared to do more than hold hands, but the sin of desire is just as accountable.

Katherine's sense returned and gave her the strength to discontinue the deliveries the day four-year-old Rosalie came in from playing in the yard to find the truck man, as she called him, crying and kissing each of her mother's fingers.

Chapter Eighteen

The bombing of Pearl Harbor had a profound effect on each American in different ways. Fathers, husbands, sons, and daughters were drafted or volunteered for military service, leaving a void filled with the fear of never seeing those loved ones again. Small, patriotic banners hung in the windows of homes identifying the double-edged sword of pride and anguish experienced by those waiting at home.

Separation was too hurtful for some dating couples, and the prospects of losing their sweethearts to war pushed them into marriage sooner than expected. After only six months of dating, Aileen and Ford were married at St. John's Rectory. Four days later, Ford reported for duty in the U. S. Army. At twenty-five years of age, Aileen and Ford knew what they were doing, but Margot hit the roof when Sean informed her of his plan to marry Norah.

"Are ya daft? You're all caught up in the romance of your sister's marriage!" cried Margot, who was ready to pull every hair out of Norah's head.

"Ma, will you calm down? Listen to me," Sean said, holding Margot by her shoulders.

"Yar but twenty, and what do ya know? Was this Norah's idea?" Margot asked.

"Let me finish. No, it was my idea and the plan is to marry in two years. My job is going well and the promotion to manager is a sure thing," answered Sean.

"Well, a lot can change in two years," responded Margot.

The change that occurred was not what she hoped for. Sean was drafted and married Norah a week before reporting to the U. S.

Army. The Lockhart family presented a supportive front, even though they were fearful Sean was taking on more than a war. Norah had a reputation of being a bit outspoken, strong-willed, and determined to have her way; much like his mother.

Still reeling from the preparations for the wedding reception given at the Bryants' home for Aileen and Ford a month prior, Katherine was emotionally drained at Sean's and Norah's reception. She enjoyed a glass or two of port, and mustered up the courage to sing "O Danny Boy" in honor of her mother's homeland, as she put it. Everyone was misty-eyed and affected by the maternal feelings Katherine conveyed through the song. The remainder of the reception required all her decency and internal strength to refrain from repeating the same travesty committed by Leo fifteen years ago when he told Katherine he wasn't her father on her wedding day. She was determined not to replicate such a selfish act at this special moment in Sean's life by telling him Margot was not his mother. The double blow of having to admit Leo and she were his parents would be unforgivable and brutal.

Following Sean's and Norah's marriage, Katherine became obsessed with constant thoughts of never seeing her first son ever again. Ted tried to comfort her, but she was overwhelmed with the care of the baby, the laundry, the cooking, and the lack of support from her childless sisters from whom she dared not ask help, because in her eyes, all they were concerned with was the fear of chipping their newly-painted fingernails. Katherine drifted along in this tunnel day after day, closed to other people's realities, until a particular phone call interrupted her self-centered reverie.

One of the nuns was calling about a complaint by a student that Sonny took money from a classmate's desk. This was the proverbial straw for Katherine, and when Sonny arrived home at the end of the school day, she grabbed him as he entered the house, throwing him forcefully against the Hoosier kitchen cabinet.

"You're a despicable son of a bitch! I'll teach you to steal!" Katherine screamed.

"What did I do?" cried Sonny.

"You stole money from a classmate, that's what," she said, as she slapped his face.

"He said I could have the eight pennies. I was going to buy you a Hershey bar!" he answered with his arms raised to protect his face.

"Don't lie, you little bastard!" Katherine screamed.

Katherine grabbed Sonny by the neck and dragged him toward the stove. She screamed at him to stick out his tongue and then pushed his face down toward the hot cover plate. Sonny struggled hard to keep his face and hands from being burned.

"I'll teach you to lie! What did you do with the money? Tell me!"

"Ma, stop! I bought two cigarettes from Harrison's older brother," admitted Sonny.

With that answer, Katherine slapped Sonny so hard his nose began to bleed, blending with his tears.

"Get out of my sight," she shouted as she threw the iron skillet at Sonny's retreating back.

Rosalie was peeking around the doorway, having been awakened from her nap by the ruckus.

"Come here, Rosalie. Sonny was a bad boy again, but we don't want anyone to know I punished him. If anyone asks you anything, say 'I don't know'."

"Yes, Mommy," answered Rosalie.

Incidents of Sonny's poor judgment grew to the point where the police were frequent visitors at the Bryant house. The turning point occurred when Sonny fabricated a story that he was helping an elderly lady clean out her cellar. He broke into her basement and piled what he could into his red wagon. He brought the stolen items home, claiming the lady had given them to him for helping her. His parents believed him until the police showed up at their front door. Being a minor, counseling was advised, because Sonny's next offense could result in being sent to reform school.

After the policeman left, Ted's disappointment, shame, and anger took him to a point he never thought possible. Katherine directed that he do something to impress upon their son that he best change his ways. She left the house to go to Saturday confession, adding that when she returned, things had better be different.

Ted escorted Sonny to the cellar, recalling how his own father used the shaving strap to curb his unacceptable behavior. Not having a strap, and knowing Sonny's strength, Ted tied his son's wrists to the Lally column after a considerable struggle, which intensified Ted's anger. He grabbed a broomstick handle, hoping Sonny would submit and apologize, but instead, Sonny spit in his father's face. Ted swung the broomstick handle and struck repeatedly until Sonny sobbed.

At this point, a screaming Teresa stood between Sonny and her father with cotton balls, bandages, and Mercurochrome.

"Don't you dare hit him again, or you'll have to hit me first. You should be ashamed of yourself! Look at what you've done! Tying up your own son; you make me sick!" cried Teresa.

By the time Katherine returned from Confession, she found Rosalie hiding under the kitchen table crying. Teresa was sitting at the table crying. She asked where Ted was, and Teresa pointed to the cellar. Ted looked as though he had aged twenty years by his demeanor. He was slouched over, sobbing loudly, as he attempted to camouflage the drops of blood on the floor with a mixture of ashes and dirt.

Running back upstairs, she asked Teresa what happened, but Teresa just sobbed. Katherine looked in Sonny's bedroom to find her answer. He had packed and left after Teresa had cleaned and bandaged his wounds. The bandage wrappers and bloody cotton balls littered his dresser.

Back in the cellar, Katherine saw what had happened. Rope rested at the bottom of the Lally column, and on the floor was an old broomstick handle with nails at the base which helped hold the straw whisks. These nails must have torn at Sonny's back.

It took a few days for Katherine and Ted to report Sonny's running away, hoping he would show up after he cooled off. Six months later, in November, police found the young teen sleeping on a pile of rope down on the Boston docks. He had spent the past months on a fishing trawler, passing himself off as being sixteen. He had been treated badly, as evidenced by the various stages of bruises on his body. He had jumped ship after being sodomized by one of the crew. Mending would be long and lengthy.

Now that Sonny was safely back, the authorities directed Katherine and Ted to arrange for family counseling or Sonny would be placed with a foster family. The parents chose to seek help through the priests at St. John's Rectory, and after what the teenager had been through, his acceptance of help was sufficient for the parole officer. Things quieted down temporarily, and Sonny returned to school.

✦ ✦ ✦ ✦ ✦ ✦ ✦ ✦

Beyond the walls of the Bryant household, World War II was completing its first year. Neighbor competed with neighbor for food at the grocery stores, as they stood in line for rationed staples with their government coupons and tokens. Fat drippings were saved and turned in at the grocery store's meat counter for a few pennies per pound; tin cans were recycled by removing both top and bottom and flattening them. These acts made each person feel they were part of the war effort.

Radios were the lifelines of the common folk. The love songs of the day reflected the need to balance the terror with memories and words of affection. Sunday specials entertained the whole family with mystery stories and popular comedians. The news always took priority. There was a need to hold on to what was dear, and hope for that time "When the Lights Come Back On."

Military mail was censored, and shrunken photo versions of letters from the soldiers were delivered in a six-inch square, tan envelope, easily recognizable, and the first to be read by the receiver. It would be weeks to a couple of months between letters due to the soldiers moving from one front to another. The time in between was similar to a period of mourning, but instantly forgotten when the response was read and reread by family members.

Another baby joined the Bryant family. Everyone was pleased with Patricia Jean, except for Sonny who had specifically requested that it be a brother. He felt outnumbered with four females in the house.

Katherine became obsessed with Patricia Jean due to the traumatic start the baby endured. She wouldn't leave the infant alone for more than five minutes.

"Sean never mentioned the picture I sent him of his new niece, Patricia Jean," Katherine sighed when reading Sean's letter. "I told him how she almost died at birth, and how I had to scream at the nurses to bring her to me, and that the milk from my breasts saved her."

"He may not have received the picture when he wrote his letter," suggested Ted, realizing Katherine's preoccupation and obsession about Patty Jean tended to close out everything else that was going on.

"Then he doesn't know that Bernard and Hank have been drafted either, because I put that in the same letter," Katherine said in disappointment.

"Katherine, Hank was drafted, but Bernard enlisted," Ted responded.

"When did you hear Bernard enlisted?" Katherine asked feeling left out.

"Did you hear the phone ring just before supper? That was Bernard asking if he and Lily may drop by Sunday to see their new niece before they leave," Ted said, buying himself time in answering Katherine's question.

"What do you mean by leave? Is Lily going with Bernard and taking Arthur? I'll have to clean this pigsty. I swear, dirt just falls out of you people," Katherine responded.

"They will tell us all about their plans when they come Sunday around two. I've fixed the vacuum and will clean the downstairs on Saturday. Teresa will make gingerbread for the company. She did a great job with the leftovers for supper. Did you thank her?" Ted asked, in an attempt to stretch Katherine beyond Patty Jean.

"And who thanks me for each and every thing I do?" sneered Katherine.

On the way down the stairs, Ted staggered into the wall, his legs collapsing under him. He was unable to regain his balance and sat down on the landing.

"Daddy, are you playing a game of hide and seek in the dark?" Rosalie asked.

"I'm hiding from Mommy and your baby sister. Don't tell," Ted whispered.

"I remember the time you fell with the blueberries and I didn't tell," recalled Rosalie.

"You're my big girl and best friend," answered Ted giving Rosalie a hug.

✦✦✦✦✦✦✦✦✦

Sunday was unseasonably warm for early December and added to the pleasure of the visiting relatives. Rosalie and Arthur played to their heart's content, as the adults sat around the dining room table while Bernard attempted to lighten the conversation with humorous recounts of what occurred during his physical for his enlistment into the navy.

Lily seemed on the verge of tears several times but pretended it was from laughing at her husband's bantering.

"So, that's the scoop. I'll be a fireman in the belly of one of those huge battle ships, for the next two years," Bernard stated, holding his nose while pretending to go under water.

"You can't be serious, Bernard," answered Katherine.

"I've never been more serious, Katherine. The government has offered, in exchange for my enlisting in the Navy, to remove from public records all indications of my prison record. I've got to do this for Lily, my children, and my family. It will open a lot more doors of opportunity once I return. I'm only sorry Pa died before knowing about this second chance for me," stated Bernard.

"Dear Lord, Bernard, what if you don't return? Have you thought about that? You're forty-one years old!" Katherine said.

"We each have a destiny, Katherine. This is my choice to alter my future. I'm taking it. Now, I want lots of letters, and only good news in them," directed Bernard.

"I'll be going back to Little Falls to live with my sister while Bernard is away. Arthur will miss Rosalie," Lily offered.

"Lily, I've been so focused on Bernard. This must be unbelievable for you. Can't you stop him? This is just too much! First Pa dies; then Sean is drafted; now Bernard enlists! What's happening to us?" cried Katherine.

"It's the times, Katherine. Nothing will be the same except our ties as a family. Now, we'd better get going because Arthur looks like he's about to fall asleep," suggested Bernard, as he helped his four-year old son with his jacket.

Standing at the front door, Katherine watched her brother as he carried Arthur on his shoulders, with Lily double-stepping by his side to keep pace. Their distant forms floated above the sidewalk as dusk melted them into the early evening light.

"Come on, Katherine. Let's close the door. The night air is cooling the house. Bernard is a strong man and he'll be just fine," Ted said confidently.

"Ted, our children are going to die. Why did we have them?" asked Katherine.

✦ ✦ ✦ ✦ ✦ ✦ ✦ ✦

The days crawled by for Lenora and Aileen without the company of their husbands, or a little one around to help absorb the emptiness they felt. Then along came an opportunity at the Boston Navy Yard. Appealing to women and wives of servicemen, the offer to train on the job while earning money won them over. They joined the thousands of women who supplemented the work force left stripped of men.

With adequate money now that they were employed, plus the allotment from Hank and Ford, Aileen and Lenora moved into two available apartments in the same complex as their mother. A reasonable rent was negotiated with the landlord, who was delighted to fill the vacancies. Each day they traveled to work together, and donned coveralls and kerchiefs covering their hair to prevent entanglement in the machines. They quickly learned the second shift paid better than the first, and before long, worked their way into the first two available openings.

The drawbacks of the second shift were quickly forming. The sisters' work routine isolated them from the family except for occasional weekends. A habit of hard drinking after work with co-workers sometimes found the sisters waking up in a stranger's bedroom around midday. Lenora and Aileen learned a lot they didn't need to know, and puffed cigarettes like a couple of smokestacks. They even began to wonder why they had settled for the men they had married, when they were so desirable, according to the group they were chumming with.

At their age of maturity, the inevitable was still a surprise to both of the sisters who sometimes couldn't remember what they had done due to overimbibing.

"Katherine, you've got to help us. Lenora and I think we're pregnant!" Aileen whispered into the pay phone.

"What do you mean, think? What have you both done to get into such a condition?" asked Katherine.

"Look who's talking! Jesus Christ, Katherine, how did it happen to you four times?" shouted Lenora as she grabbed the receiver and squeezed into the phone booth with Aileen.

"Well, I never would believe this. You two are lower than low and with your husbands' lives in jeopardy every instant. You both are unbelievable!" the older sister responded.

"Just a minute, Miss Perfect, we know what you are, and you're no better. Maybe Ted should know a few things about you and a certain S. S. Pierce deliveryman!" suggested Lenora.

"You two are no longer my sisters. After all I've done for you both," replied Katherine.

"This time, Katherine, you're going to help us and it will be private, or we'll tell Ted about Morris' fling with you amongst the grocery bags. He got drunk one night at the Wonder Bar and told us all about your sexual tête-à-tête, using the tablecloth to cover what you were doing for him when Rosalie came running in from the yard," laughed Lenora hysterically, "and what a way to get free groceries!"

"I did nothing but listen to a brokenhearted man whose wife left him. You two are disgusting. Don't ever talk to me again, and don't plan on having the holidays with us. As for your problems, they're yours, not mine. I kept mine," Katherine said, and slammed down the receiver.

Three days later, a frantic call from Aileen about Lenora found Katherine running along Beech Street toward their apartments. With no idea of what she was going to find when she got there, Katherine had asked her neighbor to watch Rosalie and Patricia Jean until Teresa got home from school.

Aileen was waiting on the second landing and led Katherine into the bedroom where Lenora was shaking uncontrollably with fever and chills.

"Make some excuse at work for Lenora, because she is not going anywhere like this. What did she do to herself?" asked Katherine.

"She hasn't eaten since we argued with you, and after work last night she took a heap of aspirins. Then she started to vomit around four in the morning like you wouldn't believe. Maybe the whiskey she drank to wash the aspirins down made her ill. While I was helping her and cleaning up the mess, she started to bleed, from, you know."

"I'm going to call Dr. Charles and present this as a miscarriage," observed Katherine upon checking Lenora.

"You can't do that! Lenora will kill us if anyone knows," warned Aileen. "By the way, I got my curse this morning. Guess this new work routine confused my body."

"We've got to get her some medical care, Aileen. I'll go to the drugstore and call Dr. Charles. He'll make a home visit for this. You stay with Lenora."

Descending the stairs, Katherine spotted her mother entering the building with a bag of groceries. Quickly, she scooted across the second-floor landing and down the hall past her mother's apartment in order to exit via the rear stairs. She was not very good at hiding her feelings, and knew Margot could read her face like a book if she stopped to talk with her.

"A nickel; here we go. Come on! Hello, Dr. Charles. This is Katherine Bryant. My sister Lenora is confined to her bed with chills and a temperature. Would it be possible for you to make a house call sometime this afternoon? Well, I believe she had a miscarriage. How far along? I'll let her answer that question. Yes, I'll stay with her until your visit. Around five would be fine. She now lives in the same apartment building where my father lived. Yes, that's the correct address; on the third floor. Thank you."

Katherine called her neighbor, who assured her everything was fine and Teresa was already home and caring for her baby sister and Rosalie. As Katherine walked to Lenora's apartment, she couldn't help feel their family was living under some awful curse. How or why these things kept happening to them when other people seemed to go along their way without much of a struggle was beyond her comprehension.

Chapter Nineteen

The holidays were acknowledged in a subdued fashion, with the absence of the male members felt by all. Ted spread himself rather thin in attempting to monitor Lenora's and Aileen's socializing on Saturday nights at the Wonder Bar. His presence tempered their drinking somewhat, but they knew he'd leave shortly after nine when the night was still plenty young for them.

The shortage of workers everywhere weighted the output required by the remaining workforce. The opportunity to make extra money was solely dependent on each individual's stamina. Along with Ted's full-time position at the Boston & Maine Railroad, he was working three nights a week and Saturdays at Bethlehem Steel. He estimated that in one year and a half he would be able to reduce his house mortgage substantially with the earnings from his second job. He lived for Saturday night to arrive, followed by Sunday, a day of rest.

Sunday was turning into a battle scene of its own in the Bryant household, totally negating the day of rest and any residual effects of Sunday Mass.

"I suppose you'll sit in that chair, now that you've filled your belly, and sleep the rest of the day until you wake for supper. Then, you'll sleep in the chair until bedtime, when you'll have a snack and go to bed; some fun!" commented Katherine, as she dried the roasting pan.

"I'm tired, Katherine," answered Ted.

"And I'm not? I wash the clothes by hand, cook for six every day, clean up after a bunch of pigs, iron all the clothes so each of you can walk out the door looking like Aster's pet mule!" Katherine responded.

"If I had the time, I'd help you more. I do the shopping at the North End and Haymarket on Friday nights! That leaves Monday night to do the bills and other paperwork we have. Saturdays I work eight to five. Is there another day I don't know about?" Ted replied, half-awake.

"Today is Sunday. Every Sunday for the past six weeks you have disappeared into unconsciousness the whole day, and I have to keep the children quiet!" Katherine complained.

"I must need the rest," Ted offered. "I'll be glad in many ways when the world gets back to the way it was before the war. Did you ever wonder how it is going to end?" asked Ted.

"Don't change the subject, Ted. I've noticed your coloring is sallow when you're resting, and you're losing hair. You should take walks to improve your circulation and burn off that pouch around your middle from sitting at a desk all day. Those cigarettes aren't helping, either!" Katherine lamented on a topic that never went anywhere with Ted.

"When the war is over, I'll have more time for walking and trimming down," Ted said in an attempt to pacify Katherine.

"It's useless to talk to you. Can we do something together, like a movie? You're acting like an old man at forty-six!" Katherine stated.

"Look! I need to rest. Then, we'll take in a matinee. Do you think you can keep the children quiet for another hour?" begged Ted.

"I'll take them for a walk over to my mother's. Some of us have the energy to think of what others need," added Katherine as she bundled up Patricia Jean in the stroller with Rosalie alongside.

Katherine had received a letter from Bernard, and thought Margot would get a couple of chuckles out of reading it. Putting on her spectacles, Margot began to read her son's handwritten letter on onion skin paper:

"…the number of ration points necessary to obtain a fresh fruit, I have none, and I cannot get any. For a glass of milk and an egg (natural) sandwich, with a layer of onion one inch thick on creamy white bread (of which I have had none for over a month), I would cheerfully lay on the counter a half crown, four shillings, six pence, two pence, half-penny, and a farthing, which in coins of the U. S. realm would be $1.48, and believe me it would be worth twice that."

Margot's eyes watered up as she dabbed her tears with her apron. To think of her son longing for an egg, a fresh fruit, or a piece of bread, and so far away from the only ones who cared whether he lived or died, saddened her deeply.

"Dear Lord, Ma, I thought it was a great letter. Had I known you'd get morbid on me, I'd not have brought it for you to read. I left one half-dead soul at home, and now you!" commented Katherine.

"Go on with ya! Sunday's a hard day for me. It's the end and the beginning at the same time. Let's have our tea," offered Margot.

"Grandma, may I play the Victrola and that record with the man laughing, please?" called Rosalie from the parlor.

"Yes, yar mother will help ya, and don't ya turn the handle. Yar too rough and will break it. Ya hear me, Rosalie?"

"Yes, Grandma, and I know the name of the record. It's *Stop that Tickling, Jack,* and the label is red," said Rosalie.

The elder mother and daughter sipped their tea, and despite themselves, laughed at the giggles coming from the parlor as Rosalie and two-year-old Patricia looked for the laughing man between the wooden slats.

+ + + + + + + +

The post-holiday weeks drifted through the winter and into spring. Rosalie was preparing for her first Holy Communion and was doing so many good deeds, she was driving everyone crazy. Cleaning Teresa's vanity got her into a heap of trouble.

"If I've told you once, I've told you a thousand times; stay out of my room!" screamed Teresa.

"Your vanity was dirty with all that powder on it," grimaced Rosalie.

"Out, out, and stay out of my room, you little brat!" yelled Teresa as she slammed her bedroom door.

Rosalie went through the house looking for other ways to do good deeds and spotted the dried laundry on the clotheslines in the backyard. Using an old chair with a missing back, Rosalie was just tall enough to pull off the clothespins, and proceeded to stuff the dried items into her father's long johns, unknowingly making a wrinkled mess of the total lot. Upon entering the kitchen with the stuffed long johns, Katherine shrieked!

"Look at what you've done, after all my hard work of hanging the clothes evenly to avoid wrinkles! What gets into you? Get out of my sight. Get upstairs and get ready for bed without your supper. Jesus Christ, why do I deserve this?" cried Katherine.

Rosalie remembered that Sister Aquina told the children they had to keep their souls clean. Before she went to bed, Rosalie scrubbed the soles of her feet as hard as she could with a face cloth. Then the tears started when her stomach rolled. Crawling into bed, the sadness she felt made her neck ache as her heart pounded in her ears. She was trying to follow Jesus' message to do good deeds, but all she did was make her family angry. Sleep transported her to the lower church at St. John's, where she was blessing herself with holy water, and heard a male voice calling her name.

"Rosalie! Rosalie! Come! You don't have to wait any longer."

A bright light shone through the ceiling which opened clear up to the sky as she walked toward the altar. Then a hand gently descended toward her, holding the sacred host. Rosalie opened her mouth and received her Lord. A serene love surged through her body as a restful peace filled her heart. The following morning, Rosalie told her dream to her father as he was fixing breakfast.

"You have some imagination, Rosalie. Did the dream scare you?" asked Ted.

"No, Daddy. It was a kind voice, and I felt happy," answered Rosalie.

Just like it was something that happens to every seven-year-old, Ted patted his daughter on the head and told her to finish the Cheerios in her bowl. Sonny was listening as he scoffed down two slices of toast, while asking Rosalie, in between swallows, how big the hand was; what the host tasted like; did she think God would talk to her again; did she think God would talk to him since he was her brother?

"Hey, Rosalie, I want you to do something for me after school today. I'll tell you as we walk to school," Sonny teased.

Between Sonny and his friend, Hanson, Rosalie's feet hardly touched the ground as they ran down Orchard Street, turned left onto Milton, crossed Mass Avenue, then down Rindge Avenue, with her riding piggyback on Sonny, and then Hanson.

"Meet me after school right here at the front gate and I'll tell you what good deed you can do for me," instructed Sonny.

At the end of the school day, Rosalie was at the appointed spot. Walking home together, Sonny explained he had to do an errand for someone at the used cars showroom and garage on Massachusetts Avenue near the fire station.

"Show me how loud you can whistle," Sonny ordered.

"Whee, whist, whee," attempted Rosalie.

"A little louder; that's good. Now, I want you to stand here on this spot, and if anyone comes along, start whistling as loud as possible. I'll be back in a few minutes," instructed Sonny, as he disappeared up a ramp toward the store's top.

Rosalie waited and waited for what seemed an hour. A police car pulled up at the front of the building and officers went inside. Finally, she figured Sonny had forgotten her and walked the rest of the way home alone.

Arriving home, she saw a similar police car parked in front. That evening, her parents and Sonny's parole officer kept going over the whole event, asking the teen why he was stealing from cars left at the repair garage. What made him think he had the right to take other people's property? How long had he been stealing from cars?

"I wouldn't have gotten caught if that stupid sister of mine had done what I asked her to do," he answered.

The next response revealed a side of their son's reasoning that Ted and Katherine kept denying.

"I'm not important like the other guys who have things, like a watch or a knife. You both say we have no money for extras, so I figured a way to get my own money. I knew you couldn't beat me again without getting into trouble with my buddy, Mr. Blanch. I didn't count on getting caught. All I wanted was a watch!" Sonny stated.

"Sonny, do you hear yourself? What if everyone went around taking whatever they wanted from other people; no one would feel safe. You couldn't trust anyone," exclaimed the parole officer, as Sonny rocked back and forth on the rear legs of the chair.

"Why do you feel you're entitled to what another person has, when they earned the right to buy or own it by their own hard work?" asked Ted.

"It will take forever for me to earn enough money to buy all I want. Why can't I have it now? I'd really enjoy it. When you get old, you don't care about those things. Mr. Blanch, Mom, and Dad have those things for themselves and can do what they want, when they want!" offered Sonny in his own defense.

"Just what do we do for ourselves, Sonny?" Ted asked.

"Well, for instance, you have a watch..."

Sonny didn't get another word out because Ted slapped him in the mouth, knocking him off the tilted chair.

"Mr. Bryant, I'm afraid I'll have to recommend that Sonny be assigned to a detention school where the instructors know how to handle arrogance without emotions getting in the way," the detention officer offered.

"He's never had any self-control from potty training on. Do you know he still wets the bed! Better clue them in for the need of a rubber sheet!" Ted stated.

"Mr. Bryant, I know this is difficult, but one day your son will realize you had good intentions. I'll process the paperwork and, Sonny you'll finish this school year with other boys who are working out growth pains just like yours. I'll pick you up around ten tomorrow. I trust you folks agree?" asked Mr. Blanch.

"I feel it is what Sonny needs; to learn the difference between what is socially correct and what is unacceptable behavior," replied Katherine.

"You both will be required to attend parent meetings with the superintendent of the detention school. Well, good night. I trust the anger has been defused?"

The following morning around 6:30 AM, Sonny knocked on Rosalie's bedroom door.

"Now's your chance to make up for the bad deed you did to me yesterday, or I'll never forgive you," whispered Sonny.

"I never saw anyone, so I didn't whistle," answered Rosalie.

"Get dressed and go out into the alleyway and stand under my bedroom window. I'm going to drop down a box. You catch it and I'll be right down," ordered Sonny.

Rosalie quickly dressed and followed Sonny's instructions, so as not to displease him again. Standing in the area of the window, she worried he'd drop the box on her head and knock her unconscious like the time he raced the old carriage she was in right into the cellar wall. Or, the time he gave her a black eye, and then the other time she got the scar which required stitches when…Sonny's window opened.

"Are you there? Here! Catch!" called Sonny

She almost caught the box breaking its fall just enough so it didn't split wide open. Peering inside she realized Sonny was running away because it was filled with his clothing. It would mean a sad time for her parents, and the house would be dark and gloomy with all the shades pulled down. Worst of all, she would get punished for helping Sonny. Picking up the box, she carried it up the front porch steps and rang the bell.

"Rosalie! What are you doing outside so early? And what's in that box?" asked her father.

"Sonny's running away again. Please don't hit him, Daddy."

"I promise not to, Rosalie," answered her father.

The whole household was up early that morning due to Sonny's screaming at Rosalie about her being a snitch. The restlessness in Sonny couldn't be controlled. The urge for instant gratification wouldn't allow him to conform to the routine of school or the expectations of the norm. He was going to have a rough ride on the road of life if he didn't receive help with his self-destructive spirit.

At ten on the dot as promised, Mr. Blanch arrived with the necessary papers for the parents' signatures, accepting the decision for Sonny's admittance to the State Reform School. He had brought along a counselor from the school as a precautionary measure, and to accompany Sonny during the hour ride to the facility. It would be time well-used if the counselor could get a handle on just how Sonny operated.

Teresa almost wished Sonny had pulled off his scheme of running away, rather than watching him be taken away by two strangers. The look Sonny gave Teresa screamed "I'm scared," but she was powerless. Her insides were petrified with fear of what might happen to her brother.

She began to spend more time in her bedroom reading, and no longer would eat the creamed foods her mother prepared with the flour, butter, and milk sauce. Nausea took over each time Katherine prepared creamed chipped beef or creamed cod fish and potatoes, sending Teresa racing to the bathroom. Her reaction would send Katherine into a tantrum, shouting how unappreciative and disrespectful Teresa was toward her, after standing at the stove for hours to prepare the food for all the gaping mouths. The yelling would be followed by Teresa turning her back to her mother, bracing for whatever Katherine threw. The missiles observed by Rosalie ranged from utensils to hamburger meat. Gradually, over the next two years, Teresa dropped thirty some-odd pounds and her severe acne subsided. The scarred facial tissue remained, but the stunning bone structure of her face, and the sparkling blueness of her eyes overshadowed any defect. People complimented the emerging beauty, and several beaus knocked at the door.

In the fall of 1945, Teresa garnered a supporting role in the annual high school play. It was the first time she sang in public, and brought the house down with, "Smoke Gets in Your Eyes." The parish pastor interrupted the play and asked Teresa to sing her song again, loudly stating that anyone with a God-given talent like her voice deserved more recognition than just three minutes. The audience agreed.

The attention attracted by Teresa's singing debut ruffled Katherine. All conversations for the following weeks seemed to wind up with her recounting all the times she sang here or there, and how many offers she received to sing professionally. Katherine rejected all offers, having been exposed to the environment of the entertainment world when her father, Leo, sang for money, and in her eyes, all associated with that element were cheap and shoddy.

College was on Teresa's mind, based on the encouragement of the nuns who taught her. Scholarships were available to the top students, of which Teresa was one.

"Just put any idea of college out of your mind," snapped Katherine, when Teresa told her which colleges the nuns were encouraging her to apply to.

"It won't cost you and Dad anything!" explained Teresa. "I'll work part-time on weekends and through the summers."

"We're counting on your full paycheck, not a few weekend hours. We can't afford the books or the clothes you'll need at college with the money we're obligated to pay toward Sonny's boarding school. Besides, you're kidding yourself. And the nuns are lying to you. They're just telling you what you want to hear. They feel sorry for you. You poor sap!" sighed Katherine, shaking her head.

"That's not true. I earn my grades, and they do not feel sorry for me," Teresa said.

"Just find yourself a husband who can take care of you," consoled Katherine.

"What? And have a wonderful marriage like you? I want a lot better than…" Teresa never got to finish her sentence due to a slap across her mouth, as Katherine screamed of how she cursed the day such an ungrateful bunch were borne to her.

Resentment grew with fewer and fewer civil words between them. Jealousy and suspicion grew out of proportion to the point where Katherine steamed open Sonny's letters to Teresa. The bond which existed between the siblings could never be broken no matter how bad circumstances eventually became.

The responses written by Teresa to Sonny were the letters Katherine should have read. They were a sister's attempts to communicate the need for Sonny to move beyond the past and treat each day as a new chance to do things right. Each day was his very own opportunity to make it better than the previous day, and if it wasn't, it was no one's fault but his own.

Teresa's philosophy never wavered, even when Sonny told her of his plans to run away from the boarding school. When he finally did, the punishment upon his return was carried out to the maximum. Sonny yelled profanities as they lowered him into the pit. The power hoses trained on his body knocked him down and choked him. He couldn't get away from the pounding as the forces tumbled and tossed him off the walls of the pit. As the minutes passed, water was entering faster than the drain could handle, causing Sonny to become buoyant. The hoses were then trained on keeping him below water. He gasped for air, only to inhale mouthfuls of rancid water. Exhaustion and lack of oxygen won out. That was the last he remembered until waking up in the infirmary.

"You're one tough specimen, Sonny," floated in the voice from the institution's physician sitting next to the bed, waiting for the teenager to regain consciousness.

"They don't realize who they're tangling with," a weak Sonny whispered. His throat hurt so badly, he couldn't swallow.

✦ ✦ ✦ ✦ ✦ ✦ ✦ ✦

It was a moment of jubilation as people ran out into the streets hitting kettles with wooden spoons while cars tooted their horns and musical instruments blasted away, spirited by the radio's news that the war was over and our soldiers were coming home! The summer of 1945 was filled with the joy of reunions. All four military members of the extended Lockhart family returned with their limbs intact, but the invisible scars were life-lasting.

The year of 1947 found maternity wards bursting at the seams with babies. Aileen and Ford had their first child just after New Year's, and eleven months later, a set of twins. In between her sister's double event, Lenora gave birth to twins, and Norah made Sean a father with the birth of a son. Margot was joyfully overwhelmed by her six new grandchildren, and Katherine's nursing skills came in handy when caring for the new mothers and their infants.

The joy of parenthood was short-lived when alcohol became more important than the vigilant care required by the innocent babies. Self-medicating with alcohol made the boredom easier for Aileen and Lenora to endure. Confinement to the home, and loss of spontaneous freedom to do what they wanted made the sisters feel trapped, compared to their independence when employed. Once pregnant, they did not work, thus money was knuckle-tight due to the blue collar jobs sporadically held by their husbands.

None of this adult-level activity was of interest to Rosalie until the afternoon she took it into mind to drop by to see her grandmother and her five baby cousins on the way home from school. Her grandmother didn't answer her door. Rosalie sprinted up to Aunt Lenora's apartment and could hear the toddlers through the door. She opened the door and found the toddlers on the floor rummaging through cookies and spilled cereal they had gotten out of the cabinet. She called her aunt's name, but Lenora wasn't in the apartment. Rosalie attempted to clean up the crunched cookies and cereal with a broom and dust pan, but the toddlers sabotaged her efforts by crawling through the crumb piles.

Placing the twins in their playpen with a few cookies, she ran through the hallway to Aunt Aileen's apartment. The door was unlocked, and her "hello" brought no response. In the bedroom, there was a woman's form in the bed wearing a slip, lying face down next to Ford. Backing out of the room, Rosalie saw one of the twins standing up in the crib with a sagging diaper soaked with urine, and runny feces dripping down the chubby legs. The dirty crib sheet reeked with the smell of ammonia.

Gagging from the smell, Rosalie cleaned the toddler, changed the crib sheet, and fixed a baby bottle with milk. The toddler was happy to see Rosalie but made no noise in contrast to Aunt Lenora's noisy twins. Placing the soiled sheet and diaper in a basin of water, she found a clean diaper for the baby. Searching for a slip of paper on which to leave a note, she spotted a book and tore a plain sheet from the rear pages. Her cheeks were on fire with anger. There was something wrong here which she didn't understand. Quickly, Rosalie wrote in the note: You shold be asshamd of yourslfs, signing it From God.

She left it leaning against three beer bottles on the kitchen table. Running through the hallway to get back to Aunt Lenora's twins, she plowed head on into Aunt Aileen, who she thought was in bed with Uncle Ford.

"Whoa, girl; what's the big hurry?" asked Aileen.

"I, I, I thought you were asleep in bed with Uncle Ford, and I couldn't find Grandma, and Aunt Lenora's twins were eating cookies and cereal off the floor and it was all over the place, and your boy baby had do-do all over the sheet, and…"

Aileen looked awful and started to cry.

"Listen, Rosalie. I just got back from the doctor and your grandmother went with me. Go down to her apartment and ask her to come up to Aunt Lenora's," asked Aunt Aileen.

As Margot and Rosalie approached the apartment, Lenora was loudly speaking words that made no sense, as Aileen was trying to support Ford, upright against the wall.

Shocked at what she was seeing, Margot approached Lenora and spoke directly into her drunken face.

"Get into yar apartment, Lenora. Have ya no shame? Get some clothes on before Hank gets home. Aileen get yar husband back to yar apartment and lock yar door."

"No, no, no, that's not what we want, do we Fordie?" cooed Lenora.

"You shut your rotten mouth," screamed Aileen.

Just as the atmosphere seemed to be reaching an unpredictable point, Hank arrived from work and summed up the situation in a split second. Grabbing Lenora, he threw his wife into their kitchen, causing her to slide across the floor and into the black-bellied stove. Margot pushed Rosalie into the kitchen, and locked a screaming Aileen and semiconscious husband in the hallway.

Hank slapped and shook Lenora so hard, she sagged to the floor like a collapsed puppet. Crawling under the black stone washtubs, she tried to escape Hank's wrath.

"You get out here so I can beat the crap out of you. I should have listened to what all the guys told me about you. You're nothing but a whore! I curse the day I met you. You rotten…" yelled Hank, as he kicked and kicked and kicked the sobbing form under the sink with his work boots.

"Almighty God; stop Hank! Y'all kill her. Stop!" begged Margot as she tried to pull him away.

Falling to his knees, he pulled Lenora out. She was not recognizable. Rosalie started to cry.

"Ma, help me clean Lenora up, and Rosalie, feed the kids for me," directed Hank, wiping his eyes.

The twins were crying and their noses were running. Fetching a facecloth, Rosalie cleaned them up and let them play on the kitchen floor while she mashed up and heated leftovers found in the refrigerator. Putting the twins in their high chairs, she sang them a song as she fed one, then the other. Hank entered the kitchen and watched as the twins finished their supper.

"Thanks, kiddo. These babies mean the world to me, and you've been a great help. Someday you'll make someone a great wife. You know, you're all right, kid," added Uncle Hank, giving Rosalie a hug.

Rosalie couldn't speak, and her thoughts were better left in silence because of the hurt in her heart over her aunts and uncles. She had survived her own mother's frequent outbursts by staying silent, and felt it was the best thing in this situation, also. A lot of growing occurred for eleven-year-old Rosalie in just a brief three hours.

"Your mother is on her way over; she'll walk you home now that it's dark," added Hank.

As they walked back to their Elm Street home, Katherine chastised Rosalie, and made her promise to never again stop in to see her cousins or her grandmother on her way home from school. She would be strapped if she disobeyed. No mention was made of what wasn't correct about the adults' behavior.

Chapter Twenty

The neighborhood around Elm Street began to change following the return of the veterans. Davis Square's business owners started renovating their stores, and new blood was evidenced by the introduction of Gilchrist. This new store was an affront to the old standby, Parke Snows, which had provided clothing and household goods to families in the area for more than two generations. Kressges and Woolworths survived the competition of being in close proximity, so why not Parke Snow and Gilchrist? Why not add a few more liquor bars in restaurants? The shopping environment became more public, and less of a family-oriented square as it was prior to 1942. Being accessible by bus and trolley attracted a varied group of patrons.

One evening, just after midnight, the Bryant household awakened to police sirens and the headlights of an ambulance reflecting from Beech Street into their backyard. Several pajama-clothed neighbors stood in the dampness of the night, watching the police and the ambulance teams lift a lifeless body onto the stretcher. The police called it a robbery, based on the woman's condition and the scattered contents of her purse on the ground.

This pushed Katherine over the edge. She wanted to move away from the area, and was relentless in pushing Ted from one realtor to the next. Embarking on her new crusade seemed to enliven Katherine with newfound energy, and lessened her attacks of depression. Ted went along with the search, but was certain they would not find an affordable home in the suburban towns in which Katherine was looking.

Ted calculated the top dollar possible for financing a new mortgage based on the maximum realized from the sale of their Elm Street home, combined with the bank's expectations and the current interest rate. He chuckled. Katherine was imagining a larger home with a yard; Ted was imagining and calculating the heating, electricity, taxes, and insurance, along with maintenance and repairs. How could he make her understand that costs for their current home sucked up his salary already? And then let her know that he seasonally dipped into the savings account to supplement shortfalls at tax time when, not to stress her, he fabricated union raises that never occurred.

He had managed to lower their mortgage with the help of his extra wages from Bethlehem Steel. Thus, if the bank saw the collateral they had in their house, plus his present steady employment, approval of a loan would be a given. Katherine would be elated and have no concern about the details, except to sign on the dotted line. This scenario played well in his mind but would not alleviate the increased operational costs of a larger home.

Sean and Norah lived in Watertown, and was one of the towns Katherine desired. They lived on the first floor of a two-family home owned by Norah's parents. After every visit to their home, Katherine would talk constantly about how good it would be for Rosalie and Patricia Jean to grow up in such a quality neighborhood.

Sean heard from a co-worker at the Watertown Firehouse, about an older home his in-laws were selling. It was listed with the Phalen Real Estate in Belmont. On his way home from work, Sean stopped by the realty office to check out the price and general condition of the home. Wanting to establish a sincere degree of interest, he asked if he could use the phone to call his sister to brief her on the house, and then the broker could arrange a viewing if Katherine seemed interested.

The news of the Belmont home's availability thrilled Katherine, but was tempered by receipt of a letter from Sonny's Naval Commanding Officer stating a medical discharge was being granted to their son. Sonny had gotten his parents' signed permission to join the Navy at the age of seventeen. Katherine prayed Sonny would take to the adventure, security, and structure of military life and make it his life's career. Now, just eighteen months since he begged them to sign for him, he was out without any future. She didn't know what she and Ted would do with him when he returned, but if this home was as good as Sean thought, Sonny could help them fix it up with the painting skills he learned in the Navy. Then he would get a job and contribute to their new home by paying rent.

They viewed the home with the realtor, but all the work that needed to be done to make it livable turned Ted off. The price was workable, but a ten-room house took a lot of heating and electricity. Yet, it was on the trolley line, and he could catch the train at the Waverly Station for North Station.

"And Ted, it is still acceptable with the town to rent the in-law apartment! The zoning laws in the area allow it because of the other multifamily dwellings on the street. And we could rent the garage, since we have no use for it without a car!"

"I was thinking that apartment would be just right for your mother, after all she has done to help us," offered Ted.

"Right now we need the rent money. Besides, she likes where she is. She has the movie theater right up the street; two pharmacies; a variety store for milk and bread, and just think, with the money from the in-law apartment, the double-garage rental, and rent from Teresa and Sonny, plus Rosalie will be baby-sitting for money fairly soon..."

"You've made your point, but don't let the realtor sense how much you want it, or I won't be able to negotiate the price to include the updating of the electrical wiring, the heating system, and overall repairs. Agreed?" cautioned Ted.

"Agreed," giggled Katherine.

This was definitely one of the highest points in their married life. They found a buyer who met the price for their Elm Street house. They were a good team when they put their heads together.

Gradually, the Belmont house resembled a home, as the familiar furniture took residence, along with a few upgrades, such as the chrome-trimmed kitchen table and chairs. Two tenants in the in-law apartment came and went the first two years. It was difficult keeping one bathroom available for the tenant's use, with six others having the same needs.

The glow of the home began to darken as Sonny gradually reverted to former habits. The current tenant found him going through her dresser when she arrived home earlier than expected from work. She was packed and gone that night. Sonny was gone by the week's end.

226

Hank phoned Katherine asking if he, Lenora, and the two-year-old twins could live in the vacated in-law apartment for two years. They would then be buying a home from a member of his family who was retiring to Florida. Hank offered to pay ten dollars more in rent monthly since there would be four of them in the apartment. The final decision was up to Ted. He had no problem with Hank. Lenora was the issue! Hank begged. He wanted more for his children than the rooftop of the Mass Avenue tenement for their playground.

The honeymoon period lasted for six months, give or take a few weeks, until Lenora started drinking again. As soon as Hank left for work, she'd pretend to be drinking coffee from her special mug. By lunchtime she was ripe, and often would try to start a fight with Katherine by using abusive language and threats of exposing her for what she really was. The jealousy in Lenora's drunken eyes was as a snake filled with venom, as she spewed forth her hurtful words. Katherine would encourage her sister to take a nap when the twins were resting, hopeful the buzz of alcohol would be gone by the time Hank returned from work.

Lenora would try to make up for the tension she had created with Katherine by inviting Rosalie and Patty Jean to her living quarters for grilled cheese sandwiches at five o'clock on Sundays, so they could watch *The Greatest Show on Earth* with their young cousins. The children knew what family was at that special time on Sundays. They laughed, joked, and hugged each other. The children's example gave the adults something to reflect on regarding their own reactions and interactions with each other.

Time was not standing still for Teresa, who was working for a Boston insurance company. She was doing quite well earning promotion after promotion. She had met a young man at her twin cousins' baptism, who coincidentally was working near Teresa in the area of Copley Square. Their relationship grew, and an emerald solitaire engagement ring conveyed Floyd's intent. It took Teresa awhile to accept his proposal, and she would not wear the emerald until he resumed his college education at night school.

A home reception followed the wedding at Sacred Heart Church. It was the first time in Ted's daughters' lives that they ever saw their father cry. He made a couple of toasts to the young married couple, and then sat down in the kitchen and bawled his eyes out. He cried over and over that it wasn't right that his baby girl was marrying that man. Sean tried to humor Ted, offering him another shot of whiskey and urging him not to say these words on his daughter's wedding day. Ted was distraught, and nothing could make it go away. He was overwhelmed with sadness over Teresa's choice of husband.

Floyd had insisted that he and Teresa live with his mother to help out with expenses since his father died shortly before their marriage. Teresa could not deal with the clinging nature and hypochondriac behavior of her mother-in-law. When Floyd took to wearing his father's clothes and smoking his pipes to make his mother happy, a six-month pregnant Teresa packed her bags and returned to her parents' home to await the birth of her baby. Floyd quickly followed.

The count was now twelve in the Bryant household. When Margot visited, Rosalie slept on the couch in the den. When Sonny crashed, having nowhere else to go, he got the den couch and Rosalie moved to the living room couch.

Then, along came another resident in 1952, changing the total dynamic of the household. Ted was her captive admirer. Her name was Vicky and her parents, Teresa and Floyd, were managing fairly well. Katherine was on duty twelve-seven, totally assuming the daytime parenting role, and encouraging Teresa to pursue her career if she ever wanted to own her own home. Floyd spent his time pursuing one interest after another in what he termed his inner development. Teresa made sure he had all the emotional support he needed with private counseling sessions.

Each evening Ted would give Vicky a ride on the imaginary elevator which took her up to bed on the third floor. She and her parents occupied the finished portion of the top floor. They were patiently waiting for Lenora and Hank to move out so they could have the second-floor apartment.

After putting two-year-old Vicky to bed one night, Ted received a phone call from his sister, Ellen. Their mother, Maggie, had died. She had fought hard to recover from an amputated leg, which was the result of a freak accident caused by a man who had an epileptic seizure and drove his car through the front of her home.

Maggie's funeral and final disposition of the home in Rotterdam Junction took a heavy toll on Ted. He was shocked to learn the money he sent her each year for the payment of the taxes on her property had never been used for that purpose. It took the very wind out of his sails. Katherine could not say a word given the grief and disappointment Ted wore on his face. He lost his mother and lost his birth home to the state.

His sadness was deepened by the fact that his widowed sister, Ellen, had taken no interest in their mother's financial situation, other than to pay rent. The contents of the home were auctioned off to pay for outstanding hospital bills. Ted bid on a settee and respectfully, no counteroffer was made by the neighbors. He brought it back to Belmont where it was relegated to the attic by Katherine.

About six months later, Margot fell in her apartment and broke her hip. She lay on the floor all night, and was discovered the next morning by a neighbor who heard her calls for help. Needless to say, her feisty disposition made hospital care a nightmare for the nurses assigned to her case. Upon her discharge, she was as a prisoner in her apartment, and fearful of going down the stairs. There was a change in the look of her eyes, and obvious incidents of forgetfulness. It was clear she could not live on her own anymore.

The attempt to meld Margot into the pandemonium of the dozen individuals living in the Bryant house brought about even more eccentric behavior. At times she seemed not to know her own children or grandchildren. In an instant, she would be out the door and halfway up the street in whatever she was wearing, sometimes only her slip and slippers. Rosalie was sent to fetch her, because others refused, as she would immediately swing to strike when approached. With the enticement of ice cream and a cup of tea, Rosalie would lead Margot back to safety.

Margot would drift in and out of these moments, but it became crystal clear on one particular day that she was no longer present as herself. She perceived Katherine to be her, and Rosalie to be Katherine. Margot turned on Katherine and began to pound her with her fists.

"Yar a rotten person to have done that to yar own flesh and blood! Goddamn ya to hell! I saw ya do it. Ya beat that child and threw her down the cellar stairs. Ya tried to make her lose the baby!" Margot's eyes were wild as her arms lashed out to strike Katherine.

"Run child! Get away from this witch! She won't harm ya as long as I'm here. Run!" screamed Margot at Rosalie.

Margot slumped into the kitchen chair. Katherine quickly phoned the family physician and Sean. The recommendation was to put Margot where she would not harm herself or anyone else. The state facility was all that finances allowed.

As time passed, Margot recognized no one, and she was so changed in her appearance it took family members a few minutes to locate her each time they visited. The attendants had curled her long hair and put lipstick and nail polish on a woman who never painted her cheeks or lips, and had great disdain toward those who did, unless they were movie stars.

Rosalie begged to visit her grandmother. The smell, as the unit's doors were unlocked for her to enter, would linger in her memory forever.

"Grandma, it's me! You look beautiful! I like the way they fixed your hair," Rosalie said, as she tried to look beyond the changes in her grandmother.

"Yar a nice young girl," responded Margot, "and ya remind me of my Katherine, but she's dead."

"Grandma, remember the trip you and I took when you were seventy-two and I was twelve years old? We visited your sister in Glens Falls and my grandmother, Maggie Bryant in Rotterdam Junction? We had a great time even though we got lost in Saratoga Springs," laughed Rosalie.

"Yar daft!" laughed Margot, "there's no place in Cork named Saratoga Springs!"

Rosalie fought the tears as she rose from kneeling in front of Margot. There was no memory of the years they shared. Leaning toward Margot, Rosalie kissed her forehead and clasped her own hands around her grandmother's.

"You're a strong and wonderful lady from Millstreet in County Cork. You remember that! No one will ever make fried spuds and pork chops like you can, and your special raisin cake with the lemon sauce will forever be my favorite. Do you still like vanilla pineapple sodas and root beer floats?" asked Rosalie, wanting her grandmother to remember something they shared.

"I'd rather some pickled pigs' feet, but they won't give me any! They don't listen to ya around this hotel," yelled Margot.

An attendant guided Rosalie toward the door, stating that Margot's medication was wearing off and she could become unruly.

"Pigs' feet; pigs' feet!" screeched Margot, with both arms raised high.

Her screeching set off several other patients, causing a swift exodus of visitors. Rosalie blamed herself for causing the disturbance, hoping none of the visitors would confront her and ask what she did to upset her grandmother. She made her way to the visitor's lounge where Katherine was waiting, and told her the unit was closed to visitors due to a patient's behavior.

"God, we traveled an hour and a half by bus only to have to turn around after thirty minutes and leave! I hope you're satisfied. You saw your grandmother and now do you believe me? She doesn't remember you, no matter how special you thought you were to her," Katherine angrily stated.

"She will always be special to me," Rosalie answered.

"If she were your mother and had done the things to you she did to me, you'd think differently," snapped Katherine.

"Well, now it doesn't matter because she doesn't remember anything," offered Rosalie.

"You shut your wise mouth, young lady, if you know what's good for you," Katherine retorted.

A few months passed, and a call from the state facility suggested the family should come quickly to bid good-bye to a dying Margot. Sean drove Ted and Katherine to the Westborough facility. Just minutes before her death, Katherine claimed Margot sat straight up in the bed looking as though she planned to pounce on them. She looked as wild as an animal with her hair extended straight out a foot from her head, then closed her eyes and fell back on the pillow.

The decision not to hold a wake for Margot seemed reasonable at the time, because she had no friends excepting the faces of locals operating the stores or bank in her former neighborhood, and they probably thought she was already deceased, having not seen her for a few years. At St. John's Cemetery she was reunited with her husband on a spring morning in 1955. The prior generation was gone, leaving the present generation acutely aware of how brief a period it was.

Raymond was unable to attend her expedient burial due to distance and his work schedule. It was a crucial period in national defense, and the project he was involved with centered on the Nautilus submarine. Bernard was able to come from Washington DC, where he worked for the government. Though it was a bittersweet reunion, Bernard's jokes and stories had them laughing so hard, they were crying. It served as a release and renewal of the bond between his sisters and Sean.

The laughter left with Bernard as he slipped on his suit jacket, kissed each female, and walked out the door. Sean drove him to South Station to catch the train back to Lily.

"Wish you would stay longer. You could have visited with Norah and me for a few days; we have an extra bedroom," Sean offered.

"Thanks for the offer, Sean, but I can't leave Lily for too long due to her condition. The doctors say she suffers from depression. The way I leave her in the morning is usually the way I find her when I return at the end of the day. She is either still in bed or sitting in the same chair as when I left! The doctors are trying different medicines to see which works best," Bernard explained.

"Just between you and me, Bernard, we might have been on the front lines during the war, but our wives must have gone through hell living each day to learn if we lived or died. It's taken a different slant with them," answered Sean.

A period of calm followed the loss of Margot. Lenora, Hank, and the twins moved to their own home. This respite allowed Ted and Katherine to do things together as a family for the first time in a long time. They took Patty and Rosalie to the movies, shopped for clothes, and even went to a church picnic the Sacred Heart parish sponsored at the Jesuit Seminary. It was too normal to last.

A call from Sonny's foreman at his place of employment alerted Ted and Katherine that he hadn't shown up to work for over a week. The fellow worker he had been living with over the past ten months had no idea where Sonny had gone or why he left. The only thing to do was to wait. Several months later, on a Saturday in January 1956, they received a call that brought all speculation to a halt.

"Mr. Bryant? This is Lt. Spangler of the East Cambridge Police Department. We have a twenty-six year old man by the name of Theodore Edward Bryant in our custody. He claims you are his father, and if so, would it be possible for you to come here so we may discuss his situation?"

"Lt. Spangler, he is a grown man and no longer under our custody," Ted calmly offered.

"I'd appreciate your presence here before we make any decisions," the officer answered.

"I don't have a car. It will take me awhile to get there," Ted informed the officer.

"We'll be waiting. Just come to the front desk at our precinct and they will direct you to my office. Thank you, Mr. Bryant. Good-bye!"

"I've been expecting this since hearing 'It's Only a Paper Moon' on the radio a few days ago," Ted reflected, as he put the receiver down.

"You and your omens, Ted; what is it this time?" asked Katherine as she poured two cups of coffee.

"Sonny is under arrest for some reason, and they're holding him at the East Cambridge Police Station. They want me there as soon as possible."

Katherine watched as Ted struggled with the decision of what to do next. Jumping up from the kitchen table, she went to use the phone in the front hall.

"I'll call Sean to see if he's available to go with you. He knows how to deal with these situations."

It was a cut-and-dried situation with nothing to deal with. At a saloon he frequented, Sonny had attempted to cut the pockets out of some of the patrons' clothing with a large pair of sharp scissors. He had come to a point of reasoning that if no one had money to loan him, then there was no need for pockets in their clothing.

The saloon's proprietor called the police, who had to restrain an uncontrollable Sonny. This sequence was presented to Ted and Sean, along with an explanation of what would follow.

There was no hope that Sonny would agree to sign himself into the hospital for a psychiatric evaluation as he had done two years prior, following his divorce. This time, he was too far gone from whatever drugs he had consumed in combination with the alcohol. The result pushed him several levels beneath human.

Arriving at the state institution, Ted and Sean watched as six strong-armed attendants removed Sonny from the police wagon, while he screamed and violently attempted to toss his body against his adversaries. Ted signed his son in and observed the attendants pinning Sonny to the ground as a doctor administered a sedative. It seemed to take forever to work as he watched the ragged, unkempt form of his son wrenching from the restraints, as the attendants held him to the floor.

Around eight that evening, Ted returned home and filled Katherine in on what had transpired. She immediately retreated to the bedroom, overcome with sorrow and the swift change from the peace of the past few months. She had no way of knowing how bad things were going to become.

The house had the quiet of a funeral parlor as Patty and Rosalie climbed the stairs to prepare for bed. Their father was waiting for them on the second floor.

"You're brother is very sick, I'm afraid," Ted began, "and should he try to call either of you, pretend it's a wrong number. We'll have to do this for a while until he is cured. I advised the doctors that Sonny is a master of escape and has gotten out of every place he has been locked up in since he was fourteen. Hope they took my warning seriously."

"That is so sad, but maybe this time he'll be cured forever," Patty said.

"How are you feeling about all this?" asked Rosalie.

"Funny you should ask!" responded Ted, attempting to make his response casual. "When I watched Sonny as they dragged him down that long corridor at the hospital, I got the worst pain in the center of my chest, about right here." Ted pointed to the area left of his sternum.

"It's only natural you felt badly. To see something like that happen to your son is awful!" Rosalie stammered, as she reached clumsily to pat her father's arm.

"It wasn't that kind of pain. I never had anything like this before."

"Did you tell Mom?" Rosalie asked.

"She's in no shape to be bothered tonight. I'll mention it later, and don't either of you tell her," Ted ordered.

✦ ✦ ✦ ✦ ✦ ✦ ✦ ✦

Later arrived one morning as Ted arose from bed to prepare for work. He fell on the floor, surprised by the inability of his right leg to support him. Frantically, Katherine helped Ted back into bed and called their family doctor. Teresa and Floyd were in a quandary trying to figure out what to do with four-year-old Vicky should Katherine have to take Ted to the hospital. Usually, she cared for Vicky every Monday and Friday, while the toddler attended Lesley Day Care the other three days.

"I can't take any time off yet. I've only been at this firm three months," argued Floyd. "How about having Patty skip school today to take care of Vicky?"

"She can't miss any more days due to the time missed when she had scarlet fever in the fall. One more day's nursery school fee for Vicky is not going to ruin us. Just give up your cigarettes for a week and your African Swizzles, and that will cover it," answered Teresa.

"You're just upset about your father. I know how it feels. We're arguing and wasting time. Just go to the phone and call Lesley Day Care."

"She's your daughter, too! Why don't you call?" pecked Teresa right back at Floyd. "I've got to do my makeup yet."

Rosalie was in the pantry making her lunch to take to work and listening to the pampered couples' conversation. A surging fear crept up from her toes to the follicles of hair on the top of her head.

"Dad is going to die!" she whispered to herself.

Climbing the stairs, she knocked on her parents' bedroom door, waited for acknowledgment, and entered.

"I'm on my way to work. Before I go, is there anything I can do?" Rosalie asked.

"Like what? Just don't lose your job; I hope you're more alert at work than at home, because around here you act like you don't know your ass from your elbow," replied Katherine.

"I'm fine, Rosalie," Ted answered. You better get going before you're late."

The decision was to keep Ted at home and see if the clot dissolved with medication. After a couple of days, his condition did not improve, and the color of his foot was worrisome to Katherine. The attending doctor arranged for Ted's admission to Mt. Auburn Hospital.

Ted had to inform the Boston and Maine Railroad of his need to go to the hospital, and to ask for an extended leave from work. He nervously dialed the phone and requested Mr. Taggart's office. He explained the need for another week of medical leave but was interrupted by Taggart with an option that floored him.

"Ma, Dad is on his knees crying on the phone," whispered Rosalie.

"Dear Lord!" exclaimed Katherine, rushing into the front hall.

"Retire! You can't mean that! I've got a mortgage and a fourteen-year-old," cried Ted as he knelt on the floor, as though praying into the phone.

"Give me that receiver," ordered Katherine. "To whom am I speaking? Well, Mr. Taggart, are you standing or sitting? Would you please stand. Now, imagine Ted on his knees before you, because he can't stand, Mr. Taggart. The doctor is going to try to dissolve a clot that is interfering with his circulation, and at the moment we're waiting for a cab to take us to Mt. Auburn Hospital. He'll be there the remainder of the week. I'll give you a call later this week. Thank you. Good-bye." Katherine helped Ted to a parlor chair and assisted with putting on his suit jacket, topcoat, and hat.

"Dad, why were you so upset on the phone?" inquired Rosalie.

"Mr. Taggart wants me to retire because of my health. Rosalie, I'm not coming back from the hospital," her father calmly added.

"Don't even think that way, Dad! You're going to be just fine. You'll show that mean-spirited so-and-so at work who's who!" offered Rosalie.

"No, I'm serious, honey. I won't be coming back home," replied Ted.

Rosalie watched as the cab driver and Katherine practically carried her father to the car. She thought of his words and wondered what had gotten into him to talk like that. She recalled her thoughts of a few days ago about his dying, and it jarred her total body. That is what her father meant. *He knows he is going to die!*

A week later, on Holy Saturday, Ted died. Both his legs became gangrenous and amputation was the only alternative. When his heart stopped during the surgery, attempts to revive him found his arteries were equivalent to that of a ninety-year-old man. There was nothing capable of mending. Years of smoking and his sedentary desk job claimed his body. There was evidence of a recent heart attack that had gone unnoticed, the doctors concluded.

The surgeon's anguished face as he reported the results of the operation to Katherine, and her reaction as she bolted toward the operating room, spoke volumes. Katherine never allowed a thought of being without Ted in her mind. He was going to get better and become whole.

"You told me, Dr. Grinski that everything would be all right. Dear God! He's only fifty-eight years old," cried Katherine, as she wrung her hands.

"Katherine, your daughters are watching you. Think of them, now," Sean whispered as he put his arms around her.

Observing these interactions at a distance, Rosalie looked back at Patty, who was attempting to blow a bubble with her gum.

"Stop that! This isn't the time or place to be doing that. I think our father just died." Rosalie calmly told Patty Jean.

"Cut it out, Miss Know-It-All!" responded the younger sister.

About five minutes later, Teresa and Floyd entered in a rapid rush, faster than Rosalie had ever seen them move. Teresa's hands covered her face as she listened to her Uncle Sean. Walking over to the area where her younger sisters were waiting, she sat down, gained her composure, and conveyed the news.

"Here's the house key, Rosalie. Take Patty home on the trolley. Get Vicky from Mrs. Arsenal, and stay inside until we get back," ordered Teresa.

"I'd like to stay here," responded Rosalie.

"You'll be more helpful by doing what I've just told you to do," Teresa stated.

The tears ran over the lower lids no matter how hard Rosalie and Patricia tried to control them as they waited for the Waverly trolley. Once on the crowded trolley, the sisters stared out the windows and dared not look at each other. A group of three men were laughing loudly, totally detached from the sorrow of the two misty passengers. Rosalie restrained the uncontrollable urge to scream at the strangers and tell them her father had just died, for fear she would be locked up like her brother.

Her thoughts toward these men and subsequent reaction drove a sharp blade of reality through Rosalie's brain, forcing her to face the fact she was, to this point in her life, totally centered on her own needs and never considered what another person's burden might be. How could these strangers on the trolley know what had just happened to her father?

Rosalie floated up toward the sky as the floor where she was standing stayed attached to her feet. There was nothing to touch for balance, nothing to hold onto. She was standing on her own two feet, and that was how it would have to be from now on.

Arriving at their stop, the sisters walked toward the house their father was so proud to have owned. It looked barren, colorless, and old. The front door opened and swallowed them into a dark, hollow hole.

In his own dark, hollow hole, Sonny did not learn of his father's death for over three months. When the state hospital psychiatrist felt the time was right, he gave Sonny the three-month-old obituary pages from the *Boston Globe* and told him to read out loud the listings for each city and town. Sonny began with Acton, Amesbury, Andover, Arlington; then Barnstable, Bedford, Belmont! The relapse was not a pretty sight. It is one thing to go through the ceremonial grieving process with your family, and it is quite another to never have had the opportunity to say good-bye to his father, respectfully.

Chapter Twenty-One

The Bryant household experienced a dramatic adjustment in roles and nonstop responsibilities in the week following Ted's death. All aspects of maintaining a livable environment, from emptying the trash to cooking supper, were parceled equally between each occupant. It should have worked, but without encouragement, guidance, and direction from the main adult, the will to persevere fell short. Katherine felt totally alone and overwhelmed by all she now had to face on her own.

Several debts Ted owed to co-workers were made known to Katherine the night of his wake. Hovering in a semicircle around the grieving widow, each whispered a reality unknown to Katherine.

"Not to be bringing up a delicate subject, but Ted owes several of us money. You know, Katherine, he liked to eat, and borrowed lunch money frequently."

"Dear Lord! He took a lunch every day!" exclaimed Katherine.

"He'd eat that at our ten o'clock break. Sometimes he'd buy an apple but generally ate the day's special with us in the cafeteria. It adds up. We have children who need the money, too!" whispered the spokesperson for the four bent, nodding heads.

"You'll have your money. Just drop me a note as to the amount Ted owed each of you. I'll trust your honesty as much as he did your friendship," Katherine offered.

This incident at the funeral parlor was just the first of a few surprises that were to adjust Katherine's view of her future from one of comfort to that of losing her house. Ted had surrendered two of his three insurance policies. In checking the surrender dates, she found one was in 1950 when they purchased the Belmont residence and the other when Teresa and Floyd were married. Katherine had insisted on a new carpet and parlor furniture for the reception at home, and catered food to supplement what she planned on cooking. Locating the savings book, she stared at the one hundred and thirty dollar fortune. This wouldn't even cover what Ted apparently owed his friends for lunches! The pension she would receive was sparse compared to Ted's salary, and they would not qualify for social security except for the allowance of having one child less than eighteen years of age.

"How could you do this to me?" Katherine cried over and over as she wrung her hands. "Why did you leave me now?"

This continued for several weeks. Teresa and Floyd were at odds with each other from the constant insults Katherine would pound her daughter with about Floyd's laziness, and how much she was doing for them by taking care of Vicky. The young couple seemed honorable and resigned to helping Katherine through the stages of her loss, but it was apparent she was not helping herself.

"Rosalie, I want Teresa to look for a flat. We need to get out of here or your mother is going to ruin our marriage," a distraught Floyd explained.

"You need to do what you need to do for yourselves," answered Rosalie.

"Will you talk with Teresa? She feels like she's walking out on you and Patty."

"It's not working the way it is, Floyd. Being here and paying Mom rent, and her caring for Vicky is making it easier for her to postpone the fact she needs to go to work," Rosalie speculated.

Teresa and Floyd found a third-floor flat they could afford on the same street that Sean and Norah lived on. They moved out of Katherine's house under tense circumstances.

Following a memorial Mass for Ted on a Saturday morning, Katherine, Rosalie, and Patty walked back home from Sacred Heart Church, and were a bit let down that no one else in the family attended the service. Katherine was in a strange mood, and by the time they were home, she started a conversation concerning expenses for maintaining the house. Patty made a quick exit for her Saturday job at the local bakery, begging off from the discussion.

240

"Rosalie, now that you're working for the Boston and Maine, I want you to give me your full paycheck. The twenty dollars you give each week is not enough," Katherine complained.

"I pay all my own expenses and need funds for nylons, clothes, and insurance; my four wisdom teeth need to be extracted and will run about one hundred dollars or so! How far do you think the money left over after giving you twenty dollars for rent a week from my paycheck can stretch? There's the money for the subway, night school payments, and you won't let me take a lunch from home, so I buy a cheese sandwich for twenty cents each day," Rosalie explained.

"Don't talk to me in that tone of voice," Katherine said over her shoulder as she stood looking at herself in the round kitchen mirror hanging over the radiator.

"Ma, you have a nursing degree. That's more than I ever hope to have. Why don't you go to work in a doctor's office or a hospital? You're only fifty-four years old."

"I haven't worked as a nurse for twenty-nine years. Oh, Ted! Why did you do this to me? Look how old you made me!" cried Katherine."

"You know, Ma, all these years Dad worried about you having a heart attack, but who died of one," responded Rosalie, with an icy air of disgust over her mother's self-pity.

The round mirror flew across the width of the kitchen toward Rosalie, bouncing off the washing machine, crashing into chunks and slivers at her feet. A dagger of glass knifed the front of her foot, causing blood to propel two feet away onto the white refrigerator.

"Look what you did!" screeched Katherine, "You and your fresh mouth."

Frantic over the blood pouring from Rosalie's foot, Katherine elevated the leg after removing the glass and applied pressure to the deep puncture. Both women were crying.

"It seems we can't even talk to each other. Perhaps I should live somewhere else for a while," Rosalie cautiously proposed.

"My God, you are the most selfish bitch I've ever known," replied Katherine, dropping Rosalie's leg to the floor.

"That's it. I'm leaving before you scar me for life. Your threats that God will mark my face one day, whenever you see me looking in a mirror, make me wonder if you might appoint yourself his messenger.

Your anger makes you capable of it, so I'm not going to stand around waiting for it," raced the words from Rosalie.

"You ungrateful little snot, get out of my sight! I curse the day I had you. I nursed you, gave you life, and this is how you repay me?" screamed Katherine.

Rosalie was out the door with just the clothes on her back, a limp and a ripped pair of nylons. Explaining what happened as Teresa checked her injury they both agreed that allowing Katherine to think someone else was going to bail her out of these circumstances was wrong. She was to be pitied for the tragedy of it all, but unless she helped herself, the future looked bleak. Her days of being a prima donna were over.

"You better plan on staying here a few days, Rosalie. I'll go down and get some of your clothes and your toothbrush. Maybe this will wake Mom up," Teresa said.

A week passed before Katherine called asking for a meeting with Teresa and Rosalie. She wanted to share a letter she received from Ted's sister, Ellen, who proposed a way they all could help each other out for a couple of years. The home Aunt Ellen was renting was being sold. Offering what she was presently paying in rent, and detailing ways she could help out with meals, laundry, and cleaning, Aunt Ellen suggested she move in with Katherine, adding that she needed to be on the first floor, and would be willing to pay for the installation of a toilet.

Katherine had been thinking of installing a first-floor toilet in a small closet off the kitchen and turning the den into a bedroom for Sonny. This way the women would have the upstairs bathroom and he, the downstairs one.

"My God, what possessed her to want to live here? Did any of you write to her?" asked Katherine as she looked suspiciously at Rosalie.

"Let's think about this for a moment," suggested Teresa. "Aunt Ellen could help with your expenses and be an adult in the home for Patty during the hours you will be taking courses to update your nursing license."

"Who said I'm going to work?" Katherine angrily asked.

"You have no choice if you want to keep your house. It needs a new roof; say nothing about your erratic mortgage payments! They're being considerate right now and accept what you send, but eventually the bank is going to pull in the rope," rationalized Teresa.

"I'll take a second mortgage when I need money," Katherine stated.

"Ma, you're making no sense. The monthly payments will be double what you are now paying because interest rates have risen, plus the bank will check to see what your income is, and know you can't make the new payments!" responded Teresa.

"Well, I never thought you would grow to be so hard and talk to me with such disrespect!" Katherine stated.

"It seems to me, Ma, that with all the intelligence you've bragged about with your double promotions and being at the top of your nursing class, you'd be using better sense. No one is going to make all this bad go away! Only you will make the difference in your future, unless you plan to marry some rich man!"

"That's just enough from you, young lady. You'd better stop while you're ahead, because from what you've told me and what I've seen of your husband, you'd better start planning for your old age now!" replied Katherine, as she turned her back and walked away from Teresa.

The tug with Katherine continued, with each daughter growing further away and more protective of their privacy. To share the smallest confidential tidbit with their mother would eventually be used to hurt them.

Once Aunt Ellen became part of the daily tapestry, she wound up in the middle several times but remained optimistic that she could make a difference in the two year's time of her stay. Her positive nature and sunny disposition sickened Katherine, who would make faces and mimic Ellen behind her back.

All Aunt Ellen's optimism disappeared the Saturday evening Sonny stumbled into the house extremely inebriated and full of anger. He had just lost the job his social worker had arranged for him upon his release from the state institution, three months prior. He stood swaggering back and forth in the kitchen as he watched Rosalie ironing her dress.

"Are you still going out with that goddamn Italian?" Sonny asked.

"Yes, if you must know, and his name is Dan," answered Rosalie.

"Well, I don't want you going out with that fucking Italian! Do you hear me?" Sonny ordered, moving closer to Rosalie.

"Sonny, just stop it. You're full of what makes the grass green," Rosalie answered.

What followed seemed to happen in slow-motion, as Sonny punched the refrigerator door, leaving a concave impression. Grabbing the Mary Proctor ironing board away from Rosalie, he bent it in half and threw it against the wall. Rosalie backed into the pantry, still holding the hot iron as Sonny cornered her and proceeded to choke the living breath out of her. A powerful, primeval scream out of Rosalie alerted Katherine, who rushed to the kitchen and wedged herself between Sonny and her daughter.

"Get out of here, Rosalie!" Katherine ordered as she tried to control Sonny.

Aunt Ellen was peeking out of her room, and whispered for Rosalie to go get her Uncle Sean and to phone the police from his home. Katherine was furious when the police arrived but agreed to have Sonny committed when Ellen hysterically told them he had choked Rosalie. The police instructed Katherine to file a restraining order against her son, and to use the attack on Rosalie as the reason. She chose not to follow their recommendation. This incident of Ellen's interference, from Katherine's perspective, was never forgiven.

"You have got to protect yourself and your daughters," Ellen cautioned.

"Aren't you just a bit worried about your own skin?" Katherine sarcastically asked.

"There's great suffering and danger in your future, Katherine. I've seen it in your cards," Ellen warned.

"Look! Maybe your being here is not such a good idea after all. Perhaps the responsibility of being a parent is unfamiliar to you, not having raised children of your own. Once a parent, always a parent, and it never ends until your last breath," said Katherine.

"Your complacency is not what Sonny needs. He is disturbed, and acts like two different people. When he's sober, there's no one sweeter; when he drinks, Mr. Hyde appears. For God's sake, Katherine, relinquish his care to trained professionals. Don't cover for him."

"I'll say it again to you, Ellen, if it is too uncomfortable for you, I'm sorry, but Sonny will always be welcomed here," responded Katherine, confident Sonny would one day make a miraculous turnaround.

"Following Rosalie's wedding, I'm moving back to Schenectady. She's the one reason I've stayed. That's all I'm going to say," Ellen concluded as she walked to her room and closed the door.

"Is that your plan?" yelled Katherine, "then let me tell you mine! If I have anything to say about it as Rosalie's mother, there won't be any wedding. I can't afford it, and I won't be humiliated by those immigrants planning an Italian wedding. So, if that's what you're hanging around for, you can leave now!"

In June of 1958, a week after Rosalie and Dan returned from their honeymoon, Aunt Ellen moved back to Schenectady. Three years later, Dan accepted a position near Washington DC. Rosalie welcomed the prospects of moving with her two-year-old and five-month-old baby, and being out from under the critical eye of her mother.

The following seven years were productive for Katherine, as she gained experience and professional respect through nursing positions at Cambridge City Hospital, Arlington Nursing Home, and McLean Hospital. Lucky for Katherine, it is never too late to grow up or to learn how to get along with others. Tantrums and sharp words or the throwing of objects are definite ways to be shown the exit door at a place of employment. Katherine couldn't risk losing her job, and was finally out from under the cloud of debt left following Ted's death. Her skills and intellect received recognition, thus reducing her insecurities.

In all public aspects of her life, Katherine was professional and secure. She began to reach out in ways that contrasted with her former personality by joining her co-workers in social activities outside of work.

Her personal life was still a partner to the familiarity of past contempt, and angry words quickly surfaced whenever Katherine felt left out of Teresa's and Vicky's closeness. They had moved in with Katherine following Teresa's divorce from Floyd, and Patty's decision to take a job out of the state. Teresa and Vicky endured Katherine's cutting remarks, given she was generous to a fault in paying for evenings out to dinner, and a play or movie. The residual feeling of companionship calmed

Katherine until the feelings of being left out or ignored threatened again, and her irrational jealousy superseded logical reasoning.

✦ ✦ ✦ ✦ ✦ ✦ ✦ ✦

As Aunt Ellen had predicted several years prior, Sonny grew more desperate and demonstrative. He could lose the shirt off his back and the shoes off his feet, but he always held onto the Belmont house key. Never knowing when he might arrive and what condition he might be in, Teresa convinced Katherine to change the locks on the doors. Sonny found this unacceptable when, one Saturday night after hours of drinking and gambling in a nearby neighborhood, he headed for his mother's house, but his key didn't work.

"You open up this fucking door or I'll break the goddamn window! You hear me, you fucking whore? If you know what's good for you, you'll open this door now, you fucking bitch!" boomed Sonny's voice in the still of the night.

Katherine, who awakened to Sonny's pounding on the door, called from her second floor window as she grabbed her robe.

"Sonny, stop your noise! It's two in the morning. Just wait a minute and I'll open the door, but stop yelling!"

Opening the door culminated in a horrific beating for Katherine. Sonny punched her several times in the face, throwing her full force against the front hall's radiator. Teresa was awakened by her mother's screams and dialed the police before attempting to intervene. The police were there in record time. Recovering from her bruises and swollen face used up Katherine's vacation and sick days for that whole year.

This time, Katherine's lawyer arranged for a restraining order against Sonny, which forbade him to come within a mile of her. To eliminate all contact, the courts appointed a legal guardian to oversee Sonny's affairs and military benefits. Katherine had fought hard to obtain disability benefits for her son years earlier based on his military records, and succeeded with the help of Senator Jack Kennedy.

Sonny was committed for observation, following his court hearing. Shortly after, he required surgery to remove part of his right lung due to tuberculosis. His drinking resulted in a bad case of ulcers. He was an accident waiting to happen; instead the accident happened to Katherine.

Crossing Belmont Street around dusk on a cold, overcast February night, Katherine was struck by a car. At thirty miles an hour, it threw her up in the air, bringing her down in a position described as 'spread eagle'. Observers said she was the one instructing the overzealous Samaritans who rushed to her aid to call an ambulance, not to move her, and keep her body warm with coats or blankets. A neighbor rushed to alert Teresa of her mother's accident.

The following day, after a tense waiting period to determine the extent of Katherine's injuries, Teresa notified McLean Hospital that her mother would not be reporting for work on Monday. The staff was shocked to learn of her accident, and further shocked to learn she was sixty-eight years old and had been working forty hours a week!

The magnitude of her injuries spoke of the painful future. Her pelvis was fractured; her right femur bone was smashed, requiring an artificial hip socket and a rod in the upper thigh; the skull fracture caused her head to swell to almost double in size; various other bones were fractured or broken, such as ribs and fragile bones in her legs and feet. The accident hadn't killed her, but fear of complications was a major concern. The care she received in the emergency room of Mt. Auburn Hospital under the guidance of the attending physician in charge that night brought her back to life.

All of the responsibilities that went with having to care for Katherine began to grate on Teresa and Vicky. They took advantage of Katherine's absence from her home during recovery and rehabilitation, and proceeded to clean out the house, attic, and basement of all the hoarded memories and worthless items they deemed wouldn't be missed. The fact that these items were not theirs to discard didn't matter. Their goal was to use the time to prepare for the possibility that Katherine may not recover from her injuries, so that Aunt Aileen would have a comfortable transition when moving into the house with them. Had Katherine known their plan, she would have exclaimed that it would only have occurred over her dead body, given the bad blood between her and her sister.

Upon returning home, Katherine needed a special bed on the first floor, and would require the aid of a visiting nurse and a physical therapist to assist her recovery. Teresa hadn't counted on strangers entering the picture. She could keep Rosalie at bay by saying that Mother needs her rest but couldn't prevent the prescribed caretakers the doctor assigned for Katherine's rehabilitation.

Slowly, Katherine progressed from sitting, to standing, to walking with a walker, to climbing steps with a cane. Patty kept in touch by phone from her new job in Illinois, begging off from visiting until her scheduled vacation time.

Teresa learned from Patty during one of their phone conversations that she had been sexually attacked and robbed in her own apartment. Her longtime relationship with a married professor went sour. The apartment they shared for their secret life became her expense alone when the wayward husband returned to his wife and family. Her name was on the lease, but her salary was no match for the rent. Attempts to reconcile with her rejecter became ugly.

Being at an emotional low, Patty's guard was down when she found her door ajar upon returning from work one evening. Her spirits lifted thinking it was her soul mate returning to apologize. Upon entering the apartment, she was sexually attacked, beaten, and robbed by a masked man. Katherine sent Patty the money to leave debt-free and return home. She looked forward to the help Patty would provide by paying rent as well as having her companionship.

Physically limited and living within the restraints of her retirement funds, Katherine began to observe a gradual increase in ways she was excluded from Teresa's and Patty's lives. They were only in the house to eat, sleep, and do their laundry. She no longer was the golden goose but a lame duck.

When Katherine's physical strength was building and she was able to walk with a cane, her mettle was tested by the death of her son in July of 1971. He died alone in a rented room, in Western Massachusetts. He had been missing from the state hospital for a couple of weeks, and the police were familiar with his habit of getting out of locked facilities and eventually winding up in trouble. Sonny had made his way to Belmont a week before his death, and had an African violet plant delivered to Katherine from a florist, well within the court-ordered mile restraint. He signed the card, "Your loving son, Sonny." Katherine did not notify the hospital about receiving the plant.

After Sonny's burial, Teresa, Patty, and Rosalie went to the police station in the town where their brother's body was found, to claim his belongings. The contents of two brown paper bags contained Sonny's polished cowboy boots, a hairbrush, a diary written in French, the old keys to Katherine's home, and a papier-mâché doll. Stopping at a Howard Johnson's along the Mass Pike on the return trip, Teresa threw all of Sonny's items in a public trash barrel.

"It is better that mother not see this junk. It will only upset her more. Her depression medicine doesn't seem to be helping. Some days her confusion is scary! You know, Rosalie, you're not realistic about what she can stand, especially when you visit with the four children," said Teresa in a controlling tone of voice.

"What are you saying, Teresa? I thought visiting with the children was good for her," replied Rosalie.

"Well, it's not. In fact it's work for her and tires her out. It makes her feel bad she is so limited," Teresa conveyed.

"We don't visit but once a month, and I always call and ask, first! We always bring pastry or cookies and clean up before leaving," Rosalie said defensively.

"It's just that when you decide to visit is not always the best for the rest of us," Teresa stated.

"Sure! If I waited for a call from you with an invitation, it never would happen. I never need an invitation to my mother-in-law's home! She loves the children to visit. That's what family should be like," Rosalie stated.

The rest of the ride on the Mass Pike was long for Rosalie, conjuring up old memories of Teresa locking her as a four-year-old in the front hall closet, and how long she cried, begging to get out. Now again, Teresa was trying to lock her out of Katherine's life, but for what reason?

Throughout the remainder of the nineteen seventies, visits with Katherine were at Rosalie's and Dan's home for the children's birthdays, Holy Communions, graduations, and holidays. Teresa would beg off from coming for the holidays, and try as she may, Rosalie could not find a way to bridge the gap her older sister seemed to prefer between them. Meanwhile, Patty married, and she and her husband found the drive to Rosalie's home too far to come due to the cost of gas and wear on their aging vehicle.

Determined not to let it get to her, Rosalie continued doing what she perceived as respectful. She would always invite Patty, Teresa, and Vicky to each celebration or holiday. Weekly calls to Katherine were brief, yet kept the door of communication flowing between times Rosalie was allowed to visit, or Katherine was picked up for a visit with her grandchildren.

One summer day in 1979, Katherine phoned Rosalie and asked her down for lunch. She had made egg salad and had all the dishes ready, with a pot of tea waiting for the hot water.

"I'm so glad you could come, because I have a favor to ask. Could you help me balance my checkbook? Teresa keeps putting it off, and I know the mistakes are my fault. I would have asked you sooner, but I didn't want to bother you during the school year," explained Katherine.

As mother and daughter sat to eat their lunch, Katherine spoke about what was going on in her house. It became apparent she was being taken advantage of, and it seemed to border on mental abuse.

"I've surprised a few people by living through all of this, and now I'm an inconvenience." Katherine said.

"You're a living miracle from where I stand," answered Rosalie. "Believe me; I wouldn't have lived through that accident!"

"They're downright mean to me, and won't talk to me. They talk to each other as if I'm not present! I'm all right for paying the bills, but not all right to talk to in a civil tongue," offered Katherine.

"Wait a minute, here! Teresa pays you rent, doesn't she? You don't have to answer if you don't want to," Rosalie quickly added, fearing she had overstepped.

"Not a cent! I pay all the expenses. She buys the groceries but not things I'd like, not ever. I gave her the money for the new car after her complaining how she wore out the old one taking me here and there for doctor's appointments. Teresa has also asked me three times for money to help pay Vicky's college tuition," added Katherine.

"Ma, you told me once about a lawyer you liked. He prepared your will, correct? Do me a favor and call him. Tell him what you just told me and let me know how I may help," suggested Rosalie.

Within the week, Rosalie was contacted by her mother's lawyer, who instructed her on calling a family meeting, along with the points to be covered. She was to report back to him periodically with the progress being made. This role that Rosalie was assigned reduced further any feelings left between the sisters.

The meeting was arranged on a Saturday morning at ten. Sitting around the kitchen table as Katherine sat off to the side, Rosalie presented the reason for their coming together due to the financial strains their mother was faced with, and to review suggestions put forth by her lawyer.

"I hope you're not intending to ask me to contribute something toward Mother's needs each month? My husband and I can just about make ends meet ourselves, with our mortgage payments and the repairs the house needs. I just about made it here this morning with that car of ours," Patty stated.

"This is a family meeting, and your presence is needed here to help sort out the present situation," Rosalie answered.

"Let me say one thing to you, Rosalie. You have no idea what it's like living here!" Teresa interjected.

"Leave! Get your own apartment!" suggested Rosalie.

"She'd be alone!" replied Teresa.

"Alone? She's already alone, and paying dearly with the heat, electricity, water, and taxes. She is enduring all of these expenses to keep a roof over your heads," answered Rosalie. "Mom could live comfortably in an apartment for a lot less than what she is spending to keep this house going. So, what do you feel you can afford to pay? I need to let the lawyer know," asked Rosalie.

"I have to pay for Vicky's college debt and now she is going for her law degree," Teresa responded.

"It seems Vicky is doing this at other people's expense. Perhaps she should get a job and continue her education at night school. Lots of people do it that way, and some even are reimbursed by the company they work for. You're only responsible for her education up to eighteen years of age. Beyond that only if you have the financial means.

From what Mom has told me, she has helped with Vicky's tuition a few times already. One recommendation by Mom's lawyer is that you pay a monthly rent, which would offset the cost of the taxes," Rosalie offered.

Watching the looks going back and forth between Teresa and Katherine, the reality came to Rosalie. Katherine was enduring all this because she must have willed the house to Teresa. That's what her mother meant when stating she had surprised them all by living so long. Teresa agreed to pay the recommended rent.

History repeats itself, it seems. Just as Margot had sought to assure her care in her final years by loaning Katherine money for the Elm Street home, Katherine was counting on Teresa to care for her, with the promise of the house when she died.

Three years passed and Vicky left for Europe, as an officer in the U. S. Army, with a large student loan in tow. Teresa felt like a ship without a rudder, and could not believe her daughter's choice. Left with only her work and Katherine, she spent as little time as possible in the house, preferring the company of her Aunt Aileen who lived a short distance from Teresa's place of employment at the university.

✦ ✦ ✦ ✦ ✦ ✦ ✦ ✦

Aileen was diagnosed with cancer during the spring of 1980, and underwent treatment at the Dana Farber Center. Teresa drove Aunt Aileen several times, and saw firsthand various degrees and stages of the disease. She never told Katherine of Aileen's illness, but wrote Vicky, relating all the physical changes their aunt was enduring. It tore at Teresa's heart to watch the suffering of a woman she cherished like a mother.

The response from Vicky included not only concern for her aunt, but a surprise for her mother with news of her impending marriage in Germany the coming August. After her daughter's marriage, Teresa sent out announcements. She never said anything about not being present at the marriage of her only child, or if she knew the groom.

In an unusual visit to Rosalie's house on a Saturday afternoon in November, Teresa explained she was just out driving and found herself nearby and decided to take a chance someone was home. Her left hand was bandaged. Teresa explained how she got a piece of steel wool stuck in her thumb while cleaning the oven. When it wouldn't heal, she went to the doctor. She was vague about what it was when questioned by Rosalie. Finally, Teresa called it osteomyelitis and said that there was the possibility she may lose the tip of her thumb.

Attempting to stay just as calm as Teresa appeared, Rosalie asked if Vicky knew about the infection. Changing the subject, Teresa brought up the news of airline tickets Vicky sent her for the upcoming Christmas holiday season in Germany.

The swing in topics clued Rosalie in to understanding Teresa didn't want to talk about the thumb.

"I'm not going, and will return the tickets because mother can't be left alone for two weeks," replied Teresa.

"You'll do nothing of the sort! Mom can stay with us during the time you're away, and we won't have it any other way," answered Rosalie.

Upon her return from the two weeks in Germany, Teresa never talked about Vicky, her son-in law, or the total experience of traveling for the first time in her life to Europe.

✦ ✦ ✦ ✦ ✦ ✦ ✦ ✦

The last weekend in January, Teresa said her doctor arranged for her to stay at the Mt. Auburn Hospital in order to take antibiotics intravenously around the clock, in a last effort to curtail the infection. Rosalie wasn't buying it. There was more to this! The infection had been going on for over three and a half months! While visiting Teresa in the hospital on the Saturday evening of her hospital stay, Rosalie ventured into her sister's forbidden privacy.

"Teresa, I'd like your permission to call your doctor and ask him just what the prognosis may be. After all, he needs to know there are people who care about you," Rosalie cautiously stated.

"If you must," Teresa answered, avoiding eye contact by busying herself with some work she brought from her office.

Upon returning home following the visit with Teresa, Rosalie left a phone message on the attending doctor's answering machine. Within forty minutes Dr. Stromberg called.

253

"Thank you, thank you so much for calling. I'm so relieved she wants you to know. Your sister has been driving me crazy. I wanted to call her mother, but she wouldn't let me. I wanted to notify her daughter, but she wouldn't hear of it. She agreed to have you as the person to notify when I spoke with her a few minutes ago," responded the doctor.

"Doctor, does Teresa have cancer?" asked Rosalie.

"Yes. At first we thought it was just an infection in her thumb, but we did a biopsy. She needs to agree to treatment; radiation or chemotherapy. With treatment, she should live well into her sixties. But she keeps procrastinating, and there is no time to waste," answered Dr. Stromberg.

"I'll talk with her, doctor. This is a big step for Teresa to let me get this close. I need to let her set the pace or she'll shut me out," Rosalie responded.

Hanging up the phone, Rosalie fought hard to keep from crying. Dan was filled with questions about her conversation with the doctor.

The phone rang; Rosalie answered.

"Hello!"

"Well, I can tell you one thing. No chemotherapy! I'll have the radiation treatments," spoke a garbled, choking voice.

"Teresa! Is that you?" Rosalie asked, as the dial tone sounded.

Two months passed as Teresa made good on her promise to see the radiation treatment through to completion. She still had not told her mother anything. Perhaps Katherine suspected there was more than an infected thumb to be concerned about. When she offered to help Teresa with the bandages, Teresa screamed, "don't come in the kitchen; stay out; stay out," knowing if her mother saw the condition of the thumb, the whole story would be known.

Stopping by after classes at Tufts University on Tuesday evening, March 31, Rosalie was surprised when Teresa began to talk about how her new medication was upsetting her stomach, and her concern about her weight loss.

"When you go for your next checkup this Thursday, tell Dr. Stromberg. You need to eat, and perhaps he could reduce the dosage or change the medicines. Everyone reacts differently to prescriptions. I'll call you Friday to see how you made out, all right?" Rosalie begged.

Friday came, but Teresa couldn't come to the phone because she was bathing her hand. Saturday, Katherine relayed the message that Teresa said she would call later. Sunday morning, April 5, Rosalie tried again before leaving for a relative's fortieth wedding anniversary celebration, but Katherine said Teresa was still in bed after a sleepless night.

Returning from the anniversary party, Dan drove to Belmont to work on his mother's income taxes. Rosalie stayed home in order to prepare her lesson plans for the coming school week. The phone rang, and she expected to hear Teresa's voice.

"Hello! Mom, is that you?" Rosalie said, trying to make out the whispering voice at the other end.

"I can't let Teresa know I'm calling you. That's why I'm whispering. She's breathing funny and looks awful! I asked her to call the doctor and she told me to shut my mouth!" explained Katherine.

"Where is she?" asked Rosalie.

"She's in the den watching television, but I'm scared to be here with her like that," answered Katherine.

"I'll call her doctor and tell him what you told me. Listen, Dan is down the street at his mother's. Would you like him to come up to your house?" asked Rosalie.

"Please!" Katherine pleaded.

Dialing the doctor, Rosalie envisioned no response, or maybe an answering service being a Sunday evening, but surprisingly a voice answered.

"Dr. Stromberg, this is Rosalie, Teresa's sister. My mom just called and said Teresa is breathing funny and looks awful!"

"Did Teresa tell you we found another lump in the upper part of her arm? Just when she agreed to have the thumb removed, this happened. We changed her treatment, and it may be a reaction. I'll send an ambulance and will check her at the Mt. Auburn emergency room. See you in an hour," directed the doctor.

Hanging up the phone, Rosalie waited a few minutes to allow for the doctor to request the ambulance before calling her mother's house.

"Hi, Mom; is Dan there yet? Good! May I speak with him?"

"Hello, Rosalie? Jesus! Teresa looks bad, and her breathing sounds like an asthma attack. She wants to wear her new robe to the hospital, but I'm having a hell of a time getting it over that bandage on her hand. The doctor called and told Teresa he wanted to see her and that an ambulance would take her to the Mt. Auburn Hospital. God! They're here already!" exclaimed Dan.

"Dan, I'll get there as fast as I can and will meet you at the emergency room," concluded Rosalie.

✦ ✦ ✦ ✦ ✦ ✦ ✦ ✦

Arriving at the hospital, Rosalie was surprised to find Norah and Sean in the waiting room with Dan.

"Your mother's neighbor called us when she saw the ambulance, thinking something happened to Katherine. This is a hell of a surprise," offered Uncle Sean.

Sean reached for Rosalie and gave her a hug. The stunned looks on her aunt's and uncle's faces begged for some rationale. She quickly condensed the past few months about Teresa's secret, but was abruptly interrupted by an ashen-faced intern.

"May I speak with Teresa's next of kin?" the intern asked.

Rosalie stood, and the intern gestured for her to follow him. He went to a small office and motioned for Rosalie to enter as he closed the door behind her. Standing face-to-face, he stared at her.

"Tell me about your sister's thumb," he ordered.

Not knowing what this doctor wanted to know or which parts were most important, Rosalie started with the beginning and raced through to the present, and added that she learned just an hour ago from her sister's doctor that the cancer was also in the upper part of Teresa's arm.

"Well, she expired," replied the doctor as he stood riveted, awaiting some sort of physical rage.

"She what?" responded Rosalie trying to decipher the word "expired."

"She's dead, and I can hardly wait to talk with this Dr. Stromberg! Why the hell wasn't he here? Why didn't he arrange for the ambulance to wait until he was here?" spewed forth the intern's words.

"I'm sure you did all you could. May I please see my sister?" asked Rosalie.

"No, I'd rather you didn't. We had to open her in several places, and now an autopsy will be done to determine the cause of death," the intern stated.

Walking back to the waiting room, Rosalie thought perhaps she misunderstood the intern's words, but recalling "autopsy" clarified any doubt.

"What did he have to say?" asked Dan.

"Teresa died! She is only fifty-one; first my brother and now my sister!"

"What? It has only been a half hour since she was brought in!" Sean exclaimed, jumping to his feet.

"I need to tell her daughter! I recall my professor at Tufts saying that the Red Cross is the contact to make in emergency situations such as this. If anyone can get Vicky and her husband home from Germany in record time, it's the Red Cross."

Fumbling through her purse for change and talking to herself, Rosalie began to shake from her ankles to her fingers. Her eyes couldn't focus on the numbers and her jaw kept vibrating.

"You need to call Katherine, first," suggested Sean.

"Mom shouldn't hear this over a phone. I'll have to tell her face-to-face and explain it all. Let me call the Red Cross, because they'll need all the time they can to arrange for Vicky to get here. I've got her rank and location info. Then, after I tell Mom, I'll call Vicky when it's nearer to morning and tell her I've contacted the Red Cross."

After making contact with Vicky, Rosalie arranged Teresa's wake, and notified the family and her sister's estranged husband through his relatives.

✦ ✦ ✦ ✦ ✦ ✦ ✦

Vicky and her husband arrived safely but with heavy hearts given the events of the last time they saw Teresa. They had sent her airline tickets for the Christmas holidays, following their wedding. She didn't want to go, but Rosalie insisted that it would be wonderful to go to Europe for the first time in her life. This was the perfect reason for going to Europe; to spend Christmas with her daughter and new son-in-law in Germany. Teresa tried to use Katherine as the reason for not going, but Rosalie removed the barrier by saying their mother would stay with Dan and her for the two weeks.

Teresa had a miserable time, staying in her guest bedroom even when her daughter held a special Christmas party in her honor. In retrospect, it was all too much to handle emotionally, given Teresa must have known more was wrong with her body than even the doctors knew.

When Vicky said good-bye to her mother for the return trip to the States, they were barely speaking. She was so disappointed in her mother's unexplained behavior. Vicky wanted to show her off to all her friends but instead was met with rejection from a person she no longer seemed to know. Now, the mystery was solved but all the reasons were dead.

Cleaning out Teresa's belongings, Vicky sought through every drawer and book hoping to find a note or letter of explanation. What she did come upon turned her stomach. Several silk scarves Vicky had sent her mother to match various outfits were rolled up in a plastic bag encrusted with something which must have resulted from Teresa being sick to her stomach following treatments. Why hadn't her mother told her the truth? Why had she shut her out? Most painful of all was the implied possibility that Teresa had decided her own end by overdosing. That idea would haunt Vicky.

On the day of Teresa's wake, Aunt Aileen arranged an early viewing to avoid seeing her family and relations. Her physical condition was dramatically shocking to those who had not seen her in the past eighteen months, but her love for Teresa demanded that she pay her last respects.

Three months later, Aunt Aileen died. Her children did not notify the family of her death, but an ardent reader of the daily obituaries noticed the names of Sean and Norah Lockhart listed in Aileen's death notice. Working in the same office as Norah, the co-worker offered her sympathies first thing upon arriving at work.

Norah was frantic, and knew neither she nor Sean could leave work to be present at the scheduled 10 AM burial. Knowing Rosalie was at home during the summer, she called with the news and time of the burial. Rosalie phoned Katherine and arranged to pick her up on the way to the Cambridge Cemetery, filling her in on the details.

Having called the cemetery for directions to the site of Aileen's burial, Rosalie explained to the caretaker that her mother, Aileen's older sister, had not been notified of the burial due to hard feelings between the sisters. The caretaker was well-versed in the absurd behavior of families and graciously met Rosalie at the entrance, guiding her to the burial site. Rosalie parked her car at a respectful distance, and she and Katherine sat in silence.

As the grieving family arrived, an undertaker began to walk toward Rosalie's car. Rosalie got out of the car and offered to leave so as not to upset her cousins. The undertaker had come with a request from her cousins for Rosalie to attend the burial but not her mother. Rosalie explained that her mother couldn't walk over such terrain to get there, and chose to tell Katherine she could represent them both at the burial ceremony. Katherine told Rosalie to go and extend her sympathy.

✦ ✦ ✦ ✦ ✦ ✦ ✦

Katherine attempted to tend to the ten-room house all on her own, with help from Sean, Dan, and Rosalie, but a series of strokes brought it all to a quick end when she didn't answer the phone, according to the daily prearranged schedule. Katherine had suffered a stroke and couldn't get herself off the floor to use the phone. Her physician, Dr. Grinski, ruled Katherine could not live on her own and required around-the-clock monitoring. She lived with Rosalie, Dan, and their four teenagers during the search for an assisted-living arrangement.

"Patty, it's so sad to see all those lonely people just sitting there waiting to die!" Rosalie said of her visits to several senior facilities.

"Whatever you decide is fine. I just can't stand the woman, so don't expect me to visit her every week!" replied Patty.

The first assisted-living arrangement for Katherine worked out well for over eight years. It was near her former neighborhood, and friends visited her. She shared many hours talking with the one person in the whole place she liked. When her friend died, part of Katherine died, and she began to take little falls which resulted in trips to the emergency room at Mt. Auburn Hospital.

On her third fall, a very sharp female intern determined by examining her pupils, that Katherine was drugged out of her mind, Seems she was overdosing on her medication, which she was allowed to self-administer being a former nurse. This privilege was taken away. Rosalie was not one of Katherine's favorite people for a few weeks.

"How did my mother get her hands on so much medication?" Rosalie inquired of her mother's physician.

"Oh, you know Mother! She's been a pill-popper from way back," was his answer.

Rosalie was shocked at his cold response, and his explanation that the elderly tend to overmedicate themselves, wishing for death, made Rosalie want to punch the doctor's lights out! She couldn't help feeling he was tired of her mother, having cared for her since the death of Ted, thirty-five years ago.

A series of mini strokes paralyzed Katherine's ability to swallow rough, textured foods. She hid this from everyone, until Rosalie was straightening up Katherine's clothes and removing some stained items to take home to wash. She found a piece or two of bacon wrapped in a napkin. Upon further searching, Rosalie found similar napkins in other pants pockets, and looking in the top dresser drawer, uncovered a collection of rolled up napkins with crushed cookies and decayed pieces of bread. Shocked by her discovery and realizing the loss of weight her mother had recently undergone was not from the aging process, but rather starvation, Rosalie braced herself for the truth.

"Ma, how long have you been having difficulty swallowing food?" Rosalie asked.

In a voice which had faded to a loud whisper, Katherine reluctantly confessed that it had been over a few weeks. She shrugged her shoulders when Rosalie explained the terrible death she would endure through starvation. Katherine stated it was time, and she didn't care.

"Well, I'm sorry, but you can't decide to starve to death. Besides, it's supposed to be God's decision as to when; not yours," Rosalie responded.

A feeding tube was recommended, followed by Katherine's directions to not use any method of resuscitation should she experience a stroke or heart attack. A copy of this wish was sent to each relative, her doctor, and lawyer.

Release from the hospital required Katherine to be placed in a nursing home. The feeding tube was one level of trauma; an appropriate nursing home was another.

After two tries, and observed roaches which led one to wonder what could not be seen, Katherine requested a Catholic nursing home. It was a fortunate match, and gave Katherine definite comfort to know a priest would be notified when her final hour arrived.

Katherine was able to go out without the feeding tube for up to three hours, but her growing lack of mobility limited where she could go. No one but Rosalie and Dan would take on this responsibility, because Katherine was unable to support her own weight, let alone balance herself when rising from or getting into a wheelchair.

Never was it so apparent that good intentions are not enough than when Katherine needed to use the toilet at Rosalie's home, and she and the hopper met but not soon enough.

"That's all right. We can take care of this. Are you all right, Mom? Now, I've got to lift you off of here to clean you up," Rosalie explained.

"Dear God! Oh! Oh!" Katherine cried.

"Am I hurting you?" asked Rosalie.

"I can't move myself. My knees won't lift me," cried Katherine.

"You're just afraid of falling, and I don't blame you. Just hold on to both my arms as I brace myself against this wall. When I pull up, come toward me," Rosalie instructed.

Working together, mother and daughter emerged from the bathroom with most of the three-hour visit time spent. Rosalie knew this would be the last time her mother would be a visitor in her home. The risk of injury was a reality too great to take.

Over the next couple of years, Katherine gradually spent more time on the custom lounge chair than in the wheelchair, and then more time in bed than on the lounge chair. She no longer had the desire to attend Mass in the chapel. Visitors were the same faces: Sean, Norah, Rosalie, Dan, and occasionally one of the grandchildren.

A couple of days before New Year's, Rosalie waited outside Katherine's room while the aides changed the bedding. They didn't converse with Katherine except to inform her when they were going to turn or lift her, and then continued their chatter in their native tongue.

"Hi, Mom; you look wide awake today. Say, these Christmas roses still look pretty good! The yellow is like sunshine, don't you think?"

"Ted!" Katherine whispered, pointing toward the foot of her bed.

"Ted? Ted who?" asked Rosalie, moving closer to hear her mother.

"Your father was here!" Katherine whispered with all her strength.

"I don't think so," a puzzled daughter responded, watching her mother nodding her head up and down.

"He was here!" Katherine whispered emphatically, as her eyes filled with tears.

"What did he say?" asked Rosalie, not believing she was asking the question.

"..time...let go, now. He...waiting f...me!" sobbed Katherine, turning her face away.

"You may have been dozing and thought Dad was here, but then, maybe he was here to let you know he still loves you. Mom, that's just beautiful! Don't be sad," Rosalie said, trying to hold the tears back.

Katherine reached for Rosalie's hand, raised it to her mouth, and pressed it against her lips. She understood what Rosalie was implying, and the look of peace and love that radiated from Katherine's eyes touched Rosalie's heart.

On January 21, the head nurse called to tell Rosalie the time was close at hand for Katherine. Stopping by after work, Rosalie found a well-intentioned nun standing next to her mother's bed, praying out loud.

"Sweet Jesus, forgive Katherine for all the wrong she has done throughout her life. Look with pity on this weak human who implores thy tender forgiveness as she prepares to meet her Savior. Have pity on this sinner who begs for your forgiveness…"

Rosalie had to interrupt. She didn't know how long the praying might go on, or how long it had already been going on, but the look in her mother's eyes conveyed the feeling that enough was enough!

"Sister, Sister, I think Jesus knows that Katherine is prepared to meet him, and whatever she may have done throughout her life to displease God, she has paid dearly for it. Dear Lord, look at her paralyzed body!" Rosalie implored.

As Rosalie glanced back to her mother, Katherine raised her eyes as though looking up to heaven, and a faint smile seemed to shout, "Alleluia!" Rosalie knew for the first time in her life, she and her mother were of the same mind at the same moment.

After the visiting nun left them alone, Rosalie told her mother of the death of Dan's mother on January 16, the same day as Desert Storm. Katherine reached for her daughter's hand and held it firmly, conveying her sympathy through her eyes.

"Yes, she was a lovely person and was very good to me. Dan and I will miss her dearly."

On January 31, Rosalie received an emergency call from her Mom's nursing home while at work. Katherine had died approximately thirty minutes prior. Released from work, Dan picked Rosalie up and sped to the nursing home in Waltham. Upon entering Katherine's room, Dan walked to the bed and kissed Katherine good-bye.

"Don't you want to kiss your mother good-bye, Rosalie?" asked Dan.

"My mother is not here. I didn't get here quick enough."

"She's right there in the bed!" exclaimed Dan.

"No, she's not. Her soul is gone," Rosalie lamented.

Epilogue

Little falls occur in everyone's lives, but what is learned from those falls, and what one does with that knowledge, is the pivotal factor. A person can choose to wallow in self-pity, twisting the facts to fit their comfort zone or own their part of it, and then move on, striving to be a better and wiser human being. Sometimes one experience is enough to make the right impression for the need to change; other times it takes a lifetime to turn it around, if one lives long enough.

The accomplishments within Katherine Lockhart Bryant's life story warrant recognition amongst the din and heartbreak of her journey. She was always there to support or bail a needy family member out of dire situations, giving of herself almost to the point of losing her own security and home. Her former support and generosity was easily forgotten and replaced with enhanced jealousy and envy as Katherine successfully resumed her nursing career after a twenty-nine year hiatus. She earned respect and recognition for her nursing abilities and proficient skills. The debts left by the untimely death of her husband were paid in full, and she held on to her home. The majority of Katherine's family rejoiced in her strength and resolve but a few individuals festered with the hurts they kept alive in their mind, versus using that energy to forgive, improve and move on.

During the last ten years of Katherine Lockhart's life, she traveled full circle in recalling memories from the innocence of a helpless Christmas infant born in the back room of a tavern, to the final crescent of her life as a helpless soul dependent on the love and care of her remaining family. This period of sharing was beneficial for both Katherine and her daughter, Rosalie; one purged her soul of shame and guilt; the younger listened with compassion and understanding of why her mother was as she was.

Patience and trust were the prime elements needed as Katherine reiterated familiar incidents Rosalie remembered hearing about or witnessed herself. The difference was the depth of each experience which Katherine never shared before. She needed to tell her side of what happened, with the hope Rosalie would forgive the physical and emotional transgressions Katherine had inflicted upon her as a child. Rosalie was indebted to Katherine not just as her birth mother but for saving her from an early death of strangulation from Sonny's hands. Katherine didn't hesitate in stepping in to save Rosalie from damage.

Hidden among Katherine's revelations of rape, incest, humiliation, bouts of depression, and physical and emotional abuse by her mother, was another secret that went unexplained when claiming she had five children. Rosalie listened to Katherine's words but didn't question them until a week later. Worried that Katherine might be mentally slipping Rosalie casually referred back to Katherine's words about having five children, explaining she only knew of her three siblings and herself. Rosalie asked if she knew the fifth child? With a restrained nod, Katherine acknowledged in the affirmative. Pieces of the puzzle fell into place answering why Katherine insisted on Sean, as her eldest son, being the one to escort Rosalie to the altar on her wedding day. The truth of the fifth child was confirmed in 2001.

The secret of who fathered her first son may rest in peace as Katherine repeated her mother's words of, "Go to yar father's bedroom and comfort and sing to him. He loves your voice." Katherine would shrug her shoulders, look at Rosalie and softly say, "What did I know? I did what she told me to do." The resentment Katherine felt for her mother was twofold: Margot betrayed her marriage vows by her extramarital affair resulting in Katherine's birth, and used the child with no more respect than Margot had for herself.

As a parent, Katherine had to frequently defend her role when her sisters appeared to have more influence over her children than she did. This tug of authority was especially damaging, given Sonny's teenage rebellion and eventual adult behavior when seeking lodging with his Aunt Aileen following his escapes from confinement at state hospitals. This enlarged the divide between Katherine, her sister, and most hurtfully with her daughters Teresa and Patty, when each of them would lie and cover for Sonny, giving him shelter and money. If there had been one mature adult amongst them, they would have realized they were enablers, pounding nails into Sonny's coffin by condoning his alcoholism.

At the age of sixty-eight, Katherine was still working a forty hour week at McLean Hospital when she was stuck by a car while crossing Belmont Street. Family members she had helped over the years were scarce now that she became a burden.

The patience of Teresa, Patty, and granddaughter Vicky grew slim during months of Katherine's recuperation, causing them to become judgmental and picky about every element of her character, from requesting bananas each week, to her reading of her prayers or her questions. Her physical improvement and healing reduced the need to take as much medication, and improved Katherine's awareness of what was going on around her, to the disadvantage of her daughters, Teresa and Patty. She was now fully aware of their avoidance of her company.

A year and a half after her accident, Katherine was struck hard emotionally by Sonny's death from exsanguinations. With the help of medication for her depression, Katherine stayed in step with what she had to do to stay alert and keep a roof over her head. Even when ignored in her own home while paying all the expenses for Teresa's, Patty's, and Vicky's sakes, she persevered until something she may have overheard or saw caused her to seek Rosalie's help and counsel from an attorney. From this point in 1978 through Katherine's last day in January 1991, Rosalie was her advocate.

After Teresa's unexpected death in 1981, a series of mini strokes resulted in Katherine having to sell her home. She lived for eight years in an independent living complex, which suited her until additional strokes rendered her unable to walk or swallow. Requiring more intense care, Katherine adjusted fairly well to tube feeding in a Catholic nursing home.

During her last two years, her world grew smaller and the television was no longer desired. Being still alert and recognizing family visitors was a blessing for both parties, yet it also suggests that Katherine was well aware she was near the end of her journey. By choosing to tell

Rosalie of her vision of Ted a few weeks before her final day was a quantum jump of trust.

Her fear of being thought senile was gently dismissed when Rosalie reasoned out loud that if indeed Ted had come to tell Katherine he was waiting for her, that was the most beautiful thing she had ever heard, adding "Dad must have loved you very much."

✦ ✦ ✦ ✦ ✦ ✦ ✦ ✦

Receiving the remaining contents of her mother's safety deposit box from the lawyer who was the executor of Katherine's will, Rosalie came upon the original newspaper copy of her parents' marriage announcement in the *Little Falls Tribune*. The dusty-rose beaded dress with dropped waist which Katherine claimed for sixty-four years as her wedding dress was the description given of the maid of honor's dress worn by Maureen Dorsey. The bride wore a dress of white monkey skin georgette!

In 2001, a parcel arrived addressed to Rosalie from the Commonwealth of Massachusetts which contained the records of Sonny's medical history at various state hospitals from 1953 to 1971. Within the parent interview are Ted's words warning that Sonny has a gift for escaping from every locked facility he has been placed in since the age of fourteen. Katherine's interview contains her exact words, "Sonny is my second son and he has three sisters."

It remains never to be learned what other bits of knowledge Katherine chose to retain to suffer over, but Ted had the right idea when he told her "It's time to let go."

Breinigsville, PA USA
12 May 2010
237899BV00001B/2/P